# Buck Up, Buttercup

Buck Up, Buttercup
Copyright © 2022 by Anna Alkire
All rights reserved.



This is a work of fiction. Names, characters, places, and incidents either are the product of the author's imagination or are used fictitiously. Any resemblance to actual persons, living or dead, events, or locales is entirely coincidental.

**I'M GONNA BE (500 MILES)**
Words and Music by CHARLES REID and CRAIG REID
© 1988 ZOO MUSIC LTD.
All Rights in the U.S. and Canada Administered by WC MUSIC CORP.
All Rights Reserved
Used by Permission of ALFRED MUSIC

*Cover design by Ashley Santoro*
ISBN (paperback) 979-8-9863881-1-3
ISBN (ebook) 979-8-9863881-0-6
ISBN (audiobook) 979-8-9863881-2-0

Water's Edge Publishing LLC
waters.edge.publishing@gmail.com

# Buck Up, Buttercup

Montgomery Brothers, Book 1

Anna Alkire

WATER'S EDGE PUBLISHING

# SIGN UP FOR MY AUTHOR NEWSLETTER

Receive exclusive content, information about giveaways, coupons, and be the first to learn about Anna Alkire's new releases. Please, sign up today!

www.annaalkire.com

# CHAPTER ONE

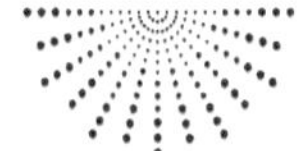

Of course, her leap of faith would turn into a plunging dive onto shards of ice-cold stress. Randi held her cell phone to her ear and forced her leg to stop bouncing.

The back of her thigh stuck to the cab's leather seat, which was undoubtedly a teeming jungle of microorganisms. Oregon should be beautifully temperate this time of year, not a steaming convection oven. She needed a shower. And a dunk into a vat of hydrogen peroxide.

"Hi, Trish, this is Randi, your new housemate," she said crankily into the hazy recording static of voice mail, fiddling with her glasses.

Sweat beaded on the curves of her nostrils—her pores were going to need a pressure washer. She cleared her throat. Would be nice if the cab driver turned his music down for three seconds.

"You haven't gotten back to me today and I'm a little worried about getting the key." She blew out her breath, trying to settle the frantic edge in her voice. "I'd hate to wake anyone up."

The wrinkles on her skirt weren't flattening out no

matter how many times she smoothed them. Her head pounded in time to the blaring pop music. After the last seventy-two hours traveling, barely sleeping, she was a moving train wreck held together by deodorant and dry shampoo. With a maxed-out credit card. Worst of all, her jaw clenched with the undeniable truth that something was off. Trish hadn't responded to her all day.

"I'll be there in a few minutes," she finished, lamely.

Her third voice mail and there were at least five text messages. Plus, the emails. And a DM on Facebook. Not getting another contact for the house had been stupid. She really should have insisted on talking to everyone.

She'd gone for it: said yes, for once, without finding all the reasons not to. The last three months teaching English in Argentina had been grueling—long hours and scraping for every tutoring job she could find—but now here was her reward. She was finally going to try living the collegiate experience, at the overripe undergrad age of twenty-four. If she could get into her new room.

Her own space. The pictures were swoon-worthy: a little cabin, actually a remodeled detached garage made into a bedroom, separate from the main farmhouse. And best of all, peaceful, clean, and a refuge from the college mania. The online ad had said her new housemates were quiet and studious. The property photo depicted a beautifully situated white farmhouse, in acres of countryside, surrounded by a hazelnut orchard. She took a deep breath—it would be fine. Trish must have lost her phone.

A needle of guilt stabbed into her stomach. Aunt Linda was probably asleep in her bed, forty miles away, still baffled and hurt. Before flying to Argentina last spring, Randi had known she couldn't do another year in her aunt's tiny two-bedroom house. She would work hard and make enough money so they could live together again comfortably, perhaps in an attractive duplex with a flowering dogwood in the front, and a connected backyard centered around a koi pond. Surely that wasn't too much to ask? This was her senior year at Oregon University, and she had to wrap it up before the debt suffocated her. And get a real job. She clamped her hands together, staring out the window at the dark country road.

She needed her own cave. A quiet place to focus on finishing an intense senior year, and building her YouTube business. What with her workload for the coming term (twenty-one credits, double the usual credit load and the max the university let her register for), other people and the long commute back and forth from her aunt's house were not things she wanted to juggle. Moving in with a group of serious students would provide the sanctuary she required, especially with her cabin-like room separated from the main house.

Her spirit animal must be a bear: solitary, happily roaming alone outside or hanging in a tree, peacefully companionless. Today she resembled a panda: sleepy eyes barely open, desperate for a leafy snack and a long nap.

The cab driver obviously smoked cigarettes and didn't use his air conditioner. Or deodorant. Randi pulled off her thin cardigan in the stuffy backseat. It still felt like midsummer down here, even with October twelve days away.

She would finish her degree and get out. *Done is better than perfect*, she told herself for the hundredth time. Companies hiring for business, marketing, and graphic design (her combined major) wanted graduates, not perfect grades. A good thing because she'd be lucky to pass everything.

At last, the car turned onto a gravel road winding into an orchard. The cab's high-beams lit up the bushy branches and thick gnarled trunks of hazelnut trees. She couldn't wait to see it in daylight.

"Shit!" the driver yelled. He slammed on the brakes and the cab jerked to a stop, swirling dust up from the gravel road. Randi gasped. Someone ran right in front of the cab, pink, naked skin glowing in the headlights.

Male butt cheeks sprinted up the middle of the road, blocking them from passing. Pale, hairy legs ended in cowboy boots. One of his hands was holding a cowboy hat on his head. He whooped and veered off into the orchard.

They sat in silence for a stunned moment. If that was somebody's boyfriend, she would be moving out.

"Did a naked guy jump in front of the car?" Randi said, taking her glasses off to rub her eyes.

The cab driver grunted.

"Do you see that kind of thing often?"

"Hazing week," he grumbled. "You want to keep going?"

She paused, her head a foggy cloud. What did he mean, keep going? Did he want her to jump out and walk the rest of the way? Not with insane naked men running around.

"Yes," she said.

Belatedly, her brain caught up with the conversation—he'd meant he could turn the cab around with her in it. A lump the size of a fist lodged in her throat. Something was brewing up ahead and it wasn't herbal tea before bedtime.

The cab rolled forward at a slower pace, veering around the largest potholes. Her clenching stomach churned with acid. She couldn't think. They rounded a bend. Cars lined both sides of the road, wedged between the trees. Women came tumbling out of one of them—young, wearing cowboy hats, short shorts, and halter tops.

Randi's mouth opened and closed. The cab kept going. Beer cans and red keg cups littered the gravel and the dirt shoulder. Noise was filtering in: shouts and high-pitched laughter. She realized the seat belt was clenched in both her fists. They drove out of the orchard. A sea of cars spread out in row after row on the grass in front of a farmhouse, like the parking lot of an outdoor concert.

People swarmed everywhere, blocking stairways, twenty deep around the sides of the house. A huge bonfire burned in front of a barn.

The driver turned off his radio. The overwhelming muddle of music, shouting, whooping, and a few hundred people talking at once brought reality crashing home. She sat suspended, unable to speak, chest heaving, panting in short gasps. Her sweating back could have been glued to the sticky leather seat.

"Hey, kiddo," the driver said, "got a pickup in twenty minutes. You want a ride back into town?"

She stared at the house number. It was correct. Not to mention the old farmhouse matched the picture online. And so did the orchard. Over the summer, Trish had emailed her back promptly, answering all her questions. This was the house of "studious women serious about school." When asked directly about parties, Trish had responded, "Little get-togethers—yes. Massive parties—absolutely not."

Anger boiled up, burning away the paralyzing fear. She huffed in dawning realization. They'd taken her savings. Conned her. After working fourteen-hour days, seven days a week for three months in Buenos Aires, she'd spent everything to secure her spot living at this house. She would get her money back, tonight—first and last month's rent, plus a deposit. Her stomach roiled.

"Meter's running. What's it going to be?"

Randi handed over her Visa. White haze blurred her vision. That card didn't have enough credit for a taxi ride back to town.

Minutes later she stood on the patchy grass, her bags piled at her feet, watching the cab drive toward the orchard. Her chest constricted and a wave of heat rolled over her. She stumbled sideways, catching herself on a suitcase. A gasp croaked out of her tight, dry throat, the flood of panic like an oncoming semitruck going in the wrong direction on a one-way street. She stepped forward, waving her hand, but the cab kept going, disappearing into the trees.

She gulped, her eyes stinging. What had she done?

"Hey, dickwads!" a man yelled from one of the cars, high-pitched and slurred. Randi jumped, clutching her bags against her chest.

"That shithead hit Kevin," said a masculine voice by Randi's shoulder.

She sidestepped, stumbling on the uneven grass. The group passed by, inspecting her like a sandwich in a deli case. A blond guy intensely tried to catch her eye, walking backward to stare at her.

Every muscle in her body wound tight. Adrenaline, hot and urgent, boiled up. She turned sharply to the right, putting a parked car between herself and the men.

"When?"

"Last week at Warren's place. Ben went after him…"

Randi weaved between groups of people standing outside the house. She kept her gaze down, avoiding eye contact with anyone. *Can a person project "leave me alone or I'll start screaming?"* Her heart banged in her chest. *What am I doing here?* The dark, crowded, smokey lawn seemed conjured from an anxiety-fueled night terror.

Gingerly, she put down her heeled feet on the path around the side of the house. Foam-lined yellow-brown puddles oozed on the ground, littered with cigarette butts. She shuddered. Her heel wobbled on a patch of soggy grass. Below her, a splatter of vomit stretched across the lawn in pink and purple chunks. Her stomach turned violently, throat burning. *Keep breathing!* She blew out a breath and picked up her pace.

In Buenos Aires her employer turned host-mother, Nicola, had liked to pat her cheek and say, "My little orphan, how are you so brave and timid at the same time?" At first, Nicola had been rigidly strict about her curfew and Randi's safety, with dire warnings about what kind of "behaviors" a conservative family would put up with in a young adult. By the end of her stay, Nicola had marched Randi into a night-club for the experience. Randi would write to Nicola about this, she decided, and tell her she felt safer riding alone on the subway in Buenos Aires than at her rented house in Riverside, Oregon.

Somebody whistled a catcall in her general direction. She didn't look around. Parties weren't her thing. Not birthday parties. Not backyard barbecues. Never, never, in her wildest moments of boredom, would she voluntarily choose to go to a party like this. Men shouted and women screamed. They were totally isolated from normal law-abiding society.

A couple by a long barn were kissing, bright sequins on the girl's shirt catching the light. Their faces pressed together violently, like fighting dogs. The barn wall thudded. Randi turned away quickly. That was way more than a kiss. Heat flushed her face.

She scanned for openings between dense clusters of bodies. Arms shaking with fatigue, she hauled her bags around the side of the house. A shocking number of heads wore cowboy hats—half of the crowd had them on, along with saucer-sized belt buckles. Walking into an enclave of country and western culture in liberal college town Riverside felt like being transported to another planet. The heads within the cowboy hats must be sweltering in the heat. She imagined herself as an anthropologist, a researcher in a foreign land. *Just keep breathing.*

She made it to the back of the house, and there, finally, the little cabin stood in front of her, lights off and the door closed. A thick cloud of cigarette smoke lingered over the concrete patio that connected the house and cabin. Coughing, she jiggled the locked door, ignoring the people staring at her.

"Hey! New girl!" a female voice yelled at her. Randi whipped around. A tall blonde waved, a sarcastic smile stretched across her face.

Randi's fingers twitched in response. Towering and broad-shouldered, the woman could have been a Viking wearing a sleeveless flannel button-up and jean shorts. Beer sloshed from the side of her red cup as she walked forward.

"Are you Randi?" the blonde said, drawing out the name in the usual tired joke.

"I rented this room. Where's Trish? This isn't going to work for me, I need my money back."

Round blue eyes blinked at her. "Sarah," she said, still smiling, pointing at her chest.

*Oh boy.* "Where's Trish?"

"Trish?" A long pause. More blinking. Up close, Sarah appeared to need an IV of fluids. Her lips were cracked, flecked with stringy white…Was that spit? Randi looked away.

"Left," said Sarah, swaying.

"She doesn't live here any longer?"

Sarah stepped sideways, her broad shoulders hitting the side of the cabin. "She's a little mad 'bout the party. Took off."

Randi slumped, rubbing her forehead. No Trish meant she would not get her money back tonight.

"Key's under the mat," said Sarah, nodding toward the door.

Randi crouched down, moving aside a battered piece of outdoor carpeting. A metal key lay lodged in the mud underneath. She wiggled the key in the sticky lock until it finally clicked over, then pushed the door open and turned on the light.

The bags slipped from her hands, thudding on the ground. Her head jerked back from the rank, musty air. Garbage coated the floor and piled up against the walls. Her "furnished" room contained a yellow mattress, bare except for the stains.

Like a blender stuffed with too much ice, her thoughts swirled in choppy circles. Hunched over, with her head between her knees, she broke down and texted her aunt. Then she called. No response. Aunt Linda didn't look at her phone much at the best of times but, with a five o'clock shift tomorrow morning, she was probably deep asleep.

Her friend Daisy wasn't an option—already drunk. The slurred story earlier, when Randi had called from the airport shuttle bus stop, had been about a Ping-Pong table, a guy with neon pink slushies, and lost purses. Which proved that Daisy and promised rides did not mix. Were college friends more than ephemeral blips?

It might have worked if not for her endless flight delays out of Argentina, and then the holdups at every layover along the way. The life lesson here pointed toward her being a hopeless loner. Maybe she should try to find some new friends.

She'd get a cab into town. The obvious choice. Forty dollars from her food budget, which fell a little short of thirty bucks. Would they wait to cash a check? Her aunt lived about an hour away and was chronically short on funds. She massaged her temples.

But the worst part about a cab was walking back out to that dark driveway, through the creepy parking area. At least here, if she screamed, someone might stumble over.

Fifteen minutes later, defeated by her bladder, she leaned against a doorjamb in the main house, waiting to use the one toilet. She felt safer. Most of the women were here. And there was light. Twenty feet away, the bathroom door finally opened and a girl lurched out. Randi took a small step forward in the line.

She needed to think. Not touching anyone occupied all of her brain, however. Along with ignoring the sidelong glances. Jell-O shots in the kitchen had taken hold of the collective consciousness. She kept her arms crossed and her gaze down.

One toilet, right next to the kitchen. How was that legal? Four women and a single shower. *Bonkers.* She needed to bang her head against a wall to restart her brain, except there were sugar ants crawling all over the kitchen walls.

Lead, not blood, slugged through her veins. The adrenaline tank had fallen off, and now she was in a disassociating haze, aware just enough to still want to pee in a toilet. The crowded room made it impossible not to touch anyone. Apparently, if you're tired enough, your phobias can't muster up the energy to make you dysfunctional. She slumped, closing her eyes.

"Buck's here," said the girl in front of her in a low tone.

Randi sniffed. The name Buck could slug it out with Randi for worst parent idea ever.

"I saw him by the fire," the girl continued.

"Where's Vicki?" said another girl.

"Not here. They're done. I don't think she's coming back to school."

"Well damn, I just might have to find that cowboy."

Randi swallowed, turning to stare at a calendar tacked to the wall. It said "COWBOY UP" in large pink letters over an image of boots. Part of her brain feverishly picked away at how to get out of there. The rest of her had the lights off. Her eyelids were sticking together and her head ached. If she didn't lie down soon, she was going to throw up.

The music changed, from a plaintive country ballad lamenting spilled beer to a jaunty two-step, and the women on the dance floor cheered. A few men drinking in the kitchen glanced over with lukewarm expressions. Everybody else in the crowded room kept talking. It was hot, steam practically wafting off at least fifty tightly packed bodies. Her head spun. Why did people do this?

The chattering around her stopped, cut off by sharply inhaled breaths. All the women in line were staring toward the open door. Randi adjusted her glasses, swaying a little as her legs wobbled.

"Buck!" shouted one of the dancing girls. A tall man in a black cowboy hat walked through the front door. "Buck, get over here!"

He jumped into the mob of drunk women with the confident look of a matador pivoting towards a bull. He grabbed a girl, swinging her around the floor in a quick two-step. The whole room turned toward the dancing, people edging forward and tapping their feet. Buck jumped to another girl, who squealed with laughter. And then he stood in the center of a crowd of women, his hands up, and looked out at the room, grinning.

The handsome cowboy caught her staring at him. Randi realized some kind of loopy smirk was plastered on her face. He winked. Her eyebrows shot up. How could he even look around with three women crawling on his chest? She shook her head at him, narrowing her eyes, glared at him a moment longer then turned away, taking a step forward in line.

# CHAPTER TWO

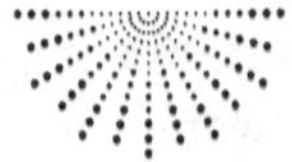

Gravel crunched behind him. He managed not to sigh, barely. These girls were like bloodhounds.

"Buck," said Angie's raspy voice. "I've got two cold beers. Want one?"

The dark side of the barn propped him up nicely, even if the distant porch light wavered a little around the edges. Some gossipy people would say he was hiding. They'd be right. But obviously not hiding well enough.

He shoved his hands in his pockets. An imaginary siren cranked up between his ears, phantom flashing lights cutting through the whiskey fog in his head. This girl didn't take no for an answer.

"No thanks, darlin'," he said. "I'm done for the night." He'd have to find an excuse to hustle away if she got much closer. "Offer that beer to Hugh. He'd like nothing better."

Angie sneered and looked away.

Well, if she wanted subtle diplomacy, she shouldn't hit on him when he was twenty minutes from passing out. Getting him drunk and dragging him off somewhere dark usually worked. But not with this one. Not with Angie.

"It's here if you change your mind," she said, almost sounding sweet, but that pissed-off brittle edge came through loud enough. She cracked open her can, foam spraying out in front of them, then settled in next to him, her shoulder brushing his.

The new girl stepped out of the back door, gripping her bag like a life vest against her body. As nervous as a plucked chicken. Or an uptight kindergarten teacher dropped into an alcohol-crazed stud party.

That little yellow dress was pretty but odd—prissy. Pinned-up honey-colored hair showed off a long neck. She adjusted the big glasses on her face and glanced around like a rabbit about to run for it.

"She's a shit-eating hippie," sneered Angie. "Fucking Trish found her on the internet. Her name's Randi, can you believe that?"

Buck blinked. "Randi," he said, a smile tugging on his face. The name fit her about as well as a burlap bag.

"Doesn't look anything like a hippie," he said. "More like a librarian."

He twitched in response and reached down to adjust his belt buckle. Prissy uptight librarian was an idea he'd thought about a time or two. Inside the house, she'd caught his eye, standing there like a flamingo in a room full of geese. He always did like the oddballs.

Sarah stumbled into sight from the front of the house, a dopey smile on her face. Her tall, sturdy body swayed like it was fighting a gale-force wind. She bumped into the side of the house.

"Sarah's done," Angie said.

He grunted.

Sarah toppled to her knees and puked onto the ground next to the new girl. Randi.

~

THROW up exploded from Sarah's hunched form, like a bursting water balloon. Randi jumped backward, stifling a scream. Sarah fell forward, landing on her hands, wheezing and gagging.

Randi shuddered. The stench of sour spaghetti sauce, gone very wrong, steamed up from the ground. A few people standing close by muttered. They kept their distance. Apparently, party intelligence was a thing, and she lacked any. Glancing down, she realized her jump hadn't been quick enough.

"Disgusting." She rubbed the side of her foot on some grass. A foul chunk stuck to the teardrop cutouts of her lemon heels. *Really?* Why was the universe punishing her?

A blond guy winked at her. "Got to let her get it all out."

"No kidding." She stepped away from the puke and toward her bedroom.

He sidestepped, blocking her. She glanced away from his yellow, hazel eyes, overly bright and intense. Objectively within range of handsome, his polo and tanned skin gave the impression of a golfer. She had noticed him earlier, with a mob of guys in the dark alleys of pasture between parked cars, staring at her. The sharp face brought to mind a predatory rat, and his gaze laser-focused on her like she'd stashed cheese somewhere in her neckline. Some men gave off creepy vibes. Words disappeared, lost in her tight throat. *Get it together, Randi!*

Crossing her arms in front of her, she took a step back and stumbled over a rock.

Quick as a darting snake, he reached out and grabbed her upper arm, his grip painful. She caught her balance, but he didn't let go. The backs of his fingers grazed her chest. Her face flamed. She tried to yank away, but he held on for another second before sliding his hand down her arm.

"You're cute. What are those…little birds on your dress?"

"Excuse me." She hated the nervous edge in her voice. "I'm leaving."

Rat-guy leaned into her, looking excited. She jerked away from his foul breath, her back bumping into the house.

"Don't do that." He grinned down at her. "I want to talk to you." He put a hand beside her head, boxing her in.

"Stop!"

He chuckled, his groin pushing into her stomach. His hand ran down the side of her dress, knuckles grazing her breast.

Randi pulled the canister of pepper spray out of her pocket and pointed it in his face.

"Move away from me," she yelled, her ragged voice cracking. Everything went quiet around them.

Rat-guy raised his hands in the air and took a step back. Randi stumbled sideways, away from the wall. Panting, her hand shaking, she held the Mace up.

"Put that away, you crazy bitch!" a female voice shouted. A blonde stepped in front of her.

Randi pushed a hand against her own quaking chest then crouched over, trying to catch her breath. Her heart stuttered at quantum speed.

"Clear out, Ryan," said a deep, cold voice off to her side. "What the hell got into you?"

"Shit, Buck, I was just talking to her."

"The hell you were."

Randi glanced up. It was the dancer cowboy from inside. The two men stared at each other.

Rat-guy sniffed and turned away. He muttered, "Bitch," under his breath as he brushed past her.

The blonde woman looked her over, a sneer on her face.

She wasn't tall, about Randi's height. Her face—angular and tan, with bright blue eyes squinted in rage—appeared feral between the strands of long, straight hair.

"You ever pull that crap in my house again and I'll knock that shit up your ass," she snarled.

Randi startled, staring back into the girl's hard eyes. Was she supposed to let the creep assault her? Anger finally burned through the hazy shock. She was getting shamed for protecting herself? She stood up straight, rage setting her jaw.

"If anyone touches me again, I'll call the police." She pulled out her phone. "Threaten me again, and I'm calling."

The girl bunched her fists, head lowering like she was about to lose it.

Randi took a step back. She couldn't breathe. The crazy woman tensed, as if ready to charge. She looked lean but strong under the simple T-shirt and jeans, the corded tendons on her neck flexing into muscular shoulders. Would the blonde's flip-flops slow her down? *Crap!*

"Whoa, ladies," said the cowboy guy. "No reason to have asses involved. That's just a waste of potential." Somebody laughed.

He grabbed the blonde's arm and pulled her back. "Go cool off, Angie. Git!"

The blonde, Angie, gave him a narrow-eyed look, then stomped off. The back door slammed behind her.

Randi slumped. Her eyes burned, and she was about three seconds from sobbing.

Cowboy-guy turned toward her. "You're all right now, darlin'," he said, his eyes hard to see under his black hat in the dim light. "That little shit, Ryan, won't bother you again."

She glared at him, blinking, then crossed her arms. "He will definitely bother me again, if he gets the chance."

He rocked back on his heels. "You scared him good. He's too chicken for more."

She doubted it. More likely he'd want revenge. And the blonde psycho undoubtedly would.

Cowboy-guy stood there quietly while she focused on breathing. Her hands shook. She shoved them in her pockets, still gripping her cell phone in one hand and the Mace in the other. Inexplicably, he seemed like a force field of protection. Or of normalcy. A little righteous indignation stirred in her belly; she shouldn't need to be standing near a man to be treated like a person.

Her heart rattled so hard in her chest that her teeth were chattering. She stared at the yoke of his cowboy shirt, trying to distract her flailing mind. A curving red line ran across his chest over the black shirt, with red roses embroidered next to his collar. Cowboy flare.

Her heart's rattling thumping still drummed through her, her pulse slapping frantically at the skin of her neck. She closed her eyes for a few long seconds, too shaky to move. If this night got any worse, somebody would find her body.

Sarah, the puker and her potential cohabitor in this hellish house, groaned on the grass. Nobody cared that she lay down there, sleeping next to a pile of her vomit.

"Sarah is on the ground," she said, pointedly.

"Yup." He peered over his shoulder.

She clenched her fists at his bland, dispassionate answer, and watched him stare down at Sarah like she was a scratched-up piece of discarded furniture. "What's wrong with you all? Are you going to leave her there?"

Without waiting for him to answer, she went to Sarah's side. The passed-out woman was sprawled out on the dirty concrete patio, limbs twisted, hair stuck to her messy face. Randi dug in her bag for a wet wipe.

A pair of boots walked up beside her. "That girl has the

lowest tolerance I've ever seen," said cowboy-guy. "Passes out on a can of Bud Light."

"Obviously, she's not safe out here." Randi tugged down Sarah's hiked-up tank top.

"Usually, she gets up after about thirty minutes and stumbles in. Best thing for everybody, when she's messy."

"Sarah," Randi called, shaking her arm. "Wake up. Time to go in."

Sarah mumbled, turning her face away.

Cowboy-guy sighed. He grabbed both of Sarah's arms and hauled her up into a sitting position. Her head rolled around on her shoulders, eyes cracked open.

"Let's go, girl." He slung one of her arms around his neck.

"Little tired," she said, smacking her lips.

Sarah was tall and large boned. Randi bit her lip, not sure if one man could lift her. She helped to prop Sarah up as he pulled. Flopping precariously, Sarah stumbled against the cowboy's chest, sleepy blue eyes gazing up at him.

"Hey, Buck," Sarah said, slurring in a flirty voice.

"Hey, puke face."

Randi realized she'd heard about Buck all night. She watched him out of the corner of her eye, irrationally drawn to someone else with a ridiculous name.

He hauled Sarah up the back steps while Randi held the door pushed open with one hand. Muscles strained under his black button-up shirt. He was lean with solid, wide shoulders. Not in his early twenties, but not past thirty either. His tan skin was weathered, like he spent all his time outdoors. He looked like he belonged in another decade, with the bottom hem of his shirt tucked in tight at the waist.

If you went for the chiseled jaw, toxically masculine type of look, he hit the mark. He had a butt chin, the deep cleft accentuating his cynical mouth. Not her type. Sarah stumbled and bumped him against the door frame. His knocked-askew hat revealed dirty blond hair—was the country filled with blond people?

Buck and Sarah staggered through the door, and someone else moved over to help. The screen door clanged shut behind them.

Randi made it into the cabin bedroom and locked the door behind her, then hauled the disgusting mattress in front of the door for good measure. The tears running down her face made it hard to see as she shoved and kicked the mess into one corner. She dumped her bottle of hand sanitizer on the wood-plank floor and wiped down a section with the last of her wet wipes.

Finally, she lay on her back with her head pillowed on one of her bags, a jacket covering her chest. And didn't sleep for hours.

# CHAPTER THREE

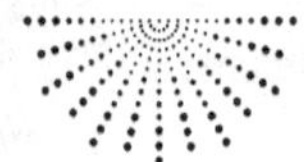

A car engine revved behind her. Randi stepped a little further to the side of the gravel road. Dust stormed over her, the cloud billowing out from the tires of an army-green Suburban speeding past. She squinted her eyes and covered her nose and mouth with her arm. The Suburban slowed down and skidded to a stop. A male head popped out of the window.

"Hey, honey, you want a ride?"

Emphatically shaking her head, she dropped her bags to signal with jerky arm movements that he should keep going. The guy quirked his eyebrows at her, his expression seeming to say, "You're a sad clown." But he drove away.

Randi forced her hands to grip and lift, even though her fingers wailed like overtired toddlers. Five minutes later, another car passed. This one didn't slow down. With the sun burning off the morning chill, the party people were rolling out of their vomit and heading home. She should have started walking sooner.

She coughed and lurched sideways, the misery heavier than her three bags. If her grandparents were still alive, she wouldn't have been caught out like this. Old familiar grief settled over her.

Randi sighed. *Lies haunt you,* she thought. *The wispy trails of what could have been follow us in our shadows.* If not for that one mistake that had realigned the entire trajectory of her life, she wouldn't be walking down a dusty road with her stomach pinching, wondering if a ten-mile hike might actually leave her passed out on the side of the road.

She had been making out with her boyfriend the evening her grandparents died in a traffic collision on the freeway. Her grandfather, who she called Papa, traveled every other week to doctor's appointments up in Portland. "Come with us," Papa and Mimi had said. "We don't like to leave you alone, sweetheart."

"Can't," she'd lied, making up a study group she had to go to.

Eight years later, the shock, shame, and certainty still burned in her stomach. She should have been with them. They would be with her now. Her foot caught on a gnarled root twisting out of the ground, pitching her forward, and she hopped on one foot, her stubbed toe burning. She forced herself to stop. To breathe. To stuff the grief back down.

Sunlight filtered between the branches. The gravel road through the filbert orchard stubbornly refused to end, instead continuing with bends and hills of endless gravel through the trees.

Birds called and sang. She sniffed, her eyes stinging. It was a gorgeous setting, exactly right for her videos. Just the area around the house would have given her new material for weeks. It was perfect. But she was going to walk ten miles to get the hell away as fast as she could.

Well, hopefully not ten. She was sixty percent sure that five miles from here would be a bus stop. And there may be something closer. Vicious, desperate growling from her stomach broke the peaceful sounds of the morning. Her vision blurred, growing hazy at the edges, and a sob caught in her throat. She could do this. Of course she could. Blinking hard, she forced the tears out of her eyes.

Another car approached. She hunched her shoulders, too late to hide behind a tree. The car took its time. She could feel eyes burning into her back.

An old pickup, with new shiny green paint, slowed down beside her until it crawled along at her pace. A quick glance sideways revealed black-hat-cowboy-guy grinning down at her.

A jolt of awareness cleared some of the fog from her head. He was more good-looking than she'd remembered, and also incredibly large above her in the truck.

"Good morning, darlin'," he called down.

"Drive on," she called out.

"Headed into town? We've got room."

"I'm going to walk." She wouldn't get into a car with a single person from that party. She walked forward, not looking at him.

"Hold up, you dropped something," he said, stopping the truck.

Randi whirled around, scanning the empty ground behind her. Her fingers lost their grip and her bags crashed down, things spilling out onto the gravel road. Her eyes burned.

Buck turned off the truck engine and leaned out the window.

"That's a lot of gear to haul all the way into town," he said, cheerfully.

"That was a dirty trick."

"I just want to talk to you for a minute."

"Leave me alone please!"

"Listen. Hugh, in the passenger seat, and I are headed in

for some breakfast. If you ride with me, this gas guzzler will have a full cab. Darlin', that's a load off my conscience."

Randi's belly shuddered and her lips quivered. The dam burst. Her hands flew up to cover her eyes and a hiccupped sob exploded out.

"I can't jump in some stranger's pickup," she mumbled through her fingers.

"Hey now," he said, the amused condescension in his voice making her glare up at him. "You hold on to that pepper spray if it makes you feel better. Land's sake, girl, we hauled around passed-out-Sarah last night. You're practically part of the family. And Hugh here has about twenty sisters, so he's well-trained."

The door of the truck opened. She took a step back, pulling up the inside collar of her dress to dab at her face.

Buck's eyes crinkled at her, a lopsided half-grin on his face. It was probably the way he looked at cows right before he lassoed a rope around their necks, or whatever. But he had helped Sarah. And her.

Her shoulders slumped. Defeated, she was beyond resistance. If they murdered her, at least she might be sitting down.

"All right?" he asked.

She exhaled. "All right, I'll take a ride to the closest bus stop. Thanks."

Buck picked up her bags and put them in the back of the truck. She hauled her heavy backpack off her aching shoulders and turned to sling it up, but Buck was already gripping the top and lifting it out of her hands.

"Hi," said a burly man sitting on the passenger side of the bench seat, a gentle smile on his face. Like she was a crazy person. Which she was. With a deep breath, she hoisted herself up into the cab next to him.

"Sorry about Buck," the big guy said, glaring at the culprit with one eye squinted. "He's devious about getting what he wants."

Buck landed on the seat beside her. "Hugh keeps the standards up. Probably why he's so grumpy all the time."

Hugh crossed his arms, leaning into the passenger door. His buzzed blond head and muscular frame brought to mind a late-twenties version of Mr. Clean, minus the jewelry.

"I ain't grumpy. Just tired of your ugly face."

Buck chuckled. Randi caught herself staring at him. She wouldn't call his face ugly, not even anything related to unattractive. More like relentlessly cheerful. And way too confident that he could boss everyone around. She sniffed, annoyed with him enough to stop crying.

The truck rolled forward, bumping on the gravel road. They sat on an old-fashioned bucket-style bench, comfortable for two people, and a squeeze for three. The middle seat offered no belt. A death trap. Because that was the logical conclusion to her week from hell. She braced a hand on the dash to keep from bouncing into the bodies next to her.

Not touching either man, holding her body tense and straight, made her neck ache. And still she knocked knees with Hugh and almost leaned on Buck's shoulder. Buck's hand on the manual gear shifter was an inch from her thigh, his fingers brushing the edge of her skirt when he shifted. Short of sitting on Hugh's lap, there was nowhere for her to go to keep from touching him.

She felt shaky, barely keeping herself together. Every time Buck changed position she noticed it, his muscular arms flexing as he drove. It was like sitting next to a tiger: electrifying, an experience you never forgot, and total madness.

"So," said Buck, flashing a grin at her. "What's your rush this morning? You just moved in last night."

Randi dug a tissue out of her bag. "I can't live in a party house," she said, dabbing at her running nose.

"A Waffle House?" said Hugh.

"She said party house, Einstein." Buck glanced at her. "How'd you end up with a room out there?"

"I was teaching in Argentina and found it online. Paid everything…" She paused, choking up, not sure why she was telling them. "They lied to me." And she dissolved again, covering her face with the tissue.

What was wrong with her? It was beyond humiliating to be crying like a child in front of these strangers. At least she'd never have to see them again.

"Huh," said Buck, tapping the steering wheel. "Well, I know Trish isn't happy about the parties."

"They got an ugly ticket last June," said Hugh. "She's on probation."

Randi sat up straighter, taking in this information. She managed to stop crying, and dabbed her cheeks clean with the tissue.

Buck rubbed the side of his face. "Is that right?"

"I can't believe you didn't know that, Buck. Jesus."

"I just look like I know everything."

"Yeah, well, one more ticket and they're facing jail time. And, of course, there were minors everywhere last night. I turned my back and they slurped down my keg."

Randi pushed up her glasses. No wonder Trish hadn't been there during the party. It revealed, even more, how shamelessly Trish had lied to her in the emails they'd exchanged about the house.

The farmland was transforming into residential housing when Buck turned onto a major road.

"That bus stop coming up will be fine," said Randi, her voice annoyingly shaky.

"No way, darlin'," said Buck. "You cry in my truck, and I buy you a coffee. Then, I drop you off wherever you want."

"No, really—"

"Hey," he said, "I put up with all the tears. So now we're going to go to this coffee drive-through and get sugary drinks to make ourselves feel better. Otherwise, Hugh over there might start his period."

"You're such a jackass," Hugh said, shaking his head.

BUCK PULLED INTO THE DRIVE-THROUGH, his hand practically on her thigh. She was still sniffling, and he clenched his teeth, the crotch of his jeans pinching. Whatever the hell was wrong with him, she was making it worse.

"Darlin', what can I get you?"

"Nothing."

There was something about this girl. Maybe the pucker above her top lip? He wanted to see her take her glasses off. Tease that grit and moral stiffness out of her shoulders. Did he have a thing for stubborn women?

"Hugh, what are we having?"

The bottomless pit leaned forward to peer at the menu. "I'll have a Sasquatch Tracks Frostbite White Chocolate Mocha, double shot."

"Two of those," Buck said, "and an iced coffee."

"Anything to eat, hon?" The woman at the window flashed a toothy grin.

"Hugh?"

"Chocolate Cream Cheese Muffin, Abominable Almond Croissant, and a Cheddar Everything Bagel. And a Big Foot Banana Bread. Plus, whatever you guys are having."

Buck huffed. Randi's mouth hung open.

"What he said times three."

"You got it," said the gal at the register, her fingers flying over the keys.

Buck handed over his credit card.

"Are you guys werewolves or something? That's a lot of pastry." Randi's voice, raspy from crying, made him think of the bedroom.

"Werewolves?" He eyed her sideways. That serious face was undermined by such sexy lips. "Hugh might be. Would explain why he's not four hundred pounds."

Hugh scoffed. "Not even close."

She sat back, unbending enough to lean against the seat. Damn, but she was tense. And sweaty. The smell of her interfered with him, making it hard to focus on anything but her body next to him as her shoulder brushed against his.

Every time he took her in, he wanted to smile. The specs did it—a pretty face swamped with god-awful massive glasses. The most deliberately nerdy glasses he'd ever seen on a woman.

*You're not interested in dating*, he reminded himself. He wasn't ready, not after that trip to hell with his ex. Lately all the women he came across were too immature, or too sweet to believe, and often enough flashed him back to being stuck in with a narcissist.

Enormous cups of whipped-cream-covered coffee smoothies appeared in the kiosk window. The warm pastries, in a greasy paper bag, followed. He pulled into a parking spot.

"Hey, darlin', hold this," he said, handing over one of the smoothies as Hugh took his.

"Thanks, man," said Hugh, unwrapping his muffin with a happy sigh.

"That one's for you," he said. She blinked up at him, her messy hair hanging around her face.

"I can't accept this," she said, solemnly pushing up her glasses.

"Come on now, a college student shouldn't pass up free groceries. And I can't drop you off somewhere if I think you're going to pass out from hunger. Better to head straight to the hospital."

She glared up at him, eyes narrowing. He took a deep breath. Well hell, something about this girl got to him.

"Hugh," she said, "will it matter if I argue with him?"

"Nope. You're his not-bad deed of the day. Got to live with it."

She sighed, blinked, and took a tentative sip. "Wow, tastes like a milkshake. Thanks."

He pulled back out onto the road headed into town, not trying to hide the grin on his face. "Where to, darlin'?"

"Bus station."

"You're already on one, the Buck Bus. Give me an address."

"No. It's safety one-oh-one. Please, take me to a bus stop."

"Some creep is more likely to follow you from one of those buses."

"Take me to the transit station downtown. That would be great."

"You're going to turn down a free ride with all of that luggage to haul?"

"I'll be fine."

"Don't argue with the lady," put in Hugh. "She's right, safety first."

"Thank you, Hugh," she said.

Buck sighed. It felt off to dump her at a bus station, exhausted and traumatized. City girls were gluttons for punishment.

He parked next to the terminal with his hazards on and jumped out to grab the bags.

"Thanks, guys," she said, smiling at Hugh. Why the hell didn't he get a smile? "You, um, restored my faith in humanity. Some of it, anyway."

Hugh got back in the truck, but Buck lingered.

"So," he said, "you've got some beef with Trish."

"Yeah, it's called fraud."

"Don't be too hard on them. They'll settle down. Go out there today and talk to Trish."

Randi scoffed, shaking her head. She glanced up at him through long lashes, her eyes green with flecks of amber in the bright light. The hairs on the back of his neck stood up. He wanted to put his hands on her.

A bus pulled into the station. He held up her hefty hiking backpack while she slid on the straps, the massive frame making her look small.

"Bye, Buck." She walked away without a backward glance.

RANDI DROPPED her bags on the concrete steps in front of Aunt Linda's house. Home. Relief flooded her. Sure, after living here for the last eight years, she dreamed of her own place with urgent longing, but she would count her blessings that she still had a roof to come back to. The key wobbled in her hand as she pushed it into the old sticky door lock.

Someone moaned. Randi froze, her foot suspended over the threshold. Rhythmic banging against the wall. She stood for a minute, her brain moving at the speed of molasses. Another moan. Definitely not the cats doing that.

She backed out of the door and closed it gently. Her face burned. She sank down onto the front step and stared at the weedy yard. Aunt Linda had been single for years. She had started dating her crush over the summer after agonizing about it for two years. Randi imagined them at about the hand-holding phase. Did a fifty-year-old jump into sex faster?

Half an hour later, she rang the doorbell, then waited a

full minute. Opening the door, she yelled, "Hello. The prodigal niece has returned."

"Randi!" her aunt called in a flustered voice. Quick foot-steps moved around in the back bedroom. "I'll be out in a few minutes."

She massaged her temples. It would be challenging to find a more awkward time to arrive and meet the boyfriend. Probably should've waited longer.

"Take your time," she shouted, trying to sound airy.

Two of the cats sauntered over, meowing and rubbing against her ankles. She scratched their heads. The house appeared the same: cluttered. Judging by the state of the kitchen, Aunt Linda's chronic pain had flared up.

Three months ago, Randi had left in a tiny, private, huff—too many cats, and the mess turned her batty. She'd realized that, as much as she loved her aunt, living in the little house made the inside of her skin itch.

She turned on the faucet and started scrubbing the pile of dishes. Even over the running water she heard voices in the back bedroom. The bathroom door opened and shut. The shower lurched on, pipes grumbling. Her bedroom shared a wall with Aunt Linda's, and the only bathroom was across the hall. Privacy was practically impossible.

She finished wiping down the counter as Aunt Linda walked out, her face a little stern and flushed pink. Randi bit her lip. The last thing she wanted to do was embarrass her.

"Sorry to barge in." Randi attempted to sound oblivious to the sexual happenings. "You look lovely…New haircut?"

Aunt Linda put her hand up to her long white hair that curled over her shoulders. "I did…a layered cut." She dropped her hand and opened her arms, stepping forward for a hug. "Amazing to see you, dear. How was your flight?"

Randi rambled on about her days of travel, ending with

missing her shuttle bus. They both ignored the noise in the back bedroom.

Aunt Linda's pink-cheeked healthy glow unwound a ball of worry in Randi's chest. Her aunt's health was shaky. After finishing cancer treatment five years ago, Aunt Linda had made many positive lifestyle changes, but her other chronic inflammatory conditions still created challenges for her.

Leisurely footsteps made their way toward the kitchen. They both turned to watch a slender man step out of the hallway. He was lanky, with a long neck stretching up to a mellow umber-brown face. A face younger than Aunt Linda's.

"Randi, this is Jack." Aunt Linda beamed, her hands fluttering.

She grasped the hand Jack held out to her and smiled back at him. Of course, since her aunt had talked about him for the last two years, she'd made sure to get a few glimpses of him at the natural foods store where they both worked. Up close revealed light freckly sunspots on his skin and bare scalp. It would be hard for her to tell his age, except that Aunt Linda knew about—and obsessed over—their eight-year difference.

"A pleasure to finally meet you," Jack said, his voice soft. "Let me know how I can help with the move this weekend. I'm totally at your aunt's disposal for the rest of the day." Jack and Aunt Linda gazed at each other.

"Thank you." Randi realized again how much she had intruded. It appeared that Aunt Linda had sprinted past the starting to date phase long ago—she was in L-word territory. He seemed far down that road as well.

Randi swallowed. Now would be an opportune time to mention how very sorry she was to intrude, but that she had nowhere to live. She opened her mouth and closed it.

"Excuse me," she said, "I'm going to go check on a few things in my room."

"We'll pick up tacos." Aunt Linda slung her purse strap over a shoulder.

"Okay, see you soon."

"Chicken?"

"Sure, thanks."

Aunt Linda and Jack hustled out the door like their feet were on fire. Randi exhaled. Aunt Linda would be taking her new boyfriend into the bedroom, and Randi would be able to hear them speaking through the wall. Firmly, she halted the progression of that thought and poked her head in the bathroom. An extra toothbrush sat in the holder. A man's razor and cream stood on the counter.

Dread spread gritty, mottled wings inside her chest. She walked over to her bedroom door. Something crunched under her feet in the hallway—was that cat litter? She peeked in her room, her nose wrinkling at the stench. Four litter boxes, overflowing with clumps, covered her area rug. Old Blackfoot, the stray Aunt Linda had taken in last spring, hissed at her from the bed.

Randi cleaned. She scrubbed and washed. And disinfected. It was the answer to the chaos of life. And as far as obsessive compulsions went, at least it was a useful one. She dealt with the cat boxes, the floor, started the laundry, took out trash, while her mind whirled like water flushing down a toilet bowl.

Aunt Linda texted her that Jack wanted to stop by his place, and to use her car to start moving. They were being very kind about it, but they wanted her gone. Her brain shifted through all kinds of useful ideas. Like, she could live in a shelter. Or, hey, why not sleep on Daisy's couch? What about camping out in the library all the time?

Still nothing from Trish. The two calls and three text

messages demanding her money back, explaining why and threatening legal action, remained unanswered.

Buck had said Trish would be back at the house that afternoon and that Randi should talk to her and work it out. Randi would work it out all right, with a court date.

When she stepped out of the bathroom, showered and wearing her sleeveless, olive-green jersey knit dress, Aunt Linda and Jack were back. They chuckled, holding hands as they walked through the front door. The implied hearts bursting around their heads made her edgy, so she forced a smile on her face.

"We picked up a surprise for you," said Aunt Linda. "Come outside for a minute."

A futon sat in the back of Jack's truck, tied down with twine, heavy and new looking.

"For you, dear." Aunt Linda put an arm around Jack's back. "So you'll still have a bed at home."

"Guys—wow, thank you."

Randi blinked, staring at the futon like it was a hammer blow from the universe. Sometimes a little thing like fate seemed possible. Her shoulders slumped and exhaustion swept over her as she took in the loving gift.

"Doesn't help me, sitting in my spare bedroom, wasting space," Jack said. "Need more room for my instruments. I hope you'll get some better use out of it."

Randi sniffed, her throat burning. "That's genuinely amazing." Her voice caught.

"Oh no," said Aunt Linda sternly. "You're not going to thank us by crying."

"Probably." Randi covered her eyes. "I'm a little wonky."

Aunt Linda's arm settled around her shoulders, her beaded bracelets jangling. She leaned into the hug, pinching the bridge of her nose.

"Well, no wonder, after traveling for three days. Come in and lie down for a minute."

"Aunt Linda," Randi said, not moving, "I—"

"You," Aunt Linda interrupted, "need a cup of tea. Let's go, toots, inside. Those bags under your eyes are alarming on a twenty-four-year-old."

Randi sank down on the couch and hunched over while Aunt Linda and Jack shuffled around the kitchen, arranging tacos and pouring drinks. Aunt Linda's deep laugh filled the room and Randi couldn't remember the last time her aunt had been so happy. There was no way she would fumble around in the way of that.

Emptiness occupied her chest. Stupidly, she thought of Buck, of that long look he'd given her before finally leaving her at the transit station. His eyes were a cerulean blue in bright light.

He was the worst person, definitely on campus, to be attracted to. And she wasn't, really. More like she'd reacted to him, producing toxic fumes. Her molecules had jumped off his and gone haywire. Then she'd made a huge, messy scene, crying. If she stayed at her aunt's, at least she wouldn't have to see his smirking face.

She pushed to her feet and went to the framed picture of her grandparents on the mantel. She touched the glass. They smiled out at her, holding Mai Tais, wearing Hawaiian shirts, in front of a beach in Oahu, Mimi's grass sun hat pushing into the side of Papa's face. Nothing was ever right without them. Eight years, as of last June, and it felt unreal, unlikely, that that much time had passed.

But she knew one thing for sure. Papa would tell her to "buck up, Buttercup." She picked up the car keys. It was time to get her money back.

# CHAPTER FOUR

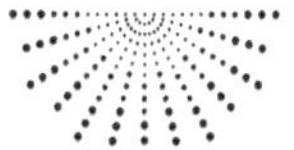

Outside, car tires crunched on the gravel, moving slowly. Buck crossed his boots at the ankle, propping them up on his beer cooler, hopeful. She probably did drive like a turtle.

"Shizzle," Trish said, looking out the front window, her voice the high-pitched squeak of a cartoon mouse. "She's here."

Buck glanced up from the game. It was about damn time Randi arrived. He needed to decide on his next move, and hustle on it.

He was worn out with living in downtown Riverside, particularly with having his trailer parked in Jason's side yard, in the gut of the college party zone. Sirens woke him up most nights. Him and Hugh were spending most of their weekends at this house to get out of Hugh's tiny apartment, watching football and firing up the barbeque. Being in the country felt right. He'd finally decided moving his trailer out here, and parking a good way off in the pasture, might not be a total shit show.

He watched Trish pace around, the heeled boots elevating

her short little body half a foot. With the black fedora hat and fist-sized gold hoop earrings, she strutted around like someone out of a fashion magazine. Except she was breaking out in hives and biting on her fingers. Why the hell couldn't girls be straight with each other?

Angie and Sarah raised their heads from the other couch. Even under the deep tan, Angie looked gray. Sarah's long length curled up surprisingly small as she lay wedged into a corner of the couch, pale and sweaty, bleary-eyed and not making any effort to hide it.

He liked these girls well enough, when he didn't end up babysitting them. Hugh knew what Buck was thinking, at least about the trailer. Enthusiastically in favor summed up the big man's opinion. But there was still one piece missing.

If Randi moved in, her and Trish would be able to force the other girls to back off the big parties. He sure as hell didn't want to be liable for one of those messes.

"Who?" Angie said, her eyes pinched and glaring.

Trish bit on her knuckle and looked out the window.

"Hey, Navajo Barbie, who the hell is it?" Angie said, pushing herself upright.

Buck felt his eyebrows go up. Belligerent Angie put herself further out on the ledge. He was surprised she still lived here after the party bullshit she'd pulled last night. Trish, part of the Tulalip tribe from Washington state, glared back at Angie over her shoulder.

"This is all your fault, Ang," Trish said, swatting at her white pants. "This girl is talking about a lawsuit, or some crap."

There was a hard knock on the door. Nobody moved.

"Door's open," Hugh boomed out from his recliner. Angie gave him a "you're gonna pay" glare. Hugh flushed, looking back at her like an eager dog. Buck held down a chuckle. That dirty bugger liked the crazy ones.

Randi walked through the front door, hard faced, spine straight, a folder of paperwork in her hand and plate-sized glasses on her too pretty, too serious face. She wore a dress again. A green one this time.

"What's that bitch doing here?" Angie said too loud, jerking her head in Randi's direction.

"Um," said Trish to Randi, clasping her hands together. "I guess you don't like the room."

Randi's gaze paused on Buck's for a bare second before she walked forward. Her hair hung down, the ends landing right where her nipples pointed out from under the dress. Buck swallowed. She cleaned up nicely.

"What you did was fraud," Randi said, her voice firm. And tough as nails. *Damn.*

"No," Trish cried. "It wasn't my fault."

Randi held up a hand. "The first step in taking you to small claims court is filing a police report. Which I will do, today. I took pictures of the party last night. Of the state of the bedroom. I documented your ad and our emails. You blatantly lied."

Nobody moved. Trish opened and closed her mouth. Hugh leaned forward and took another piece of pizza, watching the girls like he was at the Super Bowl.

"I know law enforcement has banned this house from having parties. A police report would violate the terms of your probation, Trish," Randi said. "Give me my money back, right now. I'll leave and forget about all of it."

"Get the fuck out!" Angie shouted, her face red.

"Oh yeah," Randi said tightly, "that reminds me. I was assaulted last night by some guy at your party and then Angie threatened to beat me up. I'll be sure to include both points in the police report."

Angie shot off the couch.

"Angie," Trish screamed, her fists waving, the tone of her

voice sliding into unhinged territory. "Stay out of this! If you can't, then move the fudge out!"

Silence. Buck and Hugh glanced at each other. Hugh quivered, his face pink.

Sarah burst into laughter. "You tell her, Trish."

Angie crossed her arms, face mulish. "She's full of shit. It's her word against ours, and she's obviously lying to get her money back."

"Stuff it," Trish said, hands on her hips. She turned back to Randi. "I'm sorry that happened to you. Are you saying you, um, got raped here last night?"

Randi's head jerked back. "No—no. I would have called a rape in as soon as I could. I was cornered and groped. That's assault."

"Oh, okay." Trish paused. There was a moment of awkward silence.

Randi stood up straighter. "It is not okay."

Buck clenched his fist. That little dick Ryan was a menace. Hugh caught his eye, his face grim. They both nodded.

"Listen," Trish said, her voice even more high-pitched than usual, "the massive parties out here have to stop. I'm promising you they will. So, do you think you could take the room?"

"You've got to be shitting me," Angie hollered.

"No," Randi said. "I need my money back."

Trish played with her hat. "Um, right there, we have a problem. Your money is in the government's hands."

Randi crossed her arms. "You're going to have to sort your finances out separately. And I'm betting you can. I need my money. Today."

Good chance Randi had noticed the shiny red car in the driveway. Trish had more money than she knew what to do with. Buck leaned forward, willing Trish to pull her head out of the sand and close the deal.

"Look," Trish said, "I just had to go to court last week and pay a thirty-five hundred dollar fine for a stupid party I didn't even want to have. In August I paid thirty-seven hundred. They want ten grand more out of me and October rent is due next week. My checking account is down to zero. My parents are flaming balls of pissed."

Buck whistled under his breath.

"Since I would never do anything like that, I can't really understand how you got yourself in this position, but your bill is not my problem. Money today or I go to file a police report."

Trish squeezed her face with her hands. "I want to work something out," she said, shaking her head from side to side. "I can scrounge up a hundred bucks for you. If you stay, I'll cut your rent, ten percent off."

"No," Randi said, turning toward the door.

"Wait!" Trish waved her hand frantically. "If you do the report, all of us girls here will be kicked out of school, like suspended and stuff. Sarah the math genius over there would lose her scholarship. Angie will end up in jail, prostituting her body to muscular ladies with bad haircuts."

Hugh turned a guffaw of laughter into a cough. Buck watched Randi's shoulders, stiff as she faced the door. *That's it, girl, let that heart bleed.*

"Shut up," Angie grumbled. "Let her go. It's bullshit."

"Randi, please, what would make you stay?"

Randi shoved her hands in the pockets of her dress. Dresses with pockets? It pulled the back tight over firm curves. He swallowed, dragging his eyes away.

"I can't live with a dirty kitchen and filthy bathroom, and that's only part of it. Trish, it wouldn't work."

"The mess bothers me too! We'll make a cleaning schedule."

"Oh, come on," Sarah said plaintively.

"If you don't clean," Trish continued, steel in her tone, "you pay."

"Which would mean," Randi said, "I'd end up cleaning all the time."

"If you clean," Trish said, rubbing her fingers together, "the house pays you. Fifteen dollars an hour. And the person who missed cleaning pays."

"Trish!" Sarah said.

"Thirty-five hundred dollars, Sarah. How much of that did you cover?"

Sarah pouted, lying back down on the couch.

"Fifteen dollars an hour is a joke," Randi said. "Cleaning companies charge fifty."

"Fine," Trish said, "twenty-five an hour, money deducted out of your future rent."

Randi scoffed. Buck grinned. Women were mean negotiators.

"Trish, fucking stop, Sarah and I don't agree to this," Angie said.

Trish glared at Angie, then said, "A hundred today and your rent down twenty percent."

"I'll have to live here for three months to benefit from that. You're out of your mind."

"I'll refund the deposit next month. Please, Randi, don't ruin our lives."

Randi glanced at Buck. Her black-framed specs were like those sunglasses movie stars wore, covering half her face, but nerdy as hell. Buck blinked, his stomach tightening. *What the hell?* There was no good reason this strange girl should get to him. He smiled at her. She glared at him, then closed her eyes.

An idea was taking hold of him, a chance to ride out his last months in college hell, while he finished his graduate work. Randi was uptight, serious, a hard ass in ugly dresses, and not connected to his friends. Shit, he didn't think she ever partied. The perfect decoy.

In town he was too accessible. Girls were knocking on his door after stumbling out of a bar at one in the morning. For a while, after his breakup with the immoral ex, he'd gone with it. Now he slept on Hugh's lumpy couch to escape. He was worn out, disgusted with himself, and on his way to disliking women.

What he needed was the appearance of a girlfriend. There was no way he was getting seriously involved. Not with his ticket out of here months away. She could be his fake crush. His excuse for being unavailable—most of the time.

Randi slapped the folder against her leg rhythmically. Trish bit her knuckles. Angie glared from the couch, her arms crossed. Sarah swallowed like she was trying not to throw up. Buck leaned back in his chair, grinning.

"I've got conditions," Randi said, breaking the long silence, "which I'll write out and want signed. Forty percent off my rent. My last month's rent is refunded to me and the deposit. A hundred dollars paid to me today. But first, if I stay, everything in that room gets hauled out by you all in the next hour. I'm not touching the mattress."

"So, here's the house," Randi said, forcing her voice into something that resembled cheerful. "Super cheap rent."

Aunt Linda looked around with her mouth hanging open. She stepped over a pile of broken glass and crushed beer cans.

"Randi, I'm not so sure about this."

"A gold mine in bottle deposits out here," said Jack, poking his head around a corner of the patio. The natural foods grocery store which Jack managed was, surprisingly, a hub for bottle returns. "You have a mountain of empties stacked on the patio. I know some people that pick cans on the weekend, should I give them a call?"

"Do it," Randi said.

She should be diplomatic and ask permission. Pointless. Good manners landed in the garbage disposal when a violent psychopath entered the equation. Sarah, and especially Angie, weren't going to become her friends, or even be polite. They'd stormed off somewhere, Angie's jeep peeling out on the gravel before racing down the long driveway with music blasting. Both of them had refused to do any cleaning from the party.

Randi would be in the thankless job of housemother: forced to keep the toilet from turning into a contagious cesspool of disease and hated for pointing out the rotten food in the fridge. Might as well call her Cinderella and hand her a vinyl smock—she was going to need a serious arsenal of chemicals. Either live with toxic sludge or clean up after a bunch of filthy princesses.

The biggest obstacle to renting another room was the housing crunch. Riverside didn't have enough housing for the thirty thousand students that swarmed its neighborhoods every fall, and there wasn't a closet open close to campus. She'd need a pile of money to get into anything. Randi felt her shoulders hunch. The process of taking Trish to small claims court would have been lengthy and tedious and it would probably have taken half a year to see any of her money.

If she'd chosen to live with her aunt for the year, forty miles from campus, her bus commute would have taken up at least three hours of every day. With twenty-one credits to finish each term, her transformation into sub-human zombie would have been complete.

Sighing, she wondered for the hundredth time how epic a mistake not suing would turn out to be. With her ambitious bad luck, it would probably be legendary.

"This is short-term," she said, turning to her aunt. "And since they shamelessly lied about everything, we renegotiated. The rent's cheap, and they promised no more parties."

Jack sniffed. "Once a party house, always a party house."

"I still don't understand why you're doing this," Aunt Linda said, wringing her hands. "Those cat boxes in your room were temporary...I got behind on things. But I don't want you to think that you're not welcome. We get along so well."

Randi's heart twisted. Second thoughts—no, seventh and eighth thoughts—battered through her mind. Aunt Linda meant it, even with Jack's toothbrush in the bathroom. Her vision swam, a wobbly smile on her face.

Jack put an arm around Aunt Linda, pulling her in, and Randi took her hands. "Be careful what you wish for. Living here is a stretch and won't work for long, but I want my money back. I'll be home on the weekends, if that's all right?"

"Of course. I'll count on it."

"Thank you, Auntie, it means so much to me."

Aunt Linda blinked fast, her eyes shining. "All right, enough of that. Let's see what we can do with this mess."

When Jack's can-picking friends showed up, teenagers and a spry grandparent, they piled out of a dinky Sedan, prepared with garbage bags in hand. They methodically covered the property, filling bag after bag, piling them into Jack's truck. The cleaning they accomplished turned out to be the kind of herculean feat that should be chronicled in a tome somewhere, or at least posted on Instagram. Jack generously cashed them out immediately, offering to return the mountain of bags to the store himself, then gave the family a cash bonus to recycle the red keg cups littering the ground and to pick up trash. Swore it was his environmental duty. In an hour, the house and yard went from dystopian wasteland to run down around the edges.

When Randi returned from Aunt Linda's with another load of her stuff, the lawn had been mown. The place looked like a dilapidated but charming farmhouse. Soap suds piled up in the grass around the back patio. Aunt Linda had grabbed the dish soap from the kitchen and gone to town on Randi's cabin bedroom and everything surrounding it.

She was so tired, overwhelmed, and grateful that another attack of tears leaked from her eyes. Aunt Linda pulled her in for a hug and Jack somehow conjured an iced tea. The man was turning out to have superpowers.

Buck and Hugh stepped out of the house, cowboy boots clicking on the wet patio. Hastily she wiped the tears off her face, pretending not to notice Buck grinning at her.

The guys moved the big futon into her cleaned-out room. They instantly bonded with Jack, helping him to unload boxes from the car, jabbering incomprehensibly about football. Her foggy head bobbed around from task to task, as if tied to her body with a balloon string.

Sternly, she kept her eyes off Buck's tight gray T-shirt, and the way his worn-in jeans molded to his hips. At least she thought she did. He was like an actor—not perfect, but your eyes kept landing on him, his quick smiles like flowers appearing in a magician's hands after a pop of smoke.

She sniffed, focusing on unpacking the bedsheets with total precision. What she wanted to know was why he was here. Presumably, he lived somewhere. He was nice enough, but uncomfortable to be around. Distracting as heck actually. She wanted him to go, badly.

When Buck and Hugh jumped in the green truck and

drove off down the driveway, she exhaled. Aunt Linda and Jack said their goodbyes shortly after, then walked towards the parked cars, holding hands. Randi waved as they drove away down the long gravel road through the orchard, her throat tight.

Looking down, she rolled a piece of gravel under her sandal. Leaving Aunt Linda wrenched open a black hole in her chest. They'd come so far—through grief counseling, and almost losing Aunt Linda to cancer. Finding, somewhere along the way, that they were as close as mother and daughter. Maybe closer, when you considered the respect and friendship between them. Randi would do anything for her. Except she suffocated inside Aunt Linda's cluttered house.

She needed to be on her own, totally self-sufficient. During the work week she had to focus without distractions. She wanted a quiet, uninterrupted place to get through the next term and build her yoga YouTube business. Ten thousand subscribers was her real, intoxicating goal. The ladder to a bit of YouTube success and sponsorship, finally.

Her phone buzzed with an incoming text. She pulled it out of her pocket and saw a message notification from Trish, who had taken off to her boyfriend's house after cleaning for ten minutes. Randi put the phone back in her pocket without reading the long text.

A dragonfly buzzed past her face, turquoise and iridescent green. Birds chattered in the trees. In a burst of bubbly joy, Randi turned in a circle. Alone. Acres of orchard and countryside completely to herself.

Gentle evening light backlit the orchard and made the pasture glow, white puffs of dandelion glimmering. There… she would film there. She dashed for her backpack and the pocket that held her cell phone tripod. Just enough time to shoot a video. Every muscle in her body clamored for a stretch.

With a feverish last gasp of adrenaline, she changed into yoga gear—her favorite cloudscape tights and blue halter top. Shoes on and mat under her arm, she raced out to the pasture then framed up a scene for the video.

Pausing to adjust her mat to the center of the shot, she jogged back to the phone. The text message notification popped up again. It niggled at her while she adjusted the video filters, like a swollen bug bite. Finally, she opened Trish's messages. She read them, then collapsed onto her knees, the blood draining from her face.

**Trish**: Hey good news! Buck wants to park his trailer out in the pasture and pay us rent to use the bathroom and kitchen and stuff.

**Trish**: He said you should be reimbursed first out of his rent for cleaning and money owed, and then the rest goes toward lowering everyone's rent.

**Trish**: It's perfect! We won't have to force Sarah and Angie to pay for not doing their chores! They'll just get less money from Buck! He said something about shares so you earn more if you do chores—didn't really follow that, but we'll sort it all out. Will pay cash this weekend!

**Trish**: He'll be there any minute with his trailer!

# CHAPTER FIVE

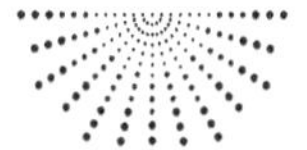

Randi dropped her paintbrush and leaned against the wall, her head swirling in the fume-saturated air. Laughter and shouting broke out on the other side of her door. Cleaning the patio that connected her cabin to the main house was reaping all kinds of consequences, and it was starting to feel like the worst Sunday morning of her life—beginning the night before with her housemates drinking all night.

She jerked back from the wall, wet paint coating the side of her arm. Hunching in defeat, she squatted to grab a rag. The whole situation was bringing home the fact that her not-sleeping kick needed to stop.

The day didn't seem real, like she had woken up and found herself transported to an alien civilization. She didn't want to leave her room and risk awkward interactions, especially with *him*. The "little" get-together that morning to celebrate Buck moving in—enthusiastically organized by all of the other women in the house, over her protests—felt like the prelude to a sporting event. Hordes of rowdy country people kept showing up and parking all over the lawn.

Her stomach gurgled and cramped. Avoiding him since he'd arrived had required all of the stealth and ninja skills she liked to imagine she possessed, and not going into the kitchen. The whole thing stank of disaster.

She wiped her forehead with the back of a clean arm. The biggest question was why decorate when she might not survive the week here? Grabbing leftover paint cans the day before out of Aunt Linda's garage had seemed resourceful and exactly what the grungy interior of her cabin desperately required. Four hours into caulking, rolling, and brushing, she could admit to being overly ambitious.

Outside her open door, people talked and laughed. They sounded giddy, and like they all knew something she didn't. What was so great about crowding together to eat cheap food?

A small part of her wondered what it would be like to join in. Engage with the party crowd during daylight hours. A shiver crawled down her spine. The rest of her wanted privacy.

Of course, they'd set up on the just-cleaned patio in front of her bedroom, because where else would you barbecue on twenty acres of farmland? Deliberately ignoring them created the sullen tone she aimed for—rude, uninterested, and withdrawn. She needed to work, not make small talk with strangers.

"Hey," said a masculine voice.

Randi startled, taking a quick step sideways to catch her balance. Her foot landed in a tray. A wet one. Beige paint covered her flip-flop and splattered over her toes. She stared at it in shock.

"Darlin'," said Buck, "the paint goes on the wall, not your foot."

With a thump, she sat down on the floor, her cheeks hot enough to melt the bottom of her glasses. "My room, my rules," she said, grabbing a rag. For her next trick she could blow snot bubbles out of her nose, which would be the logical progression of her life at that moment. "Speaking of, this space is private. You have the bad manners to set up your barbecue in front of my door, but I do not want to be bothered."

"Wow, cranky."

"All the time."

"Come out and eat a burger. Meet everybody."

"No." She gulped, embarrassed by how frantic that sounded. "I have plans."

In fact, she actually had agreed to meet up with her friend Daisy for lunch downtown at a little street festival. Also, cavorting with the enemy would not be happening, not least because she didn't have time.

He kept staring at her. The cocky half-smile on his face made her jaw clench. If she needed to spell it out, she would. She said, "Don't try to include me in the binge-drinking rituals around here. Not interested."

"Damn." He paused, leaning against the doorjamb. "There something you've decided is wrong with us?"

"Everything. Including you moving in. This is not what I signed up for—endless parties, filth, and no privacy."

He dropped an envelope on the floor. "That's my first month's rent," he said, his voice cold. Sniffing like he smelled garbage, he turned around and walked out.

She stared at the yellow manila envelope on the battered oak floor of her little cabin. Could she afford an area rug? No, definitely not. A cavernous black pit in her chest cracked open. How did someone so irritating also be a little adorable? She exhaled, closing her eyes. Pushing him away was necessary. He needed to back out of her life and stay there.

She cleaned up her painting tools using a hose by the barn. With tenacious discipline, she avoided making eye contact with anyone as she locked up her cabin and carried an empty bin to Aunt Linda's car, stiffening at the snickers of laughter behind her.

Thirty minutes later, she stood at the entrance to the Fall Festival, downtown. Hard to be droopy and depressed when a live band called Gumbo Groove played Fungrass music. She sighed, shoving her hands in her dress pockets.

Hot noon sun sizzled on her bare shoulders. She stared through the chain-link fence surrounding the festival, Buck's tight face from earlier in her mind. That look he'd given her plastered across her brain—the "what kind of monster are you?" glare.

He lived on the same property as her. His trailer was fifty yards away, so distracting barely covered it. She took a deep breath, scanning the crowd for her lunch date. She would keep her distance from him and it would be reciprocated, after their exchange that morning. It was all for the best.

"There you are," Daisy called out, hauling canvas bags on both shoulders and walking toward her from inside the gates. "I got here early and decided to do some shopping."

Daisy dropped her bags on the ground with a clunk and came barreling forward with her arms open. Brown curls bounced up and down over round pink cheeks as she ran. Randi braced for impact.

"Oh, hello," she said, stiffening. She accepted the hug reluctantly, then it stretched out. She patted Daisy's back and finally pulled away. "Um, are you hungry?"

Daisy's eyes shone as she gazed into Randi's face, smiling. "Sorry," she said, sniffling, "I missed you."

Randi blinked, keeping the smile on her face with an effort. They were friends who met for coffee once a week. There had been a lot of emailing over the summer, sure, but nothing to signal sisterhood-slash-best-friend status.

Then she felt like a complete asshole. Daisy's dad had died last spring and it had slipped her mind for a moment.

"Hey," she said, groping for words. "I'm so sorry that you lost your father. I'm here for you, Daisy."

"Thanks. I'm so glad you're finally back."

"Yeah," Randi said, adjusting her glasses. Eventually, they would need to talk about how little time she had for anything besides schoolwork. Twenty-one credits was insane, even for her. "How are you?"

"I'm okay, it's good to be away from my mother's house. Everything I did was wrong, all summer long."

"Ugh, sounds rough," Randi said. They turned and walked through the gates, entering the festival's colorful maze of booths and tents.

"I'm ready for freedom."

"Freedom fries with a side of patriot sauce? The Lion's Club can help you with that," Randi said, aiming them toward the open area lined with food carts.

"Looking at you makes me feel fat. I'll drink a beer."

"Daisy, you're lovely. The ideal of the Renaissance painters—gorgeously curvy. I'm leaning toward the Mediterranean Chicken Fusion Wrap. Fusion usually means peanut sauce, like it's some international unity symbol. Actually, I could totally get behind that. Peanuts for peace."

"You're so random. What kind of beer do you want?"

"The kind called coffee. I have a million errands to run before I head home and murder my new housemates. Things aren't going great."

"What? I thought they were a bunch of religious girls who study all the time?"

"That would be heaven. No, they lied to me. The place is a filthy party house. The night I showed up, hundreds of people were packed in and throw up was all over the lawn. It was a nightmare."

"Oh, my gawd. A party house." Daisy bounced on her toes. "I can't believe you didn't call me! Fun!"

"Daisy, you were supposed to be my ride that night but you got sidetracked by a Ping-Pong table and some kind of spiked fruity cups."

"Uh, they're called Jell-O shots. You really need to get out more. But I know, I know, if you'd just met up with me like I wanted you to, it would have been fine."

Randi decided to ignore that tangent, taking a small step forward in the line at the food truck. "Anyway, I'm staying because it's cheap. I looked online today for open bedrooms and there's nothing. NOTHING. The housing crunch is brutal."

Daisy jumped up and down, a massive smile breaking out on her face. "Randi! Move in with me! I still don't understand why you said no over the summer, but my apartment has to be better than a party house?"

"Hey, thanks for that, but I can't. You have a one-bedroom and I need privacy. I'm the world's most extreme introvert. Plus, I have a bed at my aunt's house."

Daisy wouldn't let it go. Luckily, Randi convinced her to sit next to the live music, so eventually the tirade broke. Instead, Daisy slurped down two beers, remarkably fast for someone her size, and then danced with the little kids in front of the stage.

Randi pulled Daisy out of a spinning competition to say she needed to run over to the campus bookstore. Daisy asked to go along. Blinking, with all kinds of reluctance, Randi exhaled and forced a smile, nodding.

The errand took two hours instead of forty minutes. Daisy muscled onto her side, like an aggressive mollusk. Randi tried to be patient, but the intimacy chafed. She wasn't a sleepovers and spill your heart out kind of friend, more of a workout buddy. They went to the discount shopping center together and Daisy spent thirty minutes in the homewares section, agonizing over a dish drainer. Randi finally left her to wait by the cash registers, watching the enormous clock on the grocery store wall.

It was evening by the time she returned her aunt's car, then Aunt Linda dropped her off with a container of to-go tacos and piles of stuff to put away. She dragged her feet through the front door, hauling her bags in, three on each arm. Her housemates, plus Hugh, were sprawled out on the couches, watching a football game on the television. Bags of chips and, of course, beer cans covered the coffee table.

"Hey, Randi," murmured Trish, her eyes cracked open.

"Hey."

No one else said anything. The social chill in the air was palpable. Her bags landed on the floor of the kitchen with a thunk. A good sign for a quiet night? She could hope.

The bottom shelf of the fridge that she had cleared out and cleaned in the morning was now packed with beer. Blowing a breath out through her teeth, she got to work on the lower crisper drawer, scrubbing out the moldy baby carrots stuck to the plastic. After rearranging everything, she managed to fit the beer and her groceries.

Sitting back, triumphant at last, she looked up and found Buck watching her with his arms folded, leaning against the dishwasher. The living area consisted of one large open room with the kitchen tucked into a corner. A long counter, lined with barstools, divided the space. How had he snuck up on her?

She blinked at him stupidly, still crouched on her heels, as he moved closer. There was no time to shift out of his way. Her body stiffened as he leaned in over her, boxing her in with his broad chest. The man-deodorant stench of him burned into her nostrils. He took a beer out of the fridge.

"Looks like we're going to need a kegerator out here,

Hugh," he said, turning away. The couch slugs all perked up at that idea.

She exhaled, shakily. That had been...something. Deliberately aggressive and dismissive at the same time? Him getting a view down the top of her dress? Her face flamed as she put away the rest of her groceries and then scampered back to her bedroom.

~

"Do it!"

Randi startled awake. She sat up, her heart racing. Was someone in her room?

"Crush that can on your head."

Nothing moved in the dark room. Her bike still blocked the locked door, like she'd left it. She sank back down onto the mattress. Face smashed into the pillow, she exhaled. No one lurked in her bedroom. The voice came from the patio outside her door.

The impulse to flee or hide morphed into a desire to curl up into a ball. Why were they treating her like this? Was picking on her really that entertaining?

Laughter and chatter came from the patio on the other side of her cabin wall. She jerked her bunched-up pajamas down. The party that had been in the house had just moved outside to the small patio connecting her cabin to the house. They were crushing things right next to her bedroom.

It was after ten on a Monday night. Monday night. They were literally feet away. An entire massive farm sprawled out for them to party on, not to mention a covered front porch on the other side of the house. Clearly, they were messing with her.

"Grr—argh!" The pain-filled grunt bellowed from the other side of her wall, followed by the crunch of something metal. A beer can? Cheers, whoops, and whistles erupted like the guy had scored a touchdown. Randi blinked her eyes. Her head throbbed. She didn't want to deal with these people. Why didn't they let her sleep?

She did her best not to interact with anyone. They had stayed away Saturday evening and she had fallen asleep early —until they came home at two in the morning, jolting her awake with yelling and partying until three. She'd hoped Sunday night would be mellow, judging by the hangovers she'd witnessed while putting away her groceries. But they rallied around midnight, waking her up with shouting and breaking glass. Both nights she had hidden in her room.

After she got home from school four hours ago, she'd gone to her room and stayed there, sorting and decorating, and managed to avoid talking to anyone. Her work desk stood in the back of her cabin, the equipment she used for her business organized on a shelf. She had more than enough to do and could happily not talk to any of these people ever again.

Obviously, they had different ideas about what "no parties" meant. When she'd tried talking to Trish about it, all she received was a blank look and repetitions of "but that's not a party." How were they not failed out of school?

Another crash shook the walls of her cabin, making her jerk, and then howls of laughter filled her room. That was it. Randi threw back her covers and turned on her light. She remembered, just in time, the sleepy sloth onesie pajamas. Not the right tone. Covering her eyes, she groped for her robe hanging on the row of hooks next to the door.

Before she could change her mind and jump back in her bed like a sensible coward, she wrenched open her door. Time to make it clear how seriously uptight the new house-mate could get.

Outside, about ten people congregated around a small

fire inside a barbecue grill. Sarah was roasting marshmallows while Angie tipped a beer can over her mouth to suck out the last swallow. Of course, those two.

The only other person she recognized was leaning against the side of the house. Buck stared at her. Or rather he intensely inspected every inch of her robe and slippers. Heat bloomed in her cheeks. The man was indecent, perusing her like a fast-food menu. *Gawd.*

"Hey, guys," she called out, "I'm trying to sleep." She sounded prissy and tense, which was exactly true. Nobody said anything.

She cupped her hands over her mouth. "Can you please move the party somewhere else!"

The only response was a couple of blank stares flicked toward her, and then away again. Sarah and Angie pretended like she was invisible. A guy stumbled into a pile of cans. Angie snorted a laugh.

Red haze fogged Randi's vision. That was about enough. She turned around and stomped back into her room to grab a magazine. On the way, she hit the switch for the outside light. The new bulbs in the flood light glared down on the gathering.

"Hey, assholes," she shouted through the rolled-up magazine. "Clear out or I'm calling in a noise violation." That got their attention. Angie sat up straight in her chair. Disgusted faces blinked at her from all over the patio.

She pointed at the cabin. "This is my bedroom," she enunciated slowly. "I'm trying to sleep in here. It's Monday. After ten at night."

"Fuck off, you crazy bitch," Angie shouted.

"A noise complaint would violate the terms of your probation, Angie," Randi called back through the magazine. Everyone else impersonated statues. "Do this again and I'll call it in without shouting at you first."

Angie threw down her beer can and charged toward Randi, her face enraged.

"Yeah," a guy shouted. "Chick fight!"

Randi forced herself to stay still, her stomach clenching as time slowed down. Angie stomped forward, blonde hair swinging in front of her corded neck. *Run, idiot,* the rational part of Randi's mind screamed. She swallowed into her dry throat, barely managing not to back into her room and lock the door.

Angie knocked the magazine out of her hands. Pain flared in her fingers. Randi shook her hand, holding her wrist.

"You prissy little bitch," Angie yelled, spit spraying from her mouth. "Threaten me again and I'll knock that stupid pink bow down your throat!"

Angie was going to hit her. Fear crawled down Randi's spine. She'd never been in a fight in her life. Psycho Angie probably sought them out on a nightly basis.

Somebody chuckled—was that Sarah? Another jolt of anger shot into her. The bow holding together her robe was big, dark pink, and wonderful. Angie would not be touching any part of it. She put her fists on her hips.

"Let's get something straight," she said, amazed that her voice stayed steady, "if you touch me, I'm calling the police and filing a report. For assault. I will press charges. So, if that's what you need to do, do it, because I'm going to be here for the next four weeks and I'd prefer it if you weren't."

Angie tensed, hands fisted at her sides.

Randi could feel a pulse drumming through her temples. Her vision blurred, became a little wavy around the edges. Was she going to pass out?

"Whoa, ladies," said Buck, grabbing Angie's elbow and pulling her back a couple feet. "You can't fight on a Monday. There aren't enough people here to see it."

The loudmouth chuckled and a few people muttered.

Randi took a deep breath. Another second and Angie would have wailed on her. Spit flecks stuck to her cheeks. She reached up to wipe her face, trembling.

Buck glared at her. "All right, grandma," he said, "go put your hairnet back on. Give us five minutes and we'll clear out. I was working on it before you got nasty."

Locking eyes with him, she was tempted to swat him with the magazine. Instead, she spun around, marched into her room and slammed the door. Then collapsed down the wall onto the floor.

*Breathe, just breathe.* She put her head between her knees. She'd never done anything like that in her life. Had she actually done that? How was she going to survive this until she found a new place to live?

# CHAPTER SIX

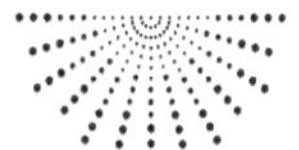

Buck cracked open his eyes, teeth clenched, ready to poke holes in the trailer wall. Another screwed-up dream about the prissy girl. It wasn't doing his body any good to be obsessed with her, so he'd appreciate it if all parts involved could move on to another, willing, female.

Groaning, he pushed the covers back and heaved himself out of bed. The pink robe last night, the black dress on Sunday that showed off her back and bare shoulders, it all burrowed through his brain, for no good reason. Randi one-upped rude and could out-nasty hostile—he couldn't stand her. And she was too damn skinny.

The old trailer cranked and hissed to life, spitting out a tepid gurgle into the shower. Giving up on the water getting warmer, he stepped into the tiny stall, jerking as his over-heated pecker deflated. His sabbatical from women motored along, making his blood pressure soar. Living with four of them was stupid, and it screwed with his resolution to stay single.

He was caught between two stages of life and had realized over the course of the summer that he didn't like where he was headed. Before he'd stumbled upon her lies, he'd been close to becoming engaged to his ex. The fallout from that breakup had turned into booze-soaked debauchery for close to a year. Finally, he was standing on firmer ground but still found himself caught up in the expectation that he was some kind of endless playboy. No man was a match for the relentless horniness of a house full of young women. He could use the appearance of a girlfriend as a buffer to keep the rest of them off.

He scrubbed with soap, gasping as the water turned icy cold. There was no space in his life for a relationship, period. Didn't need it, didn't want it, plenty of other options besides shackling himself to one person. They all lied to him, or to themselves. And he was too damn softhearted. He'd end up miserable, with someone he didn't like much crying all over him.

Over at the house, the kitchen lights shone out into the dark morning. He stepped from his trailer onto damp grass. Someone was already awake, and she needed to hear a thing or two about calling in the police.

Buck walked through the back door and froze. He blinked, taking it in. So much spandex—and a backside view. Every part of him came awake. Her ass flexed as she moved, a sculpted heart, framed by high round hips, every inch on display in skintight leggings. Lean legs stretched down to flashy sneakers, all the musculature curved and firm. Holy shit.

"Morning, darlin'," he croaked. Heaven above. Did she work out every day?

Randi glared at him over her shoulder. "Leave off with the endearments. I'm not your darlin'. And I'm not interested in small talk."

He blinked, a smile tugging at his mouth. Prickly. That

was fun. Made him want to poke her with a stick. Or something. He cleared his throat.

"You're a grumpy one, darlin'," he drawled at her, leaning back on his elbows to enjoy the view. "I'll be sure to catch you every morning, for the thrill of it."

She stuffed plastic bags of food and a tall canteen into a backpack. "Babbling is a sign of senility. You should watch out for that."

Her fitted jacket clung to high pointy breasts and a nipped-in waist. When she didn't wear frumpy grandma dresses, her skinny little body curved in pretty ways. Leaner than he went for. His eye caught on the slope of her flat stomach. He swallowed.

"Aren't you a little old to be lurking around the barely legal girls here?" She sneered at him.

"I'm a grad student," he said, eyes snapping back up to her angry face. Damn, she really had zero interest in being friendly. And twenty-nine wasn't that old.

Randi walked away, pulling a cap on over her hair, and the backpack onto both shoulders. He followed her out the back door.

"Listen," he said as she bent over her bicycle and unzipped a pair of saddlebags strapped to the back rack. "I want to talk to you about last night."

She stiffened up even more. "I meant what I said."

He sighed long enough that maybe she'd notice his frustration. The girl wouldn't know friendly if it held her hostage.

"Okay, everybody got that loud and clear," he said in the placating voice of a kindergarten teacher, "but there's no need to get the police involved. All you have to do is talk to people."

"Right, because talking to people around here is as useful as pulling off my fingernails. I'd rather deal with the police."

Randi strapped on a helmet with a flashlight attached that shone into his eyes. He squinted, eyes burning in the bright light. His jaw clenched—he wanted to rip the thing off her hard head. He sucked in a long breath, reaching deep for patience. He never lost his temper.

"Just talk to me first, I'll take care of it."

"I don't need you to take care of anything for me. Stay away from my room."

Down the road she went, butt in the air as she bounced along the gravel. Obviously, she didn't have any sense. He leaned back against the side of the house, watching her disappear down the driveway.

The next morning, she beat him to the kitchen again. News played on a small radio set and Randi dashed around like a line cook during the dinner hour. Something sweet steamed in the oven.

Buck leaned against the door frame, thinking of the ranch. His mother cooked early in the morning on the days when work started at three a.m., making crock-pots full of beans and stewed meat that fed all the hands. And always cookies, which he got swatted for stealing.

"Mornin', darlin'," he said. "Any way to sweet-talk you out of some food?"

Randi squinted at him over her shoulder, those nerdy coke-bottle glasses perched on her nose. He sighed. No spandex this morning. He walked over to his coffee maker and switched it on.

"Sweet-talking turns my stomach." She turned her back on him.

He rolled a mug in his hands. His stomach growled. "I'll pay you restaurant prices."

She glared at him, clearly wanting to say no, and he did his best to keep his face straight. What an easy mark. Too ambitious, and poor, to turn down a chance to make a dollar. He poured his coffee, giving her time.

"Wash my dishes and it's a deal."

"Yes, ma'am," he said.

A plate of oatmeal cookies thumped down in front of him. Randi snatched up the five-dollar bill he had left on the counter by his mug, still glaring at him.

"I'll give you change." She stomped back to the oven.

"Keep it, darlin'," he called out.

She grunted.

The cookies were warm, loaded with walnuts, dried fruit, oats, and chocolate. He leaned back on the barstool, popping a steaming hunk in his mouth.

He watched Randi bustle around, filling Tupperwares and putting things away. She moved quickly, darting around the kitchen with the kind of energy that was a little irritating so early in the morning. It made him think of all the ways a man could mellow her out.

He shifted in his chair. Even in baggy sweats the girl stirred him up. He was like a mangy dog who'd been handed a plate of table scraps. She'd fed him, showed off a hot restless body, and he wanted to follow her around with his tongue hanging out.

Unwillingly, he liked her. She was a worker. Abrasive, yeah, but it reminded him what the hell he was doing back in school.

And then Randi speed walked out the back door, coffee canteen and food bags tucked under her arm. Buck stood and stretched then tackled his pile of dishes.

Sarah shuffled out of her back bedroom, yawning, as the sun lit up the kitchen windows. Buck poured the rest of the coffee from his pot into his travel mug.

"Morning," he said.

"Hey," Sarah said, scratching her cheek. Her usual wide smile was nowhere in sight. "Morning."

He eyed her sideways. "Randi left a couple cookies out over there," he said.

Sarah stood up straight, her head swiveling to find the food. She picked one up and snorted.

"Healthy crap. It's a cookie not a freaking vitamin pill." She threw the cookie down, then picked it back up and took a bite, chewing with a put-upon frown on her face.

He snorted. "That bad, huh?"

Sarah slumped against the counter. "The weirdo is out there doing yoga again. That stupid crap is the first thing I see when I look out my window. I want a view of the sunrise in the morning, not some little hippy's butt in the air."

Buck's ears perked right up. If he'd had a tail, it would be wagging.

"I've got to see this," he said and headed out the back door.

Sarah followed him around the side of the house to where the property faced east, with a lawn edging the hazelnut orchard.

Buck's mouth dropped open. Randi posed in the middle of the grass, balanced on one foot, the other foot held stretched up behind her head, her chest arching out. She wore skintight pants and a bra. The rising sun shone through the curvy donut shape of her body.

"She records herself and talks into a little headset," Sarah said. "Such a weirdo."

WEDNESDAY MORNING, Randi walked through the back door, yawning. Someone had left the television on all night. Gasping, she stumbled on a stack of shoes, the size of a woodpile, left by the door. The girls were disgusting slobs. She huffed but managed to make it to the bathroom without damaging herself on the clutter.

A few minutes later, she walked back into the kitchen, looking up at the weather report flashing on the massive screen—and froze. Buck was sleeping on one of the couches, an arm slung over his eyes. With a girl next to him. Or rather, on him.

Randi stood, biting a knuckle, staring at them. The girl hung half-off the couch, one leg on the ground, high-heeled sandals falling from her feet. Her face was precariously wedged into the cushion under Buck's shoulder, dark hair hanging to one side. It wasn't Angie or Sarah. Too tall to be Trish.

Why weren't they in Buck's trailer? He'd had a girl overnight on that stained lumpy sofa? Revulsion washed over her. He passed disgusting on his way to revolting. She would never sit on any of those sofas, ever.

Her plan for avoiding everyone and staying out of the house all day had just got hijacked. She had a week's worth of burritos to make, to pack into containers for her lunches and dinners. And coffee. It was start now or not cook at all today.

Shoulders tense, she turned on the kitchen light. Buck immediately yawned and sat up. She turned away from the couches and leaned over to grab pots from her lower cupboard. Buck's voice murmured from the living room. She drained and rinsed the black beans that had been left to soak overnight. Buck coughed as he walked toward the bathroom, and she kept her back to him.

She peeked over at the living room. The girl was still sprawled out on the sofa, sleeping. *Crap*.

Her beans were simmering on the stove when the bathroom door opened again. Buck walked out, his bare chest glistening with water, a towel around his waist. Hairy, naked legs wearing cowboy boots.

Randi blinked and swallowed. His toned body shimmered with moisture—large shoulders, dark blond hair on his chest that trailed down to hard, flat abs. She turned her gaze firmly back toward the garlic on her cutting board. *Holy cats.* Her face burned. How would she scrub that image from her head?

Some little devil inside her, inhabited by her libido, was stretched out on a chaise lounge in her brain, eating popcorn, enthusiastically nodding. She bit her lip, disgusted with herself. Proximity to him was not curing her little problem.

The back door snapped closed and the girl on the couch shot up to her feet so fast she tripped on the coffee table. Managing to catch herself, she looked around frantically, her owl-like gaze landing on Randi.

"Where's Buck?"

Randi stood still, a dripping package of raw chicken in her hands. She put down the chicken thighs and took a breath. "I do not keep track of Buck," she said. Somebody shoot her. Why was the girl still staring at her?

"Crap. He was right there." The girl blinked, sniffing, pointing down at a dip in the cushions on the couch. She covered her face with her hands.

*Oh no, that sounded a lot like crying.*

"Um, yeah. He was right there, that's true."

"What's wrong with me?" Gasping, she plopped back down on the sofa, falling sideways into the saggy cushions. Sobbing.

Randi darted a glance over her shoulder, biting her lip. *Where the heck was Buck?* She needed to deal with the chicken thirty minutes ago, her schedule was already off from creeping around so the dingbat over there could get her beauty sleep.

She washed her hands then grabbed a mug from her cupboard. Muttering to herself, she poured out some of her precious good coffee.

"There's sugar on the counter," she said, giving the girl the steaming mug. The sobbing mellowed down to a trickle. "I'll be heating up some cookies in about twenty minutes," she said, stepping backward toward the kitchen. "I'll give you one if you stop crying."

"Thanks." *Sniff, sniff, sniff.*

"Yep. Well, I'm going to head back to my, um, projects now."

She shuffled back over to the kitchen. That girl was stunning, even with eye makeup smeared down her face like a sad clown from a *Batman* movie or a very puffy-lipped brunette Barbie doll. Was that Botox?

Botox Barbie shot back up off the couch. Randi startled, her hands back in the raw chicken.

"Crap! What time is it?"

"Quarter to six."

"Shit!" The girl gulped down her coffee while walking, carrying the mug with her into the bathroom. A minute later she darted out the front door, the screen door slamming behind her.

Sarah stumbled out of her bedroom as Buck walked in through the back door. Randi sighed. Way too crowded for six o'clock in the morning.

"Morning," Sarah said, plopping down on one of the barstools. "Loud out here. Can I have a cup of your coffee, Randi?"

Randi didn't bother looking up from stirring her rice.

"No, you can't. It's my caffeine and I need it. Also, I already gave away a cup this morning, to Buck's girlfriend.

She was sobbing. He left her on that disgusting sofa before she even woke up."

"Thanks for that, darlin', but she's not my girlfriend."

"That sofa isn't disgusting," Sarah huffed, stomping over to the fridge.

"What was the matter with her?" Randi snapped. The question burst out of her before she could stop herself. He was one of those people who slept with a different person every night, and then complained when they wanted to have a conversation with him. "Not good enough for dating or sleeping with twice?"

He glanced over at her. "She's not right for me."

Randi blew out a breath, indignant for the poor girl. "You just had to run away, couldn't even say goodbye to her." She glared at him. "At least have the decency to go to your trailer."

He pushed his wide body in next to hers and stuck a pan on the one open burner on the stove. She stiffened, pushing her hip against the counter to keep from touching him.

"She's stalking me," he said, his face tight. He dropped half a stick of butter in the pan. "I almost grabbed you to scare her off with your pepper spray."

Sarah leaned in to pull a box of cereal from her cupboard. "She really wanted to go 'talk' in your trailer, didn't she," Sarah said, a little gleefully. "Suzy's bird-sized brain is fixated on you like you're a peanut."

Randi put the lid on her rice. She looked at Buck, who cracked an egg onto his hot pan, his face a little haggard. She stirred her beans.

"We had a fling last summer," he said. "Now I'm thinking about a restraining order. She's a mean crier."

"A fling, ha," said Sarah. "She cornered you once when you were drunk."

Buck's body emitted heat like a sweaty furnace, and it

made the hair stand up on the nape of her neck. Her body reacted to him in all kinds of uncomfortable, overly stimulated ways. A fling, wow.

Randi huffed, backing out of the stove area. Way too much drama for the early morning. She'd appreciate it if they could finish their breakfast and move out of her way. Botox Barbie Suzy had left her mug in the bathroom—geez, classy. She washed it out at the sink, then poured herself a cup and sat down next to Sarah on a barstool.

"Well," she said, breaking the long silence, "if nothing else got through—and cuddling with her, or whatever, all night does send a mixed message—sleeping on that couch probably scared her off."

"Lay off the couch." Sarah threw her spoon down in her cereal bowl. "That's a Serta, all the way from Baker City."

"She wouldn't stop crying and I fell asleep. It was three hours past my bedtime. You girls want some eggs?"

"No thanks, Buck," Sarah said. "Eggs are gross."

"How 'bout you, Randi? I'll trade you for beans."

"Yeah, all right."

"Comin' right up, darlin'," he said, tossing her a smile.

Sarah sniffed, looking around the kitchen with a wrinkled-up face. "What's going on here?"

"You know," Randi said, inhaling the fragrant steam from her mug, "I ask myself that every day in this house."

"You opening a taco truck or some crap?" Sarah said, grimacing.

Randi sighed. What was with all the small talk? "I carry in two meals a day to campus. This," she said, pointing her mug towards the stove, "is going to turn into frozen chicken burritos for the next two weeks."

"The same thing all the time—gross," Sarah said around her spoon, shoveling in the sugar cereal she ate at least twice a day.

It wasn't the same thing every day, but explaining her rotation system would take more talking. She would rather sip her coffee and read. Getting into a cost-benefit analysis with Sarah about saving money and eating nutritiously might ruin her appetite.

Two beautifully cooked sunny-side up eggs landed in front of her with beans on the side. She stared at Buck, shocked. He winked at her.

She got up and pulled out her jar of salsa. Why did everything with him have to be flirtatious? She plopped some salsa onto her plate, then, frowning, passed the open jar over to him. He smiled at her, a patronizing little stroke for being a nice girl and sharing food. She rolled her eyes.

The image of that towel slung low over his hips kept replaying in her mind. It was making her jumpy. She forced herself not to look at him, instead finishing her food quickly and getting back to work.

An hour ago, she would have assumed, without a second thought, that he would simply sleep with someone attractive, a Suzy, if she showed up. And that he was the hookup king. That there were a dozen girls like Suzy, waiting like squirming fish strung on a line, batting their eyelashes at him.

He might be a little more complicated. Maybe. With a soft spot like a rotten orange.

# CHAPTER SEVEN

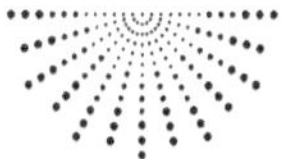

The third week of school was off to a horrific start. After spending the weekend at her aunt's, she'd arrived back on Sunday to another filthy house. It was only Monday and she wanted to leave again.

Randi picked up speed, heels clicking on the campus sidewalk, a hair short of running. The flat tire on her way to campus had risked skewering her entire day. At least the path was mostly clear five minutes before class started. She could still make it!

A crack in the sidewalk snagged her like a deer in a trap. She stumbled sideways, a nasty twinge burning through her ankle. Concrete rushed up to slap her hands and knees.

"Dammit." Pain shot along her leg. A bloody scraped knee pulsed with a burning sting, and dirt and rocks stuck to her skin. She pushed herself up into a crouch.

"Hey," said a male voice, "you all right?" A tall, broad-shouldered man towered over her.

Randi stiffened and groaned inwardly. Her dress was halfway up her thigh, the mustard fabric almost to her hip, and her slip underneath was barely managing to keep her decent. She yanked the skirt of the dress down. Now she had to talk to Sir Galahad over there, who'd ridden up just in time to savor her humiliation.

With what she hoped was a calm and composed face, she quickly gathered up her spilled bag and slung it over her shoulder. He handed her her notebook. She kept her eyes down, hoping he'd realize how uncomfortable she was and end this awkward torture.

"I'm fine," she said, standing up and dusting off her dress. Her ankle wobbled. She gasped, looking down at the broken heel of her cheap fashion Oxfords. "Just making a fool of myself, but thanks for noticing."

He laughed and Randi looked up, startled by the deep attractive sound. A russet-haired giant stood in front of her. Wavy thick hair curled out from his head, dark copper at the roots and sun-bleached at the tips. Heavily lashed hazel eyes twinkled at her. Her mouth twitched, trying to respond to his, almost, irresistible grin.

"Everybody stumbles," he said, "so don't worry about it." He sat down on a short concrete wall. "Do you want me to knock that heel off for you? I've had practice."

Randi crossed her arms. His scruffy face was boy-next-door that morphed into a football star and drove a loud car. Why did freckles make a person seem trustworthy? She was actually considering handing over her shoe to this stranger.

"Practice? Do you stalk clumsy women who wear cheap shoes?"

His eyebrows shot up. Yeah, big guy, back away slowly. She wouldn't surrender her shoe to anybody.

"Um, no. I have a sister obsessed with pageants, and my mother likes tall heels." He smiled at her like she was a crazy person. Damn straight.

With a deep breath, she adjusted her glasses. She realized that living with the alcoholics was making her even more standoffish than usual. However, being introduced to handsome men during her worst moments was a reoccurring theme in her life lately, and she was not onboard.

"Fine," she said. "I'll hand over my Oxfords, but if you're hoping for ransom payments, all I've got is a bag of popcorn."

He grinned and there were dimples. Wow, again. He leaned forward extremely slowly, like she might kick him at any moment, and laid a hand on her foot.

"Sit down," he said, "and relax. The shoe won't feel a thing."

And for some cursed reason, she did exactly as he asked, plopping down on the concrete wall next to him and letting him touch her foot. He undid the laces with slow fingers, making her blush. Her pulse jumped when his massive hand slid over her ankle to ease off the heel. He pulled out a pocketknife and bent over, slitting and wedging off the broken piece.

"Better give me the other one too," he said. And like an obedient idiot she handed it over. If her shoes got any worse, she'd be walking to class barefoot.

"That's about as flat as I can get them," he said, handing her the shoes.

Randi slipped them on her feet and stood up, surprised when she didn't wobble.

"Thanks. You actually lived up to the hype. Do you want me to promote your social media page or something? Are you prince cobbler on Instagram?"

"No, but uh thanks for the offer. I will take some popcorn though."

She sighed. "Me and my loud mouth, blabbing about the goodies." She dug in her bag.

"In class," he said. "Let's go, the lecture just started."

Randi froze. "Wait, how do you know what class I'm in?"

He sighed. "You sit in the front row, and ask questions."

"Oh."

And so, she found herself following his tall back, muscles obvious underneath a white cotton T-shirt, into Greary Hall. She stopped in the bathroom to wash out her knee, and, surprisingly, he waited for her. He walked towards two empty desks in the far back row of the arena-like lecture hall and slid gracefully into one of the tiny chairs bolted to a minuscule table, managing not to bang into it with his massive legs.

She glanced longingly at the desks in the front row. It took getting to class at least fifteen minutes early to secure her favorite spot by the aisle on the left side. Instead, she was sitting in the far back with the pot smokers—some of them actually napping. Why did they even show up? Trash covered the floor and it stank like a brewery.

"It's disgusting back here," she whisper-shouted at the giant.

She pulled out her packet of disinfecting wipes and scrubbed down the desk, battling with a pile of sticky grime on the chair. She wiped away the astringent moisture with a dry Kleenex.

The giant watched her, eyebrows raised, before looking away, a scared half-smile on his face. He tossed a beat-up notebook onto his grubby desk. An old candy wrapper actually touched his hand. It was too much for her. She leaned over him and grabbed the trash with a Kleenex, then marched to the very back of the hall to drop her pile in a garbage can.

"You're welcome," she whispered at him, taking her seat. "I don't think you should get the plague the same day you rescued my shoes."

He nodded at her, a "you're crazy" look unmistakable on his face. That was good. She didn't want an unnamed giant man thinking they were lecture buddies or something.

She pulled out her laptop and adjusted her glasses, focusing on the far away PowerPoint projected onto a screen. The professor's voice droned through a speaker.

"Popcorn please," said the giant, eyes twinkling again. "I'm Luke, by the way. We should study together."

"BITCH, don't touch my beer bottles again."

Randi dropped her grocery bags next to the front door, rainwater puddling at her feet. The fall storm gusted wind, banging the screen door against the house.

The psycho woman couldn't even wait until the door closed. Randi pulled off her jacket then shook it off outside. She sighed, then shivered, a little desperate to get into her room and under the covers.

Instead of getting better, the housing crunch was worse and there wasn't a place for her to move to. Looked like she would have to tough it out until the end of term and hope for openings over winter break. Or resign herself to commuting from her aunt's.

She'd managed to avoid everyone, for the most part. Especially Angie. But the rain and her flat tire had forced her to walk through the front door during the television social hour. And it was like no time had passed with Angie. She practically snarled.

"You gave them to a bunch of drug addicts."

"The contract is on the wall," Randi said, adopting a flat, over-worked-lawyer voice. "Take care of your bottles by Sunday, at two p.m., or the deposit money is fair game. And the people nice enough to clean up your mess are doing the community a service. If you don't like it, please, move some-where else."

Angie slammed her can down on a side table. It wobbled

precariously on the piles of junk underneath it. "Fuck that," she said, her face pinched and red.

"Take a breather, Ang," Trish shouted from one of the couches, her body taut. Everybody froze. The tiny woman became slightly terrifying when she raised her voice. "I want to watch a movie, not listen to you rage! Oh, my word, I've had it! Stack your crap in the barn, I told you that. It stinks, like reeks into the house when you put it all by the back door! I know you don't have another place to live, but PLEASE will you stack your crap in the barn."

A dark-haired guy Randi hadn't seen before sat down next to Trish and slung his arm around her.

"*Poltergeist,*" he said, cracking open a can of beer. "If anybody says *Bridget Jones's Baby*, I'm leaving."

"You really want me to be up all night?" Trish said to him. He kissed her.

"You're disgusting," Sarah said from a chair.

Trish leaned away from the kiss, a goofy grin on her face, then she cleared her throat. "Hugh picks tonight," she said, looking towards Hugh and Angie sitting on the other couch. "Don't make me regret it, big man."

Hugh cracked open a beer, his face crinkled in thought. He took a long drink from his can.

"*Independence Day: Resurgence.* The mother ship arrives."

There were equal parts groans and cheers.

Randi bent over, aiming for her bags, then paused as her glasses slid down her nose. A large pair of hands picked up the bags around her in one grab.

"Hey, darlin', I got it."

Before she could tell him, "No thank you, stay away from me," she sneezed. Her glasses fogged up. *Crap.*

He was already in the kitchen, putting her groceries on the counter by the time she squelched over, wet shoes leaving a track of damp footprints on the floor. Since beer bottles shattered on that floor weekly, her boots stayed on.

"Thanks," she mumbled at him, not making eye contact.

He'd been pestering her every morning, talking to her. It was like the nastier she got, the more he dug in his heels. Determined to do what?

She could feel Angie's glare burning a hole in her. If Buck would just ignore her, like she wanted, his psycho wannabe girlfriend could relax.

She put a pot on the stove to boil water for tea and yawned, covering her face with her hand—riding in the rain all day took a toll. She needed a hot shower. Not happening in the one crummy bathroom next to six bladders guzzling beer in the living room.

Buck stayed in the kitchen, leaning on the counter while he drank a bottle of beer, watching the movie previews on the television. Her gaze kept landing on him while she put away her groceries. His hat was off, the hair still pressed down in a crown around his head. A thin black T-shirt, soft and broken in, clung to his chest and shoulders. No, no. No more looking for her.

The truth was, she almost relished her mornings with Buck. Interacting with him gave her a little charge that she had a hard time explaining to herself. Definitely not something she wanted to exhibit in front of Angie.

"What the fuck kind of name is Randi?" Angie sneered at her from the couches.

Heads swiveled toward her, ears pricked and eyes zeroed in. Did Trish actually turn down the volume? Randi pushed up her glasses.

"Just a name," she said. "It's German."

Randi was the name her mother had given her. A bad joke. A penance. Revenge for a tough birth. Randi would never know since her mother was long gone and she hadn't had a chance to ask her. Thinking about her mother, dead before she was five, made her angry, so she tried not to.

Sure, her name was actually derived from Norse and meant lovely goddess, but the English connotation was obvious. And the setup for a childhood of bullying. She pulled a mug out of her cupboard, willing them all to look away.

"It's hilarious," slurred Sarah, beer cans stacked up next to her. "Should be Icee Queen." She laughed. "Icee! That's perfect! You should change your name."

"Randi and Buck," said Hugh between handfuls of popcorn. "Perfect name for a strip club." He chortled.

Angie stared daggers at him. Hugh put his hands up in a classic "what?" gesture.

"Movie, people," said Trish, and cranked up the volume on the television.

Randi kept her eyes on the pot of steaming water, not looking at Buck. Still not boiling. They weren't connected just because they both had absurd names with stupid sexual innuendos. She grabbed the hot water off the stove, unwilling to wait any longer, and poured it into her mug. A dash to the bathroom, while her tea bag steeped, and then she finally headed to the back door.

"Hey," said Buck, stepping in front of her, "stay and watch for a bit."

His blue eyes held hers. She blinked, adjusting her glasses. "No. Um, goodnight."

She took a step sideways, clutching her hot mug carefully so she didn't spill the steaming liquid, obviously signaling to him that he needed to move so she could get to the back door. He impersonated a rock. She edged by him in the tight space, her temper flaring. Couldn't he simply be polite?

"Hold up a second, darlin', I want to talk to you."

"No thanks."

She kept going, clumsy with the back door while trying to keep hot tea from burning her hand.

"Goodnight, y'all," called Buck. "I'm gonna hit the sack."

Randi stepped out the door before she heard the reply. Angie definitely shouted something. Then her brain grasped what was happening. Wait, what was happening?

Buck caught up to her on the back patio, underneath the tiny awning that covered the stairs. "Hey, hold up a minute," he said, right before she would have stepped into the rain to cross over to her room.

She paused, not wanting him to follow her to her door. He stood too close again under the little shelter. The rain pounded down all around them.

She looked at him, trying to project calm indifference. Her heart beat a million miles a minute. His cowboy hat was back on his head, the black rim shading his eyes. She could smell him, and see the stubble on his jaw.

Finally, she said, "Well? What's the emergency?"

His mouth quirked up in a smile. "The storm, darlin'. The rain's going to be worse tomorrow. I'll give you a ride in the morning."

She shook her head. "Stop thinking I'm soft or whatever. It's the kind of challenge I live for."

He crossed his arms, leaning in closer. Her stomach clenched. Being so close to him discombobulated her—heat was happening where it had no business being. She turned her body away from his to avoid bumping his chest.

"Falling down and beating yourself up?"

"You know what, don't worry about it. It has nothing to do with you."

She was angry. Angry was good.

She resented him for pushing her, trying to draw her out. It was condescending. At some point she would be moving out of this house, and it was her choice not to become friendly—especially with a notorious playboy who liked to tease her for his own amusement. Her massive workload came first. She didn't need, or want, any more people in her life.

"I pass you every day, going the exact same way," he said. "When it's dark and raining, you're hard to spot. There's no shoulder on that road. As annoying as you are, I'd be a little sorry to kill you."

"I'm covered in reflectors and bright lights. You know what? Stay in your lane, literally and figuratively."

She pulled the hood of her jacket up with jerky movements, her elbow jabbing his chest.

"Huh," he said. "You're a little cute when you get angry."

"Leave me alone." She stepped into the rain and marched to her door.

"Catch you in the morning, darlin'," he called after her.

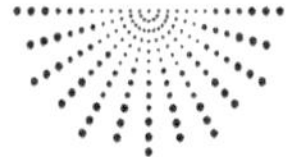

"Hey," Buck shouted at her through the driver's side window, "how about that ride?"

He drove right behind her bike, like a stalking predator, headlights illuminating the rain coming down in diagonal sheets. The early morning harassment campaign had officially left the kitchen and moved to the driveway. It was barely light outside and she already wanted to murder him.

Water and wind lashed at her lower face, the only skin not covered by her rainsuit. Her cycling goggles had fogged up. If she didn't have a demented maniac heckling her, she'd stop and fix them.

"I've got this," she yelled. "Go torture some sheep or whatever. Leave me the hell alone."

Water ran down her throat, and she coughed. The bike swerved precariously close to the ditch, teetering on the edge of falling in. Choking on the liquid caught in her throat, she veered back onto the road.

Thunder cracked in the sky above them. She startled, but kept a grip on her handles. She was halfway down the long gravel driveway through the orchard. Nearly had her first mile done. Well, half a mile. A little rain wouldn't screw up her schedule.

"It's a damn storm, you idiot," he shouted back at her.

Angry heat burned through her cold muscles. Her feet slammed down on the pedals, trying to move the bike faster. He loved to bully her. Every morning he appeared like a jack-in-the-box, waiting to trade middle school insults with her. Sure, she might be a touch pigheaded to refuse a ride in a monsoon—not the point. No way she would give in now.

It was time to show the cowboy not to mess with crazy. His little fascination with torturing her needed to stop.

"Move on or I'll dent your door with my water bottle," she yelled back at him, bending over to grab the steel bottle and then waving it in his direction.

A massive lake-like puddle came out of nowhere. Her tires hit the water and went sideways. She slammed on the ground and slid, water splashing in her face and down the collar of her jacket. Pain exploded in her right shoulder. She stopped with a thud against a slope of mud.

Panting, she didn't move. The pain of a serious injury would hit any minute—or not. With eyes closed she took a slow breath.

A car door slammed and Buck was there, calling out something she didn't catch over the ringing in her ears. He hauled the bike off her. She rolled over, spitting out dirt, gagging on the mud in her throat.

"Looks like you didn't break your neck," he said, crouching next to her. Gingerly, she moved her head from side to side and sat back on her heels. She would walk away from the fall. Bending over, still panting, the sour fungus taste of dirt coated her tongue.

He gripped her elbow, keeping her from falling over. Thunder rumbled. She stared up at him, mesmerized as water ran off his nose and dribbled from his clenched jaw. He looked like he wanted to shake her.

She groaned, closing her eyes against throbbing aches scattered all over her body.

"Why the hell would you pull a stunt like that?" he spat at her. Her ears rang, effectively muting him.

"Hey, Bucko," she muttered groggily. "If it wasn't for you, I'd be halfway to school by now." She wanted to shout at him, but clutched her middle instead. That tumble had scrambled something.

Slowly, holding onto Buck, she got to her feet. Agony shot through her ankle. She stopped moving, breathing out through the pain.

"Get in the truck," he ordered. "I'll take you back to the house."

"I'm fine. And I need to get to school. Just give me a second."

Before she could dodge his grip, he slid an arm under her legs and picked her up, cradling her against his chest. She blinked at him, shocked. In a few steps he yanked the truck door open and dumped her inside. The passenger door closed beside her with a crash.

He jogged back to her bike, shoulders flexing as he pulled it out of the mud and then carried it to his truck, his face hard. Randi sniffed. She shouldn't care that he was enraged. That's what she wanted. She slumped against the seat, squinting to slow down the spinning. She was an idiot but she really didn't want to hear about it.

With a squeaky jerk, the driver's side door opened. He sat down next to her, face like a thundercloud, water dripping from his soaked head.

"You're a real pain in the ass, you know that?"

"And you're a bully," she said, trying to be irritated instead of miserable. She cleared her throat. "Follow me like that again and I'll…" She paused, her soggy brain slogging to a halt. She wouldn't dent his truck, and the universe had called her bluff on that one. Best not to test fate.

"You'll what? Take a dive in a mud puddle?"

"I'll pour water in your cowboy hat," she said, managing to sound firm. "Does that thing actually hold water?"

"Touch my hat and you'll find out what hell feels like."

"Wow, so scary." She closed her eyes. A towel smacked her in the face.

"Wipe that mud off my truck."

He unbuttoned his soaked shirt, his dripping head bent over. A little heat warmed her cheeks. Apparently, he was going to take his shirt off. His nearness, the muscular forearms dusted with freckles, unbound reactions in her. She didn't want to feel this—all tangled up with anger. He played with her just to amuse himself.

On impulse, and because she'd hit her head, she leaned over and wiped his face with the clean towel. Her hip burned with pain but she ignored it, determined to do something so awkward he'd leave her alone afterward. He froze, his hands still on the buttons of his shirt. There was something a little gorgeous about the way his eyelashes fanned out over his sun-bronzed cheeks. She ran a corner of the towel over the bridge of his nose, skimming down to the cleft in his chin.

She wanted to irritate him, make him pay a bit for not leaving her alone. Probably because she might have a concussion, being near him turned it into something else. He glared at her. Their eyes connected and electricity jolted up her fingertips.

He smelled like a man's soap, and like rain, and something that was just him. A little color flushed his cheeks. Her pulse raced. In another life she might rub her face in the steamy musk coming off his chest. His forearms flexed. She scrubbed his chin, wiping off the last fleck of mud.

She leaned away from him, swallowing a gasp at the twinges of pain. Hopefully the dirt splattered on her face was dulling down her flaming cheeks. He stared at her, his chest billowed out, the tendons in his neck tense.

"Your face was disgusting, all covered in mud," she said, shocked at her light, detached voice. Raising the towel, she dabbed at her wet face, mesmerized by his intense gaze.

Touching him had been a mistake, definitely. The implication that she could put her hands on him—or at least he would let her maul him with a towel—startled her. She hated the fact that she wanted to. He was too much, and the last man she wanted a relationship with. Not that he'd ever offer one.

The engine revved to life and they rolled forward toward campus. He sat stiff and silent next to her. Maybe now he'd back off. Let her ride to school in a storm, carry her own damn bags, and not talk to anybody at the house. They would be strangers. The absolute best thing.

She'd been fooled before by an overly slick charmer, a lady's man. Buck was sly, teasing, and spoiled by far too much female attention. He reminded her of one of those male reality show contestants who date thirty people at once. They start out decent enough guys, but by the end of the season have the mindsets of dictators entitled to a harem of women, all there to stroke and placate their egos.

Pulling her phone out, she tried to refocus her mind. The pain came roaring back even while her stomach still hummed from that look he'd given her. Like he wanted to kiss her.

Her body could take a breather and call her later. Men would come and men would go but college degrees were forever.

The truck jolted to a halt, and Randi glanced up and saw rain slapping the windshield of the truck. The headlights glared on an empty country road, dim and gray, a downpour beating down on the dark asphalt. Her phone jerked from her hands.

"Hey," she blurted, whipping around to see Buck's back as he hunched away from her. "What are you doing?"

He didn't answer. She sat stunned, blinking gritty eyes. It was way too early in the morning for a phone abduction. His cowboy hat was in grave trouble, she decided, and turned to scan the cab for it. Piercing pain shot down her twisted back. She groaned, feeling over a bruised rib.

He tossed the phone on the seat beside her and she snatched it up. He'd called himself and entered his name as a contact. Well, she'd be canceling that.

"Don't ride home tonight," he said curtly. "I'll pick you up."

~

"OMG! What happened to you?"

Daisy stared at Randi like she'd walked in with a full body cast. Geez, so dramatic. A bandage covered her cheek, and she limped around with crutches. And so, all day long, every chatty stranger on the sidewalk thought they had to say something to her about it.

Randi sank down onto the tiny café chair, her ankle screaming for another ice pack. Walking across the street, through pounding rain, had her cross-eyed with the need to lie down. And soggy, again.

She had lurched her sore body to all of her classes by sheer willpower, and by eating candy all day. She hadn't even snarled at anyone. Now the candy was gone.

"Fell off my bike this morning." With a whack, her backpack landed on the floor. She winced; she hadn't meant to do that. "Do you see anything I could put my foot up on?"

A miniature chair materialized in front of her—a scrounged up high chair covered in food globs, squeezed in between the crowded tables of the packed coffee shop. She unapologetically plopped her foot up, barely caring about the mess. It was shocking to be injured. Made you appreciate the small things you take for granted, like having your feet on the ground where they belong.

"I can't believe you rode your bike in the storm. Why don't you get a car?"

"I'm allergic to car ownership," said Randi. She was dirt poor. If that wasn't obvious, she didn't want to explain it.

Daisy pushed a hot coffee across the table toward her. "Drink this," she said. "You look like you're about to pass out."

"What do I owe you for the coffee?"

"Forget it, crazy."

"Thanks. But don't call me crazy." Too close to the truth.

Daisy rolled her eyes and flipped her mop of curly brown hair. A group of guys two tables over held half of her attention.

Randi focused on Daisy, admiring her yellow rain jacket with a blue-and-white striped lining. "That coat is killing it. How are things?"

"Lousy. I'm still mad at you for not moving in. And you won't even go out with me on the weekends. What the hell?"

Of course, the harangue yet again. Blah blah, she's such a horrible friend, blah blah blah. In reality, going out drinking as a recreational sport walloped Daisy every time. Nothing she wanted to be involved in.

"Twenty-one credits, Daisy. I stopped watching television. I work and eat, that's it."

"Randi, you're missing out on college."

"Don't care."

From her perspective, she was fully immersed in college,

in the deep end past her hairline in all of the learning she could cram into this term and the rest of her senior year. Daisy came from a comfortable upper-middle-class family, and didn't realize what it meant to get through college without a savings account provided by your parents. Randi was twenty-four, compared to Daisy's twenty-one, because she'd had to take time off school to work while living with her aunt and doing all of her prerequisites at community college.

Daisy huffed, squinting at her. "This is the time of life to get out there, make friends, find a guy. What's wrong with you?"

She slouched, deciding to dump more sugar in her coffee. Her ankle itched under the bandage. There was plenty wrong with her. Foremost among them, this conversation.

"Men are distracting. I'm not dating this year at all."

Daisy stared at her with an open mouth. "You're not serious."

"Very. As the grave. As a heart attack. Also, it's my middle name."

"You're overreacting. Just relax."

Randi took a sip of her coffee. Daisy was a steam roller. The round, pink-cheeked face camouflaged a ruthless autocrat.

"Hey, Randi," said a familiar male voice.

Luke stood at their table, smiling down at her.

"Hey, how are you?"

"I'm wondering if you broke another heel, but fell down stairs this time. You okay?"

"Fine, a little bruised. Bike slipped this morning."

Daisy cleared her throat.

"Luke, this is Daisy," Randi said.

They all chatted for a minute about the weather. Randi

wanted to put her head down on the table and sleep. A little Tylenol and she could pass out on the floor.

Luke looked at her, a lot. If she didn't feel like the mush stuck in the bottom of a blender, she would be blushing. Finally, he worked his way up to the counter to buy his coffee, then waved to them on his way out the door.

"O…M…G," Daisy said. "Those dimples are too much. Are you going to try and tell me you're not interested in seeing where that goes?"

Randi sipped her coffee. "He's a musician. Not my scene."

If she was being completely honest, she could admit to possibly being a little interested. Not enough to date the guy —she knew nothing about him. At this point, she looked forward to seeing him in class. That was it.

"What about you?" Randi said, veering off into more comfortable waters.

Daisy talked about one of her neighbors in the apartment complex. He was a grad student in the literature department who lurked in the apartment parking lot all night, drinking. Daisy was even more infected with boy-crazy than usual. Also, she was chatting up strange men late at night. Randi bit her lip. She didn't like it and had no idea what to say.

Her phone chimed with an incoming text message, from Buck. She swallowed. It crossed a line, and there was no going back. He existed in her phone.

When Daisy left the table for a few minutes, Randi read the message.

**Buck**: When's your last class?

That was it. Like they'd already worked everything out— he learned her schedule and she rode around in his truck.

She tapped her fingers on the tabletop. Her aunt was working. Daisy's little Sedan didn't have anywhere for her bike. But riding with him was not an option. She could figure out another way.

**Randi**: Don't worry about it.

**Buck**: You at the Beanery?

Randi gaped at her phone. He knew her location. After some searching, she realized he'd enabled location sharing between their iPhones. She turned it off.

**Randi**: That's creepy!

**Buck**: Tech skills. Be there in thirty.

Randi stared at her screen. It was so beyond not okay, it was insane.

"I've got to run," said Daisy, grabbing her bag from the table. "Class in ten minutes, but seriously, you've got to lighten up. Come out and have some fun with me."

"Uh-huh. My creep-o-meter is up with your neighbor guy, Daisy. Sitting by the parking lot in your boxers, drinking Schnapps, is dumb. Reeks of desperation and bad hygiene."

Daisy rolled her eyes and flounced off.

Randi finished her coffee, staring at the wall of windows in the front of the shop, fogged over with condensation on the inside and dripping wet outside. Her mind bobbed in her skull uselessly.

Leaving was the appropriate thing to do. She could walk back over to the health clinic and ask about one of the ride services provided by the university. What she needed to do was spend five hours in the library working. She shifted, grunting. Her ankle, hip, chest, and shoulder throbbed.

A little devil in her cheered on the persistent cowboy,

reasoning with blatantly manipulative logic that he had caused her to crash, so he could bloody well chauffeur her home. But she knew what that devil really wanted.

Buck walked through the door way sooner than she'd expected him. The crowd in the coffee shop went still and silent, staring at the towering cowboy out of the corners of their eyes. He shook off his cowboy hat outside the door and wiped his boots on the mat.

She blinked, then rubbed her face. When she opened her eyes, he was still there, walking toward her table.

"Let's go, darlin'," he said. "I'll grab that bag for you."

A girl at a table next to her sighed. Randi frowned, then found herself going along with his orders, submitting like a sad cow plodding to slaughter. She didn't want to make a scene in her favorite coffee shop.

Outside, he was illegally parked with his hazards on. He stowed her bag inside the cab.

"Where's your bike?" he shouted with the rain pounding down in sheets around them.

"Across the street," she said pointing toward the covered bike rack.

He took care of it all. On the ride back to the house, she leaned back and closed her eyes, trying to ignore the uncomfortable knot in her chest.

# CHAPTER NINE

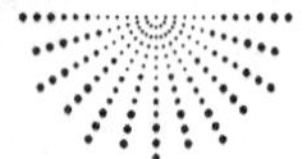

The truck bumped over the gravel road and Randi braced a hand against the dash, resolutely staring at her phone screen as her stomach turned in revolt. Her old friend since crashing her bike, the headache, was back again, knocking on her brain. The rides into school with Buck and Sarah for the last three days resembled a cruel ritual to appease a vindictive, elemental god. If only it would stop raining.

Sarah's normal ride to school with Angie was too unreliable, or late. Angie skipped class. Apparently, she was finding life tough, problems at home increasing her already sky-high stress levels. Randi wondered if there had ever been a time when Angie had been nice. Kind. She doubted it. Too much to hope that she would fail out of school sooner rather than later?

While Sarah riding into school with Buck was a useful buffer from being alone in the truck with him, it meant she had to sit practically plastered against his side. She blew her breath out, willing the ride to end soon.

"So, what's your deal?" said Sarah. "Why don't you have a man?"

There it was—Sarah's hostile conversational gambit. A regular chatty-Kathy, with an edge of vindictive spite. Randi sighed, keeping her eyes on her phone.

"Buck, Sarah's talking to you."

A rumbly laugh came from next to her. She pulled her elbow in, trying not to touch him.

Sarah inhaled in a dramatically frustrated way. "No. You."

"Too early in the morning for personal questions, Sarah." Randi held her phone closer to her face. Couldn't she finish one article?

"You're the most annoying morning person I know. I mean, yoga? If I have to deal with seeing your scrawny ass downward dogging, or whatever, you can answer a simple question."

"Darlin'," Buck said, "your ass is not scrawny."

"Can we leave my ass out of it?"

"Now, come on," Buck said. "I told you before, all I want for driving is a little conversation."

Randi shoved her phone in her pocket. Might as well feed the beasts and be done with it. They were like a couple of dogs scratching at the back door. *Gah, bad analogy.*

"Fine, one question, on the condition that you each have to answer as well."

"Generally, how talking works," Buck said.

"I'm picky."

Silence. "Uh, yeah, Captain Obvious," said Sarah. "You didn't answer the question."

Randi crossed her arms. She could feel Buck smiling at her. "Too complicated."

"Come on now, darlin', toss us a bone."

Buck nudged her with his elbow. The contact was like an electric shock down her spine. She was too close to him.

Whatever soap he used got into her brain. Talking might be good—so that she stopped thinking.

"Last year, I dated a grad student from the business school. He did everything right. Too right." She took a deep breath. Talking about it was like sticking a sword in her chest.

"We'd been dating for a few weeks when he planned a special night. Wine bar, dinner, a hotel." She swallowed. Even a year later, the memory surfaced like a punch.

"A hotel room—dang," Sarah said. She huffed, slouching in her seat. "Why didn't I ever think of that?"

Randi smoothed the skirt of her dress.

"What happened?" asked Buck.

"I got a little tipsy and decided to play a trick on him and grabbed his phone while he was in the bathroom." Actually, she had been going to take a picture of herself in the hotel room. She'd been so excited, until her legs had stopped working when she saw his screen. Like walking off a cliff into an ocean of ice water.

"He had about five missed messages from another woman. His fiancée. She was planning the wedding and needed his guest list ASAP."

"Crap," Sarah said.

"Yeah. It got ugly. I realized that I don't want to waste the time and energy on dating right now. Statistically, it probably won't work out, especially with people in their early twenties."

"So, wait, it's been A YEAR?" Sarah said, staring at her like Randi needed to saw off a limb.

Randi sniffed, feeling her cheeks burn red enough to singe her glasses. "That's another question, Sarah, and none of your business."

"Fine, but dang, Randi. No wonder you do all that yoga."

"That's rough," said Buck. "But sounds like you're missing out on being young. He's a bad egg."

She rolled her eyes. "You mean compared to the ones that want to get to know you in the sack, for one night, and create a memory?"

"At least they're straight with you."

"Well, enough about me. Your turns."

Sarah cleared her throat. "I dated Corey for the summer. He ate my food, all the time." Sarah paused, a forlorn look on her face. "I mean, sure, I'll share my Oreos, but not every damn day. And he never bought any." She sighed, obviously thinking about all those lost cookies.

Randi sucked her lips in. She looked up and Buck was smiling at her in the rearview mirror.

"I cut him loose right before school started," Sarah said, glancing at Buck. "So, I'm available. Totally one hundred percent open. Don't have a man but I want one. A good one."

The pointed hints were about as subtle as a meat hammer to the forehead. Buck shifted the truck with ease, seemingly oblivious.

Randi pulled her phone back out. "Throwing up and passing out every weekend get in the way at all, Sarah?"

"Nah. I mean, I think I need to focus on the day drinkers. The late-night crowd isn't really my scene."

"Huh. Well, good strategy. Your turn, Buck."

"Darlin', I don't have a man in my life because queer's not the way my saddle swings. Ain't got a problem with those *Brokeback Mountain* cowboys, but I'm just not curious."

"Wow, so enlightening."

IT TURNED into a wet Kleenex kind of day. Her bruises ached and her nose ran. A reasonable person might be grateful to have a not-bad-looking housemate providing transportation during an extended weather event, but she resented it. He was like the scratchy tag on the back of a sweater, bothering her all day long as she limped around campus. She was a tiny bit attracted to him —big deal. Not seeing him for a while would solve everything.

When the rainy gray turned into soggy darkness, she popped another cough drop in her mouth, hoping to soothe her viciously foul mood as well. She hobbled down toward the meeting spot. This was it, the last evening ride with Buck and sidekick. Tomorrow, she would bus to her aunt's house, stay over the weekend, and by next week she would be biking again.

Thirty minutes later, Randi limped back and forth in the bike shelter as sheets of water cascaded off the metal roof. Relentless dumping rain and freezing wind straight from a polar vortex battered the campus pavement. In the library parking lot in front of her stood Buck's truck, dark and empty.

*Call me*, he had text messaged about twenty minutes ago. He had tried calling her, twice. She didn't accept phone talking because that implied a level of intimacy she was not approaching. Texting about ride sharing hit her limit.

Because the universe was in the mood to give her a few licks, she had left her bike in her bedroom that morning, knowing what the weather had in store for the day. Bad move. Idiotic of her to believe the cowboy crowd would skip the cheap, thirsty-Thursday pint deals just because they promised to be done by seven.

Her phone rang. "Why are you calling me? I do not want phone calls."

"Wow, darlin'," Buck said, "little change of plan here—"

"No. No changing the plan."

"Come on now, take a deep breath. I know you don't want to leave Sarah in a bad place."

"What?"

"She's not walking much and I don't trust the other girls to take her to Jason's house anytime soon. I have a hidden truck key in the lockbox. The fastest thing is for you to drive the truck over here and park in front of the door in the bike lane. We'll be waiting. The key's in the lockbox under the tarp in the back. Code zero-eight-nine-eight."

She hung up on him. This situation, like dropping a blackberry into fertile soil, would inevitably lead to more thorny vines roping her into being drunk-Sarah's nanny. The girl had managed before and she could do it again.

Fists clenched, she blew out her breath. She really was an idiot. Pulling her hood up, she stomped over to the truck.

She backed the truck out of its parking spot at a crawl, gritting her teeth and stalling the engine twice. Her experience driving a manual clutch barely covered the basics. Being honked at, when she killed the engine yet again at a stoplight, did nothing to improve her mood.

She wanted to focus on school, period. Not get embroiled in the raucous, booze-soaked social lives of her housemates —especially Buck's. Fortunately, he was simply using her, probably because she was the one sober person he knew and she happened to live on the same property. Whatever pretense of friendship he was enacting was entirely untrustworthy. The gears scraped ominously as she shifted.

If she could survive this year, pass an unbelievable sixty-plus credits of coursework over three terms, she would graduate with a marketing and design major that would lead to a good-paying job. Hopefully. Probably after a few soul-destroying internships. But she would persevere. The YouTube channel was padding on her résumé, a concrete example of her producing content marketing. Maybe someday she'd actually have a business successful enough to support herself and her aunt full-time. If wishes were empty beer cans…

Any kind of relationship would be a horrible distraction that she literally had no time for. The problem was, spending time around all of the entitled pleasure-bingers, who were treating their twenties like one long hedonistic festival before the world ends, was subjecting her brain to ideas about all of the things that she wasn't doing.

Sitting up very tall in the low seat, she gripped the steering wheel with sweaty palms, easing the truck slower as she entered the party zone that was rife with tipsy twenty-somethings staggering onto the road. The bar came into view, people jammed in so tight they actually leaned on each other. She shuddered. No way would she enter a crowded bar.

Hazards on, she wedged the truck in as tight as she could against the curb. She texted Buck, then a few minutes later Sarah came stumbling out between Buck and Hugh, a happy grin on her face.

The door creaked and Buck jumped inside, pausing to drop his dripping hat in the back of the cab. Hugh shoved Sarah in, waved, then turned to run back into the bar.

"Damn it's wet. Darlin', stay there and drive, in case I need to haul Sarah out quick."

"Fine, but I'm not driving until you're both buckled up."

"All right, all right."

"Don't ask me to do this again."

"Hey, come on now, you're doing a good deed."

"Right, I'm enabling her alcoholism. Sarah needs a babysitter…that reports back to her parents."

"Relax."

"Shut up, weirdo," Sarah said, slurring and spitting the words. "Don't tell Mom."

"This will end badly and I don't want to be a part of it."

They had no idea how much she didn't want to be a part of it. This was why she didn't party, didn't take risks—something bad always happened.

"Home by eight pushing it for you?" Buck said. "Sarah's testing her limits, most kids do. She'll settle in eventually."

His arm stretched out behind her head. She exhaled, distracted by the sudden awareness of him, musk and beer, pushed up next to her. He made no effort to avoid touching her. He crossed his left leg to keep out of the way of the gear shift, which put his knee in her lap.

She exhaled, forcing herself to relax her clenched teeth. Sensation crawled along her skin, radiating out from the heavy weight of him against her side. Touching him was becoming a secret thrill—she didn't want to even acknowledge it.

All bad things come to an end, if you're an optimist, and her self-imposed sexual anorexia might be on the chopping block. It chafed. What was she waiting for? Not love, oh no, that fantasy was a fairytale told to little girls to brainwash them into conforming to male hegemony.

She was picky. After waiting so long, it would be a defeat to jump in the sack with anybody. Luke maybe. Yes, with enough planning and subtle coaching, perhaps that would be fine. Not Buck. Definitely not Buck.

"Pull over, darlin', she's heaving—quick if you can."

# CHAPTER TEN

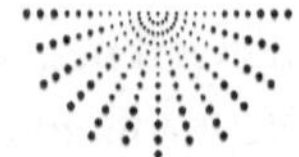

Two weeks later, Randi stared contentedly at her library table, bag of hard candy and canteen of hot tea in their places, laptop glowing brightly in the relative quiet of the second-floor rotunda. No country-house people anywhere in sight. No dirty dishes, foul beer bottles, hostile stares, or raucous, belligerent hollering. She would catch the late bus to her aunt's house at nine-thirty, stay there for two peaceful nights, and thoroughly enjoy a weekend's worth of vacation from the boozers.

Hunched over at the table next to her, he stared at her, again. The *Matrix* guy. What was a hunk like that doing in the library on a party night? The Friday-night crowd usually consisted of foreign exchange students and a few scared-looking freshmen.

He looked shockingly like a young Keanu Reeves—the kind of Asian–Anglo mix that models were made of. Except describing him as any kind of fashion icon missed the mark, considering he wore baggy clothes and hauled a backpack the size of a waste bin. It wasn't the first time he'd taken the table next to hers. She was guessing engineer…

"Hey," he finally said, "do you have a pen I can borrow?"

She handed him a pen. "Can I ask you something?"

"Um, sure."

"Are you stalking me?"

He laughed nervously. "Oh, you mean because I sit here? Uh, no, I actually study a lot. Engineering."

"Okay. I'll accept that."

He smiled at her. "Well, what's your excuse for always being at that table?"

"I own this table," she said, popping a salted-toffee hard candy in her mouth. On Fridays, she got her treat. "Paid for it with my social life."

He held up his hands. "I'm just passing through."

He took a sip of his coffee. The whipped cream swirl on top, covered in rainbow sprinkles, left a white smear on his upper lip. She respected a man who went for sprinkles.

"Um," he said, fingers drumming the table, "I was hoping to talk to you, though."

Her phone buzzed. "Well," she said absently, "mission accomplished, sir."

"Haha, yeah."

Buck had texted her. She should ignore him. Whatever it was, wasn't good. Ever since the bike crash, he'd acted like her protective big brother. He treated all the girls at the house like his flock of little chicks, organizing carpools back and forth from the house, doing potluck meals. She didn't want any part of it.

He'd worn her down in the mornings for the last two weeks. If it rained, she rode in with him and usually caught a ride home too. But otherwise, she studied and kept to herself. He texted again.

Her phone rang. He was calling her. Who did he think he was? She declined the call.

"So," said the Keanu Reeves doppelgänger, "what do you study?"

Curiosity crawled all over her skin. She couldn't stand it. She'd take a look and tell Buck to shove off. No, she wouldn't.

"Business, marketing, and graphic design. I'm double majoring with a few minors thrown in because I can't make up my mind." She grabbed her phone and punched in the passcode. She stood up. "Excuse me," she said, "I need to read this."

"Oh yeah," he said, "no problem."

Five text messages from Buck. Sighing, she opened the first one.

**Buck**: Randi, call me. Sarah needs help.

She swallowed. A niggle of worry crept up her spine. The real issue was that Sarah needed help every time she drank. Not her problem, she told herself firmly, even if she didn't want anything to happen to the tall blonde.

**Buck**: I'm sending an Uber to the library to pick you up. We're at the Dirty Bird.

She blew out her breath. He could swallow the fee for the stupid Uber. That was the last bar in town—no, the last bar in hell—that she would voluntarily walk into. The Dirty Bird fermented plagues in its soggy rotten carpeting, and at least one night a week the entrance was blocked off by first responders because that was where young alcoholics went to die.

**Buck**: Trish broke up with Jason last night. She's out of control. Sarah can't walk.

Why her? That was the mystery question here. There were plenty of people, females especially, eager to help him. They'd buy lottery tickets for the chance.

**Buck**: I'm calling you because I don't want to end up with a party out at the house. And you're sober. I drank too much to drive.

Wow, creepy mind-read. And yet, that was a massive stretch. They didn't need her involved.

**Buck**: I'll leave the girls if you don't get your butt down here.

She puffed air out, indignantly. Buck was out of his tree to throw that kind of logic at her. What did she owe a couple of self-absorbed alcoholics who treated her like sub-human housekeeping help?

She walked back to her table. Twinges of pain still jabbed at her here and there from the bike crash. Her library chair would feel a lot more comfortable than the most disgusting bar in town.

She stood, staring at her pile of books. Her plan had been to stay late and finish up the presentation due on Monday. Another two hours of work tonight, and she would have actually carved out time tomorrow for her YouTube channel.

"Everything all right?"

She popped another candy in her mouth. The first night, at the very beginning of this torture, Sarah had passed out in a puddle of her own vomit. That omen alone should have been enough to have Randi running far, far away. If only there wasn't a massive housing crunch… The clock said seven-thirty p.m. How was Sarah already comatose?

"I'm Carter, by the way," he said. "Did I tell you that yet?"

She took a deep breath. If something horrible happened to Sarah, she wouldn't be able to forgive herself. People were definitely not worth all the trouble.

"Well, Carter," she said, "what do you think about going to that disgusting dance club downtown? I've got a housemate I need to rescue from her drinking problem."

"Uh," he said, looking down at his calculator like it was screaming at him.

She slung her black faux leather bag over her shoulder. The only option, at this point, was to carry her computer into the bar. Some a-hole might spill beer on it. She should forget about the whole thing.

"You know what, yes, I'll grab a drink with you. My calculus can just wait until tomorrow."

There was a wild look on his face, like he'd agreed to rob a gas station or something.

"I won't be drinking," she said, putting her candies in the outer pocket of her bag. "I don't think I even want to sit down in that place."

"Oh, okay," he said, stalling as he seemed to think it over. He grabbed his massive backpack and slung what looked like eighty pounds over his shoulders. "Let's do it." He followed her out of the library.

Twenty minutes later, they sidled their way into the musky lower level of the bar, crammed with pool tables and poker machines. A cover band played up on a stage in the corner, belting out their version of a Pixies song. Stale beer and rotten urine reek burned her nostrils. It was way too crowded and she still had to go upstairs, to the largest cesspit in the county.

Carter stuck to her side, looking around like he'd never seen a pool hall before. Engineering students really did work too hard. They inched their way around the crowd.

Randi focused on her breathing. *You can leave the cycle of panic*, she repeated over and over in her head. She turned sideways to skim between two clusters of guys wearing backwards ball caps. *Breathe. Breathe.* The crowd was killing her. Foul steam rose from the stained carpets.

They climbed up the stairwell toward the thumping bass of dance music. It resembled Mordor, if the orcs had drinking problems and jammed to hip-hop. Broken glass crunched under her feet.

Midway up, they passed a girl puking into a corner of the stairway landing. Randi and Carter looked at each other, his eyes round saucers. She swallowed hard, fanning her face. If she made it up these stairs and her stomach stopped churning, she was going to have another candy. She clutched her bag against her side and kept climbing into the house of horrors. The den of iniquity.

The top level opened into a massive, warehouse-sized open floor plan with a long, oval bar set up in the center. She took a deep breath. Admittedly, it was half a degree less hellish than she had imagined. On one side of the room, the dance floor shook, crowded with gyrating people. On the other side stood lined-up pool tables and an exit stairway leading outside. Connecting both ends of the space were rows of tables, against the walls, all crammed with people. Tall blonde Sarah, wide smile and flannel shirt, should stand out in the crowd. Randi scanned the room three times, but her asinine housemate remained out of sight.

"I'm going to check for her in the bathroom," she said, pointing in that direction. The other end of the long room looked about a million miles away. Carter nodded and followed behind her.

They inched their way along, sidestepping sloshing alcohol, brushing by bodies crammed in so tightly together their elbows rubbed against strangers. Her pleated dress, buttoned all the way up to the neck, attracted stares from men like she was the next act in a burlesque show. It was impossible to avoid getting touched. A girl stumbled into her shoulder, glaring at her. Her long-sleeved boysenberry chiffon dress got a once over like it was an offense to nature.

She stepped away from the swaying drunk girl, adjusting the satin collar of her dress to let air onto her sweaty neck. She was stress-sweating. Fabulous.

"Hey, Randi," a deep voice shouted. She spun around and Luke materialized, waving at her. He was sitting with another guy at a table covered with jackets and purses.

Feeling like she'd sighted land after weeks at sea, she veered toward him. Carter followed close behind her. At Luke's table she slumped against an open spot of wall, fanning her face and taking deep breaths.

"Hey," Luke said, scooting over. "Cute dress. Sit down—want a beer?"

He flashed that friendly smile at her. What she wanted was a bottle of water, hand sanitizer, and teleportation out of there. How did people do this?

"No, thanks. I'm driving somebody home. Actually, I need to go and find her."

"Hang on a minute. We were just talking about a camping party while the weather's good next week. I'll send you the details. You should come. It's a beautiful spot close by."

"I'm not a party person," she said, pulling out a hard candy. She would finish that bag tonight and buy another one tomorrow, for surviving this. "But maybe. I like finding beautiful spots outdoors."

Somebody grabbed her hand and she jumped, jerking her head around to find Buck glaring at her.

"There you are. What took so long?"

She waved a goodbye to Luke then stepped after Buck. He wasn't wasting a moment. He pulled her through the crowd and people parted, like magic, for the tall man in a cowboy hat. She focused on keeping her heels, her favorite navy T-straps, out of the sticky spilled beer on the floor. She would never forgive Buck for this.

His hand was dry and warm against hers. She could feel calluses on his fingers and palm. It sent a little electric shock through her. He was rugged, a little rough, and eccentric compared to the other men in the dance hall. Almost as out of place as her.

They came to a halt in front of the pool tables. Hugh stood by a table in the back. No sign of Sarah or Trish.

She yanked her hand out of Buck's. Dirt smears speckled his grubby jeans and work boots. And his face was ruddy. Glassy eyes narrowed as he looked behind her.

"Buck, this is my new buddy, Carter. His name is really Buck, Carter. And that's Hugh by the pool table."

"Nice," said Carter. "Can I get in on a game?"

Buck's gaze veered back to her. One of his hands shot out and pushed against the wall to hold himself up. He was drunk.

"She's in the bathroom, isn't she?" Randi eyed the dark pit of disgusting that said *Ladies* on the door.

"She is," said Buck. "It's been about thirty minutes."

"Don't ever call me for this crap again." She took her bag off. "Carter, will you do me a huge favor and hold my bag for me while I go in there?"

"Oh, yeah, no problem," said Carter.

Randi held it out to him, but Buck snatched it out of her grip before Carter could touch it, then turned around and walked toward the pool table. Carter held his hands up, shrugging at her.

She took a last breath of breathable air, then pushed open the bathroom door. A single dim bulb lit up the wet floor and overflowing garbage can. She swallowed, covering her face. The acidic reek of vomit was overwhelming.

"Sarah," she called out, her arm over her mouth. "Come out of here, please. This bathroom is way too foul to sleep in."

No answer. Randi blinked, trying to adjust her eyes to the lack of light.

"Sarah, I'll find some cookies for you…"

Water dripped in one of the sinks. The one working fluorescent light dimmed in and out—the perfect setup for a scene in a slasher film. A white Converse sneaker stuck out from under a stall door. Randi slowly pushed the door in to where Sarah lay on the floor, her head leaning against the toilet seat, eyes closed. Yellow slime covered her face.

"Sarah!" Randi froze, petrified by the still, pale, waxy figure on the concrete ground. She wasn't moving. Randi jolted into action, putting her ear on Sarah's chest. It rose slightly. Randi exhaled.

"Hey! Wake up!" No response.

She wiped Sarah's face with damp paper towels, talking to her the whole time. She tried shaking her and splashing water on her face. Nothing.

It seemed like Sarah barely breathed. Like her body forgot to breathe until the very last second. She was totally unresponsive. It could be a timer counting down—how much longer did Sarah have?

She checked Sarah's pulse and it came across as sluggish. Her pale, clammy skin appeared gray in the muggy room, surely not a good sign. She had no freaking idea what she was doing. *Crap!*

At the pool table, Carter shot the white cue ball down the table, breaking up the racked colored balls. Hugh and Buck stood by, grimacing down at the floor. Buck looked up then watched her walk across the floor to them.

"Guys," she said, "Sarah needs to go to the hospital."

Hugh blew out his breath. Buck crossed his arms.

"She's passed out, in a pile of vomit, and is non-responsive. Not breathing well. She's poisoned for sure. What the hell was she drinking by the way? It's barely eight o'clock."

"The girls had a bottle of Everclear," said Hugh, looking worried.

Randi shuddered. "Well, that might kill Sarah. She needs an ambulance."

"No," said Buck. "She can't afford a three-thousand-dollar ride to the hospital. And her parents would pull her out of school. She's a big healthy girl, she can wait."

Randi bit her knuckle, afraid to walk back into the bathroom and find Sarah not breathing.

"We'll load her up," said Buck, "then Hugh goes back in to track down Trish and call Jason, the damn ass." He handed Randi back her bag.

Randi went into the bathroom ahead of them. A couple of girls stood by the stalls, sorority sisters judging by their sweaters, staring at Sarah with concern.

"It's okay," said Randi. "We're getting her some help."

"All right," one of them said. "I was about to find a bouncer. She doesn't look good."

Randi bit her lip, feeling under Sarah's nose for breathing. Shallow, but happening. She backed out to hold the stall door for Buck and Hugh.

They each grabbed an arm and hauled Sarah out, grunting with effort. She flopped between them, head rolling to the side, hair covering her face. Muscles straining, the guys hoisted her up and put their shoulders under her armpits, pinning her arms around their necks and grabbing the waist of her jeans.

Carter held the door for them as they shuffled sideways through it. They appeared to be a couple of drunk cowboys carting off a roofied undergrad. Randi swallowed, disturbed, and followed close behind them.

The stairs down were terrifyingly steep. The guys paused to rearrange their holds on Sarah, finally settling on Carter grabbing Sarah's legs in front as they went down. Randi ran down ahead of them to keep the narrow stairwell clear.

At the bottom, a bouncer stepped out, blocking the door. "Hold on there," he said.

He looked them over for a long minute. His eyebrows knit together and he sucked on his teeth. The look on his face said he absolutely did not want to deal with this. But had no choice.

"Shit," the bouncer said, scratching his beard. "She passed out upstairs?"

Buck shifted Sarah's weight on his shoulder. He pointed at Randi. "This is her roommate," he said. "We're just helping."

"Guys," the bouncer finally said, reluctance in every syllable, "I can't let you carry an unconscious girl out of here."

They all stared at him. Randi rubbed her chilled arms. The thought of standing outside for the next hour dealing with cops, ambulances, and probably a fire truck too, turned her stomach. Not to mention Sarah losing her scholarship.

"Hey," she said, stepping forward, "I live with her and will be taking her to the hospital. She doesn't have the money for an ambulance. Also, her vitals are steady." Randi swallowed. That line was straight out of a medical drama she used to watch. She was so full of it. The bouncer stared down his nose at her, obviously not buying.

"How about I give you my cell phone number, my name and hers?" Randi continued, doing her best to sound like a corporate lawyer. "I'll call you when she's in the hospital so that the bar can document that she checked in." Randi pulled out a notebook and began writing, not giving the bouncer a chance to refuse. "I haven't been drinking at all," she added. "I came in here just to take care of Sarah."

She handed over the piece of paper. He snatched it out of her hand and shoved it into his pocket.

"Fine, move her off the property. Now," he said, looking over his shoulder.

BUCK FELL into another stiff plastic hospital chair—the third one so far. At least this waiting room had a television. He hated these places. If they weren't done in five minutes he was going to grab Randi and march out the door.

There she stood, in that long-sleeved purple dress, perky as a spring foal. The dress was…like something from a *Leave it to Beaver* episode. All her clothes were strange. Every day she swished around in some feminine getup, usually a dress. None of it particularly sexy, but for some damn reason it all drove him a little crazy.

When he was a kid, a standoffish cat on the ranch had started following him around, talking at him. He called her Dog, because she waited on the porch for him anytime he left, and loved to chase after balls. It had taken Dog the cat a while to win him over, and then one day he gave in and realized he loved that unusual cat more than any animal in his life.

Randi wasn't chasing him, by any stretch of imagination, and wouldn't wait around for him, and yet he found himself on the verge of something with her. Considering giving in while knowing he shouldn't. Huffing, he rubbed his face, almost laughing at himself out loud.

He always did like people better than him. He smiled wryly. Maybe some part of him imagined they'd prevent him turning into the caricature of a drunk good ol' boy, languishing away his life in dim booze halls.

Watching Sarah come close to killing herself with liquor

had unsettled him. He'd stomped down to the bar, after Trish had called, knowing things were out of hand. Turned out to be more of an uncontrolled prairie fire.

Randi adjusted her huge glasses, listening to the nurse speaking. A hint of a black lacy bra beneath the see-through back of her dress caught his attention with a jolt. He responded, stirring hopefully under his jeans. It's nothing, he told himself firmly, just some lacy underwear, but, holy shit, he suddenly loved that dress.

She swished over to him, heels clicking on the floor. The skirt of her dress swirled around her bare knees. Damn, he wanted to slide his hands up those legs.

"She's in bad shape." Randi collapsed in the chair next to him. "Her heart rate is still too slow from the alcohol poisoning. They're keeping her overnight."

He blinked. "Is she dying?"

"I don't think so. I mean, it was hard to tell through all the hospital speak, but it sounds to me like they're being extra cautious."

He'd had enough after three hours of replying to a slurry of unanswerable urgent questions about Sarah's drinking, with the hospital staff staring at him like it was all his fault. "Did you provide the alcohol?" had been thrown at him about ten times. Randi had saved him, stepping in with cool confidence to explain, yet again, how they had got there.

"Okay," he said, pushing back up to his feet. "Let's go."

Randi bit her lip, looking down the hallway toward Sarah's room. "Leave her here alone? Without seeing her?"

"She's passed out. It's after our bedtimes." He grabbed her hand. "We'll pick her up in the morning."

He towed her in the direction of the doorway. She pulled her hand away and went over to the nurses' station. After she chatted for damn long minutes, and signed some kind of form, at last they headed into the elevator.

She leaned into a corner and closed her eyes, going from perky to wilted in a blink. A twinge of guilt pinched at him for dragging her out. The truth was, he didn't know another girl he wanted to call, let alone spend three hours in the hospital with. The thought made him frown.

Getting drunk with Hugh was supposed to distract him, flush this girl from his system. Like a prickly burr, she kept burrowing into his mind. He wasn't ready for another relationship with anyone after what he'd been through, and just sleeping with her would be wrong. She wasn't that kind of girl. Not to mention she lived yards away from him, so afterward there would be no easy way to say, "That was fun, see ya."

She was neurotic, high-strung, way too bossy—the last thing he wanted was anybody even slightly crazy in his life. Except, when she'd touched him in his truck last week, he'd been ready to pin her underneath him. Still was, every damn day.

"Who's the idiot you brought to the bar with you?" He felt stupidly satisfied when she stared up at him through her lashes, green eyes focused on him.

"You mean Carter?" She stood up straighter. "I don't know, an engineering student. Why do you care?"

They walked through the parking lot toward his truck. Why did he care? Mostly he wanted to hear what crazy shit she would say next.

"You don't know him, but you take him to bars with you?"

She unlocked the passenger door for Buck. "Stop acting like an insecure boyfriend." She walked around the truck and cranked open the driver's door. "We don't like each other. Besides, one of the girls you're actually sleeping with will get jealous. I don't do cat fights."

That almost sounded interested. He leaned back against the seat, stretching his arm out along the back. His hand landed behind her shoulder, inches away from touching her.

"Leading men on is always a bad idea. We're not safe."

She snorted. "Carter is actually a nice guy. Unlike some people in this truck. He's like a legitimately sweet, boy next door, sprinkles on his whipped cream, a bit shy, kind of person. I'm a little into it."

"He sounds like a pervert. Sprinkles? Check his browsing history and you'll have to report him to the police."

He reached out his fingers and felt her collar. Velvet. The rest of the dress was a flowy normal fabric, covered in a carpet-like old-lady pattern. But the fuzzy collar flirted. And the see-through back. All buttoned up with a hint of sex.

She tensed up, but otherwise ignored his touch. It was hard to tell in the dark, but he thought she blushed. Desire shot through his pelvis. Touching her had been a mistake. Once he'd started, he didn't want to stop.

"That other guy was there too, the STD musician."

"He's a drummer, not a testicle wart. You know, I think you're projecting your problems onto other people."

"He's trouble. I can spot a guy like that a mile away. Smokes reefer till he's dumber than a box of rusty nails, but thinks he's going to save the world with his penis."

Randi huffed. "You're an 'out-house-is-half-full' kind of guy, aren't you? I bet he does smoke pot. Maybe I'll get some from him."

He pulled his hand away and sat on it. Jumping her while she drove was a bad idea. Might dent his truck. And he wasn't going to jump on her, period. Mostly because she wouldn't go for it and was way too uptight for him. He needed someone fun, something for now.

"Buck?"

"Hmm," he said, turning back to gaze at her profile, like

an idiot. He loved her upper lip, puckered out from the deep cleft under her nose.

"What are you studying? Why Oregon University?"

"Well, I'm thrilled you're interested."

"Not that much."

"Rangeland Management and Ecology, and I'm over in Animal Sciences a bit too. I'm here because they offered me funding."

"Huh," she said, obviously struggling to stay awake. Buck blinked his own dry eyes, relieved to see the end of the gravel road.

She parked the truck in front of the dark farmhouse, exhaling with what sounded like exhaustion.

"Night," she said, tossing the keys in his lap. She jumped out the door and slammed it shut before he'd even unbuckled his seat belt.

"Hey!" He caught up to her by her bedroom door. "Thanks, darlin', for helping out tonight." He leaned on her doorjamb, crossing his arms.

She shoved past him and turned on the light to her room. He blinked in the bright glare, looking around. It was all gauzy fabric and fresh flowers in little vases. Clean and pretty. A fluffy bed, and roomy. His body tensed hopefully.

She grabbed a tote thing and headed toward the main house. He followed her inside.

"Yeah, well, no good deed goes unpunished," she said, walking into the bathroom and running the water for her toothbrush. He waited outside the door, leaning against a wall. "Now Sarah's really going to hate me."

"She'll come around." He liked the cinnamon smell of her toothpaste. "Cookies might help."

She rubbed flowery smelling cream on her face then wiped it off with a washcloth. "She might be glad I didn't contact her mother like the nurse wanted," Randi said. "But I would have if I'd known how."

She shut the door to use the toilet. He lingered like a damn dog. The answer was obvious. He needed sex, and not with her. Tomorrow he would do something about it. His self-imposed break from chasing fast women would end.

The water ran again, and then she was off, out the back door to her bedroom in the converted garage.

"Goodnight, Buck," she called over her shoulder. "I'll paint pink polka dots on your trailer if you ever blackmail me into the Dirty Bird again."

# CHAPTER ELEVEN

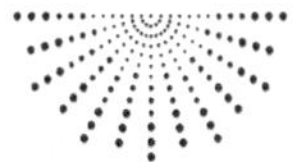

Randi glanced at Sarah out of the corner of her eye. Papers crumpled under Sarah's feet, on the floor of Buck's truck, as she ground her shoe into the pile of paperwork from the hospital.

"Let's get some grub." Buck switched on his blinker. "Here we go."

Randi groaned. "The yellow arches, Buck? Pink slime empire?"

"Lean, finely textured meat? LFTM, darlin'. Damn resourceful way to use more of the animal."

"It's pink slime," Randi said. "I want to know if I'm eating ammonia with my beef. Tumors in lab rats. Need I say more?"

"Safe enough," Buck said. "Got to feed the masses. Speaking of, what do you think over there, Hungover? Pink slime milkshake?"

"Wow." Randi huffed. "Somebody should censor you."

"Pancakes and a coke," Sarah croaked, what must be crud in her throat gurgling.

"And you, darlin'? Slime nuggets?"

"Breakfast sandwich. Are you trying to make Sarah throw up?"

"She should eat first. Bile burns, better to mix it with pink slime."

Randi shook her head. Buck grinned down at her. The little devil inside her tried to make her smile back. She resisted. She broke eye contact and leaned forward in the seat. The truck rolled forward in the line for the drive-through, then Buck leaned out the window to order their food.

Sarah wore clean clothes because Randi had brought them to the hospital that morning, but the foul reek coming from her hunched-over form was thick enough to dissolve the fine hairs on the inside of Randi's nose. Sarah's dark mood, and narrow-eyed glances, were extremely directed at one person in the truck, and it wasn't Buck.

"Hey," Sarah said, when the truck pulled forward into the long line to the pickup window, "why do you dress like that?"

"Yeah, Buck?" Randi turned toward him.

Sarah kicked the hospital papers around under her feet. "Not him, you."

Randi took a deep breath, wishing she could cover her face with a lavender-scented handkerchief—like in the days before deodorant and general sanitation. How had she let Buck talk her into coming along for this errand? "I answer one, you answer one, Sarah."

"Fine."

A little silence stretched out. Randi crossed her arms, mining for words in her dull, sleep-deprived brain.

Buck turned the radio down. "You ever put on a pair of jeans, darlin'?"

She huffed. "They have no place in my closet."

"What the heck is wrong with jeans?" Sarah burst out, ferociously.

Randi sighed, noticing Buck stiffen next to her. "I'm not part of the jeans tribe. Well, unless you mean a skirt. Or a jumper."

"So, what, you just want attention all the time?"

"Wow, hangry," said Buck. "I hope this line moves along soon."

Randi took off her glasses, then pulled out a cloth from her pocket to clean them with. "Even though you're clearly hating on me right now, I'm going to give you a real answer." She put her glasses back on, took a deep breath, and looked at Sarah. Sarah rolled her eyes.

"I, um, lost my parents when I was little—about five. Stopped talking, wouldn't eat much. Fairly normal thing for a kid to do, but of course my grandparents worried about me so they took me to therapy. I became very picky about what I wore, and that helped. No buttons. No sneakers. No pants. I changed my mind about buttons and sneakers, but loving fashion, especially dresses, stuck with me because it makes me happy. So no, I don't want attention all the time. The opposite actually. I dress this way for myself."

The truck pulled forward to the pickup window and Buck passed them warm paper bags of food.

Randi cleared her throat. "Library please, Buck."

"On a Saturday morning, with the sun shining? Come out to the football game instead. Sarah's too sick for her seat."

"Whoa, I'm not giving her my ticket."

Buck shook his head. "Eat those pancakes so you can throw your brain up out of your ass. Jesus."

"Library," Randi repeated.

Sarah shifted position. "Well? What is it? What dumb question do you want to ask me?"

Buck huffed. Randi sat still, staring forward through the windshield, not sure she cared enough to say more.

Her mouth opened, almost despite herself. "You ever lose anyone, Sarah? Someone you were close to?"

"Uh, no."

"Yeah, I didn't think so."

"Oh really. What does that mean?"

Randi turned to face her. "You black out at parties, sleep outside on your vomit, fall into toilets at bars so drunk you're barely breathing, and spent the night in a hospital because the emergency room thought your heart would stop beating." Randi kept staring at her. "You're like a kid who thinks jumping off the roof won't hurt her."

Randi looked away and finally saw the library, only two blocks away.

"You know what, screw you, Randi the weirdo. Go buy yourself a dress so you feel better."

"That's some bullshit, Sarah," Buck said.

Sarah slammed her hand down on the passenger door. "I didn't need to go to the freaking hospital," she almost shouted, then gasped and covered her eyes with a hand. "I'm screwed. I can't pay for this crap."

"Yep," Buck said. "Did it to yourself, girl."

At last, the truck stopped by the bike shelter in front of the library. Buck opened his door and jumped out. Randi slid out after him, not looking at Sarah, who was quietly sobbing. Buck lifted Randi's bike out of the back, and held her backpack up for her.

"See ya, Buck," Randi said, avoiding eye contact with him by adjusting her backpack. What she needed was a whole lot of distance between her and everyone related to the country house.

"Coming back tonight, darlin'?"

"Nope." She rode off on her bicycle, wishing his eyes on her didn't make her neck tingle.

THURSDAY AFTERNOON, Randi packed up her bag in the Greary Hall lecture auditorium, forcing herself not to look across the room at Luke. He'd been extremely late to class, and so they'd ended up sitting in different parts of the massive room. She wasn't sure he would talk to her, or if she wanted him to.

She was mildly irritated with how flippantly he treated school. Which led to the greater question of what he was actually like outside of class. Contemplating a lifelong alliance didn't fit into the picture, so how relevant was it if he had different priorities than her? He was a cute guy she'd thought about dating because her body told her to—and to end all temptation elsewhere.

He caught up to her in the small quadrangle outside the building. She forced herself to tamp down the overeager grin stretching her mouth from ear to ear as she turned to him.

"Hey," Luke said.

His face sagged, droopy-eyed, and he reeked of various smoked substances. He appeared to have missed a few nights of sleep. Randi held the smile on her face, but her stomach fell, thoughts clicking together like a lopsided Lego tower. He'd told her that he was the drummer in a band that played local shows. She realized, in a burst of clarity, the late nights in bars were not something she would do, and felt like an idiot for not thinking of it sooner.

"Hi," she said, adjusting her glasses. "Glad you made it to class. That midterm was worth thirty percent of our grade."

"Yeah." He blinked at her a little dimly, like he needed a big cup of coffee.

She resisted the urge to glance at her watch. Daisy was meeting her across the street, in front of the athletic fields, in two minutes. Probably unfairly, she felt disappointed in

Luke, or maybe it was her own cascading thought process about his lifestyle that depressed her. Must she be so endlessly difficult to please?

"Hey," he said again, leaning in closer to her. "I'm going camping out on Ebey's Island this Saturday. You should come."

"Oh." Here it was, the opportunity her body had been clamoring for, but what she felt was wary. On second thought, she wanted a proper date, if she did anything. Did he expect her to jump in a tent with him the first time they went out? "Tell me more about it?"

"We're going to raft in, leave from the downtown boat launch around two in the afternoon. I've got room, if you want to float with me."

"I have a raft I can use." Aunt Linda wouldn't mind if she borrowed the one tucked away in the garage. Besides, in the unlikely event she did go, she would want her own way in and out of the party.

"A raft for what?" said Daisy, walking up with a bright smile.

Randi groaned inwardly. *Here we go.*

"I'm telling Randi about camping on Ebey's Island this Saturday," Luke said, smiling back at Daisy, seemingly unconscious of his masterful manipulation.

"OMG, yes." The enthusiasm on Daisy's face could break something.

Randi sighed, glaring at Luke when he glanced over at her with a too innocent expression. "Actually, I have to work this weekend."

"No," Daisy shouted.

"Think about it," said Luke, flashing the dimpled grin at her. "Got to get to my next class. Hopefully I'll see you both on Saturday."

"You need to do something besides study all the time," Daisy growled at her. "The party is one night."

Daisy's phone rang shrilly. Muttering, she pulled it out and glared down at the screen. "Mom calling," she said, grumpily. "Give me one minute."

Exasperation blew out of Randi in a long exhalation. Clearly, Daisy would hammer at her about going. Could she fake a migraine and make a run for it?

She walked to the edge of the quadrangle, her attention caught by the women's rugby game on the athletic field closest to them. Angie was playing, she realized with a start, shoving through defenders on the other team with her shoulder down, quick on her feet.

The crowd in the bleachers stood and cheered when Angie broke away and sprinted down the field, leaving behind the other women diving to grab desperately at her legs. She crossed the goal line and grounded the ball to score.

Angie's teammates rushed in, picking her up on their shoulders while she grinned and pushed blonde hair out of her muddy face. A Viking shield-maiden came to mind; in another life Angie could have led insane berserkers into battle. Randi crossed her arms, leaning on a bench, a little unwilling admiration inside her.

"My mother just yelled at me for two solid minutes because I left a dirty T-shirt in the bathroom hamper," Daisy said, huffing as she walked up beside Randi.

"That's stinks. Maybe literally."

"Randi, we're going to that party."

# CHAPTER TWELVE

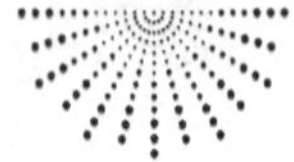

"**Y**ummy. Give," said Daisy, Saturday afternoon, obviously relishing every moment of their befuddled ride down the river with a small flotilla of stoners. Giggling, she held out her hand over the raft for the smoking joint.

Randi gritted her teeth, fantasizing about jumping overboard and swimming for shore. How could she have been such a naive idiot?

She swirled the oars to keep her raft close to Luke's in the slow-moving river. Whiskey was passed over, sloshing in a plastic bottle. Daisy held in the pot smoke and managed to gulp down a swallow, face crinkling in effort. They called the procedure a cannonball, obviously a euphemism for the brain damage. Whatever they were doing, Randi wasn't into it. The guys were zoned-out zombies. Except for one curly haired guy who talked nonstop, incomprehensibly, while staring at his beer bottle.

Daisy gasped, veins bulging out on her red face, then exploded into a fit of coughing. Randi took a deep breath. This was a monumental mistake. She would pay and pay, for hours.

Leaving was an option. Simply keep floating past the river island campsite and go down to the parked car. Ignore Daisy's screaming. Hijack Daisy's car. Watch Daisy jump out of the raft and swim back to the party, shouting curses at her. Worth considering.

"Randi?" Luke held out the plastic jug in her direction, his droopy eyelids open in a narrow slit.

"What is it?" she asked.

"Whiskey," he said.

She suppressed a sigh. "What kind of whiskey?"

His eyebrows went up. "R and R. Not bottom shelf, but it's close."

He flashed his lopsided grin at her. Even dopey, that smile was something. She took the jug and tried a taste.

"Thanks, I've never had R and R." Or been around people that partied like this. She wore her anthropologist hat again, floating into wild, undocumented lands, frightened and fascinated. "Are you a cannonballs-on-Saturday kind of guy?"

He blinked, scratching his head. These guys smoked an incredible amount of pot, and that was only in the last hour since getting on the river. They had arrived at the boat launch red-eyed and stumbling, not talking, and repeatedly misplacing the air pump. Amazingly, they'd managed to inflate their rafts.

It irritated her that Buck had been right about Luke, on some level. The guy passed baked and overshot pickled, his eyes so red she wondered if she should mention it. Luke became sly in a furtive way while stoned, and uncommunicative. Every twenty minutes he wanted her to smoke something or pop a psychedelic mushroom in her mouth. She didn't touch any of it.

If the raft next to hers had held Buck and Hugh, instead of the reefer crowd, they'd be guzzling down beer, sure, but talking. Fishing probably. She liked the two cowboys, she realized. They were straightforward, cheerful guys who worked hard. The thought made her frown.

"Lately, I can't walk into my house without having one put in my face," Luke said, finally answering her question. "They're fun, but I hide in my car and go to coffee shops to get any homework done."

"That goes to show that it can always be worse." Randi shuddered. "I thought my living situation was bad—last weekend I took my housemate to the hospital for alcohol poisoning. But cannonballs everywhere sounds like a bad civil war re-enactment. Or a civil rights violation. Why don't you move out?"

"Doesn't bother me. The hospital, huh? She okay?"

"My housemate? Yeah, I guess. She stayed on the couch for two days, watched nonstop *Friends* reruns, and ate Oreos. She's pissed at me for taking her to the ER. Would have preferred to risk dying. I told her next time I'll call her mom, so now we're not talking to each other. My house is loads of fun."

"Calling a mom," gasped Daisy, her voice hoarse, "is, like, so wrong. I can't believe you went there."

"Sarah and I aren't friends. She puked on my second favorite pair of heels and I totally hold it against her."

One of the other guys called out something to Luke and they floated apart.

"Holy crap." Daisy leaned in close. "Luke is so hot. Is he into you? I'm crushing on him a little."

"Um, I don't know." Randi paddled hard away from a sharp-edged boulder. "He likes to mooch off my Western Civ homework. And he asked me to join this madness."

The truth was she'd had to get away from her house. Especially Buck. She didn't want to be there for whatever drink-fest happened and observe him looking around for bedroom company. Or worse, wonder if he would try and get her out of her room.

When he'd knocked on her door in the evening, last week, she'd startled so hard her mug of tea sloshed. Pausing her precious work time on editing yoga videos, she got up and answered the door and said, no, she didn't want to watch a football game, or a scary movie, with the rest of the house. Nothing would convince her to hang out. Not even ice cream. He'd called her a hermit and a loner, and she'd told him to get lost.

He made her crazed. Unbalanced. Would he try again? What exactly was he doing? Why were her erotic thoughts obsessed with him?

So, when Luke kept bringing up the camping trip, then Daisy heard about it, an insane pent-up part of her had taken over and eventually said yes. Sure, she was a reclusive shut-in with no social life, but she felt a little determined to prove she could do normal college stuff, if she wanted to. Camping had sounded nice. Listen to frogs sing and, with luck, a cute guy with an acoustic guitar, hopefully part of a smallish group. And she could do some recording for her YouTube channel in the morning.

At the boat launch that afternoon, as Luke's friends had stacked case after case of beer onto their rafts and boxed jugs of hard alcohol, it had dawned on her that she was an idiot. She was totally wrong about what she'd gotten herself into.

Daisy jumped into the situation like she'd found a winning lottery ticket. She was a whirlwind of giggling, flirting energy. Underneath the brittle giddiness, Randi sensed an edge of desperation. She glanced over at Daisy, who tipped back her can of beer to finish every last drop. If they arrived at some kind of wild party, it was not the right place for Daisy. Randi's mistake. A massive stupid blunder.

She should have never taken Daisy to something like this while she was so vulnerable.

"Hey, how are you doing?" Randi said, her voice quiet. "Grieving is hard—and for a parent too. I'm so sorry you're going through that."

Daisy squinted her eyes then pushed her brown curls back behind her ears. "I was like your roommate, but all summer. Comatose, on a couch. Except, I cried a lot. Now I don't want to think about it, you know what I mean?"

"Yeah." Randi squeezed her hand.

"I feel like I need to have sex," Daisy whispered.

"Oh." Randi sat back. She grabbed for the oars and looked down at the choppy water.

"Like fun, hot sex. Not serious."

Randi swallowed, taken aback. When they had become friends in an English class last year, Daisy's openly boy-crazy antics had been funny. Daisy was a female Napoleon: super bossy, very short, a little plump, relentlessly cheerful, with soft curly hair around her cute round face. And with the will to command armies. She'd gone after a teaching assistant in the literary program like he held the key to global shipping routes.

The year before, chasing boys had been about finding a good one. Now she needed casual sex? No, not merely casual sex, a random hookup with some stranger. In the woods.

Randi bit her lip. She hated the idea of vulnerable Daisy doing that. Hated it. Was there a way to do it semi-safely? Randi bet that saying anything would make her more stubborn. Maybe she should shake her?

"I wouldn't know about that," said Randi. "I'm as prudish as a liberal person can be. Wouldn't work for me anyway. I'd want to inspect them with a flashlight for STDs, and asking them to please wash their hands first would probably kill the mood."

Daisy scoffed, shaking her head. "You're really uptight, aren't you?"

She had no idea. Sex, period, would be a huge step.

"And you sound crazed."

She couldn't let Daisy's plan go unanswered. She had to try to change her mind.

"Fun, not serious sex?" Randi said. "With some drunk stranger? It's a recipe for getting hurt by an asshole. Not to mention disease and probably self-loathing. You're not a sociopath, Daisy, you have feelings. Smart, sensitive feelings."

"Shut up. I'm on the pill, and it's not, like, something I do often. But so what if I did? You should try it. Actually have some fun."

Randi stared at her with the gut-twisting premonition that the night was going to be filled with horrors.

RANDI WALKED beside the edge of the river, trapped. Evening light sparkled on the water. Under other circumstances the location would be stunning. The island in the middle of the river was massive, with sandy beaches tucked along its sides and tall green bushy trees turning shades of gold, umber, and bright crimson.

A fraternity house of men occupied the largest section of the island. Attempting to recreate *Animal House* on a rocky beach was stupid. Worse that they were all skeezy meatheads. Their theme for the night: pimps and hoes.

*Pimps and hoes!* She glared over at Daisy, who giggled, while two guys stared at her with blank, cold eyes. She wanted to leave. It was so much worse than she could have imagined. Category five bad, with a tsunami of vicious penises staring at her.

She paced, at her limit. It would be dark in twenty

minutes. The uninhibited binge-drinking, with no police, or other sane adults, surely would end with blood.

People flooded in, packs of them hauling liquor and Doritos bags. They were hiking in from the road, using a rope someone had tied to a tree to shimmy down a steep slope then cross a shallow part of the river. A girl screamed, her foot slipping into water as she walked across a log bridge connecting the bank to the island. Someone had hauled in five kegs of beer. Guys poured it on their faces and shouted like gorillas.

She had to do something. For her, this party was like dropping an acrophobic person out of a plane and sneering at them to get over it already. Not safe, not remotely related to safe. Desperation to leave coiled in her stomach, like a hissing, cornered snake.

"What the hell are you doing here?"

Randi startled, her eyes jerking up from the pile of river rocks in her hand. What were the chances that he would be at this same party—did he find the pimps and hoes theme irresistible? It didn't matter.

"I'm paying for sins in a past life," she called out, to be heard above the music. Buck stood in front of her, and she almost threw herself on his chest.

She exhaled a shaky breath, relief flooding her. The devil she knew and all that. "I got tricked. I thought camping meant roasting marshmallows. Nobody told me it was a kegger with crazy people."

He jerked his head in a direction away from the music. She nodded, far too enthusiastically.

"Wait a sec," she called to him. "I'm going to tell my friend where I'm going."

Daisy occupied a stump, standing on it, giggling while the dumb guys drank their beer with relentless focus. Tweedledee and Tweedledum didn't speak much, especially to women. They did burp and stare openly at lady parts. One of them groped Daisy's behind. Randi swallowed, nauseous.

"Hey," she shouted, "I'm going that way."

Daisy gave her a wide-eyed look.

"Want to come?"

Still nothing. Randi pulled out her cell, pointed at it and mimed typing a text. They had service out here, so it wouldn't be hard to call and find each other. Randi couldn't stay at the fraternity beach party a moment longer. She'd lose her mind.

Both guys stared as well. They seemed tense and a little frozen, like a wild animal was crouched behind her.

Randi looked over her shoulder. Buck stood there, his black cowboy hat low, glaring toward the blasting music. They were staring at Buck, she realized. He was a little stunning, the first time you saw him.

"Are you guys coming?" Daisy said dismissively to the dumb guys.

They didn't answer.

Daisy stepped up to Randi, smiling. "Where are we going?"

Buck turned and started walking without a word. Not like him to be so grumpy with other people around.

Daisy fanned herself with a hand while looking at Buck. Randi made crazy circles next to her head, pointing at his back.

They walked single file down a trail winding through dense bushes and willow trees living in the sandy soil. Mercifully, the fraternity party faded behind them. A few minutes later the trail opened into a clearing with a fire. A group of guys, wearing cowboy hats, sat on logs and coolers.

Daisy stumbled, giggling breathlessly, red-faced and glassy-eyed. She was barely able to walk.

Randi wanted to disappear. It was all going to be too

painful to watch. She could go—climb up the slope to the country road on the other side of the river and call for a ride. Leave Daisy on her own. All of her attempts at persuading Daisy to leave had fallen flat and been ground in the mud by the heel of Daisy's flip-flop.

Buck dropped a cooler down onto the ground. Daisy sank onto it, slouching over her knees. The guys, a quiet bunch, watched Daisy out of the corners of their eyes.

"Have you been here long?" Randi said to Buck, breaking the intense silence.

"No," he said shortly. "Who'd you come with?"

"We floated in with Luke and his friends."

"Where is he?"

Randi shrugged. "Not sure. At the little stoner camp on the far side of the island, probably. Daisy decided to explore and I needed a break from the secondhand pot smoke. Those guys can't talk after their cannonballs, or whatever. I'll head back over there in a while and see if they're at the munchie stage yet. I brought marshmallows."

"The hell you will," Buck muttered. He swallowed back a long drink of beer. "Don't walk anywhere alone."

"Wow, what's got you wound up?"

He glared at her, taking a swig from his flask. "I can't believe you came out here." He shook his head, tense and scowling. "With one shit-faced friend and a bunch of dicks you don't know. What the hell were you thinking?"

Randi took off her backpack and dug around in it for her can of soda water. "Stop party shaming me." She didn't want to look at him. "I'm stuck, but I have my pepper spray. Besides, it makes you sound like a hypocrite."

She pulled out a bag of pretzels and dumped some on Daisy's lap, who giggled and leaned into the guy sitting next to her.

Buck was still staring at Randi. She sighed, rolling her eyes at him. Like she needed him to rub salt in her wounds.

"Mind sharing your liquor?"

He held out the flask. She dumped some soda into a cup for Daisy, then poured about a half shot into her can. "Camp cocktail," she said, handing him back his whiskey.

He shook his head at her. "Are you going to fall down drunk off a teaspoon of liquor?"

She glared at him. His tone was more than teasing. It bordered on hostile. Was he that annoyed with her?

"No, but my tolerance isn't anything to brag about. What about you? Planning on pissing yourself tonight?" Randi took a long swallow of whiskey-spiked soda water, blinking her eyes as the liquor burned down her throat.

He drank out of the flask. "I might not be totally in control of myself," he said. "Especially around pretty girls."

"Remember, incontinence is not attractive."

A little warm glow grew in her belly. She actually did become tipsy after one glass of wine, but getting through the evening required emergency measures.

"Keep the puke out of your teeth," she said, "and somebody out there might hold your hand."

One of the guys chuckled, looking over his shoulder at them.

"Where are your big glasses?" Buck grumbled.

"Couldn't risk breaking them, so I'm using these boring little ones. Where are all your girlfriends, otherwise known as housemates?"

"Sarah's at her parents'. The other girls, I don't know, but I wouldn't be surprised if they showed up."

One of the guys called out a question to Buck, and Randi wandered off to the edge of the clearing to find roasting sticks. She clicked on her flashlight. Oppressive darkness blanketed the woods away from the campfire. Her chest constricted, her breathing short and choppy—she was basically stuck here.

Shivering, she looked back toward the rumble of voices. Buck stood there, that cocky half-smile on his face while he talked. Her breath exhaled; she was ridiculously comforted by him being nearby. Even though he was being rude.

Absurdly, she felt like she'd known him forever. He didn't seem like a college guy, too sure of himself. He'd watched her cry, almost get in a fight, crash on her bike, and through it all he'd been a brick, dependable if not always sympathetic. No other man had ever seen her—the struggling, ambitious, brittle core inside—like he seemed to. His attention was a little addictive. She exhaled again, watching him pivot towards a couple of girls walking into the clearing.

She turned away, trying to shake off the feeling. He acted like she was an idiot who couldn't take care of herself. Obviously, he'd come here to hook up with somebody and it would happen since, apparently, he was some kind of celebrity playboy on campus. On the A-list with the cowboy crowd. He messed with her a little bit, for fun. They both knew she wasn't the hooking-up type. Definitely not.

Back by the fire, she roasted hot dogs for herself and Daisy. Hugh and a few other guys finished off the pack. Mild teasing about eating wieners ensued. Still, the group resembled adults more than *Lord of the Flies* variety horny teenagers. She polished off her can of spiked soda water, relaxing an inch.

When she stepped behind a tree to pee, Daisy tagged along, then fell into a bush, cackling like a crazy person. Randi pulled her to her feet and brushed the leaves off her back. She must be cold in her tiny shorts and flip-flops.

"Let's go to the tent, Daisy. I'm ready to crash."

"Shut up. Can't be serious." She burped, clutching her stomach for a moment. "This is fun. I need another beer…"

"You're falling over."

Daisy walked away, scoffing, stumbling back toward the group around the fire.

Randi herded her back to her seat. They ate roasted marshmallows, then wasted half the pack watching them sizzle in the fire. People wandered in and out of camp, mostly staying. Soon, the little clearing became uncomfortably crowded, blaring country music competing with the dance pop down the island.

All kinds of women showed up, half of them obviously focused on Buck. Odd. He was good-looking, sure, but she must be missing something. A blonde jumped up and wrapped her legs around his hips. Stupid jealousy choked her, which she firmly decided to ignore. She stared resolutely at the fire.

She chatted with a few people, mostly Hugh. Daisy flirted outrageously with the muscular bald man, who blushed to the tips of his ears.

One of the dumb guys, from earlier at the frat party, wandered into the clearing and zeroed in on Daisy. Randi bit her lip, anxiety fluttering in her stomach. Daisy was too drunk. She was barely tracking what happened around her. She would be totally vulnerable, alone with some strange guy who was too smashed himself to make good choices. Grabbing Daisy's hand, she pulled her away, keeping her back to the oncoming disaster.

"I'm going to the tent to sleep," Randi said. "Come with me. Let's call it a night."

"What?" Daisy squinted at her. "You're joking right? Still early. No way I'm going to sleep."

Randi took a deep breath, trying for calm. "Listen, do the hookup thing with somebody you know. Those dummies from earlier are total strangers. Daisy, it could be bad, and will definitely be disappointing."

"Hey," said the dumb guy behind Daisy.

Daisy whirled around, a full smile lighting up her face. "Hi."

They all stood there for a few long moments. Randi crossed her arms. Daisy giggled.

"Want to go for a walk?" the dumb guy said, flat eyes focused on Daisy's cleavage.

Randi covered her face, swallowing down the tirade she wanted to yell at both of them. The guy could be categorized on the acceptable-looking side—in a backwards ball cap, nice haircut kind of way—but he turned her stomach. Rude, obviously exploitative, and about as bright as a cracked keg cup. Randi had very little experience, but she guessed he was lousy and selfish in bed, or worse. And they wouldn't have a bed.

Daisy, on the other hand, was intelligent and sensitive—and desperately wanted someone to fall in love with her. She was vulnerable from grief and loneliness, close to passing out drunk, and reckless in a way that was self-sabotaging and destructive. An unstoppable train wreck.

"Did you bring beer?" Daisy asked coquettishly, cocking her head to one side.

Randi glanced through her fingers. He held up one half-empty keg cup and nodded his head. *Wow.*

Daisy walked off without looking back. Randi gulped, tears burning her eyes. She pinched the bridge of her nose.

It will probably be fine, she told herself. She was uptight and scared of intimacy, and negatively impacted from "abstinence only" programming during primary school. Other people jumped in headfirst all the time. Hooking up was a thing, and plenty of people did it. At least Daisy had the pepper spray and the little flashlight Randi had given her.

She glanced up and found Buck's eyes on her from across the clearing. Depression, and exhaustion, sat like a hundred pounds on her shoulders. She swallowed, gave him a little wave, then turned away quickly. No doubt Buck would hook up with somebody. Of course he would, that was the point of a wild party in the woods. Simply not for her.

Watching her step, not interested in talking to anyone, she walked toward the trail. Done. Hanging around waiting to see if Daisy would remember to find her was pointless. What was she going to do, stalk behind them like a creeper and wait till they finished? Not happening. The girl could call her if she needed her.

On her own, everything made her skin crawl—sinister rustling in the woods and sordid laughter from strange men. She patted her pocket with the mini can of pepper spray, she always carried two with her, then slipped her hand inside to hold onto it.

The flashlight in her smartphone made a thin triangle-shaped beam of white light. A square foot of ground in front of her glowed brightly, and beyond it, thick darkness. The path through the woods stretched ahead, an overgrown thicket, the ground an obstacle course of thorny vines, rocks, and beer bottles. Getting back to her campsite was going to give her an ulcer.

A guy about to urinate against a tree blinked, caught in the glare of her light. His wobbly head turned toward her. Gasping, she jerked her hand to turn the beam away from him, taking a quick step back. She tripped, squealing. Her phone slipped out of her hands, immediately disappearing into a clump of grass. *Shit!*

A rapid stream of urine surged nearby, disrupting the stillness of the dense darkness. The guy belched. Randi scrambled over the ground, groping for her phone, swallowing the whimper stuck in her throat. The sharp thorn of a viny plant cut into her wrist. Pain burned up her arm as the urine blast began to taper off. Her hand found solid plastic then the screen of her phone lit up. Shivering, she stumbled away, her pulse hammering under her skin.

She forced her feet to move faster, but not run. Running would attract attention, possibly bring out the inner predator lurking inside the hearts of young, testosterone-saturated men. What if some creep followed her? She shuddered, her heart punching her ribcage.

A woman screamed. Randi jumped, swinging wildly around, pointing her flashlight into the dark trees. The scream turned into squealing laughter. She sagged, forcing herself to breathe, pressing a hand hard into her upper chest.

A twig snapped behind her. She whirled, pulling out the pepper spray and stumbling backward.

"Good lord," said Buck, "you're scared out of your mind."

Randi crouched down, sitting on her heels and putting her head between her knees. She wanted to punch him.

"Did you have to sneak up on me?"

"Darlin', what the hell do you think you're doing? I told you to wait for me."

Randi pushed up to her feet. "None of your business. I've got this." She turned away to march down the path.

She lasted about five seconds. Pausing at a fork, she peeked over her shoulder. He stood right behind her.

"Why don't you make noise when you walk?" she whispered at him, not sure why she was whispering. "It's creepy."

"Do you know where you're going?"

"Yes, of course I do. I don't want to go through the fraternity party, so I'm trying a new route."

"Your tent's downstream on the west side?"

"Yes."

He pushed past her and walked confidently into the dark. Randi huffed. He treated her like a helpless idiot or an annoying kid sister. Either one was wrong. And possibly chauvinistic. Except she felt pathetically thankful he'd chosen to walk her to her tent. It didn't make her less of a feminist, she decided firmly, hustling to catch up to him.

Twenty minutes on a tight narrow trail later, angling their bodies to avoid thorny vines, she spotted her tent. The little nylon dome sat on a patch of dry grass overlooking a small beach below. A few other tents were visible in the clear spots nearby.

Randi sighed in relief. Moonlight glinted off the water, breaking up the darkness. The rushing river muted the sounds of alarming debauchery. Nearly peaceful over here, far enough from the chaos that she felt almost safe. Some warm fuzzy goodwill grew toward Buck.

"Thank you for walking me over here." She pivoted to face him. "You saved me from a little anxiety. Thanks, Buck, I really appreciate it."

"Yep," he said, taking off his hat and rubbing his head. "Glad you didn't have a heart attack, darlin'. The house would be kinda dull without you around."

"Wow, that warms my heart." She took off her backpack. "Don't fall into the river and drown tonight in a drunken stupor. The girls will blame me and someone would end up in jail."

Buck walked away. Randi exhaled, pushing hair out of her face with shaky hands. Definitely best he left. Of course. His chivalrous instincts were strong, especially toward perceived kid sisters, and she could simply accept it and not become depressed about the stupid ache in her chest.

She grabbed her jug of water and toothbrush and walked a few paces away to clean her teeth. At least he was sort of her friend—in an "I'll laugh when you fall" kind of way. She trusted him, mostly, which was odd.

She pulled out her phone, checking for any messages or SOS calls from Daisy. Nothing. She typed out a quick *I'm at the tent* message, then stuffed her phone in her pocket and turned around.

Buck was sitting in front of her tent, pulling off his boots. She stared at him. A bug buzzed by her face. She closed her mouth. Why would he pull off his boots at her tent?

"What are you doing?"

"Waiting for you to finish with that water. Toss it here."

"Is something wrong with your foot? Why are you taking off your belt? Buck, what's happening?"

He unzipped the tent and peered inside. "Is the other girl gonna show up here?"

"Daisy? Uh, yeah. I mean, I hope so. Her sleeping bag's in there."

"Some men might get excited about the idea. I find it terrifying. You're going to have to sleep in the middle. I don't want to wake up and find her trying to rape me."

Randi rubbed her face, struggling to comprehend what was happening. "Buck, you can't sleep here. That's my tent."

He tugged the water out of her hands. "Relax. I've been up since four this morning, I'm exhausted, and tired of dealing with a bunch of hyper kids who want to party all night. They won't find me out here. I'll be asleep before you're warm in your bag."

She crouched down to untie the laces of her boots, watching him finger-brush his teeth with her toothpaste. He acted like it was all totally reasonable and normal for him to sleep in her tent. With her.

"Not my problem," she said. "I'm sure plenty of girls would let you hide in their tent for the night. I'm not one of them."

He dropped the water jug onto the ground next to the open door. "You're not staying out here alone," he said. "That little tramp with you might bring some asshole back."

Randi swallowed. She hadn't thought of Tweedledum showing up.

"Don't talk about Daisy like that."

Buck ignored her, squeezing the back of his neck. "Not to mention the hundred horny guys wandering around, piss drunk, and not a quarter that many women. You're single, too hot for your own good, and you skip around with your head in the clouds. More than one of those dickheads is thinking about surprising you in your tent, believe me."

Randi crossed her arms. "Hey, I appreciate the gesture, but I'm okay. Nothing is going to happen. On the off chance, I have pepper spray and know self-defense."

"Spray that shit in a tent and you'll be blind, as well as raped and beat up."

"Buck, this is crazy."

"Darlin', I'm staying."

They stared at each other. The worst part was, she wanted to give in.

"You don't have a blanket."

"Go do your thing in the bushes and then get in here." He crawled inside.

She gazed up at the moon, her heart racing. Not ready to be inside a tent with him—it was too sudden. Unplanned. Getting into her pajamas would be so tricky. Should she ask him to step out?

A couple of guys stumbled into view, headed down to the water. Drunk guys were everywhere. Her little window of privacy was going to end at any moment. She hurried over to a dark patch of bushes and "did her thing."

The tent crinkled and shook as she stiffly crawled inside. Buck lay on his back with his cowboy hat covering his face. Her hands shook as she pulled up the zipper and tied the flaps closed on the tent door. He didn't move. *Get ahold of yourself!*

It was supposedly a five-person tent, but his massive body took up half of the space in the little nylon dome. She grabbed her extra fleece blanket from underneath her sleeping bag and tossed it on his chest.

"Hide under this when Daisy comes in." She slipped into her bag with her pajama pants in her hand. Awkwardly, she squirmed into them.

Buck stretched the blanket out and the hem didn't reach his knees.

"What happened with that guy you came out here with? Going to show up at your tent?"

"Luke?" Randi stuffed her leggings and cardigan into her backpack. She'd sleep in her T-shirt dress. "His girlfriend showed up. Or his hookup partner. Whatever. She was pretty hostile. He sat there like a lump, too stoned to speak. I'm not into it anyway. That guy's way too cool for me."

"Good riddance."

She pulled the sleeping bag up to her chin. Buck didn't move, as still as a stone statue. She was restless, the brush of fabric almost painful against the rigid skin of her nipples. The little devil inside her pointed frantically at the big warm man next to her.

She told the devil to hush. What was she going to do, jump on him?

"You've been busy," she said. He'd been elsewhere the last few nights, his truck not parked in the usual spot when she went to bed. The weather had been gorgeous, so she'd skipped carpooling—and, stupidly, not seeing him in the kitchen in the mornings had shadowed her entire week.

"Yep."

"Are you, um, seeing someone now?" She gulped, pinpricks of heat and ice stabbing into her cheeks. The alcohol was fueling her mouth, blabbing hugely personal, none-of-her-business questions to Buck like an idiot. "Are they going to show up with a shotgun and start screaming about your promises?" She should stop, just stop talking.

She waited, holding her breath, then exhaled. A long minute passed. She rolled away from him, facing the empty side of the tent. Not going to answer, which meant he didn't think she had any business asking. And, yeah, he poked around. What did she expect? He was notorious for leaving bedrooms all across campus.

"I'm not sleeping with anyone," he said. "Not since before I met you."

"Oh."

Chewing on her bottom lip, she turned enough to peek sideways at him. He was lying with his back to her, an uninterested brick. "So," she said, "you made it through five whole weeks of celibacy. Wow. Somebody should give you a sticker."

"Go to sleep."

She lay awake, thinking crazy thoughts. Like if she didn't stay away from the cowboy, pathetic would hardly describe the needy ache lodged in her pelvis, and the slutty little devil inside, dancing a mamba.

# CHAPTER THIRTEEN

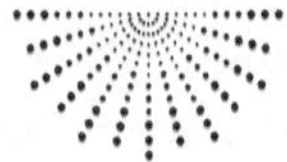

Her ear tickled. Randi blinked, disoriented by the light coming from above her. Must already be after seven —she'd overslept. Tent. Other people breathing. One of them pressed against her back.

Her eyes snapped wide open. Buck lay curved against her, spooning, one of his dense arms like an oak log on her side. A hefty knee pinned her thigh. She was half off her sleeping mat, and he was half on, with her pillow smooshed between them. He wheezed into her ear.

She took a deep breath. *Don't panic. He's keeping warm. How intolerably awkward for him to wake up right now. Sneak out before he does.*

The unbearable sensation of him against her was…hot. Heat tickled her insides. His breath on her ear tingled, wet and, mostly, disgusting, and yet she quivered in her belly with every exhalation. She bit her lip. Actually, that tickle morphed, at mutant-lightning speed, into a heavy and startling arousal. *Crap*. She needed to scoot, fast.

She inched away from him, holding her breath as his hand slid along her side.

His arm jerked, tightening around her. "Where are you goin'?" he mumbled into her neck.

"Yoga videos," she whispered. "Quiet, don't wake up Daisy."

His scratchy cheek rubbed against her neck. He nuzzled! She gulped. He bit the lobe of her ear and she gasped, her whole body jerking.

"You shouldn't have woken me up," he said. She groaned at the feel of him, his hot front pressing into her, the hard ridge down below against her backside.

Panting, her eyes fluttered closed. Molasses and warm honey ran beneath her skin. She didn't want to move. A wave of heat expanded under her spine. They lay like that for a few long seconds. His hand gripped her hip and rocked, slowly. She swallowed a moan. The intense throbbing between her legs tensed every muscle in her body. This was new—unbearable. She tilted her head back, shivering as his lips slid along her jaw, his breathing ragged in her ear. She arched against him, her knees opening.

Daisy moaned and rolled over. Randi froze, holding her breath. Buck stilled. Horrified with herself, she pushed out of the sleeping bag. She kept her eyes down, unable to look at him. By the time she'd opened her backpack of clothes and peeked over her shoulder, Buck was stepping out of the tent door.

Her face flamed. What had she been thinking? With jerky movements, she pulled on her warmest yoga gear, scrubbed her face with a T-shirt, and took a deep breath. She didn't want to go outside and face him.

Daisy muttered in her sleep. Vaguely, Randi remembered Daisy stumbling in late. She'd come in alone and hadn't seemed to register the hulking man hiding under a throw blanket. She examined Daisy anxiously. Facedown on top of her sleeping bag, arms tucked under her body in the cold air, she was sleeping in the same shorts and thin hoodie she'd worn the day before. Otherwise she appeared normal. No obvious bruises.

She put her sleeping bag over her. Screws of guilt tightened in her chest. She shouldn't have left her alone last night and could have done more. Not cut out for the party scene was an understatement for Randi attending a toddler's backyard birthday fest. At a bacchanal in the woods, she was like an old woman who'd been dropped into a sinister music video—and then commanded to breakdance or die.

Her old-woman bladder needed to squat outside five minutes ago. Time to put her big girl pants on. *Get it over with, coward.* She took a deep breath and opened the tent door.

Buck was waiting for her outside. She couldn't meet his eyes. Huddling over her backpack was an excellent excuse for turning away from him. Everything would change now—how could they have a snarky pseudo-friendship when she knew what his dick felt like? Would he try to finish what they'd started in the tent? It was all ruined. There were decisions to make—did they sleep together? Did she move out before anything happened?

"Wait for me," he said. "I brought a fishing pole." He walked off, long legs covering the ground fast. She watched until he disappeared up the path.

The fog of panic cleared. Clearly, his hard-on wouldn't turn him into a crazed sex maniac. Erotic morning encounters were a dime a dozen for him. Nothing special here.

She splashed water on her face, and the tense bubble in her stomach deflated. She swallowed a cookie and washed it down with a can of cold coffee. *Just be calm.* Later she would figure it all out. Buck clearly wasn't going to drag her off under a bush. Excellent. Definitely. And she was the stupidest girl on that island for being disappointed.

"You've got this," she spoke out loud, talking to herself. Shaking her head, she started working before she lost her mind.

She was looking down on the beach, adjusting her cell phone on a portable tripod, when Buck appeared. He winked at her. Her pulse took off like a scared rabbit. She was in so much trouble. He glanced away, casting into an eddy of water beneath a sprawling willow tree.

Closing her eyes, she blew out a long breath. He wanted to hang out and pretend like nothing had happened? Tensely, she turned the idea over in her mind. If she did bring it up, the next obvious step would be to state what she wanted. *Don't break my heart.* She flinched at the stark revelation of her fear.

Liking him, a lot, didn't make him the right man for her—it made her vulnerable. Yes, she would finally admit to herself that she bordered on moonstruck. One benefit of having a mental breakdown at sixteen, landing her in a psych ward for a few months after her grandparents died, was she had sat through a lot of therapy. She knew what positive self-care involved. Jumping into bed with someone who was only physically attracted to her and not available for a relationship would not be a healthy choice.

Nope, she didn't want to talk about it either. He moved further away along the river, casting his line with unconscious grace and beauty. Smothering away hope with rational thinking didn't always work, stupidly. Instead, she would stay busy.

She filmed a twenty-minute shoot, deciding to voice-over later so the microphone would pick up the ambient sounds of the riverside. A cacophony of birds whistled and called all around her. Dragonfly wings buzzed past her ears as they dove for the gurgling river.

Buck didn't appear to be watching her. Finally, the movement and breathing rescued her sanity from the confused lust pit it had fallen into. Her sore and tense back softened.

They stayed within sight of each other for the next hour, him fishing and her doing a series of yoga shoots on the west side of the island. The sun rose into a clear blue sky, warming the air from frigid to promising a little heat in the afternoon.

Resolutely, she kept her brain turned off, refusing to ask any questions of herself or Buck. The morning of exploring the island over rocks and through tall grass felt like an escape, peaceful yet charged with the changing energy of autumn. It helped that they didn't talk much. In the moments when a rogue thought slipped through, her heart squirmed, pounding about the startling, tiny, merry buzz in her chest.

By the end, she was warm, even possibly cheerful, her quarter-zip fleece tied around her waist. Buck stood up from stowing his fishing gear in a raft. She handed him a couple of cookies out of her bag, taking a bite from another.

She zipped her backpack closed, the camera gear stowed away in a dry bag. Smiling, she rose to her feet.

"That was a good shoot," she said.

He grinned back at her. Quick as a darting bird he leaned forward and kissed her on the mouth. He stayed there for a moment, soft and feathery. It left cookie crumbs on her lips.

"I like fishing with you," he said. "Those yoga moves are sexy."

They stared at each other. Randi's lips tingled. Was it possible for your whole body to flush?

She was frozen, and cracked open, by the simple kiss. She tried to push down the welling emotion quivering up. His little peck wasn't anything more than fleeting affection. She realized that.

"Didn't know it was so easy to make you quiet." He rubbed her mouth with his thumb, stepped back, and put his hat on. "Go roll your girl into a raft. Let's get before the drunks wake up."

RANDI TOOK a picture of the water. The light on the river glowed, soft and warm, gold shimmering on rippling dusky blue and green as the raft floated downstream.

So far, she wasn't freaking out. Spending the morning with Buck had helped her realize that yes, they both had slipped up in various horny ways, but life quickly went back to normal when the cold air of reality gusted in your face. And still, a ridiculous little butterfly fluttered in her stomach.

She could let something happen. The idea simmered in her belly, delicious and full of heat. She closed her eyes, taking a deep breath of musky river air. In a moment, her wits would return and she'd remember all of the countless reasons she shouldn't. He really had released some endorphins that morning...

"Hey," said Daisy, her voice hoarse, "what are you doing today?"

Randi glanced toward the huddled figure on the other end of the raft. Daisy lay on her side, pale, curled into a ball under the fleece blanket.

Randi cleared her throat, seriously attempting to push thoughts of Buck into a container, where they belonged.

"Cook and work at home, I think. Unless my housemates are on a bender. Or have destroyed the house again. Ugh. I should move out. They're all crazy alcoholics at my place, with one puke-covered bathroom."

She swallowed, pausing the rambling. Seconds ticked by. Was Daisy more than extremely hungover?

"I've looked a few times, but the only housing left are

dark unfinished basements or actually sharing a room with a hairy guy named Dick."

No response. She took a drink from her water bottle. Daisy stared at the side of the raft.

"Um, what are you up to? Want to come help me cook?"

"Yeah, sure." Daisy pulled the blanket around her face. "I don't feel like going back to my apartment yet."

Randi put her camera away. Buck and Hugh were far behind them, fishing. This was an opportune time to talk, even if she dreaded it. "Hey," she said, "what happened with that guy last night?"

"He's an asshole." Daisy covered half her face with the blanket. "It was stupid. He was lousy."

"I'm sorry."

"This hangover is killing me." Apparently, that encompassed all she wanted to say.

Randi bit her lip. Daisy clearly needed help, and she was completely unqualified to offer any. People weren't her thing.

"Why does this blanket smell like a man?" Daisy stared at her.

Randi swallowed, her cheeks heating up. "Um…"

"I woke up for some water in the middle of the night and thought I saw someone with you…" Daisy blinked a few times, then glared hard at Randi's face. "That was real."

Randi started rowing. Daisy had turned the tables on her, and she was not ready to talk. About anything.

"He's a friend and nothing happened." A small lie, but technically they hadn't kissed in the tent. Overall, not too far off. "He wanted to hide from some girl chasing him."

"Are you serious?" Daisy sat up. "Randi. Holy shit. Who is he?"

Well, at least she wasn't catatonic anymore. Randi rowed harder. She genuinely didn't want Buck to overhear them.

"I'll tell you, but don't say anything in front of anybody

else. Especially my housemates. I don't want people to develop the wrong idea and think something happened—is happening… You know."

"Fine. Who was it?"

"Buck," Randi whispered.

"What?" Daisy shouted, slapping the side of the raft. Good grief. Why did Randi put up with this?

"Calm down. He's just down the river, so be quiet."

"You are in so much trouble," Daisy said, eyes sparkling, clearly relishing every moment. "That guy is a player. I mean girlfriends-in-different-towns kind of player."

Randi flinched. "He can be a bossy jackass." She managed to sound nonchalant. "Thinks of me as a kid sister too stupid to live."

"That's twisted." Daisy sat up straight, totally energized now. "He's so, like, tough. And a little mean. A manly man. I don't see it with you two."

"Yep, a disaster." Randi paddled, her stomach lurching as she navigated through choppy water.

The conversation brought home what she already knew but had avoided thinking about all morning. She had to stay away from Buck. Letting him hurt her could derail everything she had worked for, and spiral things out of control. She couldn't handle the fallout.

She needed to stay on her schedule and follow her routine. He would toy with her and then disappear. Letting herself fall in love with him was too much of an emotional risk for her mental health. A relapse would mean not finishing school for who knew how long. How could she even contemplate risking everything when the finish line was so close?

"Look, there's your car," she said, her voice hoarse. "Get ready to jump."

~

"So, you're sleeping with Glasses now?" Hugh said, spitting the words out like an accusation. Buck glanced away from the road toward Hugh's set face. He was scowling so hard his lips puckered out.

"What, you hoping for a report?"

Hugh sighed. "If you're going to fuck around, why pick a girl like that?"

"Calm down, old man. She's not one of your sisters."

"If you had sisters, you'd know how screwed up they get, 'specially the sensitive ones." Hugh huffed, fidgeting in his seat.

Fucking perfect. Hugh was working up to one of his lectures. Buck gripped the steering wheel. Time for the ugly.

"Glasses is on her own. No parents. Grandparents passed a few years ago."

Buck shifted, taking in her history—trying to. No family besides the aunt. Damn, he couldn't wrap his head around that one. He exhaled a long breath.

"That's rough."

Hugh cleared his throat. Here came the moral tirade. "Vicki worked you over." He sniffed. "You're in a black place. You shouldn't take it out on that kid."

He had to say the V-word. Vicki's name made him go to dark corners in his head. Women were all liars. Wait long enough and they showed their true colors.

Was Randi a liar? She lied to herself, he thought, about not needing people. The truth was he didn't lump her into that category of women. She was more of a neurotic and cantankerous handful.

"Damn, Dr. Hugh, what do I owe you for the session?"

Hugh didn't answer. The silence grew heavy.

"The truth is," Buck said, "I'm done with all the party bullshit. I want to wrap up my grad work and move the hell out of here."

Hugh grunted, but left well enough alone. The man was softhearted. Sleeping with the meanest, nastiest bitch he could find had become Hugh's twisted way of dealing with needing sex and not wanting to settle down. A way to dodge being stuck and miserable. For Hugh, the worse they treated him, the better. Twisted go-nowhere logic. Back in Texas, before Buck had dragged him up north, his girl had beat on him. Hugh pretended like that was all right.

Buck stared out at the country road. Randi didn't resemble his ex, in personality or looks. Vicki, the spoiled princess, got whatever she wanted from both parents. Vicki had manipulated him into a relationship without one honest moment. He'd never met such a practiced liar, and she could cry on demand. The sex clicked, a warped kind of good, and he'd made it work. For a while. Problems were everywhere else in their relationship. The ugliness carried over into all of it.

Randi didn't want to jump in his bed for kicks, or to trick him into a relationship. Sleeping with her would be a feat worthy of a Greek ode. Last night it had gone from "fun to chase her," to "finish line in sight." He still didn't quite believe it.

Mostly, they bickered. And he looked forward to it every morning. He liked making her mad, breaking her out of that stiff remoteness. Early in the morning, she bounced around like a pinball, lobbing insults at him. Reminded him of home. She felt like his, which was crazy.

She wasn't ready to sleep with him. Hell, she froze up over a kiss. All he knew was he wanted her to be right there with him. Not a drunken hookup—that wasn't an option with her. If it happened, she would choose it.

Hugh was right. He shouldn't mess with her. She needed

some limp little dick, like the kid from the library, who would make her feel safe. He gripped the steering wheel hard, clenching his teeth.

They drove out of the orchard onto the gravel road in front of the house. There she sat, in a lawn chair by her cabin. He parked next to his trailer. Dragging her behind a door and finishing what they started in the morning was what he wanted to do—and wouldn't.

"You ever take a look in that barn?" Hugh stared hard at the barn closest to Randi's cabin.

"Floor's concrete. Big mess inside."

Hugh set down his twelve-pack of beer and headed toward the old building. Buck sighed. When Hugh got a bug in his nuts about something, the man couldn't think straight.

They walked past Randi in her lawn chair, working on her computer. Long, bare legs stretched out of a cute little dress, pretty feet crossed at the ankle. He swallowed. Something about those dresses made him want to throw her over his shoulder like a caveman.

Another girl dozed in the other chair, wrapped up in a blanket. He nodded at Randi. She gazed up at him through her lashes. His dick twitched. Dammit.

The wide sliding door of the barn came open with a jerk. Buck walked up beside Hugh.

"Hot damn," he said, "somebody cleaned up all the crap." Somebody sat in a lawn chair, watching them. What the hell was she up to in here?

A fast-flying swallow swooped past their heads. The attic of the barn, old plywood nailed to the rafters, was a mess of bird guano and nests. Otherwise, the clear floor spread out in the huge space. It had been recently pressure washed too.

"Huh, this ain't bad," Buck said. "Except that far left wall is about to shit out." The soft wood was rotten and pitted with holes. On second thought, dumping every spare minute into the place sounded like a stupid way to spend his free time.

Hugh crouched down, examining the water pipe coming through the wall.

"Somebody might grab that barn stove if we don't pick it up today," Hugh mumbled. Buck rolled his eyes. Hugh was already gung-ho on the project.

"The thing weighs four hundred pounds. We don't need to rush over on a Sunday."

Buck walked along the long open space, at least seventy feet. On the right-hand narrow side, a door led into a little end room, a shop at some point. He opened the interior door.

Counters lined the room, their wooden surfaces clean. A little space heater sat in one corner. A few cabinets held office supplies, and one wall was pegboard. Windows on both sides of the room let in bright light. Corkboards blanketed in index cards and sticky notes hung on the walls. A foam presentation poster lay half done in front of a cabinet.

"What are you doing in here?"

And there Randi stood, arms crossed, looking pissed off and ornery. He smiled. The pink in her cheeks was cute as hell.

"Do you work in here? The space isn't half bad."

She took a deep breath. Were those squirrels and foxes on that little red dress? Normally her dresses weren't so sexy. Her bare shoulders were sun-browned, golden with a flush of pink. He put his hands in his pockets. How was he supposed to resist her when she was so damn gorgeous?

"Look, I'm using this space and the big room too. I'm the one who cleaned and cleared everything out."

He leaned against the counter. "This is shared space, just like the kitchen or living room."

"There are two other barns!"

"Yeah, with dirt floors made of old animal shit. Not to mention fewer walls."

"So, what, you're going to take over so you have a new place to get drunk?"

The big glasses slipped down her nose when her face puckered. He tried to press his smile flat. She was all worked up.

"All right, let's negotiate. How about I leave this room all to you? Also, we'll put in some desks and tables in the other room."

She glared at him through her lashes. He hardened. If they were together, he'd pull off those glasses, prop her up on the counter, and kiss her until she forgot what day it was. She would be about the perfect height… He swallowed.

"And what, you turn the barn into a party space? You know this is twenty feet from my bedroom."

She stomped around, straightening up notebooks. If she bent over, he would lose it.

"Hey, I'm not opening a frat house. I'm too busy to party much. Relax, darlin'. Hugh found an old barn stove at a demolition site and some other free stuff. We might end up with another shower in there."

That got her attention. His too. Desire cooked his blood. Renovating the barn sounded better. Except keeping his hands off her might kill him.

"Fine. But remember what I said, I'll call in a noise violation."

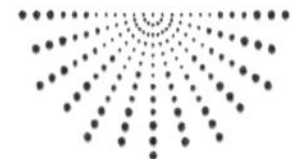

The following week passed about as pleasantly for Randi as for Sisyphus rolling a boulder uphill. She desperately needed a brutally productive work session out of her library time. A bead of sweat rolled down the back of her neck. Mountains of coursework were avalanching her to-do list, and her end-of-week midterms would be served up in approximately fifteen hours.

"So," Carter said, his round, puppy dog eyes scanning her face, "uh, what kind of music do you like?"

Randi's phone buzzed by her hand. She flipped it over on the library table and saw Buck's name flash on the screen. What was wrong with that man?

"I like everything," she said, not opening her phone. "What about you?"

"Classic rock, mostly."

Carter drummed his fingers on the table, his face red and a little sweaty. Whatever he was working up to, it was taking him an eternity to arrive there. Spiders of impatience crawled up her spine. The stuffy library closed in on her. Her phone sat buried under a notebook, sucking up her energy like a fathomless black hole. Everything was out of control, and she couldn't find a moment to herself. She needed to work, dammit.

He cleared his throat. "So, a Battle of the Bands is happening this Friday. I mean tomorrow. Over in the main quad. We could go check it out at some point, if you're planning on coming to the library. Or if you're not too busy..." Carter stared down at his mechanical pencil, his thumb clicking the top at the pace of a whacked-out speed drummer.

"Yeah, maybe. I don't care for crowds." She tried to keep her voice from sounding tight. She didn't like people, period. And nice guys were torture.

What was wrong with her? She should be jumping at the chance. This wholesome guy had asked her on a date. After, they could spend long evenings together, doing homework, in the library. They'd go out for coffees and see comic-book movies on the weekend. He made sense. Dating him was normal and right.

She adjusted her glasses, hating the beaten-down look on Carter's face. "But stepping outside for a minute would be refreshing."

He nodded his head. "Awesome, yeah."

Her phone buzzed again with an incoming call from Buck. She hit ignore.

"Excuse me," she said, standing up from her table, peering into the stacks for a somewhat private spot. The big idiot required a phone call.

The library crowd was finally thinning out. She walked toward a tall window overlooking the dark quad. Wind lashed at the trees outside, streetlights illuminating flurries of leaves spiraling up on the walkways through campus.

She sighed, opening up Buck's text.

**Buck**: I'll wait for you in the truck.

Randi rolled her eyes up to the ceiling and tipped her head back. Why did that man think he needed to babysit her? She wanted to work late. Three text messages, delivered to his phone, had clearly explained her plan.

She dialed his number.

"Hey," he answered on the first ring.

"Buck, go home."

"Well, darlin', I'll do that as soon as you're done."

"I can't concentrate when I know you're down there waiting for me like some kind of martyr. Why are you doing this?"

"Hey, now, I'm going to hang up if you keep yelling at me."

"Look, I'm not a child, I can get myself home. My bike works great. I need to burn off some energy."

A longish pause stretched out between them. She should hang up on him and send a clear message about their lack of ride co-dependency. She was an independent woman, dammit.

"It's cold, windy, and dark. And, if I wait for you, I don't have to drive."

There was the meat of it, the crux of the issue, the thing hobbling her life—she drove his truck back at night, and he hung around town drinking beer. The other girls in the house rode in with Buck so they could bar hop too. About time to put a stop to that nonsense.

"If you need to burn off some energy, darlin'," Buck continued, "come cuddle with me tonight."

She drew in a breath, mini lightning bolts zapping through her head. Did he just ask her to sleep with him?

"No. No cuddling," she huffed. Did he think she would casually go to bed with him late on a Thursday night? "And hey," she gasped, hating the catch in her voice. He'd just asked her to hop in bed with him. Gawd. "I'm not the damn drunk-truck chauffeur. I'm riding my bike."

She hung up on him. There, that would break up their pseudo-friendship whatever. Definitely past time to set some firm boundaries.

Her forehead bumped against the cold window. He made her want to punch something. Or rip his T-shirt open. Or jump in a fast river and float away until she couldn't remember what he looked like.

He wanted her to cuddle with him. That euphemism was absolutely wrong—you cuddled with a teddy bear or a kitten. He wanted to lie on top of her and pin her to the ground. Pound his hard cock into her. Heat rolled over her face, her stomach, between her legs. The thought pressurized some bubbly place under her spine, desire for him threatening to burst out of the can she had stuffed the little devil in.

Ever since camping with Buck, strangely only four days ago, she had become painfully conscious of his body. In the morning he smelled like old dusty leather, sharp fresh soap, and the canteen of coffee next to him in the cab. At night he was musk and sweat, all hardworking man. It made her want to run her hands over the ropy muscles on his shoulders.

He hadn't touched her all week. Granted, Angie and Sarah had been going out of their way to not leave them alone. At times, she and Buck were nothing more than testy carpoolers, enduring the bad weather that had rolled in Monday morning, squashed in the cab of his truck with another girl from the house. But then he would glance at her in that focused way, his eyes lazy, his mouth cocked in a half-smile, and she melted all over the floor. It was chaos. It resembled a pile of weird old trash nobody knew what to do with, crammed into the corner of a rotten barn. There was no future there.

Randi stood up and smoothed down her gray chambray skirt. She adjusted the necktie of her blouse. Her transparent ghostly reflection looked back at her in the window. Single. Accomplishing things. She took a deep breath, turned away, and marched back to her table, low heels clicking on the floor.

She needed space. If she had to be a bitch, so be it. Otherwise, she would sleep with him. And not call it cuddling.

She sat down at her library table.

Carter leaned forward, his earnest face stretched in an expectant smile. "Are those hot air balloons on your shirt?" he asked.

"Yep." Randi opened her laptop. She was not going to run down and make sure Buck left. She would get back to work.

"They're cute," Carter said.

Randi glanced at him and he quirked a smile at her, all awkward sweetness.

"I mean, hot air balloons are cute, I guess. My father is a bit of a balloonatic. He stores a Montgolfier aerostat in our garage. It's a beast to load into and out of the truck—my job, of course. But, um, I meant the way you dress, is, um, cute."

"Thanks, Carter," Randi said, swallowing irrational annoyance. Cute? She aimed for uptight academic trapped in a vintage boutique. The c-word was about as flattering as fingernails on a chalkboard.

What was wrong with her? She needed a long bike ride or a ten-mile run.

"Show me a picture of your dad's balloon sometime," she said, managing a tight smile. "Now, shall we get some work done?"

She put her phone in her bag. Checking if Buck had messaged her was absolutely out of the question.

Carter's leg bounced up and down, shaking his table. He was fidgeting like a toddler on Halloween. She wanted to throw something at him or trap him in a pack 'n play in the basement.

Her brain wriggled like unset Jell-O, sloshing around in messy splashes. The wind battered the library windows. Twenty minutes crawled by. She stood, gathered up her things, and said goodnight to Carter.

With jerky pulls, she yanked on her rain pants and jacket in the women's bathroom. "Don't be a spineless hormone ball," she said to herself in the mirror. A throat cleared in one of the stalls. She fanned her red cheeks and left. Resolved to be firm, she marched out of the library double doors.

Cold air slapped her in the face and leaves flew past her feet, a twig catching on her shoe cover. She tugged her cap over her ears and, with her head down, trudged over to the bike shelter—a massive tangle of packed wheels and twisted handlebars.

Ten minutes later, she finally sat on her bike, helmet on, lights blazing. It was invigorating. What she needed. And when she got home, she would be asleep as soon as her head hit the pillow, not lying there thinking about a grubby man within walking distance.

She pulled her phone out of her pocket to check it one last time. Still blank. He was long gone, back at the house by now, getting shoulder rubs by a line of beer-soaked women.

Resolutely, she steered her bike away from the parking lot. The path veered to the left down a steep hill. Something painful twisted in her chest.

She jumped the curb back to the road and swung her bike around, bumping a parked car painfully with her leg. Riding against the wind, teeth clenched in contempt for herself, she worked her way back to the library, following the sidewalk until the leaf-covered parking lot came into view.

There sat his truck, long tail sticking out into the road. Inside, a man-sized lump leaned on the passenger window.

Her bike squealed to a stop. She opened the driver's door. "Are you too drunk to drive?"

He sniffed, rubbing his face. "Hello to you too, darlin'."

Huffing, she walked around to the tailgate, which squeaked as she yanked it open. As she laid her bike on the bed of the truck, she paused, swallowed, and stared down at the ground. Buck had always insisted on loading the bike for her, and her bag. He was chivalrous down to the heels of his fancy leather boots.

Wind blew the hood off her face as she set her bag down next to her bike and closed the tailgate. Apparently, she had finally succeeded in making him annoyed enough to stop treating her like his weak little woman. Or something was wrong.

She pulled open the driver's side door and jumped in the cab. A gust of frigid air slammed the door shut next to her. Buck grunted, his face scrunched up.

"Hey, you okay?"

"Fine, let's go."

The ride back was quiet. He sprawled out with his eyes closed, muscular arms limp at his sides. Hay and horses permeated his clothes, and mud smeared his jeans. She bit her lip. He was obviously injured.

On impulse, she parked the truck in front of his trailer door and turned off the engine. He lay there, not moving. The dim cab light outlined his tough tanned face, a little haggard and pensive as he slept.

The uncomfortable ache in her chest crept back. Inexplicably, he was in her life. He actually worried about her—for the wrong reasons. Even when she yelled at him, he stuck around, the lump. What would happen when he was gone? Longing pulled at her, working something loose.

Her mind was split, unbalanced by the worry that something had hurt him. She was exhausted with fighting the physical longing to touch him. There could be relief in giving in, jumping in the flow, and being carried away. Impulse drove her and she took off her glasses, making a decision, knowing she would regret it, but unable to stop herself.

She leaned over and kissed him on the mouth. They both held still except for their chests rising and falling. She liked the pillowy softness of his lips, the heat of his body in front of her. She did want to cuddle with him, to lay her face on his chest and fall asleep listening to him breathe.

His mouth moved under hers, a slow glide back and forth. Alarm bells clanged in her head. The kiss was about to turn into something else, pivot from sweet to expectant. She yanked away fast.

"Wake up, sleeping beauty," she croaked, putting her glasses back on, barely resisting the urge to jump out of the truck and run to her room.

He blinked at her, his eyes narrow.

"I don't know why you waited for me, but thank you." They looked at each other. She bit her lip. "Text me if you need an ice pack or something."

He stared at her, unmoving.

"Or a kick in the ass to hustle you out of this truck and into your bed?"

She pushed open the creaky door and jumped out. He slid out of the passenger side and leaned on the side of the truck, hopping on one foot to catch his balance. He was hurt.

"Why didn't you tell me you were injured? I almost left you in that parking lot."

"Darlin'," he said. "You can bring me something anytime."

She stepped away from him and turned to unload her bike and bag.

"Buck, stop screwing with me. I'm not going to be hookup number ninety-seven, or whatever. Rise above the novelty of someone telling you no and move on."

He crossed his arms. "You kissed me. The screwing would go both ways."

"That's a horrible pun. I shouldn't have kissed you. It was a mistake."

"Let's really kiss and then decide."

"Go to bed, Buck."

She walked away from him, sensing his eyes on her the whole way to her bedroom.

SHE STARED at the wall of her bedroom. What had gotten into her? The answer was so obvious she didn't want to think it. She paced back and forth on her creaky floor.

Her phone buzzed. Buck.

She froze, staring at the phone on her bed like there was a burning fuse on it. Nothing right would come of looking—yet another broken boundary. He had actually texted her at night.

She picked up the bomb, because she was wildly out of control. When you didn't want to lead a guy on, had in fact decided to end it—whatever "it" was—there were some things you didn't do. Like kiss him.

**Buck**: I want an ice pack.

She blinked. Remembered babbling something about helping him with his injury. Had she offered to bring him an ice pack? *Dumb!* She'd practically thrown herself at him.

**Randi**: Wanting is different from needing. If I offered an ice pack, it was in good faith it was for your injury and not other nefarious reasons. Other nefarious reasons are off the table. Period.

She bit her knuckle. The man was turning her into a basket case. And she had on her Sleepy Alpaca Romper—a fleece button-up onesie with long sleeves and very short shorts in fuzzy pink with little alpaca faces on it. She couldn't leave her room.

**Buck**: I've got a baseball sized bruise on my calf. I need an ice pack.

**Randi**: I'm sure any of the other girls would be thrilled to help.

**Buck**: No. I want an ice pack, painkiller, and some water. From you.

**Randi**: Since when did carpooling together mean I wait on you hand and foot?

No response. Randi stared at her empty bed. She was not sleeping any time soon.

Leaning her head back to stare at the ceiling, she exhaled, making burbling raspberry sounds like a lunatic. It was all temporary. Before long, one of them would be gone.

She grabbed a jacket and slipped into her flip-flops. In and out. Leave the goods in front of his door then run like rats were chasing her.

She stepped into the house. Three heads swiveled toward her with hopeful looks on their faces. Sorry girls, she wasn't a cowboy.

"Hey, Randi," Trish muttered and turned away, deflated. Sarah crossed her arms and swiveled back towards the big flat-screen.

Angie glared. Randi raised one eyebrow at her and pretended to make tea. After a long moment, Angie rotated back to the television. There was a cease-fire between them, and no diplomacy. It helped that Randi stayed in her room at night. Until now.

The major, monumental, flaw in what she was about to do, now occurring to her, was the girls noticing her go out to Buck's trailer. Shizzle would fly.

A sitcom played on the television, pounding out cheap laugh lines. She glanced at the clock. The show would be over in five minutes. After that, Angie would probably take up a guard dog position in front of Buck's trailer, gnawing on an old beer bottle. She was so screwed.

She swallowed. The kitchen window looked out toward the pasture, his trailer in the center, a little light illuminating the steps up to his door. Getting caught going out there would be a disaster, and the thought of another confrontation with Angie made her gut clench. She bit her lip. On the other hand, dropping off an ice pack, and not going inside, was sketchy but acceptable and could be shrugged off. And she would dangle the bait of Buck's injury and deflect them right into playing obsessive nurses.

As inconspicuously as possible, moving slowly enough to not make sound, she slid the kitchen window curtain closed and turned off the back porch light.

Tense, heart racing, she slipped out the door. Getting to his trailer took long minutes of picking her way through the overgrown pasture. Their television show was over. She stopped, ankle-deep in the long grass, and turned around. The curtains were still closed. Shaking her head, mouth dry, she hustled forward until she tapped on his door.

"Come in," he shouted from inside.

Out of breath, she stuck her head in, keeping her feet fixed to the grass.

"I'm not. I'll put everything here."

"Darlin', come on, this leg is killing me."

"Do you want the whole house to see me go in here? Not happening."

He paused. "Doesn't bother me. Besides, they watch some doctor soap opera now. They're all glued to the TV."

She hesitated, looking back at the house. There weren't any enraged faces staring out at her.

"Fine, but you're a horrible person to ask me to do this."

She stepped inside and couldn't stop herself from looking over every detail. The interior of the trailer hadn't been new for at least twenty years. Dark wood paneling covered most of the surfaces, with worn orange tweed upholstery on the cushions. Mostly tidy but dusty. Open packages of disposable plates and plastic cups sat on the cracked, off-white countertop.

Buck lay on a massive bed, past the little kitchen and table, in the back. The king-size mattress took up a quarter of the space in the entire trailer.

The quilt underneath him caught her eye: a gorgeous collection of brown and blue fabrics, pieced together in a modern improvisational flow of color and pattern. He had his grubby work clothes on the quilt, like a handmade work of art was as everyday as a polyester comforter from a thrift store.

"I finally got you in here," he said, a half-smile on his face. "And I'm too busted to do anything."

She huffed then startled, seeing him in the bright light from his kitchen. "Buck, what happened to you?"

His pinched face, tight and gray, gleamed with a patina of sweat. Only one boot was off, his white-socked foot on the bed. His other leg hung over the side, like he'd collapsed and had been lying there for the last hour.

"Do I need to take you to the hospital? What happened?"

"No." He pushed up on an elbow as she opened the painkillers. "Wild horse today in the Ag barn and I stepped in to help. Tool shelf fell on my leg. I doubt the bone's broken, only a bad bruise. I'll be fine." He swallowed four pills dry.

She shoved pillows behind his back before handing him water. A full gallon jug and two different kinds of painkiller landed on the small fold-out table next to his bed. He needed a thermometer—his pale, cracked lips scared her.

"Not buying it," she said. As gently as she could, she peeled back the bottom of his jeans to peer at the injury. A purple and black mass of swelling bulged out the elastic rim of his sock.

"Doesn't look good," she said, propping his foot up on a pillow and wedging ice packs over the bruise.

He hissed, his head falling back. Her stomach twisted and she pulled off his other boot.

"What else do you need?" She wanted to smooth back his hair. Biting her lip, she shoved her hands into the pockets of her jacket.

He blinked up at her. "Stay with me. If this gets worse, I might have to think about doing something tonight."

"Text me." She took a step backward.

"Come over here," he said, "or I'll chase you down."

She huffed. "Bluffer."

"I want to see one of your videos."

"Well, fine. Tell me what you think later. Just don't leave gross comments."

"Grab that tablet on the table and get over here," he said. "Otherwise, I'll be staring at the ceiling."

"Buck, don't force me to start an awkward conversation neither of us wants to have."

He closed his eyes, rubbing his forehead.

"Doesn't sound pleasant, does it? I will hand you the tablet though."

She brought it over to him, stretching her arm out so she

didn't go near him. Instead of taking the tablet, he grabbed her hand.

"Darlin', give it a try." He stared up into her eyes. "Nothing serious is going to happen tonight."

His hand was warm and rough around hers. He tugged. Like a melting popsicle, her will to resist him dripped away, and at any moment she would plop onto the ground as a sticky puddle. She sat down. Her chest worked like a set of bellows. She couldn't manage a full breath.

"What, exactly, do you want me to try?"

His fingers played with the cuff of her jacket, setting off tingling goose bumps all over her arms. He smiled up at her. "Cuddling."

She sat up straight, pulling away from him. "If cuddling is a euphemism for sex, the answer is no."

"It's not. This fuzzy thing you're wearing is nice. Are those little alpaca faces on there?"

"I think you should rest."

"I'll rest better if you keep me company. I can't roll over, so you're safe tonight. An opportunity, now that I think about it, for you to be totally in charge. Get over your nerves a bit."

"My nerves? I don't know what you're talking about."

"Uh-huh. Skittish as a filly in her first heat."

"What?" She blushed to the bun on the top of her head. He'd nailed it.

"And I'm the nicest, gentlest stud you're ever going to meet. You could kiss me again. We'll rub our noses together."

"Humph." She fiddled with his tablet.

"Help me shift over, and then get comfortable. Pull up the videos that keep you so busy."

She swallowed. "I..." she started and stopped. Cleared her throat. "I am worried your injury is worse than you think. So, I'll stay for a few minutes, on the condition that whatever cuddling may happen—because I'm too exhausted to sit up anymore—is a one-time deal. Tomorrow, it never happened."

"I never kiss and tell. Wiggle over here."

Carefully, she slid over the pillow cushioning his injured foot. His eyes narrowed as he shifted his hips, face pinched in pain. As soon as she pushed the pillows over, his head fell back on them and he patted the narrow sliver of mattress next to him on his non-broken side.

"You act like this is all nothing. I couldn't find a less safe person to be involved with on campus if I tried. You're not going to be happy until I'm a brokenhearted drunk, chasing you around with a cigarette hanging out of my mouth."

He startled, shooting her a frightened glare.

"Still want me to stay?"

He gulped. "Don't tattoo my name on your stomach."

"Did somebody do that?"

"They brought up the idea."

"What is it with you? These girls think you're the Prince of Sheba."

"I'm a good cuddle."

"You're trouble."

"Get down here." He pulled on her arm.

Lying down on his bed was a horrible plan. She did it anyway. She was on her side, her leg touching his. Her body hummed in giddy happiness. Her mind thundered with agonized storms.

She held the tablet up between them while her YouTube home page greeting video played in a corner of the screen—a montage of her in the lotus position from different filming locations, spliced together in editing.

"Lot of views," said Buck. "And subscribers too. Making some money yet?"

"Starting to." She scrolled down to play a recent shoot she'd done in the orchard.

"Perverts stalking you?"

"I've blocked a few people."

She played the video from the camping trip, a little spark of pride in her chest for the mix of images she had put together. Instead of keeping the camera trained on herself, she had woven in imagery of water, trees, and sky. The Ken Burns slow glide of the camera angle, edited in during post-production, gave the video the new age feeling of something on a screen at a spa, or a meditation retreat. The production felt polished.

"Do you mix your own sound? I remember those bird calls."

She smiled, leaning into him a bit more. "Yes, for the most part. I buy some stuff, and make simple mixes with the ambient sounds from shooting. Lately I've been using a few percussion instruments layered over drumbeats."

"Huh." He pulled the tablet down on his chest, flipping out a stand built into the back of the case. For a cowboy from the country, he used a lot of tech gadgetry. Probably a stupid assumption that he wouldn't. When she let go of the tablet, he took her hand in his, lacing their fingers together.

She swallowed, a warm, scared tightness in her chest. Her eyes stung. The moment didn't seem real. Somebody, most likely Angie, would ram the side of the RV in a drunken rage at any moment. She didn't deserve to be happy—it wouldn't work out.

"What's next? How do you make your videos in the winter?"

She cleared her throat and forced herself to remember she had some pride. She wouldn't dissolve into a weepy mess just because he held her hand. And wanted her with him.

"Warm clothes. I do some filming inside, but I need to invest in big lights." She tilted her head up to examine his face. Probably she was a total fool, but he appeared to be actually, really and truly, listening to her. "What I want is to film with baby goats."

"Yoga with hyper little goats butting your backside?"

"More like balancing on my back. I used to have my aunt's cats involved. That's what got me started. One of the videos went viral for a second." She smiled, thinking of the hours, months, she'd spent coaxing the cats into those few viral moments that had made a tiny name for her online.

"Traveling too," she said. "Warm places with sandy beaches." She yawned, blinking. How could she be so exhausted while he nuzzled into her hair? Not that she'd ever be able to sleep with Buck lying next to her. Zaps of desire darted around her pelvis because their feet were touching. She stared at his neck and wanted to touch the hollows there. With her tongue.

"Randi."

"Yeah?"

"Kiss me."

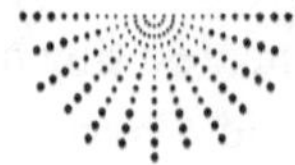

Randi's eyes snapped fully open. His mouth nuzzled against the top of her head—all he could reach, apparently. Then he surprised her by pulling off her glasses, slowly, so they didn't snag in her hair. She froze, petrified against his side. He sat the glasses down on the little table.

"Come on now. I won't even bite. This time."

It was undeniably clear—she wanted to kiss him. And she didn't trust herself to kiss him. She would unravel.

*Courage*, the little devil inside her shouted. She pushed up, leaning her head on a hand, her elbow sinking into the mattress.

"I don't understand." She stared at him. His face burned into her brain; she'd remember the slope of his nose when she turned eighty.

"What's that?"

"Why me? I mean, we're from extremely different backgrounds and are, no doubt, diametrically opposed politically…"

"Teacher talk turns me on."

"And I'm not your type. I heard about your history. It's

been all surgically augmented sexpots for you. The most porno-licious arm candy."

He looked at her like she was crazy. "Right, cos gossip is real reliable."

"And you're not my type either. I imagined an emotional man, a self-deprecating vegan. He backpacks into wilderness areas and protests animal cruelty at the vet hospital. He'd convince me to never use plastic and I'd eventually trick him into eating cheese."

"You're rambling." Buck's calloused finger ran along the scooped neckline of her onesie. "Sounds like you're imagining, more than living."

She swallowed. Pretty much all of her cuddling experience was imagined.

"I almost got there once, with the guy engaged to marry another girl. Explained why he used two different phones."

"Should I beat the shit out of him?"

She huffed. "I broke up his engagement to the rich girl. It's cool."

"Good girl."

"I'm an idiot to want to kiss you."

"Best thing you'll do today."

He had an answer to everything, except why he wanted to be with her. What were they doing, starting this? Where would it go?

"Hey," he said, "I'm tired of pretending I can stay away from you."

She frowned in concentration, constantly sidetracked by actually lying next to him. Did he mean he needed to sleep with her and get it out of his system—would that work? She knew, with a sudden and disapproving certainty, that she wouldn't be able to move on with her life if she didn't kiss him.

His body radiated warmth—a massive, hot man who

turned her on by walking into a room. And he couldn't move. Best thing indeed.

She leaned forward and set her lips against his, surprisingly plush for such a firm mouth, or maybe he was puckering up. His fingers slid into her hair, pulling her head down, and her mouth opened with his.

Her hand landed on the other side of his head as he licked into her mouth. She hadn't kissed in so long, his tongue was startling. Wet. His hand pushed down her spine in a firm glide, stopping on the curve of her backside. He groaned, thrusting his tongue between her lips.

Heat, already simmering, boiled over, releasing tingling steam on her skin. An almost painful lasso wound down her body, snake-like, biting into her clenching center. She floated in aching desire. Her body tensed, throbbed, vibrated with the realization that finally, finally, she was with a man. With this man. She arched into him.

He pulled his mouth away, lips sliding down to her jaw. "Mmm," he rumbled. "Going to be so good between us, darlin'."

A little of her frenzied desire cleared. "Think you know all about it, huh?"

He chuckled, the tickling movement on her neck sending shivers down her spine.

"Tomorrow night you'll be shouting, your pussy shaking under my mouth." His hand on her backside gripped her hard, pinning her against his body. The pressure on the swollen nub of her clitoris pushed her into a wave of pleasure. She hummed, rubbing her cheek on the bristly side of his face.

"We shouldn't do this again," she said, her body heavy. She wanted to, now.

"Stop that," he said, sounding a little angry.

She started to pull away, but he pinned her on top of him

with an arm. Instead, she slid sideways, curling up along his side.

"You need to sleep." She realized she'd completely forgotten about how much pain he must be in. "And so do I."

"Stay with me."

"I can't sleep in here."

"I need you."

She startled, a little taken aback. He kissed her head, the solid muscle of his arm moving underneath her face as his hand stroked her back.

"All right, I'll stay a little while, but I want to rest. No nefarious kissing."

He pulled a blanket from the corner of the bed and dropped it on her legs.

"Cover those things up before this hard-on kills me," he said.

He flipped a switch and the lights went out. She blinked, a little unsettled by the total darkness, more alarmed by herself. What was she doing? The last hour had been like stepping off a cliff. She should be running through the pasture screaming.

HE WOKE her up at three to go to the hospital. She lay cuddled against him, still in her jacket, the blanket tucked around her. He'd spent most of the night messing with that blanket, which was too damn small.

She smacked her lips and mumbled, "Hospital?" Her eyes flew open as she sat up, looking him over with a startled rabbit glare. Her cool hand felt nice on his forehead.

"Yeah, I better go. But twenty more minutes isn't going to kill me. Go get dressed, darlin', and make us some coffee."

Her hair tumbled down her back as she sprang up. Something in his chest turned over. Getting through all of her freak-outs, grumpy with pain, wasn't going to be simple. He wanted to skip over all the nonsense and go straight to the in-his-bed-every-night phase.

He stared up at the ceiling, trying to muster up the will to move into the bathroom. The door closed behind her and quiet descended in the trailer. At some point during the last week he'd decided to be with her. Or to stop resisting wanting to be with her. Truth was, he didn't know what the hell he was doing.

Twenty minutes later, she started the truck. He hopped down the aisle of his trailer, bracing against the counter and table to lift himself up and keep weight off his busted leg. Randi fussed over him in her quiet way after he landed in the passenger seat, putting his coffee in his hands, dropping a bag of cookies on his lap, and handing him a new ice pack.

The next hours were torture. The only thing keeping him going was her, sitting next to him in the blue-striped dress with little flowers stitched on the front, like an old lady's hankie. They watched the morning news in the waiting room. She tapped away on her laptop in between helping him to the exam room and grabbing coffees.

The white collar of her dress was stitched with a bumblebee in the corner. The only good thing about the tiny exam room was how close she sat next to his hard, narrow bed. Not a thing sexy about that dress—loose, long-sleeved, buttoned up to her neck. The blue-striped material resembled a man's shirt. Except, on her, he wanted to trace the hems with his fingers. The middle cinched in around her tight little waist and the bottom showed off her pretty calves. Still didn't explain why he couldn't keep his eyes off her.

If his leg didn't throb like it'd been caught in a blender, he would nuzzle his face into her lap. Work on those tiny white buttons that ran all the way down the front with his teeth and tongue. One thing from last night became clear: she might not have much experience, but her body was eager as hell.

"Don't you have class at ten?" he said to her.

She glanced up from her computer. "I do." She adjusted her glasses. "But the professor knows me. I can miss if you need me to stay."

"Midterm this week, right?"

"Yes."

She stayed stubbornly distant. He swallowed coffee, frustrated in all kinds of ways. Did she have to act like they were remote coworkers?

"They want to dig around some more on my leg and look for a hairline fracture. Take the truck to class, darlin', then come back and pick me up when you're done."

"All right." She left without a backward glance—or a kiss—her honey-colored hair swinging down her back.

He dropped his head against the back of the chair. The pain tried to crack open his head. A niggling urgency bothered him, like he would run out of time with her. Why did he care so much about some lonely girl who would be out of his life in six months? She really wanted to pretend like last night hadn't happened. And he was too damned tired, and busted, to do anything about it.

RANDI STARED at the text message.

**Buck**: Come watch a movie with me.

Feeling guilty was stupid. She'd been away from the house for two hours. Buck had woken up from his afternoon nap and she was gone. So what?

She was acting like Soft Head, the little cat with a dent in her head that Aunt Linda had adopted. That cat took ten wrong turns getting to the food bowl. Soft Head didn't live long, poor thing.

"They're loud but freakin' awesome," Daisy shouted at her.

Luke's band was playing on stage, inspiring the crowd to frenzied dancing. Daisy bounced from side to side, her head nodding to the beat. Carter bobbed up front, his giant backpack like a turtle shell, shoving back the other dancers behind him.

She was having fun. Like sneaking out of the house late at night and finding a convertible waiting for you.

"The trumpets are great," she called back.

"Carter's cute," Daisy said.

"Yeah?"

"Yeah."

Daisy pirouetted. The song ended and the audience erupted in cheers, hollering for more.

Randi looked down at the text, the phone still in her hand. She needed to reply. Say something, anything would be better than nothing.

**Randi**: Can't tonight.

She punched the keys slowly, stared down at her taciturn message, and nothing more came to her. She hit send.

**Buck**: Where are you?

His message shot back fast. For a cowboy, who presumably grew up around cows in the middle of nowhere, he rapid-fired back at her like the champion of a speed texting competition.

**Randi**: On campus.

**Buck**: Doing what?

**Randi**: At a concert with Daisy and Carter. Luke's band is playing.

She took a goofy picture of herself to send to him. Changed her mind and took a sneering picture, then sent off the goofy picture before she could change her mind again.

**Buck**: How are you getting back here?

A prescient question, and she didn't have an answer. Daisy had wanted to go out and had badgered her mercilessly. She'd worked at Buck's table in his trailer because he asked her to stay. The man had an issue with being solitary. After he'd finally fallen asleep in the afternoon, she snuck out, glad to have time alone.

Restless and unable to focus, she'd given in and let Daisy pick her up. On the condition they stayed for only a couple hours. And so she took Carter up on his offer to go to the Battle of the Bands, after all. The event was crowded but not bursting. And she discovered that outside she could handle the crush of a live show—even love it.

**Randi**: Playing it by ear for now. I'm not drinking, so I can drive Daisy's car.

The problem with that plan was Daisy had already swallowed down three beers in the last two hours. She didn't want to end up with Daisy sleeping over.

**Buck**: Having fun?

**Randi**: Yeah. It's not bad.

A yawn surged out of her. The lead singer of Luke's band finished his thank you speech while the rest of the guys busily cleared their gear off the stage. The pause in the music reminded her of being in bed—if only she could float there. Then the next band was warming up on the other stage, heavy metal emo guys with dyed black hair and ghostly white faces.

"Randi!"

She turned and saw Luke, sweaty and grinning, drumsticks in his hands.

"Hi. Great set."

He pushed hair dripping sweat away from his eyes. His gaze aimed down, looking over her dress. She flushed. Was he staring at her chest?

"Thanks." He paused, a sheepish look falling over his face. "I'm glad I finally ran into you. I've been wanting to tell you —apologize—for my, uh, friend showing up. When we were camping."

"Yeah, Emily." Randi couldn't help smiling at him while he looked like a kid caught with his hand in the chocolate chip bag. Couldn't a guy ever be excited about his girl, ready to claim and boast about her? Everyone was so sly, or guilty. "I explained to her we're friends." She'd explained about three times before finally walking away.

Luke looked down, shuffling his feet. "Her and I are just friends," he said, peering over his shoulder like she might pop out of a bush and jump on him. "Got to go, we need our gear moved, but let's study this week sometime. I thought we could meet up on Tuesdays, make it a regular thing."

"You know where I work in the library."

"Yeah. Really good seeing you."

Luke strode off through the crowd, curly head towering above the masses.

Her phone buzzed.

**Buck**: Done yet?

She rubbed her face.

**Randi**: Yeah. I'm pretty done. A whiny heavy metal band is screaming about something. I don't like it.

**Buck**: I ordered an Uber. It'll be in the parking lot by the library in fifteen.

**Randi**: Buck! I'm here with Daisy. You're going to eat that fee.

**Buck**: You were up at three in the morning. Come home.

Home?

**Randi**: Ready for two and a half kids, huh? Plus two dogs and a few cats?

**Buck**: Don't forget the baby goats.

**Randi**: You're freaking me out.

**Buck**: I will, all night long.

**Randi**: No, no freaking tonight. I heard the doctor. 48 hours of total rest. And not moving.

**Buck**: We'll cuddle.

**Randi**: We won't.

**Buck**: Come home.

**Randi**: When I do, I'm staying in my room. So cancel your Uber because nothing is going to come of it.

**Buck**: It's not like that and you know it.

**Randi**: I'm going to find Daisy.

**Buck**: Twelve minutes till the Uber.

**Randi**: Cancel it!

She shoved her phone in her pocket. How could one man justify to himself being such a bossy a-hole? She exhaled, scanning the crowd for Daisy. That stupid Uber timer made her shoulders ache.

Daisy stood in line with Carter for the beer garden.

"Hey guys," Randi said, "I'm headed home."

"What?" Daisy blinked at her, thin eyebrows pinched together hard. "It isn't even nine o'clock."

"I go to bed early."

"Wait, how are you getting back?"

"I'll take the bus."

"Just stay here. You can crash at my place."

"Not tonight. One of my housemates broke a leg yester-day. I don't want them out there alone."

"Oh yeah?" Daisy's eyes narrowed. "Who's that?"

Damn, the girl was a bloodhound for secrets.

"Buck."

"What?"

"Do you have to shout?"

"How did he break his leg?" Carter asked.

"He helped a new guy with a problem horse—saved him, I think. A heavy tool fell over and landed on his leg. Hairline fracture and a nasty bruise."

"Ouch," Carter said.

"Yeah, he's not too happy." An understatement. He'd glowered at her all morning like a cornered bear.

"But," said Daisy, "he's stuck in bed and needs to sleep. What are you going to do for him?"

"Goodnight, Daisy. Night, Carter. I'm actually dozing off on my feet a little."

She walked toward the bus stop. Incidentally, also in the direction of the parking lot by the library. Her resisting Buck might be a little pointless, but if she stopped, he would become intolerable. She shook her head.

Him caring about her was alarming. It set her on edge, like someone suddenly all over your social media accounts, obsessed with everything you said. You block that creeper.

Except Buck wasn't a creeper. A control freak maybe. A dominator with far too much charm and cunning? She blushed, thinking of him growling what he would do to her. It was hot, and frightening. She might tease him about her future self turning mindlessly submissive but, in reality, that was not happening. She would fall in love with him, and shatter to bits.

She imagined falling so hard she could already feel the air rushing past her face. He would own her heart and use her body. In the end, the strength holding her together would all crumble, leaving her wrecked and broken. She'd spent months in that place and didn't want to go back.

Another man would be better. Someone she respected, who was a bit distant. They would be polite and respectful, agree on politics and challenge each other's recycling habits. He might be gluten intolerant, which would be irritating to accommodate all the time, but they'd write a blog about it…

Her phone buzzed.

**Buck**: The Uber is two minutes away.

**Randi**: You buying me things creates expectations. Let's not go there. I'm taking the bus.

**Buck**: Get on the bus and I'll drive out to the stop to pick you up.

**Randi**: NO you won't!

**Buck**: Get in the Uber.

Randi stopped herself from writing that she hated him. She took a deep breath. Couldn't he leave her alone for one night? She needed to process…for a few weeks. Or years. Being a basket case was no cakewalk.

**Buck**: Please darlin. I'm sorry. This leg feels real shitty. I need to know you're safe.

"I WANT to pay for my ride. Can't you change the setting or something?"

"No. The ride is paid for before I pick up."

Randi forced her limp, exhausted body out of the sporty little car. The driver reversed and sped off down the driveway. Another Uber ride in a car that resembled any other college maniac driving too fast on the road.

"Where's your bike?" Sarah called down from the front

porch, her voice mock-concerned. She and Angie were sitting on the beat-up recliners, a pile of empty beer cans between them.

"It had the day off, Sarah," Randi said, turning to walk away. "Goodnight."

"You took Buck to the hospital today," Angie said, loud enough to make her head pound. Randi stopped walking and turned to face them.

Angie spit into a cup, the brown stream shooting out of her snarled mouth like a bullet. "That's fucked up you kept it from us that he broke his leg. We're his friends. You don't give a shit about him."

"If Buck wanted privacy, it's not my place to let everyone know. Now, I was up even earlier than usual, so I'm going to go—"

"You need to stay the hell away from him," Angie growled, brown spit bubbling from her mouth. She wiped her sleeve across her face.

Chewing tobacco, ugh. The pieces came together in Randi's head—the bottles full of dark nasty goo were spit. Her stomach squeezed. How could anyone…?

"You're a stuck-up bitch who doesn't give a shit about anyone but yourself," Angie continued, her voice cold. "His friends, who don't like you, won't put up with your shit. You need to move the fuck out and leave him alone."

Randi swallowed, her throat tight. She dug her nails into her palms. No telling what Angie would do when she was drunk—attack her like a starved dog that had pulled its chain off the wall, for instance. And Sarah, as a witness, would egg her on.

The moment stretched out. Angie and Sarah sat up on the dirty front porch, drunk and haggard. Randi bit down on her bottom lip. So many truth nuggets she could fling back at

Angie ran through her head, like, *Have some pride, he's not into you.* Hard to resist.

"Nope, not the way it is. Other people don't have the same feelings as you, they have their own. Buck's real friends will support what he wants. Which isn't you." Oh, crap, she hadn't meant to let that last bit slip out.

Angie surged to her feet, knocking over a can from the table. Liquid sloshed onto her clothes and chair. Randi took a step back. Angie really was drunk.

"You fucking bitch, come say that to my face!"

Brown sticky spit dripped from Angie's front. Randi wanted to laugh, point her finger and hysterically cackle, but more of her wanted to cry. Shockingly, some part of her wouldn't back down.

"What, that you lack empathy? Or that you're too self-absorbed to take no for an answer?"

Angie sprang up and surged toward the stairs down the porch. Cans toppled around her. Something banged, taking Angie's legs out from under her. She face-planted on the floor with a thwack. Randi held her breath. Angie lay still, not moving.

Sarah chortled, then burped.

"Better run, Randi," Sarah said, a slur in her voice. "She's a little dazed…won't last long."

Randi did her bathroom routine in record time, her pulse hammering. Angie and Sarah opened the front door right as she slipped out the back. She got into her room, locked the door, then collapsed on her bed.

Angie was an unpinned grenade and a terrifying drunk. The thing with Buck, whatever it was, was going to send her over the edge.

*You don't give a shit about anyone but yourself,* replayed in her mind. Not true, but the people she deeply cared about wouldn't fill the fingers on one hand.

Her phone buzzed. From Buck. She buried her head in her pillow.

**Buck**: Hey.

**Randi**: Hey.

**Buck**: Come check on me.

**Randi**: No way. Angie is off her chain tonight. If she saw me going out there the police would have to dig up my body.

**Buck**: You can dodge her. Don't be a coward.

**Randi**: I'm totally a coward. Also she outweighs me. And has the rage.

**Buck**: She'll deal. Hide behind me if you get scared.

**Randi**: No thanks.

**Buck**: I need help with the ice packs.

**Randi**: No you don't. All your supplies are next to your bed. I packed the cooler for you with food and drinks. You're welcome.

**Buck**: I need a cuddle.

**Randi**: You need sleep. And to not move. I'd be asleep if you weren't harassing me.

**Buck**: Fine. Fluff your pillows.

Randi blinked at her phone. But a fine was fine and she accepted it. The stupid thing she didn't want to admit to herself was that she might dart out the door and army crawl to his trailer to see him, belligerent Angie be damned.

The threat of dealing with a couple of drunks held her back, partially. She wanted to rub her face on his chest, those spongy muscles rising and falling under her cheek. Touch must be addictive. If she didn't restrain herself, curb the emerging wild libido, next she'd be settling for random hookups, desperate for any little crumb of sexual attention.

She rolled over, face down on her pillow. The little devil part of herself, tied up and handcuffed in a dark part of her head, desperately shouted, *Hey, idiot! Take it while you can! You're not going to find another one like that. Go for it! A drunk could kill you on your bike tomorrow*—and she'll be a blonde, driving a Jeep with a "Cowboy Up" bumper sticker.

Three loud knocks banged on her door. Randi startled, then froze. The doorknob rattled but the lock held. She swallowed. Had Angie finally come to murder her?

"Open up," Buck said.

Randi wrenched open the door. "What are you doing?" She looked around nervously at the dark patio and empty windows.

"Move over, I need to sit down."

Before she could think, she stepped back. He hobbled inside, swinging on his crutches, and shut the door behind him. Then he grabbed her, his mouth landing hard against hers.

His mouth softened, both of them sinking into exploring nibbles and licks. The little devil in her head was grinning like a lunatic and shooting off fireworks. Buck swayed when she leaned into him.

Coming back to her senses with a snap, she pulled away.

"Sit down." She glanced around, frantic to find something for him to land on other than the bed.

In a few big strides he was sinking into her mattress, resembling a humdrum, average guy from the suburbs, wearing sweats and a T-shirt, his head bare. With a groan, he lay back on her comforter, turning to lift his leg up onto the mattress.

"What do you think you're doing? I said no."

He gave her a sideways look. "Do you want me to leave?"

She huffed, stomping over to him. Gently, she tugged off his one cowboy boot (the other foot only had on a sock) and set it by the door. "I want you to take me seriously."

"If I didn't leave the trailer, or have you visit me, I was going to lose it. I've been cooped up in there all day."

"For a guy that grew up on a ranch, you struggle a lot with being alone."

He grunted, a "you got me" smile on his face. "Don't spend much time alone on a big ranch, actually." He scratched his head. "I don't mind working solo. During the evening is when I want a pretty lady around."

"Uh-huh. Well, you're here, you damn parasite, might as well ice your leg before you head back."

"Come over here and lie down. You get grumpy when you stay up late."

"I'm always grumpy."

"Mm-hmm."

"I'm genuinely irritated about the ride thing."

"I'm irritated you're always running away from me. We're both happier when you don't."

She crawled around him to the side of the bed against the wall, on his good side. Her legs were too tired to stand up anymore. When she yanked the covers down, he scooted them under his hips and pulled the blankets over his chest.

"It's cold in here," he said, fluffing a pillow beneath his head.

"You're incorrigible."

"Trying to start something with the teacher talk?" He leaned over and turned off her bedside lamp. The nightlight by the computers blinked on, a faint warm glow.

"Nope. You're suspended."

He found her hand under the covers and laced their fingers together.

"Yeah, I suppose I am. For tonight."

Her chest rose and fell like a normal person, but on the inside, freaking out barely covered it. She stared at his profile in the dim room, that stubborn masculine chin jutting out. He lay on her bed. Reality needed to fly home from the extended vacation. Her body wanted to do something urgently, even as waves of sleepiness pulled her down into the mattress. Her mind spun in drowsy circles. What did it mean? How did she get rid of him? Why her?

"Night, darlin'."

Her eyes fluttered closed. She was in so much trouble.

# CHAPTER SIXTEEN

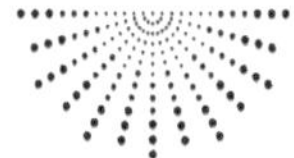

"Stop working, darlin', and dig in." Buck slid the egg and vegetable scramble toward her.

The booth table overflowed with steaming plates of potatoes, bacon, ham, omelets, and basically everything else on the breakfast menu, plus tall glasses of Bloody Marys, taking away all her workspace. She saved the essay on her laptop while she held up the computer with one hand.

"Never seen anybody doing homework in a bar," Hugh said, his eyes on a college football game playing on about twenty screens above their heads.

"Twenty-one credits, Hugh. There aren't enough hours in the day." Explaining her workload to people made it feel heavier, like a weight lifter pausing too long and losing their momentum.

She closed her laptop and slid it carefully into her bag. The guys picked up their forks, taking deep breaths, as if preparing for battle.

"These servings are insane." She picked up a fork and wiped it off with her napkin. "I had no idea the Dirty Bird could be so generous."

"I told you, the food is good." Buck cut into his fried chicken and waffle combo. "She didn't want to come in here," he said to Hugh, then turned to Randi. "What'd you say... worried the flashbacks would have you retching in a corner?"

"I'm surprised my shoes aren't sticking to the carpet."

"Then she wiped down the booths and table with hand sanitizer."

Hugh looked up from his plate of food. "You should wipe them down again after Buck's done. Protect the public's health and all."

Randi startled, her eyes darting to Buck. She had no idea if he was clean. How could he be STD-free after sleeping with half of the student body?

"Wow, buddy, I'll remember that one. I'm clean." Buck looked at her, the corner of his mouth lifting for a moment. He thought her concern was funny? "Got checked last month."

Randi blinked and remembered to take a breath. All they'd done so far was kiss, but still, saliva was almost as dangerous as the rest of it...

"Hugh's the dangerous one," Buck said. "Too Catholic to use a condom."

"Not true." Hugh blushed to his hairline.

"Let's eat, before anyone loses their appetite," Randi said. "You guys might have to hollow out a leg to finish those plates."

"This ain't nothin'." Buck dumped syrup on his plate.

"Where are the other girls?" Hugh asked.

Randi didn't answer. The puke all over the bathroom that morning flashed into her mind, and the broken glass on the floor, and a kitchen so cluttered there wasn't room to make coffee. Not to mention beer cans all over the living room. Earlier, the mess had made her blood boil. Then depression had settled in, along with a bone-deep exhaustion with cleaning other people's messes.

"They're crawling out for water about now." Buck finished his Bloody Mary. "Angie and Sarah polished off a twelve-pack last night."

"I'm surprised they didn't go to Jason's. He bought a couple kegs of beer. Trish was there."

"Her and Jason back together?"

"Maybe," Hugh said. "I'm tired of it. Old worn-out drama. But not as old as all the ladies asking about you. Worried sick you're bored and lonely with a busted leg."

Randi put down her fork. The toast in her mouth turned into cement. She stared at the beads of water on the plastic sides of her iced tea.

Buck grunted. "Is that right?"

"Excuse me," she said. Hugh moved out of the booth, making way for her to scoot out.

She smoothed down the skirt of her dress. Buck stared at her as she left the booth, like he knew she was sinking deep into her head. For a moment she looked at the propped-open door leading outside, an escape route into the open air, but she went in the bathroom instead. Her face in the mirror frowned at her.

Alone together, everything else faded to blurred irrelevance. An illusion. She washed her hands in cold water, staring down at the cracked yellow sink. Her and Buck were like a set of mismatched salt and pepper shakers: together they got the job done, but bring in the fancy pepper grinder and she became a thrift store find that didn't fit in.

She twisted her hair back into a tight bun. Pushed up her glasses. She didn't know what she was doing. Part of her desperately wanted to stick around and finally have sex. He was the only person she'd ever wanted like that, where you forgot about everything except what your bodies did together. Her past experiences had been exciting, but awkward, and ultimately she chose not to go there. Since losing her grandparents she hadn't really tried.

And now, he'd somehow charmed and forced his way into her bed, and a dam inside her was about to break. He was becoming one of the people in her heart, terrifyingly fast.

Of course, they wouldn't last. Buck wouldn't settle down until someone coerced him to with a baby. Not her, not in this lifetime.

Either move back in with her aunt or sleep with him. Really sleep with him. She bit her lip, standing up straighter, the seed of an idea coming into focus, a third way and a compromise. Damage control. She would dip her toes in the water and still have time to run like hell when the horror music started.

Randi crossed her arms, shaking her head. Buck flat-out refused to go back to the house and lie in bed.

"Maybe tomorrow when I can do something more interesting than stare at the wall." He winked at her. She blushed, glaring at him. Hugh stood right there.

"Yeah, you can stare at the corner." She pushed him away when he tried to kiss her.

After three hours at the bar, watching football and stacking up empty beer pints, Buck wanted to see a movie. Randi rolled her eyes and closed her laptop. The guys were tipsy, and depressed about the home team's unmitigated loss. She pulled the truck up to the entrance of the bar, helped load in Buck, and then drove to the theater while the guys remorsefully detailed the lacking defensive strategy of the Oregon University coaching staff.

"Let's go, girl," Buck said, after she snagged a prime

parking spot at the movie multiplex. "This won't be any fun if you're not with us."

Hugh covered his chest with his hands. "Well, that hurts."

"Look, I'm broke. You already bought me breakfast, even though I didn't want you to, but that's it. No more, Buck. I'll run some errands and be back to chauffeur you to your next delight when the credits roll."

"You an English major?" Hugh asked, his head tipped to the side. "Spell chauffeur and I'll buy your ticket. Long word."

"I'm buying the damn tickets," Buck said. "My idea and my party."

"No. I'll go to a movie when I can pay for my own ticket."

Buck took her hand and started kissing her fingers. She tried to pull her hand away. He gnawed on her knuckle. A giggle slipped out of her. "Stop, you maniac," she said. "No kissing with your bestie in the cab."

"Yeah." Hugh crossed his arms. "Gives me heartburn."

"Darlin', listen to me, I have plenty of money. If I want to spend some cash entertaining myself and the two people I like best, it's right. Won't set me back a bit. Makes me happy and I need that with this bum leg. Some other asshole, who thinks you owe him for throwing down ten dollars on a movie ticket, yeah, steer clear of that bullshit. You don't owe me anything, not even a smile. I only want the real ones."

She closed her eyes to block out his, and shook her head. "Buck, I didn't think you were that kind of guy, but, still, I have a lot of work to do and I'm not comfortable with you spending money on me."

"Nope, you have your presentation done and you've started your paper. Relax."

"I can't handle him on my own," Hugh put in.

She bit her lip. Why was he so hard to resist? "Not the car racing one. You two might want to leave me behind to enjoy all of that scenery."

They compromised on a *Star Wars* movie. Buck went all-in on the experience, buying huge tubs of popcorn, candy, ice cream, and monster-sized sodas, and was generally over-the-top ridiculous. She walked around with a stupid grin on her face.

He grabbed her every time Hugh turned his back on them. She walked around in humming, tingling awareness of him. He leaned in for a kiss and the television in her head switched to static and white noise. Kissing him, whether he tasted like beer or popcorn, took her on vacations to warm and giddy places.

"What are we doing?" she whispered to him when he came up for air from nuzzling around her neck. "Two days ago, we didn't touch each other and now we're necking in public. It's too fast. I'm not sure I can do this…"

"You are doing it." His thumb smoothed over her cheekbones. "And you love every minute, when you're not thinking too much."

"You never asked me. You just barged in, like an imperial army. I should resist you to make a point. The little people have a voice too, dammit."

He smiled, his eyelashes fanning out on his cheeks when he looked down. Sometimes he was so gorgeous she wanted to smear dirt on his face to bring him back down to humanity.

"I'm with you, darlin'." He stared into her eyes. "I'm your guy." He huffed, a smile turning up his lips. "I've been damn patient."

She blinked hard, attempting to swallow down the lump of soggy emotion in her throat. Without a doubt, she was a total pushover.

"I don't think you know what patient means," she choked out, her voice rough.

Buck tweaked her nose. "Not trying is waiting too long."

"We're not right for each other."

"We are. I want to spend time with you outside of bed, and in it. That's rare." He played with the skirt of her dress. "And you like kissing me. Kiss many people, darlin'?"

She crossed her arms. "No."

"You want me to kiss you." He nuzzled her ear. She wanted it way too badly. Her whole body shivered, a throbbing wet mess.

Hugh scooted back into his seat from the aisle. "*Star Wars* time, you sick rabbits," he said, tossing a piece of popcorn at Buck's head.

Randi took a deep breath, trying to focus on the iconic words scrolling across the screen. Was she doing this? Her little devil danced a jig, pointing at Buck like he was a pot of gold. The chemistry between them bubbled out of its test tubes, hotter every time he touched her. The logical, brain-based part of herself understood with rational certainty that getting close to him would hurt her. Not hurt, devastate.

Buck tickled her face with a licorice stick, then teased her lips open with the tip. When she puckered around the long stick, letting him slide it in and out, he leaned back in his seat with a groan, grinning at her. She bit off the tip and grinned back, snatching the stick out of his hands.

*Just stop freaking*, her body screamed at her. *Win! Win the sex!*

After the movie finished and they'd dropped off Hugh, Buck demanded to go shopping at one of the massive super-center grocery stores. He ordered her to push a jumbo-sized shopping cart, then commandeered an electric scooter.

"Always wanted to ride one of these." His scooter jerked backward and forward in the store entryway, like he was testing out a bumper car. An older couple smiled at them. Randi covered her face with her hand.

He pointed his crutch like a general. "Restaurant Randi-Buck is stocking up."

She cracked a small smile, already resigned to the fact that he had to make a joke out of their names. Sometimes it seemed like the man could get away with anything.

First, they went to the meat department, where Buck filled up half of the cart with a huge pork shoulder and shovel-sized brisket.

"There isn't a roasting pan in the house large enough for these monsters," Randi said. "And they'd take about six hours on your grill. Besides, don't you think thirty pounds of brisket is overkill for one man?"

"For us. And friends. I'm driving to home wares."

He ended up buying two Crock-Pots and a dutch oven, picking her brain the whole time about what they could make with the meat, and throwing in a few of his own ideas. Gleefully, he decided to look into electric smokers. An hour later, they loaded a mountain of food into the truck.

Randi blew at a chunk of hair hanging in her face. "The Randi-Buck has hours of cooking to do." She slumped at the thought.

"Tomorrow. Now we go to pizza. Normally, you'd have some input, but since I'm injured, you're indulging me."

She couldn't stop smiling. When was the last time she'd had so much fun? Mostly they teased each other, lobbing soft insults, and making absurd observations. Other times they were quiet, shoulders touching, or holding hands.

By the time they'd boxed up the leftover pizza, she could tell he was very tired and struggling with the pain.

The farmhouse was dark when she drove up the driveway, all of the cars gone. She exhaled.

Getting Buck to go lie down in his bed was, yet again, a futile endeavor. He wobbled up the house steps with his crutches and then collapsed on one of the disgusting couches. She brought him a painkiller and an ice pack, then was forced to clear cans off the side table to set down his water glass.

Turning to the kitchen, she took a deep breath, unclenching her teeth. Somebody had swept up the broken glass from the party the night before. That was it for cleaning.

"Well," said Buck from the couch, "at this rate, they're going to pay you to live here."

"It's different now. I can't take your money."

"You're taking their money. If you're sick of cleaning, then don't do it. But if you do, at least you're getting paid."

"I can't live with this. I'm not going to last here much longer."

Buck fell asleep on the couch, watching football highlights on the television. For two hours she cleaned. If she was being honest with herself, she needed the distraction. Her emotions rattled around in her brain like clanging pots in a windstorm. She felt out of control, feverish, ready to take off on a twenty-mile run.

She checked on him often, changing out the ice pack. His skin was a little hot and there were blue smudges under his eyes. Heaviness pushed on her chest while she stared down at him. How did she let him coerce her into running around all day?

By the time she walked out of the shower and peeked by the bathroom door, he was standing in the kitchen, drinking a glass of water. The rest of the house remained quiet. The girls weren't home yet.

Buck hobbled his way in beside her. Her comb froze midstroke through her wet hair. How did he think bathroom invasion was acceptable? His eyes scoured over every inch of her, then he nudged her over with his hip and grabbed her toothpaste.

Bedtime. Her pulse jumped in her neck. Would she ever settle into the idea of having him, a brawny man, next to her in bed? No, no, she wouldn't. Because it was unreal.

"There's that robe." He smiled, his eyes running down her body, his finger tweaking the giant bow at her waist. "Prettiest present ever."

"I'm more grenade than present."

"I can't wait to make you explode."

She flushed, her nostrils flaring. "Don't get me worked up. I might hurt you."

He pulled her in for a kiss. "Worth it."

Instead of kissing him, she put her forehead against his mouth. "I want to talk to you. About how I can do this."

"You want to be on top? Works for me, darlin'."

"Listen, Monday's coming and I'm freaking out, like not-able-to-focus-on-school freak-out. I need a plan."

She pulled away and pushed him into a chair in the kitchen. The slobs would arrive back at any moment, but she had to set limits, right now.

"All right, darlin', lay it on me."

"First, I'm a private person. I want to be very discreet, especially from the other girls."

He leaned back, scratching his head. "They already know."

"What?" She stared at him, her illusion of security shattered.

He shrugged at her. "It got out that I stayed in your tent. Also, us spending mornings together, riding in to school and back home, you taking me to the hospital, it all puts out the impression that we're together. Which we are. Not something I blab about, but we're a done deal."

She paced around. "Well, still. Hugh is one thing, but I don't want to be coupley around your other friends."

"Coupley, huh? What else?"

She chewed on her lip, her voice paralyzed with embarrassment and doubt. *Say it.* Buck's eyebrows crept up, and the side of his mouth twitched. Laughing at her. Fabulous.

"I think we should sleep together," she blurted, forcing the words out. "When you're better, for a limited term," she qualified, "and it makes sense for our schedules."

A satisfied, happy grin spread across his face. Definitely laughing at her.

"Forget it." She turned away from him. She couldn't do this. Waiting so long, she had obviously missed the workshop on how to negotiate the details. She should walk out the door and move out of the house, even if she had to roll her possessions down the driveway in a pull cart.

He yanked her down onto his good leg before she could set herself to resist. She crossed her arms. His whiskers tickled the skin on her neck. She gasped, shivers running down her spine.

"Yep, with you there," he nuzzled more. "We should sleep together."

"We should sleep together for one week."

"Start out with a bang? Nonstop sex for a week would mean missing a few classes."

"What?" she gasped as his rough hand ran over her bare stomach. Deep in her stomach clenched. Head tipping back, she panted, making a total fool of herself. She gulped, heat flaring in her cheeks.

He pulled her forward until her mouth landed against his, the roughness of the kiss startling her. Her body ignited like a rocket engine and the rest of the house, the unlocked front door, were tiny flecks in the distance as she accelerated. She wanted to be with him too much. Nothing admirable would come from it, but she soared, beyond lost.

He flinched underneath her, and she realized her weight was jostling his bad leg. She shot to her feet, pulling her robe closed.

"I'm sorry. I hurt you."

"I'm fine," he growled, his eyes pinched closed.

"We shouldn't do this."

Footsteps banged up the porch steps. Angie pushed open the front door, her face flushed. She stumbled a little, landing in a chair.

Randi froze, hastily tightened her robe, then walked to the kitchen sink. Hand shaking, she filled up a glass at the faucet.

"Fucking Buck!" Angie shouted happily.

The door slammed open. A couple of guys Randi didn't recognize staggered in, Sarah propped between them. They dumped her on the closest couch—the one that smelled like urine and never dried out. Randi cringed.

"Hey, Ang," Buck said, rubbing his face. "Sarah gonna live through the night?"

"She's fine."

"She spewed," said the burly guy. "Better than a stomach pump. Probably wake up in an hour and want more beer."

"Damn heavy to haul up those stairs," said the other guy, falling on a couch.

The guys appeared...normal. Not giving off blatantly pervy vibes, anyway. Sarah's chest rose and fell regularly, her skin color rosy, not gray. Not Sarah's nanny, Randi reminded herself. She stepped quietly toward the back door, ready to slip out.

"Hey, darlin'," Buck practically yelled at her. "Grab my crutches for me, and the pills from the pharmacy."

She turned around, clutching her bathroom tote against her stomach, everyone's eyes on her.

"What the fuck," Angie said, her eyes narrowing, "is happening here?" She rattled a brown bag, pulling out a can of beer. "We'll help you, Buck, but sit down and drink with us first."

"Too tired," Buck said. "Drank a little today and the mix with these pills knocks me out. You all fill up and enjoy for me. I'll catch up when this leg mends."

Randi stood stiff, her teeth almost breaking open her bottom lip, holding the door for Buck. Beer cans popped behind them. Any minute, Angie would charge out. Or she'd drink four beers and set fire to Randi's bedroom.

"Oh, Randi," Angie called out, her voice a parody of sweetness, "congratulations on your paycheck. I could get used to a live-in maid."

Everything in Randi hardened. "I doubt you'll live in a clean house again, Angie. Except maybe your mother's."

An emphatically pointed middle finger was her only response.

Buck managed to hobble down the shallow back steps. Exhaling a deep breath, she followed behind him, clicking the door shut.

The motion sensor light kicked on, flooding the back patio with a blueish glare. She squinted, angling her head away.

"I'll walk you to your trailer and carry this stuff for you, then I'm going back to my bed."

He didn't say anything, instead turning away and hobbling across the patio, straight to her bedroom. He held the door for her.

"Put your bathroom tote down, darlin'."

She sighed, relieved he was being reasonable.

"You're right, I don't want to drop anything in the grass."

When the door shut and locked, she spun around to glare at him.

"Don't kick me out." He collapsed on her bed. "I'm not sure I'd make it across the pasture."

"You know that psycho in there is going to murder me, right?"

"She outweighs you, sure, but you've got stamina. You can outrun her."

"There was nothing discreet about the way we left the house together."

"Take off the robe and come over here." He bunched her pillows under his head. "Pull my boots off for me."

"Buck, I'm serious about putting a time limit on this thing. I hate difficult conversations, so I want to give us both an easy out, no hurt feelings or expectations. Two weeks. And then we stop." She'd tacked on another week—seven days was a little short.

"No," he said, wincing as she pulled off his boot.

"If you put this boot back on tomorrow, it stays on. I probably re-injured your bone."

"My bone is fine. Except the one in my shorts."

"We are not doing anything tonight."

He sighed. "Yeah, I guess we aren't."

"All right, one month. Not that either of us is obligated to finish the entire month, but thirty days does bring us close to the end of term and the start of winter break. I'll be moved out by New Year's."

"You're calendaring our breakup?"

She pulled her glasses off and set them on the nightstand. "I'm a planner."

Ten minutes of staring at the dark ceiling later, her heart pumped fast enough to power a race car. He lay next to her, in her bed, and she couldn't sleep with the synapses firing at every nerve cluster in her skin.

There comes a point, probably in every mammal's life, when the body stops listening to the brain. *Procreate!* Every female organ focused on the sweaty warmth of him mere inches away. She was spiraling down a rabbit hole into a place where abstaining became meaningless. How had she made it this long? Like standing on the roof rack of a moving vehicle, balancing in your socks while the car dropped down a hill.

Buck's hand touched hers. She jumped. Gawd, she was embarrassing.

"Darlin'."

"Yeah?"

"What happened to your family?"

Her fist gripped the sheets as her heart shifted to an entirely different rhythm.

"I thought you were sleeping."

"Nah."

"Oh." He wanted to know her tragic history? She crossed her arms. "You should be."

"Come on now, tell me a little about yourself. I promise it won't be one-sided. I'll tell you all about my two jackass brothers, workaholic dad, and food-obsessed mother. Tonight, though, is about you."

She stared up at the ceiling fan, a dark X above her. The grief swelled, always there, easy to sink into.

"Hey, come over here and cuddle with me," he said, tugging on her arm.

She turned, tucking herself against his side, too tired to resist.

"What happened, darlin'?"

"Wow, you really know how to show a girl a nice time."

"Give me six hours."

His hand roamed over her shoulders, lightly rubbing. Surely in six hours this would all be a bizarre dream. Her and Buck? It didn't compute.

"I'm unlucky," she finally said. "More than that, people I'm close to die. My daddy died when I was a baby. Military. My mom, brokenhearted, followed not long after." She'd left so much out, like her mother's addiction, the crushing horror of it. Condensing the most devastating moments of her life into pillow chat made her head ache.

"Papa and Mimi, my grandparents, took me in. I was always worried something would happen to them. Wouldn't let them out of my sight for years. They died in a car accident when I was sixteen. Eight years ago, last June."

Buck's hand went still. He blew out his breath. "I'm sorry. That's a lot of grief for a kid."

She swallowed. Strange, to talk about it all in the dark, with him. "I dropped out of high school. Stopped eating," she heard herself say. "Blamed myself for my grandparents' deaths, because I should have been with them, but I snuck off with a boyfriend instead. Ended up in a psych ward for a few months. Then my aunt nearly died. I realized she needed me —if I didn't pull myself together, another death would be on my hands. So, I did."

He kissed the top of her head. "Not your fault anybody died."

She trembled, weirdly relieved to be saying her story out loud, to tell someone who wasn't a therapist. And tomorrow he'd realize she was too much for him. Too broken and sad. Too whatever. Which was for the best, obviously.

"Aunt Linda recovered from the pneumonia, and cancer, and I became a bit of a health nut."

"Yeah, a bit."

"It helps that she works at the Natural Foods Co-op now. I have reinforcement. She acted like giving up cigarettes meant life wasn't worth living."

The words dried up. There it was, her dark history condensed down into a snack-size portion. She exhaled, shakily.

"Hey," he said.

"Yeah?"

"Thanks for telling me."

"Well, I'm doing my best to scare you off."

"Didn't work."

She yawned, turning her face against his arm. "That fracture is probably my fault. You were perfectly fine until I came along."

"Worth it."

∼

"So, how's the little wife?"

Buck grinned; the big man sounded jealous. "Oh, mighty fine. Attentive to my every need."

Hugh, hunched over and frowning, rowed the boat with more force than a lazy Sunday called for.

The truth was, Buck was randy as hell and pissed. She'd snuck out of bed before he'd woken up. His raging hard-on had twitched in frustration as soon as his eyes opened. He'd texted her to hightail it back to bed. Twenty minutes later he finally heard back. She was already at the library.

"Always saw you with one of those rich girls, members of the country club and all that," Hugh said. "Still the plan?"

"Plan? What the hell are you talking about?"

"Hey, you can play dumb, but I know I'd sure be tempted."

Buck cast his line into a little shaded eddy on the side of the river. "Money don't matter. I want to be happy."

He stared at his line disappearing into the water. There had been plenty of women in his life, from the very rich to the barely eating. Five years ago, back in Texas, he'd been close to settling down with the kind of girl Hugh was talking about. But, like a cliché of a cowboy, he'd ridden west into the sunset, too restless to settle down at twenty-four.

"Why the hell does she cook so much?"

"Randi?" Buck glanced at his phone. She still hadn't texted. "Because she has a forty-year-old's soul." Hugh stared at him, forehead wrinkled in concentration. "You think your diet of Doritos and canned chili is going to cushion you into a healthy old age?"

"Wait, Randi's only twenty, right?" Hugh asked.

"Twenty-four."

"Damn, still."

"That's old for an undergrad." Buck reeled in to check his bait. "Angie's twenty-one."

Hugh's head whipped around to stare at him. "Shit."

Buck hooked on another worm. "Maybe she'll outgrow the crazy."

"Doubt it." Hugh sighed. "She punched me the other night. Was spraying the beer from a keg I bought. Soaked the T-shirts of a couple of cute girls that showed up at Jason's house. They left crying. I got socked in the face for taking my beer away from her." Hugh cracked open a can, his face beet red. "Later, she kissed me."

"Damn, boy, another abusive girl wailing on you. You need therapy."

Hugh grunted. "Not more'n most people."

Buck leaned back against the side of the raft, propping his aching leg up at the same time. Sometime in the last year, wild parties had lost his interest. And wild women…not as entertaining as they used to be, not since Tiff had dragged him down to hell and back.

Planning for Tiff's pregnancy had changed him, even though it had turned out to be fake. Thinking he was going to have a kid a year ago had flipped a switch. He'd fallen in love with a little baby that didn't exist. And grieved for it, too. He'd never settled back into his old self again.

"I think I'm done," Hugh went on. "With Ang."

"That a boy."

"I want to finish the rec room in that barn at your place.

Be out there when she isn't shit-faced drunk. Actually talk to her."

"Don't sound like you're done."

"I'll get friend-zoned."

"Friend-zoned? More like beat up."

"Yeah, well, maybe Randi will bring around some nice girls."

"Hmm," said Buck. He doubted it. Randi worked all the time, until he forced her away from the computer. As soon as he got done fishing, he would do that.

She was insecure and nervous as hell, and actually serious about the one-month nonsense. What she needed was to stop thinking so much and to trust him. He was taking Randi on a date.

"Fine by me," he said to Hugh, reeling in his line. "Pool table would be good."

# CHAPTER SEVENTEEN

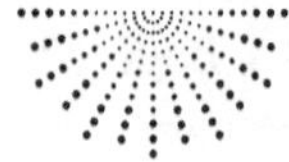

"Oh my," said the girl at the table beside Randi's. "Somebody's going to have a super night."

Randy rubbed her tired eyes. She had been in such a rush that morning to escape from Buck that she hadn't brought any treats to keep her going. The coffee was long gone.

Something thumped on the table in front of her. She startled, sat up straight, and blinked. A massive bouquet, in a vase, stood on her table. A heart-shaped box thudded down next to the vase. Chocolates.

"Pack up your crap," Buck ordered, looming over her and leaning on one crutch. "You're coming with me."

She closed her mouth and covered her face with a hand, putting her head down to giggle.

"Move it, girl," he said. "We're going to dinner."

"Sushi!" Randi squeaked twenty minutes later as they sat down on pillows at a low table. "How did you guess I love sushi?"

He raised an eyebrow at her. "Because you're a city slicker."

Beautifully garnished plates arrived, and Randi marveled

at Buck's graceful use of the chopsticks. He tried to convince her to get drunk on rice wine. Every time their eyes met, she blanked out for a moment, a pulsing drumbeat in her ears.

It was all very clear where the romance was leading. He wanted to take her to bed, to do more than sleep. He was being blatant about his intentions, and surprisingly, up-front worked for her. She had always wanted her first time to be special, not an afterthought on a rumpled bed or in a cramped car. This qualified.

He held her hand as they walked out of the restaurant. "Come to my trailer tonight," he said.

She bit her lip, not answering as he opened the truck door for her. He wanted her to drive. Grunting, he climbed into the cab on the passenger side. Obviously, his injury still hurt him.

"What about your leg?"

"It's fine."

She didn't say anything.

"Okay, it aches, but I'll behave and let you do all the work."

And, just like that, she couldn't take a deep breath. She gripped the wheel with white knuckles and swallowed hard.

One thing was clear, she was not cut out for this. When she could speak again, she would apologize, before running into the orchard.

"Darlin'?"

Randi just shook her head.

"What happened? Tell me."

Randi slowed down to turn onto the gravel drive through the trees. They were almost there—oh no. NO.

She cleared her throat. "Buck?"

"Yeah, darlin'?"

"You realize I'm a…that I haven't…"

Silence.

She blinked back tears. Of course, he didn't want to deal with that. He wanted some fun for a month and already, before even having sex, she'd degenerated into a pathetic mess. Too anxious to try.

He huffed. "How the hell did you make it to twenty-four?"

"Later. Too long of a story. Being a loner and a workaholic helped."

"Huh." He scratched his face. "Turns me on a little. I can't wait to watch your face. During. After." He groaned.

"I mean, I masturbate—advanced masturbate. I'm not some innocent out of a Victorian period drama."

"Shit." He shifted on the seat. "You're going to have to show me that sometime."

She huffed. A little heat stirred in her belly.

He unbuckled his belt and slid over next to her. "Let's go cuddle at my place and see what happens."

"That cuddle is definitely a euphemism."

His hand touched her thigh, sliding up under her skirt. She jerked, gasping as his fingers grazed over the crotch of her underwear.

"Park next to your room and grab your night tote," he said, his fingers circling on the fabric between her legs. "Then we'll drive over to my trailer."

"You have water over there?" she said in a breathy voice.

"Toilet, shower, it's all ready. And a bottle of wine in the fridge."

"Wow, fancy." She never thought a sentence with the word toilet in it could turn her on, but then it was definitely his hands that deserved the credit.

"Get a wiggle on," he murmured into her ear, "or I'll put my mouth between your legs right here."

~

THE TRAILER DOOR closed behind them and Buck was on her, pushing her against a wall, his mouth hot and hard on hers. She arched into him. His hands slid up the skirt of her dress to grip her bottom.

He groaned. "You wore a thong."

She hummed in reply.

"You're a naughty girl. Go lie on the bed before I bend you over on the steps."

"Pretty scary," she mumbled against his neck, molten heat throbbing between her legs. She didn't want to take the time to move.

Broken bone, she reminded herself firmly.

Her heels wobbled when she pushed away from him, forcing herself to turn and walk up the three interior steps into the trailer. Buck grunted behind her as he used a crutch to jump up the steps on one foot.

Worry doused her like a bucket of cold water. She slid onto the bench at the little table by the kitchen.

"Buck, you broke your leg." She paused, trying to count in her befuddled head. Less blood in her brain? "Three days ago. What if we get carried away and you end up like the crooked man, living in a crooked house with a crooked cat…"

He limped past her, all the way to the bed. "Scared?" He tossed the word over his shoulder, a challenging edge in his voice.

She swallowed, putting her face in her hands. Her throat tightened, a sure sign that she was perilously close to breaking down. Scared didn't encompass the chaos. *Dammit!*

Buck grunted in pain. She peeped through her fingers at him. And, like an out-of-control emotion roller-coaster, her state of mind leaped over the chasm and scrambled to the other side. They'd agreed on one month—check mark the plan in place. She would "hook up", surely an experience worth having at least once in her life, and finally lose her V-card with someone she was crazy attracted to. Buck. Who, through a freakish twist of the universe, was her friend.

She stood up and walked down the aisle to where he lay on the bed.

"I'm a little scared." She reached down to pull off his boot. "I have a lot of pent-up sexual frustration. What you need is a safe word. Like platypus. I'm not sure you're healed up enough for me."

He shook his head at her and pulled her down for a gentle kiss.

"I'm not going to need a safe word, but I do want you to help me with these clothes."

He got his jeans down his hips, propping himself up on one foot. She worked slowly to move them over his swollen leg.

"I have a question for you," she said.

"Shoot."

"What changed? I mean in the last week or so. You avoided me for a while, after we took Sarah to the hospital."

He looked down, working on the buttons of his shirt. She folded his jeans and sat them down.

Finally, he said, "My last relationship, it got me as near to hating women as I've ever been in my life. The girl, she told me she was pregnant. Lied about it to keep me with her. I thought there was going to be a kid. Thought about the baby constantly, making plans, even read a couple books about it."

Randi gasped. She reached out and squeezed his fingers. He didn't look at her, but he gripped her hand back and sniffed.

"Well, I came home early from work one day. We'd moved in together when she told me about the pregnancy, about three months before. Was real hot that day. We were going to go buy an air conditioner that night. I slipped in through the open back door and heard her on the phone with her mother. She shouted that she 'couldn't fake it any longer.' So I went back outside and stood by her window while she whined about lying to me. Not pregnant again that month, would have to fake a miscarriage, and on and on. That was fifteen months ago."

"Unbelievably horrible," Randi said, aching for him. How did people work themselves into those kinds of deceptions?

"It put me off my time here. Like nothing good could come out of this place."

She lay down next to him, curling her body around him as his story sank in. She kissed his shoulder.

"Sounds like a lucky escape, though, from a sociopath. They're ten to twenty percent of the population and incredible at hiding it."

He huffed, turning to look at her. Their noses touched. "You're not a sociopath."

"You're not a sociopath either."

"Please take your dress off and get in bed with me."

"Have more romantic words ever been spoken?"

He kissed her, his mouth a lingering sweet caress. Was that the closest she was ever going to be to hearing how he felt about her? Her eyes fluttered closed as their noses touched again, then their lips, exploring each other for long minutes. The kind of kiss that could happen at the edge of the bleachers during a football game, or outside your front door. Sweetly tantalizing, a coaxing invitation.

They parted like two long-distance swimmers emerging from the water after a twenty-meter dash, remembering how to breathe regularly, eyes blinking in the air. He smoothed the hair back from her face.

"Sit up and undo that zipper," he whispered.

Abruptly, she knew it was time. She wanted to do this and she was ready, comfortable and safe. The monolith V-card would come down tonight and she would experience it with Buck. She didn't think they had a future together, but she knew she was falling in love with him. Tonight meant something to her.

With a shuddering breath, she pushed herself up, stunned she didn't wobble and fall over on her shaky limbs. She sat with her legs off the bed and her back to him. First thing was to take off her glasses and set them on the side table. The other side of the trailer became blurry and unfocused.

Buck groaned. "You take off your glasses and I get hard. Harder."

She peeped at him over her shoulder. "My secret sex weapon? One of these nights I'll keep them on and whisper in your ear to be quiet, young man, or you'll be seeing the principal."

He shook his head. "Don't get ahead of yourself. You're going to be too busy in my bed to talk much."

"This mouth has a mind of its own."

"Take your dress off and then bring that mouth over here."

She took a deep breath, removed the thin leather belt around her waist, and forced herself to reach up and undo the toggle clasp at the back of her dress. Stretching, she pulled down the long zipper that ran down a hidden seam on the back of the fitted bodice.

She turned her head to look at Buck, terrified of what would be on his face, desperate to not lose her nerve. His heavy-lidded gaze was on her, his face flushed. She drew in a breath and, slowly, an inch of shoulder at a time, pulled the dress forward.

The flared skirt fell further down her legs, covering her bare knees. Finally, she stood up to step out of the fabric, realizing too late that she had left her heeled sandals on.

With rare grace, she managed to not trip over the bunched fabric around her ankles.

Buck groaned behind her. For a moment she stood with her back to him, wearing nothing but a thong and a sheer black lace bralette. She sat down on the bed and worked on the straps of her shoes.

"Darlin'," Buck's hand was skimming over her back, "you are sexy as hell."

He sat up and yanked his undershirt off over his head. Pulling her down to sit beside him, he kissed her shoulder, the sweetness of his gentle lips and gliding hands drawing up a lump of emotion in her throat—it felt so good, unreal, to be that close to another person. She turned her body to face him, running her hand down his chest.

He dragged one of her legs over his hips, positioning her over him while he kissed her neck and chest, grumbling happily. Then he slid down further, while holding her hips steady.

"Oh," she gasped, as he yanked her pelvis forward to meet his face. Her hands landed on the wall behind his head with a thump. He jerked the thong down her thighs. Hot wet lips touched her clitoris, then he sucked the pulsing nub inside his mouth while his tongue circled and swirled.

Her eyeballs rolled back as quivers ran down her spine, and a sensation like ice sliding on her skin. His mouth on her was more than she could bear, and everything she'd never known she wanted. Shaking, head thrown back as she panted and groaned, release burst inside her, white-hot gunshots ripping through her.

All she could do was breathe, her body humming like a revved engine. After one last lingering kiss that had her shuddering, he pulled away. Roughly, he jerked his boxers over his hips, kicking them down with his good leg. She was making urgent little moaning noises as he opened a condom wrapper and pushed it on over his long erection.

She straddled him, and he gripped her hips, rubbing her clitoris up and down the length of his cock. When she gasped, shivering in a quick burst of rippling pleasure, he thrust into her, sinking into the moist throbbing entrance of her sex.

Her head went back, and she vibrated, a high-pitched keening coming from her throat. She was pushing down on the hot thick length of him, the inside of her stretching with a pinching tightness. Incredible that she could take him all in. She paused, looking down at his open-mouthed face, tan skin stretched across his cheekbones, narrow blue eyes glinting at her. The pain ballooned inside her stomach.

"Come here," he said, his heavy-lidded eyes meeting hers.

She bent forward until her lips touched the roughness of his cheek. The change in position opened her enough for him to slide further in. She buried her face in his neck, gasping at the fullness inside her. His hands slid up and down her torso, cupping her breasts, gripping her backside. He rocked her back and forth. The movement reawakened a pulsing need to move against him, despite the pain.

Bracing on her elbows and knees, she moved, letting Buck's hands guide her hips and set a rhythm. She gasped and shuddered, calling his name. His grip on her tightened, his slitted gaze watching her face. The pressure built, expanding, until it burst in blinding pleasure. She cried out, clenching around him, her entire pelvis pulsing in shock waves of bliss.

He ground her down hard on his hips, his head thrown back on the pillow, groaning and shivering against her.

She collapsed on his chest, tingling, still riding the after-shocks, gasping at the sensation of him inside her.

He rubbed his cheek against the side of her head. "Darlin', we've got so much cuddling to do."

IN THE MORNING, she woke up to a hard Buck against her backside, one of his hands groping her chest.

"Oh."

"Come for another ride," he rasped against her shoulder. "Condom's on."

"Hmm, presumptuous. I don't know." Her body cranked into hot and ready in two breaths. She liked the feeling of him behind her. A lot. How shocking, probably something wrong with her. "More than once a week just doesn't seem proper."

"I'm breaking you in. We should stay in this bed all day."

Wild urgency throbbed between her legs. Pushing him back on the bed, she straddled him, humming when he slid inside her. She was out of control. And giggly. He growled and swatted her backside, making her laugh harder, while she bounced on top of him.

After, she jumped out of bed, invigorated, a no-doubt goofy smile on her lips. How had she missed out on this for so long? No wonder people became sex addicts.

Buck's shower was tiny, with about three minutes of tepid water. He squeezed into the bathroom.

"Hey!" She wiped water out of her eyes. "I'm going to need more flowers before I'll watch you on the toilet."

"All part of life in a trailer, darlin'. Bathroom romance."

He grabbed her after she put on her clothes for the day: a navy-blue stewardess dress, tight in the bodice and flared in the skirt. The striped bow at the neckline matched the sleeves, giving the impression of a dressy, and a bit provocative, uniform. She hadn't wanted to wear this dress for a long time.

"Too sexy for a Monday." He looked her up and down.

"This is a modest dress, Buck. Long sleeves, a skirt down to my knees." She adjusted the striped blue tie around her neck. "Maybe you're sensing sex pheromones. I wonder if people will look at me today and notice a glow. Men will sneeze, overcome with my pheromones."

"I can't let you leave the trailer like this." He pulled her forward for a searing kiss.

After a blissful minute, she pushed away from him. "Let's go. I skipped the gym for you, but I won't be late for class."

Ten minutes later, Sarah caught them kissing in the kitchen.

"Um, morning." Sarah cleared her throat like it was full of mucus.

Randi jumped, spilling coffee when her arms jerked. Buck was plastered to her back, pinning her to the counter. She forced him backward with a sharp jab of her elbow.

"Morning, Sarah," Buck said. He bit into a cookie, his face mellow and peaceful. Randi swallowed down a giggle.

"Morning," Randi called out, far too cheerfully. She coughed. "Take a cookie, Sarah." When you're desperate, and live with a violent psychopath named Angie, resort to bribery. Cookies might buy her time.

She sensed that Sarah had mellowed out recently, mostly because the blonde occasionally talked to her again. Sarah didn't appear enraged, more like disgusted and resigned.

"So," Sarah said around a mouthful of cookie. "You two… are you like, going public?"

"No!" Randi twitched at the bullhorn volume of her voice. She swallowed. "Okay, way too early in the morning for, um, going public. Or even talking about it."

"Huh." Sarah took another cookie.

Randi frantically gathered up her things and Buck's, hustling him out the door.

"You're jumpy." Buck tossed his crutches in the back of the truck.

"Don't play dumb with me. You understand, as well as I do, that now I have a price on my head."

~

"WELL, HI STRANGER," Aunt Linda said in her phone. "I wondered when I would hear from you."

Randi closed her laptop. She stood up to gather her things then stepped away from the people working at the library tables. Aunt Linda had that tone in her voice that indicated things were far from right. Either her health problems had flared up or she was falling into a depression. Or both.

"Hi to you, too. You own a phone, it goes both ways, but what's going on? Has something happened?"

"You know I always sense I'm disturbing you. If you're at the library you have to gather all your things and go outside, or you're in class, or making a yoga video. Besides, I realize you have better things to do than talk to a boring old lady."

Randi put her face in her free hand. Aunt Linda was in full meltdown mode.

"Auntie, what's going on? Did something happen with Jack?"

"When you're fifty-eight, you comprehend a thing or two. One of them is no one wants an old woman."

Randi took a deep breath. The lingering giddiness in her stomach withered and died. "I'll be at your house in two hours, old woman, so kick your booty into shape. You'd better scrounge up a bottle of wine. You're going to need it when I apply the thumbscrews and you tell me everything."

She hung up the phone without bothering to wait for a reply.

Two hours later, she sat on a bus headed to her aunt's, still not texting Buck about it. What was she waiting for?

Her phone vibrated with an incoming call. She pulled it out of her bag, expecting Buck's name on the screen. Not him.

"Hey," she said in a low voice, moving to the back of the bus. "How are you?"

"Um, I've been better." Daisy's voice shook, more high-pitched than usual. "Where the hell have you been? Your text messaging sucks."

"Look, I tell you every weekend, I'm not a bar person."

"It was a wine bar."

"I have no money, and if I don't work on the weekends, I won't pass my classes. Twenty-one credits."

"Ugh. You're such a nerd. One drink on a Saturday night isn't going to tank your five-year plan. What bullshit."

"Wow, deep breath, fireball. Why don't you go punch your pillow for a while and call me back when the tantrum's over?"

Daisy cursed her out and hung up. Randi exhaled, looking up at the shiny beige bus ceiling. Obviously, fate would make her pay for actually enjoying herself last night. Get a little sex and the universe comes crashing down on you with histrionic bat cases.

Eight years ago, before the nightmare, she'd had friends, a boyfriend, all the normal teenage stuff. Did her desperate best to be normal. She was the quieter, less open one, but being close to others gave her a thrill. She craved it. Fascinated by people with parents in their lives, she compared how she was different, trying to soak up some of that experience, marveling at their security and entitlement.

Then she'd lost everyone that mattered for the second

time in her life and had fought her way back from insanity by learning to rely on herself. And only herself.

Daisy wanted a closer-than-sisters best friend. The more withdrawn Randi was, the more of an irresistible challenge she became to Daisy, it seemed. Or she wanted a thrill-seeking partner, someone to go drinking and carousing with. Probably both. Either option made Randi shudder.

Yet, it poked at her cold heart. More practically, Daisy and Aunt Linda went together like ham and biscuits, served with a generous helping of melodramatic gravy. Randi had watched them drink a little wine then happily excavate their personal lives for juicy nuggets of psychoanalysis. Dissecting their emotions actually made them happy. She picked up her phone and texted.

**Randi**: Come to my aunt's for dinner tonight. I'll be making some kind of mess of beans and rice. You can both yell at me for being a horrible person and I'll get it all out of the way.

**Daisy**: Fine! But I'm bringing wine and I don't want any judgey looks about it!

**Randi**: Bring chocolate too and there will be no judgment.

# CHAPTER EIGHTEEN

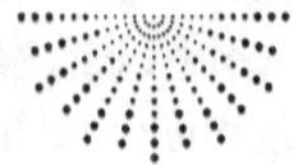

"Oh, it's you," said Aunt Linda from where she lay sprawled out on the couch. A news program blared on the television. She raised a smoking joint to her mouth and took a long draw.

Randi waved the air in front of her face. "I'm opening windows, this is cat abuse."

"They love it." Aunt Linda sipped from a fast-food cup. "I won't bother offering any to you."

"Twenty-one credits." Randi shuddered as she walked past the kitchen, the countertop buried under two layers of stacked dishes. "How long have you been living on that couch?"

By the bathroom, the cat boxes overflowed with clumps, and litter was tracked all over the floor. Randi took a deep breath then bent over coughing, a definite tickle in her throat. Cleaning for her aunt wouldn't help.

"What time is it?" Aunt Linda's eyes drifted shut as her head rolled back on the cushions of the couch.

She should call Buck. She stuffed an empty garbage bag into Aunt Linda's bin. If they were a normal couple, of course she would. After finally managing an evening away from him, with time to think, she knew she was making a mistake. *Dear Buck,* she could write to him, *you are a hazardous addictive substance, a class three narcotic, actually, and I'm far too uptight to deal with your euphoria-inducing symptoms. I'm starting to like you way more than I should and you were just supposed to be a little innocent experimentation. A one-month thing. I'm realizing I have a problem with you.*

As breakup letters went, probably a little oblique.

She sent a quick text to Buck, deciding to stick to the facts: her aunt was a lump of dysfunctional despair and she needed help.

No, hooking up for a few more weeks wouldn't kill her. She would think of it as an elective course—he did know what he was doing. The problem was, her head and heart didn't play nice with each other.

When Daisy bustled in two hours later, the cat boxes and floor were clean and Randi was swallowing painkillers to deal with her headache. She put a casserole in the oven to bake, then collapsed in a chair, her hands cupped around a steaming mug of tea.

Thirty minutes later, her phone buzzed. Buck was calling her, like a considerate adult. Why couldn't she do that?

"Housemate calling," Randi said, as lightly as she could force her tight voice. She didn't want to talk to Buck, and she didn't know why.

"The word is roommate, Randi," Daisy said irritably. "Housemate sounds weird."

"Weird is my middle name."

Aunt Linda refilled Daisy's wine glass, and they settled into the couch, back to talking endlessly about men, chatter flowing out of them like water from a faucet. Randi hadn't said much, and not a peep about Buck—too tired. Her connection to him felt fragile, like loud voices might shatter it. Or her. Apparently, the sex glow was long gone, because neither her aunt nor Daisy suspected a thing.

She needed time away from Buck. He'd hijacked her solitary existence, like an unplanned day at the beach—messy fun that took over all your plans as soon as your feet sank into the sand. He was a vacation that wouldn't last.

"Hey, darlin'," said his deep calm voice from the phone. "Your aunt doing okay?"

Of course, texting with him would not be enough. He had to poke his big hat in and manage her.

"She's inside getting tipsy with Daisy. They go together like a couple of long-lost drama queens."

"When should I pick you up?"

"Hey, I already texted you that I don't need a ride tonight."

"Yeah, and when I ask how you're getting back, you're not answering."

"Because I can manage it myself."

Silence on the line.

Why was she being such a bitch? She took a deep breath. Yes, she didn't want to be steamrolled, but she could muster up an explanation.

"Auntie's in a rough spot. She and Jack are on the outs, and her health issues are flaring up. I'm going to stay here and help her out for a bit. Probably for a few days."

"I'm sorry to hear she's having a hard time. How can I help, darlin'?"

She smiled. Sometimes she didn't believe he was real.

"Well, don't let Angie burn down my cabin in a fit of jealous rage. How's your leg?"

"Still there. Are you running away because you're tired of playing nurse?"

"I'm not running away," she said. "A few days to think things over isn't running away."

"Did you make up that stuff about your aunt?"

"What? No."

"Well, one minute you're helping out your aunt and the next you need to think things over."

"Wow."

They were fighting. The third person upset with her today. Did she complete the cycle? Could she return to her normal, quiet, sane life?

"Listen, I've got to go and clean two weeks' worth of my aunt's dishes. Dirty plates follow me wherever I go, alas."

"Darlin'?" he said, speaking the word like a question. Silence followed. A small eternity passed before he continued. "I'll call you tomorrow."

She sat down heavily on the back step. A tight ache pounded in her sinuses, and her body seesawed between heat and chills. No, not sick. That would be extremely bad right now—the mountains of work granted no leave. She rubbed her temples. Dealing with intense relationships overwhelmed her skill set. They made her sick.

Her aunt had pushed Jack away, refusing to meet his family. Daisy remained unhappily single. So, here she was, cooking and cleaning for them, instead of curled up with Buck.

It shouldn't matter and she couldn't let herself start to need him. They would be together for a month and then things would change. A learning experience. Lesson one, not talented at hooking up without emotions. Lesson two, nothing easy about getting involved, at all.

She went to bed early, desperately hoping to sleep off her cold. Daisy and Aunt Linda stayed up, watching a reality show about dating and finishing the wine. In the morning, Daisy lay on the couch, softly snoring, with cats snuggled around her legs.

Randi dragged her sneezing, miserable self to school, then

back to Aunt Linda's to make a pot of soup and collapse back into bed.

The next day she met up with Luke for a brief study session in the library. He looked concerned with her for wearing a mask, insisted on buying her a coffee, and gave her tickets to one of his shows coming up over the weekend. After thirty minutes she called it quits and headed back to her aunt's.

Buck kept up a steady text conversation with her. When she'd mentioned meeting Luke, flat silence, and a possibly angry lack of response on his side. She realized she didn't want to hurt him. Finally, she had resorted to pictures of her sick self in skimpy pajamas and buried under cats. He texted her back. Clearly, though, not happy with her.

Fussing over her with essential oils pushed Aunt Linda out of her funk. By the time Jack knocked on her door two days later, Aunt Linda opened the door, her gorgeously coiffed, tense self. When Jack took Linda in his arms and kissed her, Randi stepped into her room to leave them alone and pack up her bag, pulling out her phone to text Buck.

**Randi**: Hey are you still on campus?

Buck answered after a few minutes.

**Buck**: Give me an address and I'll be there.

**Randi**: I'll come to you.

**Buck**: Darlin', don't argue. Where?

**Randi**: If I give you this address you'll know the location of my secret lair. First you have to complete the labyrinth and fetch a Golden Fleece.

**Buck**: Give me the address. I'm getting in my truck now.

**Randi**: Anyone ever tell you you're a steamroller?

**Buck**: Burning gas here.

Twenty minutes later, Randi jumped when the door rattled with a loud knock. *Oh no*, he was at the door. She had been planning to run outside and jump in his truck before Aunt Linda had a moment to think about it.

She sprang off her bed to sprint to the door, took the hallway corner too fast and slid across the slick hardwood floor on her thick socks, stopping with a thud against the bathroom door. Before she could get there, Aunt Linda opened the front door with Jack by her side, one of his long arms around her back.

Buck took his hat off and balanced on his crutches to swing through the door. Randi swallowed, the bottom of her stomach dropping out. She hadn't forgotten what he looked like, it just blanked out her brain if she wasn't used to it.

Hard eyes raked her up and down. That square jaw, shadowed with stubble, seemed firmer than usual. Dark blond hair smashed down from his hat and those brawny shoulders on his tall frame made her mouth lift in a smile before she could stop it. She was such a goner.

"Oh." Her aunt glanced over at Randi with round eyes. "I didn't realize you two had become friends."

"We have," said Buck. "She's the only girl I've met that wakes up earlier than I do. Knocked my socks off." Randi's stomach clenched. Did he have to talk about getting up in the morning?

Buck shook hands with Jack. "Hi, Jack, Linda, nice to see you both again."

"Sounds like you're, uh, close friends." Jack gave Buck a long stare. "Are you spending a lot of time at Randi's house?"

Randi blushed. The conversation was torpedoing south, fast.

"Buck is paying rent out there, actually," she said. "He has a travel-trailer RV. That thing needs a lot of space, so he parked in our pasture."

"We're dating." Buck picked up her bag and slung it over his shoulder.

She glared at him. "You broke your leg a week ago. I can carry my own bags."

"Not fractured, only a bad bruise. Saw the doctor yesterday."

"Well, my goodness." Aunt Linda stared hard at Randi. "I thought you were being awfully quiet. We'll have to talk again soon, dear."

Jack grinned, for some unfathomable reason. He grabbed the rest of Randi's bags, and they all shuffled out to Buck's truck. Randi bit her lip while her face burned. Buck had practically announced they were sleeping together. Her aunt beamed like a kid on Christmas morning.

As they drove away, Randi said, "Too bad I can't let you handle the thirty questions your little outing of us is going to create." Like some kind of absurd send-off, her aunt was still waving when the truck stopped at a red light.

"You ashamed of me?" Buck's face tensed.

"No," Randi huffed and tried to gather her thoughts. "This is all new to me. And private. I'm still waiting for you to realize how many hot blondes you could be sleeping with."

The truck veered off the road. She clutched the taut band of her seat belt as her body clunked into the passenger door.

"What's going on?" Randi glanced behind them, expecting a police car.

"Come here." He reached out a hand to her.

She stared at him. The little devil took over. She unbuckled her seat belt and flung herself in his arms. He kissed her like he was desperate for it. Before Buck, she'd had no idea kissing could be like this. Other kisses hadn't even existed in the same dimension. His hands moved over her, shaping her body, pressing her closer. He was responsive and demanding. She ran her hands over his back, hungry for him. Completely lost.

A horn honked and somebody whistled from a passing car. She drew away from his mouth, resting her forehead against his.

"Crawl over me," he said, and her pulse picked up. "Driving hurts my leg."

She kissed his cheek then rubbed her face along it, liking the scrape of his bristle.

"As you wish," she whispered, then used the door on her side to hop out and go around.

"What happened to 'as you wish?' I wanted more honking before we drove home."

"I'm onto you and your ideas of fun." She shifted the big truck into gear. "Another reason for staying at my aunt's was to actually give your leg a rest."

"Wrong there. Without my minion around I had to do everything myself, plus drive, and so you did my leg more harm than good."

"Minion?"

"The other girls can't even make a decent cup of coffee. And a starving dog would turn away their cooking."

Randi spluttered. "So, you're a Neanderthal who wants a minion to cook and clean for him?"

"Every man's dream. But if they're wearing a hot little black skirt like that one, the minion gets to wear clothes."

Randi sat up straighter. There was a definite edge to his voice.

"You know what, you can take your primitive brain and sleep with your chauvinism tonight."

She jumped when she felt his hand on her leg. "You really do have the prettiest legs." He ran a finger under the hem of her skirt.

"What's going on with you?" Randi swatted his hand away. "Are you demeaning me because you're upset?"

His arm landed behind her head. "You take off for a week and you have to ask me that?"

"Three days."

"If I disappeared after the first night we'd been together, you'd stop talking to me."

Randi adjusted her glasses. "If you took off it would be because you didn't want me. That's not the case with me. And I didn't take off exactly, we talked every day." Randi swallowed. What she was, to put it simply, was a coward. "I'm a snail without a shell, Buck. I needed to catch my breath. You've done this, many times. It's all déjà vu for you."

"Right, because my Neanderthal brain is fuck and repeat."

They sat in angry silence as she pulled up next to his trailer.

"Hey," Randi said, "I'm still getting over the cold. I'm going to go sleep in my bed and I'll see you in the morning."

She turned away, ready to dash to her room. He gripped her arm.

"No." His jaw clenched.

"Buck—"

"Wait, darlin'." He took a deep breath. "Hang on."

They glared at each other. The creases on his face appeared deeper, like he'd barely slept the last few nights. She swallowed. He looked so haggard. His hand slid down her arm until he held her fingers.

"Come in. I've got a drink for us in there."

"Um…"

"Please."

Did the man ever apologize? She doubted it. Yet, strangely, his emotional reaction triggered a little hope deep in her cynical heart. Blowing out her breath, she thought back to what he'd said, which basically amounted to teasing—with a dash of emotional manipulation. Also, he'd announced to her family that they were dating, like their "hooking up" was a relationship that would last for longer than a month. Her cheeks heated. He really was determined to break her heart.

She sighed, capitulating yet again. "Don't you ever get tired of getting your own way?"

His eyes crinkled a bit at the edges. "Your fault for always making me chase you."

That smile. Her whole body softened, leaning into him. Gawd, she couldn't resist him.

"Right. Blame the rabbit."

"A skittish, soft bunny. Hmm, keep up that sexy talk and we won't make it out of this truck."

"Sexy talk?" She scooted away from him toward the door. "Your painkillers are too strong."

"Hop to it, honey bunny, into my lair."

"Are you trying to keep me away from the house because the kitchen's a total disaster?"

"Might be."

"I need a minion."

They moved themselves inside the trailer. Buck hobbled back to the bed and collapsed, putting his leg up with a groan.

"Pour that wine on the counter into a couple of mugs and come back here and snuggle with me."

Randi pulled his boots off then propped his leg up on a pillow and wedged an ice pack over the bruise. She frowned. It didn't appear better.

"So, Linda and Jack are back together?"

"Turns out Aunt Linda was being a little dramatic. They never broke up. He wanted to introduce her to his family, she said no. Couples function like that, by the way, one person says no and the other person accepts it. They had a minor squabble, and then he left for a week to travel down to California."

"Why wouldn't she go with him?"

"She's eight years older than he is."

"Yeah."

"Yeah. That's her reason. Doesn't want to take a chance now and be devastated later."

"That's not living. More like hiding."

Randi put her head back against the pillows. She completely understood where her aunt was coming from. "I don't know," she said, "maybe we only have so many heartbreaks we can take. That kind of pain doesn't make you stronger, just bruised."

Buck took the empty wine glass out of her hand and set it down on the nightstand.

"You're strong. I like it."

She huffed. "I'm a soft-bellied turtle—"

He kissed her, and whatever point she was trying to make melted away in a surge of heat.

"You're tough." He slid off her glasses. "I like it. A lot."

He pulled her down onto the mattress and rolled on top of her. She blinked, surprised to feel his full weight, to be pinned down.

She blew out a breath. "Phew, those bones are heavy. Good thing I'm so tough."

He kissed her hard and long. With a will of its own, her body took over. Her knees parted, her calves wrapping around his back when he leaned into her. She was arching into him by the time he pulled away.

His eyes were dark as they stared down at her. She swallowed, trying to stop herself from panting.

"I'm crazy about you," he said.

Treacherously, her heart jumped up and down, clapping. He was crazy about her?

A little while later, when he entered her, and her whole body sang yes, she called his name, and thought whatever happened in a few weeks, at least she would know what it was to melt.

BUCK WOKE up one second away from making love to her in his sleep. They'd slept naked, her soft body spooned in front of him, that round bottom massaging him into a stiff rod. He was ready to shove inside her and rut like a red-eyed beast.

She moaned, turning her head toward him. He nearly lost it. This damn strange girl was twisting him inside out.

"Not a condom close by," he croaked out of his dry throat.

"That's not very Boy Scout of you," she said.

"I'm no Boy Scout."

When she arched back into him, his restraint broke. He lifted her leg and pushed inside her. The slick hot feel of her without a condom sent him into an ocean of bliss. She squirmed against him.

"You want this," he grumbled, trying to prepare himself to pull out. To deal with her freak-out.

"Yes," she whispered, already quivering around him.

He pushed harder into her. She wriggled into him, almost as frantic as he was.

She was always ready for him, so hot and wet and lost to her passion. Like her body was desperate to squeeze him any chance it got.

He rolled her over, ass up, then grabbed the pillow and

threw it out of the way. She braced on her forearms, and he pulled her hips up high. Then he was pumping into her from behind, and she was gasping and shuddering around him.

She shouted. He held out for another handful of seconds until she softened.

Groaning, he yanked out of her and came hard, pressing against that perfect heart-shaped bottom, pleasure jerking his body.

He wiped her off, his hand a little shaky. She murmured something happy sounding. He collapsed on the bed and scooped her into his arms.

Too damn good.

"Another first," she said, stretching like a cat in front of him.

He kissed her shoulder. "You make me wild." She didn't know the half of it. He wanted to tie her to the bed. For the next week.

Randi rolled to face him, propping her head up on one hand. She stared down at him, her preoccupied eyes deep green pools. The morning light on her face and long hair made him catch his breath. So beautiful.

"We're going too fast, aren't we?"

True, way too early to go bare. "The no condom thing? You're on the pill. And I bet you never miss one."

"I'm too busy to menstruate, so technically I shouldn't even be ovulating."

"Yeah. I follow you."

"But…no barrier. The probability of a baby went up a fraction. A few percentage points. How does anyone deal with the stress of this?"

So honest, laid it all out there to take or leave. He nuzzled into her hair. There was always a sweetness to her, like cut grass. Even her body odor tempted him.

The thought of her pregnant made his inner caveman

pound his chest and grunt. She wouldn't run from him any longer. He swallowed, alarmed at himself.

"Fatalism," he said. "And you sleep with people you like."

She tensed up. What a handful.

No, he wasn't ready to get anybody pregnant. Having a hunch didn't mean you started a family after dating for less than a week. Usually, the idea of getting a girl breeding set off tea kettle whistles in his head, and thoughts of running like hell.

"Relax. Fairly tough to conceive, animals or humans—the right conditions have to exist. That little window of time, sometimes only hours long, when the egg's dropped in position. Granted, you're hot and young, all favorable signs for any buck like me. But between the pill and pulling out, we'll be fine, darlin'. And most of the time, I'll wear a sack, to be tidy."

"Do me a favor," she said.

"What's that?"

"Knock on wood."

"Go get dressed. I'm taking you to Darlene's."

At the diner, he read the paper while she tapped away on her laptop. He'd missed her the last few days—the sex, yeah, although he'd barely had a taste of that. But mostly this. Their mornings with her insanely perky energy, the huge glasses slipping down her nose, them together tackling another day of work with hot coffee and breakfast.

She always sat up so straight, reminding him of a little dancer. She was so solemn all the time, and when she did smile, it felt like the sun coming out.

There had been other girls he'd enjoyed spending time with. He liked having a girl with him. But he could slip into silence with Randi, like sitting beside a river fishing, waiting, moving in and out of sunlight. He caught her, and let her go, over and over.

Panic crept up on him. There wasn't that part of him holding back, he was close to all-in, and not willing to be. Also, she might actually be serious about the one-month thing. About not being ready for him.

She didn't know how good they were. She might need to go out and sleep with a few idiots before she understood the reality of dating. He was as pissed as a caged bull, thinking about it.

# CHAPTER NINETEEN

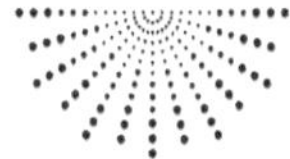

"Sexy moves, hot stuff!" a guy hollered from the sidewalk.

Randi ignored him, counting in her head as she held downward dog. The red recording light shone on her cell phone in the corner of her eye. Eventually, the big golden retriever running around unleashed would knock over the tripod, but it didn't matter. Filming would go on until the inevitable disaster. She hadn't posted anything in two weeks. Even if this video was a complete fiasco, she would finish it and edit like hell.

Bright sun filtered through the yellow leaves above her as she progressed into a standing backbend. The Riverfront Park was crowded. Bicycles dashed by on the wide path by the river, weaving between dog walkers and baby strollers.

She moved from warrior one pose into warrior two on the grass lawn, a little sideshow of freak, talking into a headset. A frisbee floated by over her head. Someone laughed. Probably one of her more interesting shoots yet. "Heckled for Yoga" could become a meme…

A whistle pierced her ears, but she didn't glance up at the

guy. Some people could make alarmingly high-pitched noises with their mouths, as attractive as someone slapping you in the face to get your attention.

Doing yoga in the downtown park, during the busiest part of the day, was a surefire way to encounter men with sledgehammer mating tactics. She should have been here at sunrise. But her mornings these days were spent energetically, and exclusively, in Buck's bed. Not doing yoga.

Warmth rushed into her face, and she bit her lip to keep from smiling. Heat stirred in her middle, the desire a simmering pot that could boil over just by thinking about him.

Addicted, definitely, with no rehab in sight. For the last week, since returning from her aunt's, she and Buck had spent every night together. Not right, healthy, or sane to want him so much. She was on the edge of tumbling into some crazy place she couldn't climb out of.

*Breathe in. Breathe out.* She forced herself to count, looking at the bright surface of the river. You can't force peace, but you can breathe until the body stops fighting and remembers how to relax.

This thing with Buck didn't feel like her life. More of a glitch, like she'd clicked on a pumpkin recipe but the link popped to a flashing emergency screen demanding her credit card number. Obviously, going any further engendered the kind of mistake that public service announcements should address. KEEP YOUR CREDIT CARD SECURE AND PLAYBOYS OUT OF YOUR BODY.

She flashed back to him cupping her face with his hands that morning, their sweaty bodies still joined. He'd run his thumbs over her cheekbones, his eyes dark and intense on her face, then rested his forehead against hers.

"Hey," Daisy shouted.

Randi wrapped up her recording with a bow, holding the pose for five seconds.

"What is this?" Daisy said, dropping her bike sideways on the grass. "Were you making a yoga video?"

"Hi, yeah." She rolled up her mat and stowed it in the bag, along with the mini tripod for her phone.

Daisy unwrapped a burrito from the taco stand down the road, staring at her as she pulled on her T-shirt dress.

"Uh wow, that's weird. The homeless guys liked it, though."

Randi pulled out the packed sandwich from her bag and stared back at Daisy, who was wearing red horns on top of her head, a spot-on costume. "I thought you had no illusions about my weirdness, but if I'm downing your game, I'll take my lunch and go."

Daisy rolled her eyes. "Calm down, sheesh."

Randi sat down on the grass and took a bite of her sandwich. Where was her patience? Living at the country house was sharpening her edges.

"So, are you, like, making money on YouTube?"

"A little," Randi said. "I'm barely over one thousand subscribers, the minimum to make ad money. I've got a lot of work to do over the break, promoting."

She swallowed, the shedloads of marketing and video creation she needed to do as soon as finals were over was looming like a thirty-pound file in her backpack. More important than the YouTube creation was researching internships, hopefully jobs, not too far from Aunt Linda. Buck flashed into her mind—surely he wouldn't be around long enough to affect her plan? She locked that depressing thought away, firmly.

"Huh. Your yoga gear is super cute. So weird to see you out of a dress though. But tell me about your crazy home life. How's the country house?"

"Hell." Randi popped a grape in her mouth. Hell was an exaggeration when you took Buck into account, but not by much.

"What happened?"

"My bedroom got TP'd."

Daisy's eyebrows hit her hairline. "Are you serious?"

"Two of the girls out there hate me, the one I took to the hospital, and the one who plays rugby."

"Well, you did threaten to call that girl's mom. What did you do to the other girl?"

Randi toyed with the lid to her Tupperware. Past time to say something to Daisy, but she would rather take an organic chemistry final.

"Well, as strange as it is to me, I'm actually seeing someone right now. And that girl, Angie, has made it clear she wants him. Claimed him like he was a piece of property. He didn't reciprocate."

"Wait, you're seeing someone?"

"Yes."

"Randi! Who is it?"

Randi cleared her throat. "If you start screaming, I'm going to stand up and leave. Not joking, Daisy."

"Shut up, who? Wait…not Buck?"

Randi nodded. Didn't seem right to say it out loud, like tempting fate to call down three lightning bolts on her head.

Daisy screamed. Falling sideways on the grass, she slapped a hand over her mouth. Randi took a deep breath and stared down at the river.

"Oh, my freaking gawd. How long? Why didn't you tell me?"

Randi fully opened her eyes. "Because you're a screamer."

"Is his RV trailer thing still out there? Are you his booty call?"

Randi jerked, a jolt like someone had thumped her on the back. Was she a booty call? That made a kind of sense. Close and convenient. Adjusting her glasses, she took a deep breath.

"I don't do booty calls. Buck seriously injured his leg and asked me to help him out. I guess one thing led to another. So, we're together. For now."

"You're together? OMG I might have to murder you just to see him at the funeral."

"Yeah, get in line. It's like he's the pied piper of women in cowboy boots. Or their cult leader."

His crowd did things like upside down beer bongs—standing on your hands, on top of a keg, while beer shot up your throat. She wasn't just a fish out of water, she was a fish up on a dartboard with drunk girls throwing missiles at her bulging eyes.

"His friend is such a dork. That beefy, bald guy."

"Hugh? He's great actually. For some reason he's stuck on the sociopath I live with."

"Which one? Wait, is there more than one?"

"One sociopath—the short blonde who wants to murder me. I think she knocks him around, and then they hook up. He needs an intervention."

"What? You say the weirdest stuff sometimes. But seriously, I can't believe you haven't invited me to any of the parties out there."

"Daisy, I don't go to parties. And they're on probation after a blowout last summer."

"So, what are you doing tonight? You can't skip Halloween on a Friday night."

"Are those devil horns on your head?"

"Duh."

Randi fingered the pumpkin broach on her bag. "Usually, I eat a few pieces of candy and call it a night."

"You can't do that. This is your senior year and you need to enjoy it before it's over."

Randi rolled her eyes. The last thing Daisy worried about was Randi's enjoyment.

"Come on," Randi said, standing up. "Let's head back to campus."

"Call me if you end up going out tonight."

"Not likely."

"Just promise."

~

THREE HOURS LATER, Luke found her in the library.

"Let's go grab a coffee downstairs," he said, a dimpled grin on his face.

Randi smiled back and glanced away, grabbing her bag to pack up. He was standing a little too close. The situation was suddenly a bit swampy. On the surface he was friendly and easygoing. Did she smile at him too much?

"All right, I'll go down while you buy yourself a coffee and attempt to steal my homework, as usual."

"Not stealing if you give it to me," he said, leaning toward her. She blushed, turning to walk quickly towards the wide stairway down. Was that an innuendo?

Coffees in hand—he'd insisted on buying, and she'd compromised on a small, fifty-nine-cent cup of black—they squeezed into one of the tiny round tables in the café next to a fogged-up window. She inhaled smoky, nutty steam, wrapping her fingers around her hot mug.

"So," he said, eyes twinkling at her over his cup, "what are you doing tonight?"

"Oh, you know, the standard exciting five hours of library study time. I'll head home with Buck at some point when I start feeling guilty about him waiting for me in the parking lot."

He sat back, a surprised look on his face. "Buck Montgomery?"

"Yep. What were his parents thinking? But I have that in common with him."

His eyebrows knit together. "You're dating that guy?"

Was that concern on his face? Or shock because the popular cowboy went for the nerdy library rat? No wonder. It still didn't make any sense to her either.

"Yes, surprisingly. Total mystery why we're together. Never saw myself with someone who wears yoked shirts, or silver belt buckles the size of dessert plates. Did you know those cowboy hats are shockingly expensive?"

"I'm not surprised at all that he likes you. You're about the hottest girl on campus."

She sat up straight in her chair, almost spilling her coffee. The espresso machine behind the counter hissed and whirred, frothing milk. "Hardly," she croaked out. "I'm more like the freakish loner."

"You're not, and I'm an idiot for missing my chance."

She closed her mouth then took a hasty sip of her coffee, burning her tongue. His chance? The conversation was colliding into thorny undergrowth.

That was flirting. And now she would carry around a nugget of guilt for going to coffee with him, which was lame. It was a sneak attack, and she hadn't seen it coming. Sure, she enjoyed his good looks, and, if she was being brutally honest, she got a little thrill out of being friends with an attractive guy. The free music tickets didn't hurt either—his band put on a good show.

"I'm not sure what to say." She needlessly straightened her notebook on the table.

"Hey, but watch out, those country guys are all old school

chauvinists when you get down to it. And assholes. They don't respect women."

Randi adjusted her glasses. She blinked, trying to tamp down the surge of protective indignation she felt for Buck. Yeah, he'd slept around, but from what she understood, he was respectful. How did Mr. Luke Casanova dare to make that criticism? And why the heck was she so worried about it?

"He's a decent guy. Drinks too much, but then I'm an extremely boring person who hates parties and avoids alcohol."

Buck's need to consume alcohol like a duck waddling after pieces of stale bread didn't sit well with her. What was so entertaining about literally poisoning yourself? Currently, he was at a Halloween barbeque party, cutting the workday off early so he could start drinking at two o'clock in the afternoon and call it socializing.

She firmly turned the conversation with Luke back to their coursework, then sighed in relief when he stood up five minutes later.

"Come down to the show tonight," he said. "I'll buy you a big glass of non-alcoholic soda."

**Buck**: Darlin I need you to come save me.

**Randi**: Buck, if you can text, you can walk away from a party. I'm staying at the library.

**Buck**: I'm scared.

**Randi**: You're full of it.

**Buck**: Get over here. Chase off these freaky people.

HER PHONE DINGED with another incoming text.

**Daisy**: It's Halloween! You promised me! I'm about to find you at the library and use my devil prongs on your ass!

Randi covered her face with her hands.

"Hey," Carter walked up to her table, more like waddled. He wore a head-to-toe unicorn costume. Randi sighed, her willpower cracking at the foundation.

"Happy Halloween." Carter reared back, neighing, waving stubby front unicorn hoofs in the air. "What are you up to, Randi?"

Behind Carter, a couple of guys were mock fighting, one of them in an inflated sumo wrestler outfit. It actually looked like a gigantic pillow squeezing his body on all sides, with a little electric motor blowing in air to keep his magnificent puffiness fully inflated. The other guy sported a rainbow rhythm gymnastics getup, using a ribbon apparatus as a fighting tool.

Randi huffed, giddy approval bubbling up in her chest. She had, on a whim, packed a dress in her bag. Just in case. At the grocery store last weekend, she had even sprung for a ninety-nine-cent pack of face paint.

The bars were the problem. They had obnoxious drunk people. Yet, in that moment, she realized she couldn't sit in the library any longer. Also, she probably did need to rescue Buck, whatever that meant.

"I'm shocking myself a little, but I think I actually want to go out."

"Well, yeah, it's Halloween."

"You know what, Carter, when an engineering student

closes his books before I do, point A, I win, and point B, I need sugar."

"I concede." Carter made a formal bow. "You've won the study battle this eve."

"Unicorn talk? Cool." She stood and dramatically shut her books. All three guys whisper-cheered.

"I need to change and grab Daisy. Then onward ho, dudes."

Walking downtown with her motley crew of friends, her grinning face could have belonged to another girl, someone wearing wings. Daisy poked her devil prongs into the sumo wrestler, making him squeal and run down the sidewalk, inflated puffiness seeming to levitate him upwards. It felt like the entire city was out on the sidewalks, capering below the big maples lining the roads, unleashed from adulthood for one night. Randi practically bounced on the pavement.

Carter rammed Mike-the-Sumo-Wrestler yet again as they walked up to the doors of the music hall. His bodysuit farted out air, and they all dissolved into helpless snorting.

"Randi, you came!"

Luke stood by a brick wall, smoking with his bandmates, surrounded by a thick crowd of people outside the music hall. He walked over to her, a dimpled smile on his face.

"Damn, you're dressed to slay. Never seen you without your glasses on."

"Well, face paint and specs don't go together. You guys play soon?"

"Really soon. Hey, it was so good seeing you today. I look forward to our little dates more than I want to admit. It sounds dumb, but getting coffee with you is like the highlight of my week."

Randi put her hand up to adjust her glasses, and gripped empty air. She scratched her nose instead.

"Luke, I'm—"

"Taken," said Buck, making her jump. "She's with me, so back the fuck off."

~

BUCK WATCHED Luke raise his hands up in the air, an expression of bewildered innocence on the scumbag's face. So smug. Buck wanted to punch his oily face.

"All right, see ya, Luke." Randi grabbed Buck's elbow and pulled him away, down the sidewalk.

He stumbled a little. Damn. There was something not right with him. The last five hours were a bad dream he wasn't sure had happened, except it was the only thing that explained how fucked up he was.

Eyes squeezed shut to block out the spinning, he let Randi pull him wherever she wanted. Why were his cheeks numb? Everybody and their sister had pushed alcohol on him all day at that foul party. He'd hardly tasted a beer because the girls were all determined to pour liquor down his throat. Jell-O shots. Tequila shots. Whiskey. Bourbon. Somebody handed him a "Muff Chaser," which he'd passed over to Hugh. The sight of all that whipped cream started a bile blender going in his stomach.

Finally, she was there, looking over her shoulder to eye him sternly then pulling him toward a dark alley in a businesslike way. The whole day he'd wanted Randi with him. By the time he'd texted her to "save him," he was dead serious. Being cold and dismissive to women went against the grain with him. But they'd been like a pack of hyenas, with Angie egging everyone on to new levels of debauchery.

A wild bunch of girls had rolled in during the barbecue. Somebody said they were strippers. Thirty minutes later, they'd been next to naked, humping the air beside the Tiki bar in Jason's shitty backyard. One moment he'd been thinking about leaving, then the next he'd been too messed up to get off the couch. What the hell had happened? Twerking asses, in thongs, had materialized in front of him while he'd sat there, clutching a sick stomach. Ryan, the asshole who'd grabbed Randi her first night at the house, had showed up. Went straight to pound town with one of the crazy girls on the floor in the living room. The spell had broken. Buck had staggered outside, retched, then called Randi.

Now she was here, standing in front of him, dressed like a dangerous witch, wearing a tight burgundy dress and black thigh-high stockings, which made his alcohol-poisoned penis try to rouse itself. Dark purple was painted all around her eyes and on her lips. It was a little frightening. And sexy as hell.

"Hey." She cupped his face in her hands. "You look messed up. Want to go now? Or maybe puke in the alley first?"

He pulled her into his arms, resting his head on top of hers. "I'm mad about that prick. Fucking coffee?"

She rubbed his back. "You're too drunk to be mad." He felt her pull his truck keys out of his pocket.

"You're gonna get it when I wake up."

"Uh-huh. Where did you park?"

"Hugh drove. We can't leave…just got here."

He stumbled away and puked next to a dumpster.

Ten minutes later, he staggered back to her, the roiling in his stomach down to a manageable level.

"Feel better?" she asked him.

"A bit. Gonna grab some water, and whatever you want. Go bounce around on the dance floor."

"Aye aye, captain. Heave-ho!"

He grabbed her hand and drew her toward the door. Tight knots were pulling in his chest—for this girl.

RANDI POKED a straw into Sarah's mouth. Her head lolled to the side, drool dropping from her lips. Her eyes blinked open.

"Hey, drink up some water. We're leaving."

In her inebriated state, Sarah was back to talking to her again—had actually given her a sloppy hug and muttered how happy she was to see "good old Randi." Then Sarah had followed her around with that wide grin on her face. The transformation was completely baffling but something had happened at the barbecue to make Sarah avoid Angie.

Daisy crossed her arms, her foot tapping. "You can't leave now. Luke's band is playing, we just got here."

"Carter's staying, and so is Trish. I think Hugh's still on his feet. Not sure what happened to the cowboy crowd today, but it was lethal."

Buck, his back to the bar, stood on the other side of the music hall, surrounded by women. A crazy group had shown up twenty minutes ago and mobbed him. Last time she'd checked on him, that cocky smile had been stretched across his face, but he'd looked ready to drop. An hour dancing was more than enough time for her.

"Screw those guys," Daisy said. "Buck doesn't need you and he's going to pass out. We're having fun."

Randi had been having fun. At one point, she'd stood next to an elaborate dirty tampon costume and a topless Dolly Parton, the plastic-molded bare breasts on proud display. The kind of weird moment that burns into your memory like a pyrograph etching done with a blowtorch. The music pounded upbeat and joyful, the crowd goofy and enthusiastic. Hugh bounced around in his construction-worker getup, a bloody stick protruding out of his chest.

She didn't recognize herself. It was like all the Buckinduced endorphins had unclogged something in her brain—being out at night, in a crowd, had transformed from sinister to slightly exhilarating.

"Stop yelling at me, or I won't do this again." She spoiled the effect by smiling.

"Hey, weirdo," Sarah croaked.

"You're awake. Dig deep and stand up now. We're leaving."

"Okey-dokey," Sarah slurred. "Got Polly." She patted the parrot puppet strapped to the shoulder of her pirate costume.

Hugh materialized and hauled Sarah up. "We'll be at the door." He grunted, one eye pinched shut from the strain. "Go grab Buck."

Randi pushed her way toward Buck's stool at the bar. A red clown nose perched on Buck's face, his concession to Halloween. One of the girls in front of him laughed, pulling down her low-cut top to show him something on her breast.

Randi saw red. She slowed down. Fists clenching, she was tempted to turn around and leave him.

Angie stumbled toward her, eyes vicious in her square face.

"Hey, freak," Angie said too loud, droplets of spit flying from her mouth, "guess what Buck had earlier."

Randi didn't say anything. She froze, words eluding her. The happiness crumbled—she knew what was coming. Saw it in Angie's triumphant face.

"A lap dance from that girl." Angie sneered at her, gleefully watching her face.

Heads swiveled to stare at them. Randi blinked, the room spinning.

"Oh yeah," Randi said weakly. "How much did you pay the girl to do it?"

"Mm." Angie shook her head, a vindictive smile on her face. "That was all him."

Buck pushed his way over to her, stumbling uncharacteristically—Randi had never seen him so befuddled and wrecked. He slid an arm around her waist in a firm grip. She glared up at him, tears stinging the back of her eyes.

"Goodnight, ladies," he said, and pulled her toward the door.

She walked with every muscle in her body tense. In the lobby, she steered them into an empty corner by a staircase.

"So." She swallowed hard. "Angie tells me you had a lap dance earlier with the girl that was hanging all over you."

"No." Buck rubbed his face.

He leaned against a wall then stared at her, eyes bloodshot in his pale face. He looked like a stranger. Why did he need to drink like this?

"Not a lap dance," Buck said, holding on to one of her arms. "Darlin', those crazy girls showed up at Jason's, I don't know who they are. She tried to dance with me. I told her no thanks then I left. That's how it went down."

"More happened than that." She wiped at her cheeks, violence uncoiling inside her like a hissing cobra, ready to smack his droopy-eyed, dazed face. She stared at him, every muscle clenched. A tide of black grief washed over her and she hunched over, unraveling.

"Hey, stop crying, darlin', please. The day got out of hand. I didn't like it. The whole time I wanted you."

"So, if I'm not by your side like a guard dog, you let women pull down their shirts in front of you and, no doubt, grind on you earlier. I can't do this, Buck! I'm done!"

"No, listen to me. I didn't lay a finger on any of those girls. And I didn't want to. I'm too soft with women, have a hard time telling them to get lost."

She vibrated with rage, everything ruined.

"Let's go home," he slurred, wobbling against his braced hand. "We'll talk more, later. Don't let Angie mess with you. Girl's got it in for you, darlin'."

She took a shaky breath, closing her eyes. She would drive them home.

"Ask Hugh about it." Buck gripped her hand. "He was there."

"No," said Hugh ten minutes later, "Buck didn't get a lap dance. He jumped up and hid behind a couch." He guffawed, scratching his head. "It was weird. We were grilling burgers and betting on corn hole toss. Jason had the blender out, making slushy drinks for the girls, playing some crap pop music. Normal stuff. Out of nowhere, a bunch of strange, unhinged girls show up. Act like they're performing at some dick's bachelor party."

Hugh shook his head, glancing over at Buck sitting in the cab of the truck with Sarah. "He's no cheater…too honest."

The drive back was silent. Icy. She kept her eyes on the road, fuming. Couldn't believe he'd had the nerve to give her a hard time about Luke. About coffee!

She parked the truck in front of Buck's trailer, then realized that her stony silence had been completely ignored. Sarah was snoring softly, her face pressed against the passenger window. Buck's head was tipped backward over the seat, his mouth hanging open.

"Wake up! On your feet, drunks!"

No response. She collapsed forward on the steering wheel. The inside of the cab fogged up with foul breath and the reek of bile. Buck and Sarah had passed out. She was so sick of this. And done. Done.

She left them there. She grabbed her tote, locked up her room, and went into the house to shower. At that moment, numbness reigned, carrying her forward with dry eyes. What had she expected? That Buck, the most sought-after cowboy on campus, would stop flirting and boozing with women who were trying to sleep with him? Change his life for a mousy hermit with no social skills? He drank, all the time. On the weekends he binged until he threw up in the street. It disgusted her. Not something she wanted in her life.

She put on her oldest, ugliest set of sweats in the bathroom. When she opened the back door and stepped outside, Buck blocked the door to her bedroom, hunched over in a rickety lawn chair.

"Buck, I'm too tired to talk. Please leave me alone. I want to sleep by myself."

"Fine," he spat, his face hard. "I plan on a shower in any case."

She waited. He didn't move.

"Good," she finally replied.

"This is bullshit." Buck rubbed his face. "You know what I said when that girl pulled down her shirt in front of me at the bar?"

Randi crossed her arms, but she couldn't resist. "No."

"I said, 'You've pissed off my girlfriend, and I've had about enough. Move away from my chair. Now.' And you know what? I'd been sayin' that to her for the last ten minutes. She was deranged."

He looked up at her, his face haggard. "The thing about being a big man is this…when a certain kind of crazy woman corners you, what you want to do is shove her away, violently. But you can't lay a hand on her, and I wouldn't, no matter how irritating. So, I kept talking about you. Hoped you'd hustle your ass over and help me."

Randi shifted and swallowed. Help him? Her perception of Buck tilted on its axis. A part of the reason he wanted her around was as a barrier between him and crazy women? She wasn't sure what she felt about that.

"Angie gave me some fucking drug-spiked Jell-O shot at

the barbecue, that date-rape shit. Lucky for me, I could move, but I was messed up, seeing stars and stumbling. Been sitting here thinking about it. About what the hell happened. I called Hugh and texted Jason. They agree with me."

She blinked, digesting his words. Buck involuntarily drugged? It defied her expectation of his control and invulnerability in a party situation. Which was asinine. Of course bad things could happen to strong men.

"I'm sorry that happened to you. Are you telling me you couldn't have walked away from those girls at the bar tonight?"

"Darlin', next time I will. I was sick, about to toss my cookies again."

Randi stood still, trying to take it in. He'd been drugged? The muscular man sitting in front of her had needed help. And she had dismissed it.

"Believe me?"

She wanted to argue with him, make him pay. Instead, she took a deep breath. The night had been long enough and she was ready for peace—although she knew she wasn't done thinking.

"You drink too much, Buck, but I'll leave it for now." She put down her tote and helped him stumble up to his feet. "I'm sorry I wasn't there for you. That I didn't take your SOS for help seriously. It won't happen again."

His mouth twitched. "You're my champion."

She sniffed. "Go shower. I'll grab clean clothes for you. I'm not cuddling if there's even a hint of throw up."

# CHAPTER TWENTY

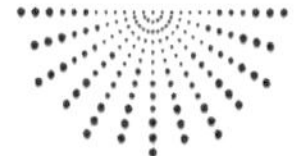

Randi adjusted her thick scarf to cover her chin. The clear, freezing day was poignantly sunny as winter crept inevitably in, reaching icy fingers into the last fall days.

Orange and yellow leaves tumbled down the street and around the farmers market tents. Every available inch of space was occupied by busking musicians, sunflower and dahlia bouquets, tables covered in apples and squash, meat, eggs, pastries, cascades of vegetables, and the trinkets of a hundred hopeful artisans.

Both hands wrapped around her hot cider for warmth, she drew the steaming cup in close to her body. She inhaled, willing herself not to chew on the paper side in anxiety. Finals were less than a month away. Worse were the projects, presentations, and papers she had to finish before then. Too much to do. She was brittle. Stretched dangerously thin.

Buck wasn't happy. He needed her to do time-consuming things like eat dinner with him and not work after seven o'clock in the evening. Her aunt was complaining about lone-liness. She wanted to see her niece more and get to know Buck. Daisy threatened to stalk her. The girl had a piece-of-cake, eleven-credit term and could not wrap her brain around the fact that Randi couldn't spend every weekend seeking out exciting ways to consume alcohol and watch Daisy chase men.

"Randi," Daisy called from a bread stand. "Over here." She resembled a shiny white marshmallow in a big puffer coat.

Randi weaved between the packs of people and fluffy dogs.

"Hey." She pulled Daisy in for a hug. "How are you?"

Daisy shivered. "I'm taking us to lunch. It's too cold out here." She tossed her empty coffee mug in a garbage can. "I'm hungover and need carbs."

"I won't turn down a few carbs."

They landed in one of the boutique restaurants along the riverfront, complete with vaulted ceilings and sprawling crystal chandeliers. Way too dear for her meager budget.

"Randi, you can order more than breadsticks."

"I'm fine, I already ate."

"Yeah? Did you have to serve Buck a three-course meal before he'd let you leave for an hour?"

Randi put her face in her hands. Lately, Daisy's sharp edges had exhausted her. She said through her fingers, "Are you going to harangue me because I won't allow you to buy me another appetizer?"

"Yes. What's with you these days? You're like with him all the time. Cutting out your friendships for a man isn't healthy, you know."

"I barely see him. Twenty-one credits, how often do I have to say it?"

"Really? You couldn't come out for one drink last night?"

"Hey, we were out last weekend on Halloween. Never done that before. I worked at the library last night, by the way. But, wait, I told you that about five times in text messages."

Daisy sniffed; her mouth puckered.

Randi rubbed her temples. "My workload is insane. I'm not sure I'm going to pass everything, but I can't afford this freaking tuition so I have to. I've been sleeping at my aunt's more, just to be able to study at night."

"Oh, Buck works you pretty hard, huh?"

Randi turned bright red thinking about it. The truth was that he did. She'd cut out going to the gym to accommodate the nighttime acrobatics.

"The whole messy house distracts me. I found a bottle of chewing-tobacco spit next to the toilet the other day. Who does that? There's one bathroom and it's making me lose my mind."

"I saw that blush. Tell me about the sex."

"No way, but I will listen to you if you don't gross me out with details. How was your night?"

"Hideous. The girl I partied with was wacked out, like stumbling, from some pills she took and one drink. Her friends took us to this apartment with, like, literally nothing in it but dirty laundry. Then they got stupid stoned and didn't want to go anywhere."

"So, you had an early night?"

"No, I screwed the guy that girl has a crush on, in the laundry room. She's all pissed about it. Whatever."

Randi blinked, trying to take it in. She adjusted her glasses. She needed a book, or a degree in psychology, to help her out here.

Daisy stirred her drink a little violently. "I don't understand why you don't want me to go out to the country house. Your place is fun and filled with hot cowboys."

"Honestly?"

Daisy glared at her.

"Your wild phase is a little terrifying." And she'd probably get mad at her about something and try to screw her boyfriend. "You're a Scorpio, aren't you?"

"Yes. Why? What are you, the weird and prude sign?"

"Um, what? Why am I weird—never mind. My aunt's a Scorpio, too. My point is, you're pinching at me. When a Scorpio gets mad enough at you to pinch constantly, time to duck for cover."

"You're the one treating me like shit. I'm over it."

Randi sat her coffee down. "Look, we've become close friends and I hate that we're fighting, but I'm going back to work."

She pulled a five out of her wallet and left it on the table. The one breadstick in her stomach scraped around like a chunk of asphalt. Hands shoved in her pockets, she walked out the door.

"Hey. Want half a beer?"

Randi forced herself not to stare at Sarah's beer and cringe. The can is cold, she reminded herself.

"Okay. Thanks."

The beer sloshed pale yellow into a glass, exactly how it would appear coming out the other end. Randi shuddered. She was an alcohol snob, but really, there was more to beer than cheap ethanol—like flavor.

"What are you working on?" Sarah leaned over, peeking down at Randi's laptop screen.

"Video stuff for my YouTube channel."

The bonfire crackled in front of them, sending sparks up into the dark. Randi yawned into her hand and closed down her computer. After shooting a video, working at the library, and helping Buck host this barbecue for his visiting brother, she was ready to disappear under her blankets. The social demands with him bordered on exhausting. Massive meals and bigger cleanups.

"You're on YouTube?" Sarah said.

"Yeah."

"Huh." Sarah swallowed down beer. "I watch stuff on there pretty often, I guess. For school."

"It's a great resource."

Sarah was chatting with her, while sober. Randi held very still, afraid the earth would shift beneath her.

On the other side of the fire, Buck laughed. He caught her eye and winked.

She snorted, trying to ignore the champagne-like bubbles in her chest. He lived so easily in their relationship. Happy. She went around with her heart about to burst out of her ribs, her stomach clenching with the certainty that a cliff was coming. Any second now.

Her plan to end the relationship at the one-month mark had sort of fizzled out of her mind. They were there, together since he'd injured his leg thirty days before. *It could work out*, said the confident devil inside her, tossing back her hair. Most of her planned for the fallout, organizing strategies to survive losing him, hopefully with dignity.

His brother Chase watched them, a frown on his face. Chase was stockier than Buck, quieter, and seemed a little cold, mostly to her, but then she wasn't exactly a part of the group. The only person that got past small talk with her, besides Buck of course, was Hugh. And now Sarah too.

Buck's friends over for the barbeque were mostly other graduate students in the agriculture department. A decent group of people, as far as she could tell, and a refreshing change from the wild and loud crowd Angie drank with.

She glanced back at the burning logs, shivering as a chill breeze blew against her neck. The fallout from Angie drugging Buck had been incredibly less than the psychotic blonde deserved. Buck had confronted her and Angie had claimed it was an accident, wasn't her fault, on and on. He'd let it go. Randi clenched her teeth every time she thought about it; she didn't buy for a second that the drugging was an accident.

"Is Angie, um, away for the rest of the weekend?" she said to Sarah.

She fervently hoped so. The house remained actually cleanish, the people present relaxed. No one proposed keg stands. No topless girls chicken fighting on top of drunk guys' shoulders. She didn't twitch like a cat with a rabid bitch nearby.

"Missing her already?" Sarah grinned at Randi. Not Sarah's drunk grin, yet, but edging over into tipsy.

"I'm counting the days of peace. What about you? Jonesing for your binge partner?"

Sarah had distanced herself from Angie over the last week, along with everyone else in the house. She wouldn't say much about the drug-spiked Jell-O shots, except that she'd learned about them after Buck had eaten one. Randi believed Sarah hadn't been part of the drugging plot, but knew she was protecting Angie too.

Sarah snorted and took another swallow of beer. "Angie's with her mother, who's finally leaving her asshole father. Angie's pissed as hell about the divorce. It's been messing her up—she didn't used to be so, um, angry."

"Oh, that's rough." Surprisingly, she could feel a trickle of sympathy for Angie.

"I'm cutting back," Sarah said abruptly.

Randi blinked at her.

"On beer."

"Well, I knew you didn't mean vegetables."

The big grin returned. "Realized I had to either cut back on drinking or cookies, if I want to fit into my clothes. The cookies won. Barely."

"Not blacking out around strange perverts will be a nice bonus…and the perverts you do know."

"Yeah, right." Sarah sighed. "If you weren't such a weirdo, I think I'd like you."

"Call me a weirdo again and you won't touch any more of my cookies."

"Those aren't cookies, they're health biscuits."

"Goodnight, and from now on, enjoy the packaged sugar bombs you call food."

"Hey. Calm down, I did the dishes, remember."

Randi rose from her chair and made her way around the fire to where Buck stood talking to his brother. Immediately, he put his arm around her waist.

"Hey, darlin'."

"Hey, I'm stopping by to say goodnight."

"Is it bedtime already?"

"You don't have to—"

"I'm ready. Chase, I'll see you early enough to snare some steelhead at the coast. Poles are in the truck."

"You will."

"You sure you don't want to come, darlin'?"

"Twenty-one credits, Buck. I'll have time to go fishing when penguins are ice-skating in hell."

Chase looked them over, his eyes narrowed. The guy seriously disliked her.

"Think about what I said, Buck. We need you in the spring, working on the ranch. Finish up here and get back home where you belong."

Her stomach flipped and dropped. The spring? He would be done at the end of winter quarter?

He'd always talked vaguely about it, but had implied he would stay for at least the year. Instead, his truck would haul the trailer east, out of town, before spring break.

"Yeah," said Buck, "I heard you the first time."

Chase took a swallow of his beer. "I forgot to tell you. That girl you were engaged to in Texas, she wants to come for a visit. She and Mom are friends on Facebook."

"All right, night, jackass."

Buck gripped her hand hard, steering them toward his trailer. Her face ached like she'd been slapped. Pebbles of dread, and understanding, filled her lungs. She couldn't get a full breath.

They were at the trailer and Buck pushed her through the door. That was good, it would be better to talk inside. She didn't want a crowd of people witnessing this.

"Darlin', stop freaking out."

"Your brother doesn't think I'm going to be around for long."

"He's an interfering asshole. And jealous. That boy needs a woman before his head explodes."

"Well, he made a point of making sure I realize you're leaving soon, like by spring, only a few months away."

"Five months."

"You've avoided the obvious. Did you plan to text me on your way out of town?"

"No. Calm the hell down, I haven't lied to you."

"Listen, Buck, I'm a crazy person. This thing between us is fun for you, but it will leave me unhinged. Dysfunctional."

"No, it won't, and no, you're not. Reckless on that damn bicycle, yeah, and a little deranged about your work, but not crazy."

"You don't see it."

"You don't let people in easy, I know, but that's not crazy. It makes sense after what you've been through."

"I was in the psych ward—involuntary confinement. They forced me to eat, to keep me alive."

"After your Papa and Mimi died?"

"Sophomore year. It was a full year before I went back and finished my GED. I lost it."

Buck drew her into his arms and held her tight, kissing the top of her head, rubbing her back.

"Too much grief, and only a teenager. Makes sense you went through a rough patch."

"I'm not strong enough to lose people. I need a plan, Buck. You're leaving soon and I can't hang around until you're kissing me goodbye. I can't. We need to end this at Christmas."

"No."

"Then we'll end it now."

He held her tighter, a little painfully.

"Darlin', things are going to change, they always do. I'm not going to live in this trailer behind a rented house for the rest of my life, and neither are you, but we can't let that make us run scared."

She sobbed. "No, Buck, I can't… let me go."

"No way. Hey"—he cupped her face with his hands—"I'm yours, Randi. Don't run away right when it gets good."

She kissed him hard, wrapping her arms around his neck. She felt his body shudder, his mouth bruising against hers. He grabbed the back of her thighs, hoisting her up, and she wrapped her legs around him while he bore her back on the bed.

He jerked her skirt up and yanked her underwear down, his movements fierce. She panted, her knees falling apart, tears still streaming out of her eyes. She loved him. The certainty bludgeoned her. She would lose him, and she couldn't stand it.

His mouth landed on her, on the hot aching part of her that always wanted him. He sucked and stroked her with his tongue, and she was ready to explode almost immediately.

She arched, heat rolling over her, everything else swept away for a handful of heartbeats.

The click of his belt buckle and then his pants were off his legs. He crouched above her, placing her ankles up over his shoulders, sliding deep inside her.

Her head rolled on the pillow. She was so full, the pleasure building in shattering waves. He moved slowly, watching her. She rose against him, wanting it hard and fast, needing mindlessness and oblivion. He grabbed her hands and pinned them above her head. She groaned and closed her eyes, frantic as the pressure built again and again, only to be halted by him pulling back.

"Hey," he said. She opened her eyes and met his glare, intense and focused. "Don't leave me."

She swallowed. And realized she couldn't, not today.

"Say it."

She moaned, thrusting up against him.

"I won't leave."

He let go of her hands, and she grabbed him as he finally pushed them up toward the edge. One of his fingers found her clitoris and rubbed the aching nub. She shattered, falling hard and long, taken to a black, vast part of herself.

He gasped and shuddered above her, pushing harder into her and spasming with release.

They lay unmoving for a long time, breathing, wrapped up together on the bed. She reeled, exhausted. The panic evaporated in the emptied-out, enervated space inside her. The little demon inside her flashed a thumbs-up, sated. Completely in control of the ship.

Buck roused, forcing them both to sit up. He stripped off her dress and guided her into the bathroom. When she was done, they crawled under the covers, his body wrapping around her back.

"We're together now, darlin'. There's nothing crazy about it."

THREE UNFINISHED PROJECT stacks were lined up on the library table like soldiers. Randi glanced at the organized piles, a bead of sweat trickling down her neck. She had to finish her art history paper in the next twenty minutes.

November was nearly over and this Friday turned out to be a linchpin to her entire term. If she survived, and actually finished everything, she'd celebrate for a minute with Buck on Saturday.

She chewed on a cinnamon-flavored toothpick. She wanted hard candy—crunchy, sticky, sugar-coated gravel scouring her insides, keeping her going. Every addict had to face the music, and she'd run out two hours ago.

Buck texted her, again.

**Buck**: Hey darlin, send me a picture so I remember what you look like. And breathe. You're working too hard.

**Randi**: Too busy

But he'd broken her flow. She gulped down the last of the water in her bottle.

**Randi**: Fine. Xx

She sent him a photo of the gnawed toothpick.
"Hey, bitch, I'm going to talk to you."
Randi snapped up, knocking her stainless-steel water bottle sideways off the table. Angie stood in front of her. Dizziness bubbled up from Randi's stomach; the edges of her

vision blurred and bent like she was stuck in a claustrophobic tunnel with a squinty-eyed blonde blocking the exit. That was it; she was not working at this table anymore if Angie knew where to find her.

Angie had stormed back into the house a few days ago after a week-long hiatus out of town, presumably at her mother's house. She'd been drinking even more heavily since returning and everyone was tiptoeing around her. Randi doubted she was still attending her classes.

"Angie, this isn't a good time, or place—"

"No, you're going to fucking hear what I have to say. I am so sick of your shit." Angie stumbled sideways, shooting out an arm to catch herself on the library table. "You turned him against me. I finally figured out what you're doing, Miss Innocent acting like the perfect little wife."

Randi pushed up her glasses. Everyone in the crowded room resembled department store mannequins, unable to do anything but listen to Angie rant.

Swallowing down the lump in her throat, Randi lurched clumsily to her feet. "You need to stop, or I'll be calling library security," she said, keeping her voice low. Angie reeked like the piles of empty beer cans she left all over the house, and was actually swaying. There was no point in trying to reason with her.

"Shut up." Angie leaned forward and knocked a stack of Randi's books onto the floor.

Someone laughed, nervously. Angie whipped around like a cornered bulldog. Randi forced herself to take a breath and move. She stuffed everything in her backpack, hands shaking.

"You're after his money just like all the other prissy bitches. You know his grandparents are going to give him millions and can't resist using your pussy to get some of that."

Gasps from the room. The round-eyed women at the next table leaned over and whispered in each other's ears.

"I have no idea what you're talking about."

A grinding headache drilled into her skull. Her thoughts splintered, unable to encompass the new reality of Buck, incredibly wealthy. The idea had never occurred to her. Stupidly, she couldn't stop picturing his battered green truck, the sides splashed with mud.

"He's from one of the biggest ranching families in the country and you have no idea? You're either lying or stupid."

"Are you done?"

"He's using you. Warming his bed until he leaves. You ruined his last year in college so now he's leaving early. Getting back with his rich girl from Texas."

Angie's rants were so deliberately malicious, grasping at anything and everything to knock Randi down. And yet, the words echoed in her head. On some level, Buck was using her. He belonged on a ranch and she would chase a career in the city. Of course, they wouldn't end up together.

A searing blush burned the skin on her face. Her favorite pen skittered away from her hand, rolling off the tabletop and disappearing under a chair. Everything else was, finally, haphazardly shoved in her backpack. She didn't bother to close the top.

The familiar faces of the other library regulars in the second-floor rotunda, the most beautiful room in the library, became unfocused at the corners of her watery vision. None of them were friends, exactly. More like comrades—they occasionally borrowed office supplies and huddled with her in the library trenches, confident enough in each other to dash to the bathroom without packing up. She took a shaky breath, not making eye contact with any of them.

Angie leaned on the desk, one hand propping her up, glaring down like she needed to catch her balance. Randi slung her backpack over one shoulder and turned toward the arched exit. Truly, she would miss the beautiful space. After this debacle, she wouldn't ever show her face in the second-floor rotunda again.

Walking quickly, she made it halfway across the room before Angie moved. Something crashed behind her. Glancing back, she saw Angie stagger forward from a pile of toppled chairs. People at the other desks stood, backing away.

"Don't you walk away from me, bitch!"

Angie charged her, shoulder down and arm out. She brought to mind a WWF female wrestler—Blonde Menace, or Rabid Cowgirl. All she lacked was a sequined headband. Time slowed, each of Angie's stomps like a thunderclap in the silent room. *Do something!* Where was a cream pie when you needed one?

Her primitive reptile brain switched into gear, swinging her backpack in front of her torso, turning her body away from the oncoming collision with none of the grace of a matador dodging a bull, just the fervent hope for a similar result. Angie pounded forward. The collision came and Randi leaned sideways, flinching as Angie stamped hard on her foot. Even while Angie missed the full-body hit, the backpack ripped out of Randi's grip. Things exploded all over the center of the round room: snacks, notebooks, pens fanning across the carpet. Her poor laptop clunked to the ground ominously.

Angie tumbled down, landing on her elbows, and stayed there. Spitting and shaking her head like a gagging dog, her back arched and vomit spewed down onto the library carpet.

Randi stared at her, shocked. Was anything worth being in contact with this monster? Weirdly, pity unfurled in her chest for the ferocious, wild girl.

She flashed back to the beginning of the term, remembering that the blonde breaking out of a scrum of fighting women, jumping, and dodging the grips aimed at her, had been Angie. She'd powered through the entire rugby field, sprinting over the goal line. The team had hoisted her onto their shoulders, her bloody face photographed for the school newspaper.

Angie was a warrior. Her talents—if she ever surfaced long enough from alcohol to find them—were misplaced in an academic setting. Living past her twenties would be an accomplishment. Perhaps her fixation on Buck had been an unconscious distraction, an obsession that allowed her to forget about her real troubles.

Randi covered her eyes, unable to stop the tears tracking down her burning face. All feeling morphed into grinding misery and desperation to escape any ties to this savage person terrorizing her life.

# CHAPTER TWENTY-ONE

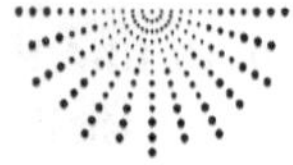

The day from hell wouldn't quit. Waiting out the aftermath was a torturous cherry on top of the disaster sundae, eating up another hour of Randi's work time. Library security ran in, followed shortly by campus security, all demanding answers to the same questions. Finally, Angie left, escorted by a phalanx of tense people in uniform. Randi walked out of the second-floor rotunda then cried for thirty minutes in a bathroom stall.

The hard-won morsel of peace and happiness she'd found with Buck had shattered. It didn't matter that Angie's rant had spun vicious nonsense—or mostly so. How rich was Buck? Why didn't she know more about his life?

She stumbled around, her head rattling like a box with multiple jigsaw puzzles jumbled together inside. Her mind brutally replayed the confrontation with Angie over and over. School deadlines relentlessly loomed, hammering down on her, while questions about Buck clattered on top of it all.

She glanced at her watch; her economics professor had given them until five to turn in their projects, which meant forty minutes left to finish. She shoved up from the table to find water. Her new work spot, the dark back corner of the sixth floor, swirled with dust. The clammy underside of her shirt stuck to her skin when she pulled on it. Stress-sweating. Lovely.

Her phone vibrated with an incoming call in her pocket. After glancing at the screen, she hit accept. "Hi, Aunt Linda, how are you?"

A long pause, broken by a sniffle. *Oh, no.*

"Auntie, what's going on?"

"I broke it off with Jack."

"What? Why?"

Randi sank down, landing on a chair. *This was bad.*

"I'm tired of pretending that we have a future together. I'm an old woman."

"Auntie, he really loves you. Why now?"

"The holidays are coming and he brought up meeting his family again, and wouldn't let it go."

Randi swallowed. "I'm so sorry. Are you working tonight?"

A gasp and swallow. "No," said Aunt Linda.

"I'll swing by in a couple hours."

By nine o'clock, after squeaking by on one project deadline and begging an extension on another, Randi was extremely tempted to stay the night at Aunt Linda's house, but Buck had texted an SOS so she borrowed her aunt's car and forced herself into it. They needed her at the house ASAP, he'd said.

She drove down the long gravel driveway with the window cracked to keep herself awake. Aunt Linda had taken a leave of absence from work, starting about a week ago. She was "fasting," which meant lying on the couch with a flare-up of colitis, starving herself until she broke down and ate crappy fast food. And the cycle continued.

Aunt Linda couldn't be left alone and Buck wasn't going to be happy about it. He acted a little put out with her all the time for working constantly, anyway. They all claimed to hear her when she said twenty-one credits, but apparently the nodding heads signaled non-computing brain space. Her four-way rubber band act was about to snap.

She stopped the car, and a nauseating tide of déjà vu swamped her. Cars were lined up along the gravel road, parked on both sides. Unrolling the other windows, the raucous sounds of hundreds of people swarming her house intensified.

Randi bit her lip. Why hadn't Buck warned her? And where was Trish, who might actually go to jail if the police found out about a raging party out here again? She picked up her phone and dialed.

"Hey, Trish, what's going on? Are you at the house right now?"

"No, and I'm going to sue those backstabbing barf breathers," Trish slurred the words, practically yelling into the phone.

Randi swallowed. "Did you try to send people home? What about Buck? I don't understand how this happened."

"I stayed at school all day, like finishing a late exam, then went for a drink, when I get a call from a friend asking me where I am. She's at my house, at a ten kegger blowout. Did I know Angie's doing a wet T-shirt contest? Freaking-A, Randi!"

Trish dissolved into hysterical laughter, hiccups, and sniffling. "There's no freaking way I'm going back now and risking getting blamed, AGAIN, for Angie and Sarah's bullcrap. And Buck started it. Put a pool table in the barn, bought a bunch of beer, and invited people over!"

Randi bit her lip. She didn't think Buck would start a

huge party. "You're still liable, Trish, for damages, because you're technically the one leasing the property."

A glass slammed on Trish's end. "I hate them. I just paid off their last ticket, five thousand dollars this week. Those A-holes."

The line went dead. Lights came up behind her, cars bumping along the gravel road going way too fast, trucks and dinky sedans stuffed with more people wanting in to the party.

Ten minutes later, she pushed through the crowd on the side of the house. The door to her cabin swung wide open. All the lights were on. She always locked her door, every morning. A volcano exploded inside her. She ran forward, pushing people out of her way. Standing in the doorway, she saw a couple on her bed, other people at her desk, and somebody twirling in her office chair.

"Out," she shouted, hardly recognizing herself. Every muscle in her body flexed. They didn't move, staring at her with their mouths open.

"I'm taking your pictures," Randi pulled out her phone, "and I will be reporting this to the police, if I find a single paperclip missing."

"Wow, bitchy," said the girl at her desk.

"What's wrong with you? You are trespassing in my bedroom. What kind of trash do you have to be to think this is okay?"

"Shit, we're sorry," said the guy, pulling his girl after him. "Door was open—I thought—well, sorry, ma'am. We won't do it again."

"Are you even twenty-one? If you're underage, leave the property now otherwise there will be arrests. A noise complaint has already been called in. The police are coming."

Muttering, they left, arguing amongst themselves about staying. She could only hope they spread the word. The police coming and the filed noise complaint were flat-out lies, but would be true soon enough. Desperation clawed at her—how could she get rid of so many people?

Tracked-in mud clumped on her floor and was smeared across her comforter. She ground her teeth. Her computer sat on the desk, shiny metal exterior gleaming with vulnerability.

She gathered up the beer left on her furniture and a glass pipe reeking of marijuana, and threw it all in the trash bin outside, her hands vibrating then clenching into fists. Music blasted from the house and the barn. Even more people were crowding the property than on that first night she'd arrived. They all looked like kids. Definitely not just the cowboy crowd.

Heat built inside her, boiling, until her shallow pants of breath in the cold air looked like steam escaping. She shoved her way through bodies back into her bedroom. Her door lock was broken, the knob bashed to the side and the screws missing from the base. The last thread of tolerance inside her snapped. She pulled the tablecloth off her nightstand, uncovering her upside down storage totes.

Thirty minutes later, the totes were packed as full as she could stuff them and loaded into the backseat of her aunt's car. She walked into the barn and spotted Buck, lounging next to his pool table, wearing a cocky grin. Suzy, the gal that had slept next to him on their couch, smiled at him, her front pressed against his side. Giggling, she leaned forward, whispering in his ear, and his arm slid around her back.

Randi turned away, thrusting through the crowd to the other side of the barn, towards the old shop room that they'd turned into a study office. Sarah and Buck used the space sometimes, and Randi kept her big school projects stored inside.

She pushed open the unlocked door, stepping over the

padlock on the ground, and flipped on the light. Ears buzzing, she stared. The kaleidoscope image in front of her made no sense.

Not just trashed, it was more like a hurricane had blown up the inside of the office space. She stumbled sideways, thumping against the doorjamb. Her marketing poster and design boards were in pieces, stomped on. Weeks of work torn up and flattened.

Nails were being hammered into her chest. She covered her face, crouching over, trying to breathe through the rattling sobs.

"Shit," said Buck from behind her. "When did you get here? Darlin', I didn't want you to see this. Everything's all crazy tonight."

He put a hand on her, but she lurched away and wiped her face before turning to him. He reeked of beer and cigar smoke. Her stomach turned.

"Buck, I'm leaving, and I don't think I want to see you again."

"What the hell are you talking about?"

"Everything. The drinking, the fact that you're about to move away, that you put your arm around a girl when I walked in here."

"Hey, I was pushing her away."

"Sure. There you are, playing pool, getting drunk, while hundreds of people show up here, mostly minors, and crawl all over my bedroom. My unlocked bedroom. I can't do this anymore. I won't. And I'm sure as hell not sticking around waiting for the police to arrive."

Trembling, she stumbled through the door to the outside. She needed to leave, get in the car, and drive before she turned around and started punching him.

"Hey, listen to me! Angie will be moving out tomorrow. This bullshit was the last straw."

Buck grabbed her arm, yanking her to a stop.

"Let go of me. Now," she snarled the words at him.

He glared at her, shoving his hands in his pockets.

"I'm done. All you do is drink. It's disgusting. And you lied to me about us, you knew you were leaving. You could have told me about this party happening, but instead you tricked me into coming out here. For the last time. You don't respect what I'm trying to do—you can find some other naive idiot to fuck."

They stared at each other. Part of her heart clenched.

Buck's face was hard. She had never seen him so angry. "Are you done? Because I've had about enough. I don't know how you can even think those things, let alone say them to my face. Don't respect you? Wow."

A sob leaked out of her. She swallowed, covering her mouth with her forearm. His jaw flexed.

"Goodbye, Buck." She turned and walked away.

BUCK STARED at the puddle of beer on the kitchen tiles. He hoped Angie would slip in it. Knife-sized pieces of broken glass she could land on lay scattered all over the floor.

The instigator herself stumbled out of her bedroom and staggered into the bathroom. "Fuck," she yelled, and crashed, making a satisfying smacking sound. Hopefully she'd landed ass-up in the pile of vomit and spilled toilet water. Someone had managed to break their only shitter last night.

The door creaked open and Angie came out, clutching her head. Made him feel a tiny bit better. He handed her a cup of coffee.

They drank for a while in silence. He forced himself to take deep breaths.

"Cops come?" she said, picking at her fingernails.

"They did."

"Fuck."

"Yep. Almost went to jail."

"Damn, how bad is it?"

"We didn't get a ticket."

Angie blew out a big breath and she slumped, leaning against the counter. Like that was all it was about. He sniffed, shaking his head.

"Shit, that's good," she said.

"You blacked out?"

A pause. "Yeah, I guess I did. That whiskey was a mistake."

He put down his coffee, and she glanced at him sideways.

"I'm gonna jog your memory. I bought a few kegs of beer for myself and my friends. Planned on drinking those for the next few weeks."

"Shit, Buck, listen, I'll pay you back…"

"Next thing I know, there are hundreds of kids running around out here, most of them minors, taking my beer, breaking our stuff, and threatening to put me in jail if anyone notices the shit show happening all over our house."

Angie rubbed her head, her eyes closed.

It had been a close call. Made his gut clench thinking about it. After Randi had stormed out, he'd switched off the electrical breakers to the house, then the barn too, and had shouted at everyone to get the hell out, the police were coming. When the officers had arrived, two hours later, he'd managed to talk his way out of a crap pot of trouble and gotten away with a warning.

"That was it, Ang. We're all done. Not going to live with you anymore. Trish is talking about a lawsuit and she's serious."

Angie snorted, standing up straight. They stared at each other. She smirked, like she expected him to smile at any moment. Give an ah-shucks and crack a beer. His teeth clenched.

"Shut up, Buck, it was just a party. I'll clean this up, pay for whatever. Y'all are getting stuck up. I know Sarah wants me to stay."

A throat cleared. Sarah stood in the hallway, her arms crossed.

"Ang," Sarah said, "I love ya, but I'm tired of all the fighting with Trish. You still haven't paid her rent for this month. You're out of money."

"Well shit, fuck you too." Angie pushed away from the counter, knocking over a glass bottle with her elbow. It tumbled to the tile floor and shattered. More bottles fell, like dominoes, tipping over the counter ledge and bursting on impact.

The three of them stood around the pile of broken glass, staring at the floor, watching liquid ooze across the tiles. Numb, sick, disgusted. Angie shook her head then gasped, covering her face with her hands.

They were the angriest tears he'd ever had the misfortune to witness. Angie clenched her fists and her face was bright red, her shoulders tensing like she was about to knock over the rest of the glass stacked on the counter.

"Your parents need you, Ang," Sarah said.

Buck put his hands in his pockets. He'd forgotten that Angie's folks were going through a nasty divorce.

"They're assholes," Angie choked out, swiping at the tears on her face. "I don't want to move back home."

He pushed away from the wall and went for the big box of donuts Hugh had dropped off that morning. He grabbed one and, without giving her a choice, placed the sticky thing in Angie's hand. She sniffed, looking down at it hanging from her fingers.

"Here's what's going to happen, girl." He handed the box

to Sarah. "Angie, you're going to do what I tell you to do, and it'll be all right. I'll talk Trish off the ledge. Someday, you'll even thank me for saving your sorry ass."

Angie flung the donut down on the counter and turned her back to him.

"We're moving you out today. Hugh's renting a truck right now and picking up boxes."

"That ass wipe," Angie growled through her heaving and slimy tears.

"You're gonna be gone before Trish gets home," he said, then sighed. Throwing her shit out in the dirt was the least of what she deserved, but she was Hugh's abusive, sort-of girl-friend, so she got donuts, a pat on the back, and shipped the hell back to her parents' house.

He walked outside, letting the screen door slam behind him. Randi had packed up her aunt's car last night. She'd left him. And he was so angry with her he was almost glad.

THE RIVER RAGED along the banks, scraping away grass and rocks from crumbling edges, its current violent and ruthless. Upper branches of submerged trees waved above the water-line like drowning arms.

Randi stared out at the gray water. Colder and colder. If she stood there long enough, the biting air might freeze the sharp-edged tangle of thoughts making her head throb. The churning edges of the river lashed the muddy bank, pounding hard enough to subsume a body and beat it down into the frothing rapids.

Cyclists whizzed by on the bike path, and one person walking about ten little Pomeranians and Chihuahuas wearing tiny four-holed sweaters hustled past, the dog-walker also covered from head to toe to keep out the cold.

Randi's breath puffed out in white clouds. She couldn't convince herself to move.

**Buck**: I miss you.

His text, at seven-thirty in the morning, had sent her into a tailspin, knocking her out of the angry, but functional, place she'd been. She resisted the urge to take her phone out and glare at it again. Nothing had changed. Definitely not Buck. Or her, for that matter.

The to-do-list voice in her head, that she imagined as a plump imp with purple glasses, was pacing back and forth, muttering things like *I told you so*, and *How could you do this to us?* Mountains of projects required hours of drudgery before she could finish the term. But she'd walked out of the crowded coffee house and come down to the river. To stare at the cold water.

"Hey! Randi!"

A cyclist screeched to a halt in front of her. She recognized that huge backpack. Carter pulled down the scarf covering his face, smiling.

"Hey, haven't seen you in a while. Was actually thinking about calling you, if that's okay, since you weren't in the library all weekend. I mean, at least that I know about. Also, I don't have your number. Did you change tables or something?"

"Hi, Carter. I'm not studying in the library anymore."

He leaned his bike against a park bench and walked closer to her. "You look a little cold. Are you, um, all right?"

She swallowed, her throat tight. Saying it would make it more real.

"Buck and I broke up a couple nights ago. The aftermath is a lot harder than I thought it would be."

He was the first person she'd told. She blinked, trying to get rid of the stinging in her eyes.

"Oh," he said, staring down at the ground, hands twitching in his pockets. "Wow, I mean, didn't see that coming."

"I did." She'd planned for it, at first.

Googling Buck's family had been a mistake. The magazine articles and gossip columns on the Montgomery family made her realize the magnitude of her oblivious foolishness. Every other girl in his orbit, probably on campus, knew that his family was ranching royalty and one of the largest landowners in the country.

Her mother had died a drug addict. Her father had gone in a military accident before she was born. She'd lost her grandparents and gone crazy. All of it molded her into the simulacrum of a woman, hollowed out and hard. There was no absurd corner of the universe where she ended up with someone like Buck.

Carter scratched his chin and looked at her like she was a badly built computer he wanted to fix. "Let's go find a hot drink," he said. "Right over there at that restaurant."

"I can't."

He didn't say anything, just bent over to lock his bike to the park bench.

"My ex broke up with me in September," he said, standing up. "I almost took the term off… Shopped for plane tickets to Europe, and rail passes. Needed to go and walk around by myself. Probably should have done it."

He took her freezing hands, rubbing them between his gloved ones. She gulped. Gawd, she didn't want to cry.

"Come on inside for a minute."

She let him pull her toward the big condo building with restaurants on the main floor. The heated indoor air burned her cheeks. She sat down at the first empty table she saw and stared at her hands.

She missed Buck. Three days ago, they'd slept together, even though he'd been angry that she wouldn't make time to meet with him during the week. Yeah, she'd admitted, she'd avoided him. Too much work. Then she'd discovered that, even half dead with exhaustion, she could still take a bliss rocket ride. Three times.

A bowl-sized mug of hot cocoa landed in front of her as Carter settled in the other chair at the little table.

"Thank you," she said, holding her fingers in the steam rising above the mug. "Chocolate makes everything better."

A relieved smile broke out on his face. "Anything you need, Randi, just tell me."

They sipped their drinks for a while. Of course, his had sprinkles.

"I'm not much of a talker," she said, "about feelings, but I'm glad I told you. I think I needed to say it out loud."

He fidgeted with his napkin and looked up, taking a deep breath.

"I know it's too soon to ask this, but I feel like I'm always missing opportunities, especially with you." He swallowed, smiled, looked extremely uncomfortable, and flushed.

"Come to dinner with me," he said. "Not tonight, after term ends, or when you're ready. As a friend, with no pressure or strings. I mean, I like you, and I'm happy to be your friend and to wait until you might be ready for something more."

The image of Buck with his arm around that girl burned through her mind for the hundredth time.

Carter tapped his fingers against the table, and she realized she'd been staring at him.

"Yes," she said, then hated herself when his face broke out in an ecstatic smile.

RANDI PEDALED the last block to her aunt's house, her bike's light barely penetrating the dark. Cold rain splattered on her face. Of course, she'd forgotten her hat that morning.

During her days, she ran from place to place, darting to her next class, frantically submitting papers and turning in projects, stumbling with constant exhaustion. Finally, when her head at last sank onto a pillow, Buck burst into her thoughts like a burning shot of caffeine. Her nights were a blur of agonized wakefulness.

She pushed the dripping hair out of her eyes. The paralyzing mourning of her failed relationship with Buck needed to end. Her well-being, not to mention work, future, and sanity, all depended on her moving on.

Aunt Linda's house sat dark in the overgrown gardens around it, except for the dim porch light left on. A tall shape shifted on the tiny concrete entryway step, the only place with a sheltering overhang. Leaning against the wall stood Buck.

Randi's heart froze in her chest, then started beating again like she was a marathon runner crossing the finish line. Her hand squeezed on the brake, and she jolted to a stop, bracing herself on the handlebar.

He straightened up, and she forced herself to awkwardly lurch off the bicycle and walk up the short driveway.

"Jesus," he said, his voice hard, "do you have to ride that at night in a rainstorm?"

"What are you doing here?" She didn't want this. Her head and hands were shaking.

He huffed. "Get in here out of the rain."

When he reached toward her, she took a step back, stumbling into her bike.

"No, Buck, don't touch me. Please."

He stared at her like she was a crazy person. That was appropriate, she was a few breaths from leaning over and vomiting on Aunt Linda's azalea bushes.

"Fine." A muscle clenched in his jaw. "I can't think when you're standing there like a drowned cat."

She didn't move. "I have to go inside."

Buck glared at her, his face bleak. "Darlin', you don't need to do this. That party was a shit show that came out of nowhere."

Her heart was a battering ram. Black edged in around her vision.

"I'm dating Carter now," she said, blurting it out, spit and rainwater flying from her mouth.

The bag in his hand dropped to the ground with a thud. His face twisted into a sneer. "That didn't take long."

She looked away, hot tears mixing with the cold rain on her face. Her ribs constricted like something had kicked her in the chest.

He cut across the yard rather than walk past her. She stood frozen, staring at the side of the house. A moment later, his engine revved and he drove away.

Her empty stomach heaved acid up to her throat. She crouched down, spitting into the garden bed next to the front steps.

A white bag caught her eye. Buck had dropped it. Inside were two take-out burritos from the local place. Her face scrunched up as she stared at rainwater soaking into the paper wrapping.

Next to the bag, an ivory envelope had landed in a puddle of water. She wiped it off on the inside of her jacket. The soggy envelope read "Randi and Family" on the front. A thick invitation for a Christmas party slid out in her trembling fingers.

She stared at it, shaking her head, gulping sobs.

*Dear Randi,* read a handwritten message, inked in big loopy cursive on the back of the cardstock. *Buck has told me so much about you. I know he's having a hard time convincing you to travel out to the ranch. Please come, I want to meet you very much. With a hopeful heart, Buck's mom, Dolly.*

# CHAPTER TWENTY-TWO

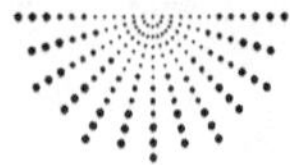

"Hey! Crazy girl!"

Randi startled, knocking her steel water bottle off the concrete bench. Sarah plopped down next to her, in her usual outfit of blue jeans and a flannel button-up, a big grin stretched across her face.

"Hey, um, drunk girl," Randi said, scanning the area around Sarah for other blondes. Finals week on campus stayed relatively quiet, but Randi found the wide-open spaces made her more tense, not less.

Sarah huffed. "You know what, I'm takin' a breather. Had to sober up for the final stretch."

"Huh," was all Randi found to say.

"Trish and I were talking about you last night. Wondered when you were coming back."

Randi blinked, then reached up to rub her face. The exhaustion hung over her constantly, as oppressive as a cloud of cold gray fog.

"Sarah," Randi said, "I'm not coming back. I moved out."

"You still have a bunch of stuff in your room."

"Well, yeah, I'm paid through to the end of the month, so

I'll clean out everything when you're all home for Christmas."

"Oh."

The silence stretched out. Sarah slumped forward, picking at a loose string on her jeans.

Randi cleared her throat. "So, what happened with the big party, were you lucky with the police?"

Sarah glanced sideways at Randi. "Buck didn't tell you?"

Randi's head jerked back. "No, of course he didn't. We're not together anymore."

Sarah sighed. "Oh shoot, he didn't say anything. I mean, we don't see him much anymore, and he's grumpy. Guess that's why."

Randi flinched, then swallowed hard. She looked up at the sky filled with fluffy clouds.

"Anyway, yeah, we did get lucky with the police," Sarah said. "Buck took care of it. Kicked all those kids out right before the coppers showed up, then pulled his good-old-boy charm on their butts."

"Oh. That's good."

"It's been real quiet ever since."

"Angie in jail or something?"

Sarah grinned. "What, you don't even know that? Buck kicked Angie out the next day. She's back in Baker City."

"She's gone?"

Sarah shoved Randi in the shoulder. "Don't look so happy."

"Wow." Randi sniffed, forcing her cold hands deeper into the pockets of her trench coat.

The campus bells started ringing, signaling the end of the lunch hour.

Sarah stood up. "I'd better head toward my last final," she said.

"All right." Randi forced a smile on her tight face. "Well, good luck…with school, and the healthy living."

Sarah smirked at her. "You're such a mother hen."

Randi adjusted her glasses. "That's the most absurd thing you've ever said."

"Don't be too hard on Buck. He's a pretty sad cowboy without you around."

~

HER PHONE WAS RINGING. She reached for her bedside light, eyes sealed shut. The term was done, finally, and she had ten days of sleep to catch up on. If it wasn't an emergency involving dead bodies, she might turn it into one.

The caller ID flashed Daisy's name. Randi blinked, sitting up. Her and Daisy hadn't spoken for weeks, not since Randi had walked out on their lunch together.

"Hey, Daisy, are you all right?"

Nothing. Randi turned up the volume on her phone. A premonition tightened her shoulders. She could hear muffled male snickering, or grunting. Was this a butt dial?

Then a gasp. Definitely Daisy—she was next to her phone but sounded like she couldn't breathe.

Randi shot out of bed. "Daisy," she yelled into the phone. "Can you speak? Where are you?"

"Fuck," a male voice muttered close to Daisy. The line went dead.

Randi froze, her stomach twisting. She stared at the dark screen, panting; Daisy was not okay. Wrenching herself into motion, she called back Daisy's number, putting the phone on speaker while she grabbed for her shoes. The call went to voice mail.

She called again, snatching her aunt's car keys from the

wall hook, flying out the door with a jacket in her hand. Her untied shoes slid on the icy path to the driveway.

Halfway down the road in front of Aunt Linda's house, she remembered to buckle her seat belt and turn on the headlights. Her phone rang. She slammed on the brakes, skidding sideways.

"Daisy! Where? Where are you?"

A pause on the other end. "Darlin', this is Buck," he said, his voice slurring the words. He cleared his throat. "Daisy okay?"

Randi held the phone away from her head. There was Buck's name on the screen. She didn't have time for this.

"Buck, I have to find her. She called me, but couldn't speak or breathe well. I heard some guy with her, and then he hung up. She's not answering. How do I locate her phone? Do you know about any parties tonight where I could look for her?"

He fired off a few questions. "Text me her number and email, Facebook, everything you have. I'll call you back. Wait for me."

Randi called the police while she drove. Twenty minutes later a detective spoke to her. She answered all of the officer's questions, her leg shaking with impatience.

She shot down the road, pushing her speed as high as she dared.

Thirty minutes after Daisy's call, she pulled into the parking lot of a convenience store close to campus. The core of the party zone surrounded the little all-night shop, including the fraternities.

Another ten minutes crawled by. *Too long...* In another five minutes she would start searching, house by house if she had to. She paced back and forth under the fluorescent lights glaring down on the shop entrance, sipping a cup of sugary coffee. Young guys and giddy girls streamed in and out, carting out cases of beer or canned energy drinks. She resisted the urge to grab them and shake them until they told her where the parties were.

Her phone buzzed. Buck.

"Hey," he said, "I've got something. She posted her location on her Facebook page three hours ago. There's some other stuff we could do, but it takes longer."

"Where?"

He paused. "Darlin', you can't go charging in alone. I'll be there in five minutes."

"Dammit, Buck, tell me right now!"

He hung up.

She closed her eyes, massaging her forehead with the knuckles on her clenched hand. In minutes, he would be there.

Treacherously, the little devil inside her batted her eyelashes, clutching her hands beneath her chin.

She looked down at her ragged pajama pants, mangy sneakers, and her aunt's grubby yard work coat covered in cat hair. The snarled lumpy knot of hair tied back from her face was pulling, making her scalp twinge. Nothing about her appearance would inspire desire. That was good. Definitely.

Buck and his friends walked up with hard red faces, dark cowboy hats perched on their heads. Four guys, Buck and Hugh in the front, and it looked like Jason, Trish's ex, in the back. The other guy she didn't recognize.

All drunk.

Randi swallowed. They were holding themselves like boxers about to jump into a pit with the guy who had robbed their grandmas.

"We'll pile in your car, darlin'," Buck said. "It's the Beta house about a mile away."

She forced herself not to stare at him. He didn't give her

the same courtesy. He leaned on the car's center console while she drove, putting his shoulder next to hers.

"You call the police?"

"Yes. They're busy, though, and the officer leveled with me about not having time. I'd call them now, but I don't want to be told not to go in there as soon as I find her."

Buck grunted agreement. "We'd rather not deal with the police tonight. They make Hugh nervous."

"I ain't crazy about 'em," Hugh said.

The back of her neck burned. There was way too much masculine intensity and bubbling testosterone in the car.

"Guys," she said, "I can tell you've all had a few, let's not turn this into national news, if we can avoid it."

Grunts from the backseat. "Whatever shit did this needs to learn a few things," Hugh said, angrier than she'd ever heard him.

"It could be more 'n one," Buck said, the Texas accent strong in his voice.

"Fucking frat guys," muttered the guy she didn't know.

They found the fraternity house—a huge colonial-style mansion with tall white columns and lion statues by the door. Randi illegally parked in the crammed parking lot behind the house and put on her hazards.

Her heart drummed in her chest. The dark house sat strangely quiet for a supposedly massive party night. The double front doors had been left cracked open. She pushed inside, hope sinking at the lack of people, and they all stepped onto the white marble floors of the spacious balconied foyer. No party didn't bode well for finding Daisy.

The inside of the fraternity house displayed battered grandeur. The old oak balustrade on the grand staircase was noticeably gouged and scraped, the red carpet on the steps littered with trash. Abandoned keg cups lay scattered over the dull white marble floor.

"Hello!" Randi yelled. "I'm looking for a lost person."

A head popped out of a bedroom on the balconied second floor.

"What the fuck do you think you're doing in here?" a stout muscular guy called down at them, stepping out to the upper railing. Other guys piled out behind him.

"I'm searching for my friend, who called me unable to speak. She posted this location earlier tonight."

The guys on the balcony froze, tense looks on their faces.

"Let her search, you fucks, or come down here and stop us," shouted Hugh. He stepped forward, all flexed up, his burly frame bulky with muscle.

"Hold up, Tank," Buck said. "Give the guys a chance to explain."

Upstairs, the fraternity brothers argued with each other, one of them waving his hands around. Randi's stomach clenched. She couldn't make out their words, but the intensity was obvious. They knew something.

"Tell me where she is," Randi yelled, "or I'm calling the police in right now!" She was about three seconds from charging up there herself.

"Wait," called down the short guy with dark hair. "Relax, we didn't do anything to your girl, but I think she's here. Come upstairs and I'll show you."

"Is she okay?" Randi shouted, racing up the stairs.

"Willy found her in the supply closet," the short guy said, meeting her at the top of the stairs. "He heard a phone ringing, so he opened the door. Some fucker was in there with her. Nobody knows him. He ran out of here."

"I knocked him," said Willy, pushing bright red hair out of his eyes, "but the shit kneed me in the groin."

They pointed to an open door in the middle of the hall. Randi ran. She skidded to a stop in front of a spacious janitorial room, the size of a walk-in closet. Daisy lay on the floor, sprawled out oddly, a blanket covering her. She sank down next to her, calling her name and feeling for her breath.

She was breathing but unresponsive. Randi peeked under the blanket and saw that Daisy's pants had been pulled down to her knees, her shirt and bra shoved up to her neck.

Buck stood in the doorway, arms crossed, facing away. The other guys stayed out of sight. Randi wiped the hot tears off her face, gasping, trying to calm down enough to speak.

Black swirled in her vision and she reached out to put her hand on the wall. *No, no, no* repeated in her head, cutting through the layers of her brain like an expanding bullet. Not bright and vibrant Daisy, *no, no, no…*

"Buck," she said, her voice hoarse, "I want to talk to that guy, Willy."

She walked a little way down the hallway with him. He was red-faced, his freckles dark on his strained face.

"Hey," she croaked out, "tell me what you think happened in there. Everything. She'll need to know."

Willy swallowed. "He had his pants down and his dick out —sorry, I mean his, uh, penis."

"Just tell me. I don't care what words you use."

"Okay." He cleared his throat. "His pants were down, but still over his knees. I think I got there in time. I mean, the fucker had her exposed, but her pants were still too high, I, um, noticed." He sniffed, looking away.

"Why didn't you call the police right away?"

He blew out his breath. "Yeah, we fucked up. I told the guys first, the leadership. Everybody panicked. Our frat is in serious shit, no matter what. They cleared the party out first and nobody wanted to touch her… Fingerprints, and shit. I put a blanket on her. It's only been about an hour."

She walked back to the group of guys. The cowboys and fraternity brothers eyed each other belligerently, not saying much.

"I'm calling nine-one-one now," Randi said.

"Fucking hell," one of the frat guys yelled.

"Watch your damn mouth," Hugh yelled back.

"I talked with Willy, and hopefully she wasn't raped, but I think she was drugged."

She spun away from them and dialed, then was put on hold.

Buck interrupted her pacing. "Darlin', we're gonna go. We'll make it more complicated and you're all right here on your own. Call me when you get to the hospital."

There would be no calling him. She stared at the dark blond stubble on his cheeks, blinking her eyes. "Thank you, Buck," she whispered, "for coming to help."

The corner of his mouth cocked up in a grin. "I'll always help, darlin'."

Then his arms came around her, pulling her into his warm body. She gasped. The scrape of his stubble on her cheek sent shivers down her spine. A little warmth blossomed in her body, and a painful ache familiar and dreadful. She couldn't resist putting her forehead down against his chest, letting him kiss her temple, letting him hold on to her for too long.

"Hello, what's your emergency?"

She pulled away, wiping her wet face on the sleeve of her coat, and walked a little way down the empty hallway. She answered all the dispatcher's questions as the cowboys moved down the stairs, their voices a deep rumble fading away until the front door of the frat house clicked closed behind them.

Hours later, the hospital confirmed that Daisy had been drugged but not raped. Randi stayed with her for the next week.

~

Two weeks later, Randi carried the refilled bowl of popcorn back to the couch and plunked it down on the coffee table. It was Christmas Eve and they were watching *The Godfather Part II*, because they wanted no happy endings. Or romance. Or cuteness.

"I hate Christmas," said Daisy, wiping at the mascara smudges under her eyes. At least two pounds of tears saturated the throw blanket tucked under her chin. Randi met Aunt Linda's eyes. Whatever Daisy needed, they were failing.

"Ladies," said Aunt Linda, pausing to gulp down half a glass of wine. She hiccoughed—had she finished the second bottle? "Ladies," she said again, "this will not do."

Randi rubbed her face. Her ability to pretend to be okay not only missed the mark, it was buried in the weeds. Finals were done, she'd passed her classes, two sponsors had emailed her about yoga, and she wanted to hide beneath her blankets and stay there for a month.

"I'm sorry," said Daisy, starting to cry again. "I shouldn't have come..."

"No, stop," Aunt Linda said, raising a finger like a general with an insubordinate. "Daisy, I'm extremely grateful you're here. I need your help with the lump of misery over there."

They stared at her. Randi stopped rubbing her forehead. The numb deadness inside her glanced up, hardening to face this new assault.

"Lump of misery is probably a better name than Randi," she said. Then shoved a handful of popcorn into her face.

Daisy sat up straighter. "What's the matter with her? Wait, is it Buck?"

Randi's heart clenched, viciously. "Can we leave it be? I don't want to talk about it."

"I thought he was home for winter break. You broke up?"

Randi's head fell back against the sofa. At least Daisy had stopped crying. *Masterful move, Auntie.*

"She broke up with him," Aunt Linda said, standing up with her wine glass dangling precariously from one hand. "And I still don't understand why."

"Randi," Daisy said sharply. "Did you lose your mind?"

Randi jerked, then shot to her feet and across the room. She clenched her teeth. It was so like them to poke at her, a couple of bored kids with long sticks.

"Hey, honey," Aunt Linda said, "I only want to try to understand."

Randi turned to face them, only realizing she was crying when the hot splatters dropped off her chin.

"You're one to talk," she said, wiping her face on her sweatshirt. "You broke up with Jack for no good reason."

Aunt Linda stood still, staring at the woodstove. "Maybe so, I can be a stubborn old bitch sometimes."

"Linda," Daisy said, her eyes round. "I would never think of you that way."

"But," Aunt Linda said, "I'm not letting you off so easy, Ms. Randi. I found this."

Aunt Linda turned and plucked up a familiar ragged white envelope from the cluttered shelf next to the fireplace. It was the invitation from Buck's mother to the Christmas party at the ranch. Aunt Linda handed the heavy stationery over to Daisy.

"A Christmas Day shindig at the White Horse Ranch," Daisy read, her voice rising with each word, "come glitter, sparkle and be merry—food and drink provided. Randi, what are we doing here? We all have to go!"

"Daisy, calm down. The ranch is a seven-hour drive and there's no way I can go. Buck and I broke up."

"Hey, put on your big-girl underwear," Daisy said, rolling her eyes. "That man is a prince. He's invited you to a Christmas Ball."

So easy for them to talk when they weren't contemplating

total humiliation for themselves. She pressed on her cheeks, trying to dislodge the stuffiness behind her nose.

"Did he cheat on you?" Daisy said.

"No."

"Did you realize he has a gambling addiction?" Aunt Linda asked, cocking her head.

"No!"

"Is he actually gay? Oh, my gosh," Daisy said, fanning her face with a chocolate bar wrapper. "I just flashed back to *Brokeback Mountain*. RIP Heath Ledger."

"No," Randi said, sinking into the overstuffed chair temporarily free from cats. "He drinks too much."

Daisy scoffed. "Compared to you, which is, like, meaningless."

Aunt Linda put her glass down, her other hand covering her heart. "What happens when he drinks too much?" she said in a quavering voice.

Randi blew out her breath, crossing her arms. "He lets horny women flirt with him," she said, belligerently.

They stared at her. Daisy started tapping her foot. "Then he goes home with you?"

"Look, he and I, we don't fit. He's from some rich and famous ranching family. I'm a poor nobody. He'll be done with graduate school in less than three months and be gone. I don't want to wait around to get dumped and be broken."

"So, you broke up with him first?" Daisy said, her face horror-stricken.

Randi stood up again, unable to stay still. She paced back and forth.

"Randi, honey," said Aunt Linda, "I'm sorry to say this, but you sound like a coward."

"Uh, yeah," said Daisy.

Randi flinched and then walked out the back door.

Ever since seeing him at the fraternity house, a persistent

devilish voice in her head, from the box she'd locked it in, shouted that she was making a mistake. It was over, though. Buck wouldn't wait around for her. No doubt he'd made plans with the girl from Texas who his brother liked so much.

Running into Sarah on campus, hearing about the day after the party, had been like sticking needles into her skin. She'd realized how much Buck had been trapped out there with that crazy party. And, Aunt Linda and Daisy had confirmed her fears about herself. She might be a blockhead, but she was definitely a coward.

The door opened behind her, and she wiped the tears off her face as Daisy walked up to her holding a jacket.

"Here, it's freezing tonight."

Randi sniffed. "Thanks."

"I can't believe I didn't know you and Buck broke up."

"You had a lot going on."

Daisy shivered, stuffing her hands in her pockets. "I'm sorry, Randi. I'm sorry about how I acted in the restaurant right before we stopped talking. This whole year I've been a self-absorbed mess. And you've been the best friend I ever had." She choked on a sob. "I'm so sorry."

Randi blinked, the iceberg in her chest melting. She held open her arms. "Thanks. I'm not sure why you like a boring, sober coward like me, but I'm glad you do."

Daisy snorted, pulling away to wipe her face on her sleeve. She shuddered in a breath. "What happened at the fraternity house...you saved me. That pervert was about to rape me, but you kept calling, and he got caught."

Randi kept an arm around her. "I'm so sorry it happened."

Daisy gulped, her hand over her face. "I was lucky...and I'm still so— I hate myself."

"It wasn't your fault. Hey, you're going to get through

this. And they caught that asshole, he's the one who should feel ashamed."

"You stayed with me at the hospital, drove me home. You handled all the police stuff, even my mother." She broke down into sobs. "I would have lost it," she choked out.

They stood there for a few minutes, arm in arm, looking out at a bright moon in the clear night sky. Some little hole in Randi mended that she hadn't realized was there. Daisy wasn't the best friend she'd expected, but here she was, as close as a sister.

"You're special," Daisy said, wiping her face. "Buck's a lucky man."

Randi scoffed. "Lucky to have escaped. Someone told me I'm a mother hen."

"Ha! That's so true."

"I don't see it."

"Hey, Randi?"

"Yeah?"

"We're going to that party."

# CHAPTER TWENTY-THREE

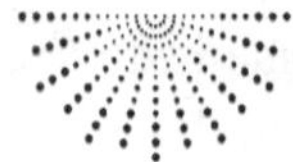

Randi woke up early and stared at the ceiling, wide awake. She got out of bed then tried doing yoga. After five minutes she rolled over and started push-up sets. The cats glared at her reproachfully from the sofa, curled up around a sleeping Daisy.

Two hours later, Aunt Linda shuffled out of her bedroom, wrapped in a fluffy blue bathrobe, one hand over a face a little haggard from too much wine. "We've got to get on the road," she croaked, reaching for a mug in the cabinet. "Research gas stations, honey, I'm not sure what's open on Christmas Day."

Daisy stirred on the couch, one hand pushing at the cat sprawled out on her neck. "Is it morning? Crap."

Randi blew out a breath, watching her aunt pour a cup of coffee. "Better make some sandwiches, hon," Aunt Linda called over her shoulder. "We won't find much today."

Daisy sat bolt upright. "Clothes! We have to go by my apartment!"

"Stop." Randi paced back and forth in the kitchen. "This is crazy and I can't go to his parents' house. I haven't spoken to him in two weeks. What if he's there with another girl or throws me off the property? We don't have anywhere to stay."

Aunt Linda's coffee mug thudded down on the kitchen counter. "Do you want to live the rest of your life wondering what if? Trust me, not fun."

Randi bit hard on her bottom lip and gripped her hair.

"Come on, Randi. Road trip," Daisy said. "Road trip. Road trip."

Aunt Linda joined in the chant. Randi swallowed, glaring up at the ceiling. Inside, her heart was having a broadsword fight with her brain. She picked up the invitation, looking again at the handwritten note from Buck's mother.

"Fine," she said, then slapped a hand over her mouth. Aunt Linda and Daisy cheered.

It took them three hours to start on the highway headed east. Randi kept looking at the clock on the car dash as if it might say something different. They wouldn't be there until after seven p.m., and that was if they drove without stopping. You couldn't show up that late on Christmas Day.

"We're too late," she said, for the fifth time. There was no use arguing with Google. Dirt roads must be involved, and of course the mountain pass, not to mention three hundred and seventy-one miles.

"Honey, it'll be fine." Aunt Linda waved her hand around like she could waft away doubt. "And I think Google is wrong about something. It's not that many miles."

Five hours later, they all staggered out of the car and walked stiffly to a general store on the side of the mountain highway.

"That road had too many curves in it," Daisy said, holding her stomach.

Randi stared at the two sets of doors in confusion. Aunt Linda jiggled the first set, shrugged, and walked down to the other entrance. A long row of gleaming Harley-Davidson motorcycles leaned on their kickstands, parked in a line along the building's front.

The swinging double doors opened into a hazy bar. Twenty eyes examined them. The bikers all wore black leather, their long-bearded grizzly faces practically replicas of ZZ Top.

Daisy giggled. Randi took a step forward, scanning for a bathroom. A long oak bar stretched down the length of the room, pool tables lined up along the other side, and flat-screen televisions played a football game.

"Gotta buy somethin' to use the can," said the gravel-voiced woman behind the bar.

"Coffee please," croaked out Randi.

She slid onto a barstool and put her head in her hands. Aunt Linda and Daisy ordered before dashing for the toilet. Burnt vegetable oil permeated the air. Her stomach clenched in knots; eating was not happening.

Buck hadn't texted her back. The entire trip was a complete, unmitigated disaster. They were going to show up at his parents' ranch, in the middle of unpopulated eastern Oregon high desert, at the end of the party, a total surprise, leave in humiliation, and have to drive another three hours to find somewhere to sleep.

A burly man sat on the stool next to her and made throat-clearing noises from behind his beard. "That's a glum face for such a fetching gal. Tell Old Mack what I can do to cheer you up."

Randi turned off her phone. Staring at the blank screen wouldn't change anything.

"I'm driving almost four hundred miles today to chase after my ex-boyfriend. But I realized, one, he doesn't want me, and two, I'm making a stupid fool of myself." She cupped her hands around the mug of hot coffee. "So, please, help me convince my aunt and best friend to turn this disaster around and head home. I have a chocolate bar waiting for me on my nightstand that'll cheer me right up."

Old Mack sipped his beer, looking at her contemplatively. "One time I chased after a woman. She pulled a shotgun on me." He chuckled. "Hell of a night. We got hitched for a few years after that. Love is dangerous shit. You love this fella?"

Randi sniffed, pinching her nose. "Yeah," she said thickly through her clenched throat. "I do."

A watermelon-sized hand thumped her on the back. "You gotta go," said Old Mack. "If it don't work out, come back here and I'll get you drunk. We ain't pretty, but we know how to party."

Rigid with nerves, her hands clenched the steering wheel as they pulled back onto the highway. The open road twisted away in front of them, winding through the yellow high desert like a snake. Ahead, the Steens Mountain lay like a slumbering giant, mauve, white, and ultramarine blue. Daisy and Aunt Linda, buoyed by whiskey shots with the bikers, sang along to Christmas carols on the radio.

They traveled into tiny Burns as the sun set, the last place to buy gas for a hundred miles. Randi shivered, pulling her coat tight around her as she ran for the bathroom. When she glanced in the mirror, haggard eyes gazed back. She'd dropped weight lately, which made her bony, pale, and hollow-eyed. Who was she kidding? This would end badly.

What the hell was she going to say to him? *Hey, I was just on my way to Idaho...Merry Christmas. By the way, I'm a lost sad sack...*

It didn't matter. Her dignity didn't matter. He was worth it. Or rather, her future doubt and self-recriminations were worth it.

Two hours later, they bumped down a gravel road to a

post and lintel arch. Tall white letters spelled "White Horse Ranch" across the long wooden beam.

"There it is," Daisy said, pointing at a small mansion covered in sparkling white lights.

Randi blew out her breath. Her mouth was dry. He was here. His parents and brothers too, about to be embarrassed by one of Buck's women crashing the party.

"I don't know if I can do this," she said.

Aunt Linda gripped her shoulder. "YOLO."

"What?"

"You only live once, Randi," Daisy said. "Get with it, girl, and put on some lipstick or something, you're a little peaky."

"Oh my," said Aunt Linda. "I wasn't expecting modern architecture. Shows what I know. Those windows are as tall as my house."

Randi focused on her breathing. If she just got this over with, it would be done.

It looked like THE party in the lower quadrant of the state. Shining pickup trucks lined up along the lawn, close to a hundred vehicles. Strung globe lights and massive paper lanterns gleamed everywhere. Garlands of evergreens wrapped the windows and doors, giant red bows at the apexes. It could be the centerpiece of a Martha Stewart magazine.

Daisy and Aunt Linda bustled around, putting on makeup and digging out clothes. Randi couldn't let go of the steering wheel. It hadn't been real until this moment.

"There's music in the barn, Randi, and a bonfire by the big open door," Daisy said, sticking her head in the passenger side door.

"I can't do this."

Aunt Linda opened the driver's door. "Come on now, honey. Put your jacket on, and we'll walk over there."

Randi let herself be coaxed out of the car, realizing she did want to have it over with. They walked through the parked trucks toward the intimidatingly large house. The tall double front doors were unlatched and inside she glimpsed what appeared to be the family, laughing and busy. A big crowd was on the other side of the house inside an open, lit-up barn.

A few people, standing outside the house, eyed them curiously. Randi stopped.

"I need to talk to Buck before I go to the party. Go ahead, I'll come find you."

"What? He's probably over there," Daisy said.

"It's okay. I'll wait for him here."

Aunt Linda hugged her. "All right, don't keep us wondering too long."

She watched them go, grinning a little at the bounce in their steps. Whatever happened to her, at least they'd all gotten out of the house and weren't crying in front of the television.

Ten minutes passed. She paced, trying to warm up her frozen legs. People walked past her, chattering happily. An older man pointed at the barn and told her, "Party's that way." She nodded, forcing her face to smile, and stayed where she was.

A woman in a beautiful mauve cardigan over a red dress bustled out of the front door. Her pinned-up hair was gray and pearl white, her layered silver jewelry flashing.

Randi smiled back at her friendly but puzzled gaze.

"Dear, do you need something? Everything's set up for the guests in the barn."

"Thank you. I'm hoping to speak to Buck. Is he here tonight?"

"Well, yes, of course, he is. I'm sorry to ask this, but were you invited, dear?"

"Yes, ma'am, I was. Buck gave me the invitation himself about a month ago."

"Huh," she said, looking skeptical. Randi didn't blame her, maybe she wasn't the first ex-girlfriend to show up tonight. Mortification engulfed her. She wanted to crawl into a clam and disappear.

"I'm sorry to be so awkward. I'll just wait here a bit longer for him, if you don't mind. Then I'll leave."

Before the woman could reply, someone called out to her, the tone implying it was an urgent concern involving catering. Randi slumped further into her jacket, horrified with herself, as the matronly woman bustled back inside.

She couldn't take much more of this loitering around like a stray cat at the door.

Five minutes later, a kid—somewhere around seven or eight years old—ran out the door and held a paper cup full of hot cider up to her.

"Oh, thank you very much."

He grinned at her and scampered off.

Her icy hands were almost warm when the house doors swung wide open and a familiar chuckle mixed with feminine giggles. It was Buck, with his arm around a gorgeous redhead.

Randi took a step back, looking down. Her ears were ringing. This was wrong. She wouldn't ask to speak to him now. Her stupidity was over. She turned around and walked toward the car, her heeled foot stumbling on the gravel walk.

Vertigo clawed up her wobbly legs, like when she dreamt of falling then woke up with her stomach a quivering pancake of soggy dough, and the sensation that the room was spinning. She wheezed and gasped, veering into a thorny bush by the path. *Drive the hell out of here.* Once they were on the road, she would be able to breathe again.

She stumbled, grabbing onto a fence post. A big hand gripped her elbow.

"Randi," Buck said, his voice a low rumble.

She glanced over at him once, a little behind her right shoulder, catching a glimpse of his shaved cheek. A pleasant drift of bay and rum and woodsmoke came into her mouth and nose when she gasped in a breath. Her brain split into five different thoughts, the uppermost wishing for a clue in the one word he'd said to her so far. She pushed herself away from the fence, gathering her tattered dignity.

"Oh, hey," she said, voice cracking. "I feel awful interrupting you here. Very late now, we'd better start traveling—"

She stopped, blinking in dazed surprise. He was smashing her against his chest, both of his arms wrapped around her.

"You came," he said.

Maybe three hundred and seventy-one miles was all worth it for this hug. She inhaled and let a long exhale out, telling herself to step away.

She pulled back enough to say, "Hey, I don't want to keep you from your guests, but I do want to apologize for leaving the way I did, and for what I said to you. I'm sorry. You're a good man, Buck."

He cupped her face with his hands. She wished he wouldn't do that. Her thoughts melted. Finally, she looked up into bright blue eyes, crinkled at the edges.

"What's this now?" he said, wiping the tears off her face with his thumbs. "You want to run away again already?"

"Buck," she said, a little heat burning into the marshmallow sadness smothering her. "Don't treat that girl poorly. I'm sure she's waiting for you."

He gazed down at her, inspecting every inch of her face. The grin stretched into a full toothy beam.

"Darlin'," he said, then stopped, chuckling.

"Yeah?" she finally answered, working to hold a stern expression on her face, managing not to cling to him in desperation.

"She's my cousin."

"Oh."

She blinked, trying to take in his words.

"And, no, not a kissing cousin. I can see that dirty thought wiggling around in there."

She glared up at him. "My thoughts do not wiggle."

"I missed you," he said, running his hands up and down her back.

She blew out her breath. Swallowed. Forced herself to say, "I missed you, too."

He smiled. Laughing at her.

"I realized a few things while you were gone," he said. "First, you spoiled me for any other woman. Flat-out. You leaving made it clear. Tried cooking a couple times with the other girls at the house and had to take the spatulas out of their hands. Trish gave me a plate of burned broccoli that a starving goat wouldn't touch."

She held on to his coat. Her heart was racing. "You've always been a broccoli racist."

"Also," he said, eyes twinkling down at her, "I decided I rushed things a bit and had to give you time. You needed a breather. Dating Carter, though, that pissed me off." His grip tightened on her. "Till I thought about it for ten minutes and realized you were lying."

She put her forehead against his chest. "Yeah," she said, "I was."

Texting Carter to tell him that she didn't think of him that way had been brutal. But stringing him along would have been vicious.

"Hey," Buck said, forcing her to look up at him. "Why did you come out here? Drive almost four hundred miles on

Christmas Day to stand outside and nearly freeze to death. Tell me."

Here it was. She swallowed. The words would come out all wrong. She wasn't ready.

She closed her eyes, took a deep breath. *Now. Speak now.*

"I knew, before we broke up, maybe even before we slept together, I don't know, my feelings, they're like darting fish, or knives, when they turn on…my feelings, I mean, I fumble around, not sure what to do with them." Her words were a rambling mess. Like a crazy person.

She bit her lip, forced herself to go on. "When Mimi and Papa died, I shut down. But you, you…" She paused to swallow, opening and closing her eyes again, trying to ignore the tears running down her face. "You broke my heart wide open. I love you. I love you so much it terrifies me. Of course, I don't expect you to feel the same, I mean, you're a normal person, but I want you to understand about me. The real reason I left. I'm not cornering you, or attempting to trap you into something you don't want. But that's what I struggle with. All those ugly things I said to you don't matter. I've told you because I want you to have the truth."

She exhaled shakily. He pressed his forehead against hers, not running away. Her hands shook.

"Wow, darlin', I was reviewing CPR in my head. Your face is bleach white."

She stared up at him, her heart in her throat.

"Okay," he said. "I was more obvious than a purple cow, but with your emotional disability, you haven't picked up on me floating around like an idiot with an arrow in his chest."

He rubbed her arms up and down, not saying anything while a little group of people passed by without seeing them. She stood suspended, watching his mouth, barely able to take in his words.

"What I really want to do is kiss you and carry you off to

my room, but I better say this clear, so you straighten a few things out in your mind. I knew, practically from the start, that you got to me. Like nobody has before. I fought it for a while, cos it snuck up on me out of nowhere. There you were, all of a sudden, fallin' off bicycles, traipsin' around in pretty dresses, looking at me like you could crawl inside my skin."

He kissed her on the mouth, a quick soft peck. She wrapped her arms around his neck, knees wobbling.

"Then we started sleeping together…I was a goner. I love you. You had until New Years. After that, I was going to barge back in and force you to talk to me. I need you. You're stuck with me, especially now that you came all the way out here and fessed up. We're a done deal, darlin'."

She pulled his mouth down to hers and kissed him, hard and fierce. After one fleeting moment of bliss, she had to pull away to cry on his shoulder.

"Are you sure? I don't know, we've only known each other a few months…"

He rubbed her back. "Take a deep breath. We'll find you a stress ball to squeeze, or a therapy dog, once I finish my grad work. Gives me enough time to put a fence up around the trailer."

"Aren't you moving back here?" she said, choking a little on the waterworks coming out of her face.

"Nah, they offered me a temporary job at the university, helping to wrap up a few research projects with the animals. I'll come out to the ranch a few times when they get real busy, but I won't be able to stay away from you for long."

He kissed her again, hoisting her up against his chest. She straddled his waist. That little wound-up part of her pulsed to sudden burning life. He groaned, turning so her back bumped against the fence post. The skirt of her velvet sweater dress slid up her thighs, and she shivered, the hard length of him pushing against her pulsing center.

"Buck!" a matronly voice yelled. "Buck Montgomery, bring that girl inside before she freezes to death."

Randi jumped off him and onto her feet, hastily smoothing down her velvet skirt. Her cheeks were about to burn off her face. His mother had spotted them, on their way to mindless copulating.

"I'd better start driving," she said. "I want to make it back to Burns tonight."

"What?" he said. With a grunt, he adjusted his pants, focusing on her face. "You're not going anywhere but my bedroom. First, though, you have to meet everyone."

"Oh no," she said, taking a step backward, adrenaline shooting into her veins. "I'm in no shape for meeting your family, way too soon for that. Besides, Aunt Linda and Daisy are with me. We can't all sleep in your bedroom."

He smiled down at her, his thumb running over her cheek. "We're going to my trailer. I dragged it all the way out here so Ma could give one of the cousins my bedroom. Linda and Daisy will stay in the bunkhouse. There will be plenty of room with most of the cowboys gone. Now, get a wiggle on, and come meet my mother."

HE COULDN'T STOP LOOKING at her. The long jacket swished around her legs, a soft evergreen-colored dress peeping out from under the hem, and tall boots that stopped at her knees. The Christmas gift he wanted. He ached with wanting her.

He pushed her inside the front door, ignoring the frantic looks she threw over her shoulder. At least she didn't cling to the door frame.

"Buck, is that you?" his ma said, shouting from the

kitchen. She bustled over to the entryway a minute later then stopped, focusing on his arm around Randi.

"Ma, this is my girl. Darlin', this is Ma."

Randi was as rigid as a field post. "Nice to meet you, and sorry to intrude on your party. I wanted to speak to Buck, but I don't want to disrupt your night in any way."

His ma cocked her head for a moment, like a confused chicken. "But honey, we're so glad you're here. About broke my heart when Buck told me you weren't gonna come out. Now, like a Christmas miracle, here you are."

Randi smiled shyly. "Thank you," she said.

His ma hugged her and pinched her cheeks. Randi stayed still, a smile fixed on her face, tolerating the petting with round rabbit eyes. He didn't blame her. His ma was a force of nature.

Ma herded them into the kitchen, right into the middle of party headquarters. His brothers skulked by the hearth in the family room, lurking. Chase glared at Randi like a terrorist had walked through the door.

"Darlin', you put up with Chase last month, that sulky-faced sack of resentment over there. The tall blond one's Austin. He's the oldest and the quietest. We poke him with cow prods to get him talking."

"Howdy," said Austin. "I can speak just fine."

"I thought you two broke up," Chase said, barging in like a battering ram.

Randi froze on her barstool, and Buck dropped an arm around her shoulders.

"You forget your manners somewhere?" Buck said to Chase, clenching his jaw.

"Came back for the money, girl?" Chase said, staring at her like she was a disease on legs.

Randi adjusted her glasses, her hand shaking. "I'm not sure what you're talking about," she said.

"What's going on?" Ma shouted from the far side of the kitchen. "Y'all better make this girl welcome."

"Chase," Buck said, "shut your gob. You don't understand shit about her, or us. Any more and we'll talk in the hay barn."

Randi stood in the awkward silence, dusting off her jacket. She stared at the door like she couldn't wait to make a run for it.

"You haven't told her," said Austin. "Well, shit."

Randi glanced at him sharply, poised like a deer startled by a gun cocking.

"You're both jackasses. No, Randi doesn't know everything about my investment portfolio. Come on, darlin', let's go find my pa, and the torture will be over."

He grabbed her hand and pulled her outside. She looked tired and too thin again.

She yanked him to stop on the path behind the house. "Hey," she said, "I hate that your brother thinks I'm after your money, but I don't understand, what did I do wrong?"

"Nah, darlin', he's the one with the loose screw. We'll talk more later. Now come on before I give up and carry you to my trailer like a caveman."

It was a dodge, and he knew it. He'd tell her tomorrow.

# CHAPTER TWENTY-FOUR

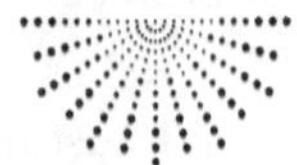

Randi danced with Buck to "Have Yourself a Merry Little Christmas," sung by Sam Smith's hot-chocolate voice. Buck gazed down at her, a half-cocked smirk on his face, like he knew she could barely breathe.

No part of her recognized this, like an alien wandering into a happiness theme park and going straight for the biggest roller-coaster. Her brain shouted warnings that the sun would set on this moment, and she'd be back on the other side of the gates, looking in.

"Hey," Buck whispered in her ear, "we can sneak out of here now."

She swallowed, her heart rate picking up at the thought.

"I'll go check on Aunt Linda and Daisy," she said, shivering as his rough cheek nuzzled against her temple.

Aunt Linda was sitting in a chair against the wall, a plate of cake in her lap.

"Well, my word, what a relief to see some color back in your cheeks." Her aunt smiled smugly at her.

Randi couldn't stop the smile from breaking out on her face. She sank down onto the chair next to her aunt and leaned into her side. "Do I tell you I love you enough? I don't think so. I love you, Auntie."

Aunt Linda sniffed, pulling her in tight with one arm. "I love you too, niece-e-poo. Thanks for not screwing up your life, makes me proud. And like I had a tiny hand in it. College degree, almost, hot little business, and a hunk of a man. Your parents and Mimi and Papa would be proud."

"Proud of us. But speaking of men, we made a deal on the car ride here."

Aunt Linda chuckled, dabbing at her face with the little hankie she carried around. Randi blinked, blotting her own tears on her sleeve. This lady was her blessing. Moving out, and away from her aunt, to find her own life, would be ridiculously difficult. But new things were around the corner, bright and shiny.

"Yes," Aunt Linda said, "I remembered. I called Jack and wished him a merry Christmas. He wants to make me dinner next week."

"You said yes?"

"I said yes."

"Well, we've just about sorted out all the lumps of misery. Are you sure the bunkhouse is okay for you?"

"Yes. Go. If you make a baby, your auntie would be very happy."

"Oh no, don't start with that already."

"I talked to Buck's mother about it. We think you should strike while the grandmothers are healthy. And I want to be Nanna, by the way. Not Grand Auntie, or Great Auntie. Dibs on Nanna."

"Wow. We're dating. This is Christmas, not our wedding."

"Have a productive honeymoon and don't rush out of there in the morning. Fun things come to those who wait, naked."

Randi rolled her eyes and walked away, exhaling. She

picked up a glass of sparkling wine on her way to the bonfire, the liquid a cold burn down her tight throat. She was as nervy as a virgin again. Except now, it would be sex with a steady boyfriend, the person who actually loved her back.

Not real. Not convinced they belonged together. Why her? It terrified her to be with someone who had so much to offer when she had so little. How would they ever balance the scales?

Daisy bounced by the massive bonfire in the midst of an impromptu dance party made up of a handful of women. They all grinned a little self-consciously, moving to the Mariah Carey song that everyone played to death during the holidays.

Randi finished her champagne, the bubbles like silly sparkles landing in her stomach. She put down her glass on a banquet table set up by the fire. Without pausing to think, she joined the dancers. Her dress fanned out around her legs in green velvet ripples.

Daisy squealed and hugged her. Randi adjusted her glasses, cheeks burning—she would rather not draw every-one's attention to her non-existent dancing skills.

"Hey," Randi said, "I'm exhausted and going to, um, head to bed. You all right?"

"What?" Daisy said, her face morphing into open-mouthed disappointment. "Randi, it's only eleven o'clock."

She shrugged, biting her lip, not able to hold in a smirk.

Daisy's eyes narrowed, realization dawning on her face. Before Randi could say anything, Buck was suddenly there, sweeping her off her feet and up into his arms.

She found herself squealing and giggling, covering her burning face with one hand and clutching his neck with the other.

"Night, Daisy," said Buck. "Stay outta trouble."

Daisy snorted. "You're one to talk," she said, but Buck was already striding away.

"Buck," Randi said.

"Yeah, darlin'?"

"Put me down right now."

The eyes of the entire party watched them as he dragged her off to his trailer, like a caveman.

"This is payback."

"What?"

"For the last month."

"How long are you going to punish me for that?"

"Till I feel better."

She gave up and covered her face.

He carried her until the sounds of the party faded. They were on the other side of the massive lawn, the bitter cold like pinpricks on her flushed skin. With a grunt he heaved her up, so she lay belly down on his shoulder in a fireman carry.

"Oomph," Randi grunted, giggles leaking out from between her clenched teeth. "Buck, I have two perfectly working legs."

"Tell your legs to hold on, I'll be with 'em in a moment."

He got the door open and hauled her up the steps, each bumpy step squeezing out another giggle. Finally, they landed on the bed at the back.

Buck collapsed next to her. "Damn, I didn't think that would be so hard."

"You're a maniac."

He grinned, rolling on top of her. "And you're mine, little lady. I hauled you back to my cave and now we're settled."

"Good thing I like you so much."

"You more 'n like me."

"Yeah."

"Say it. Makes me feel better."

"I love you, Buck. Even when you're a caveman."

Then he kissed her. And, it turned out, making love with him was easy. They handled each other's bodies like extensions of their own, not holding anything back, even their hearts.

$$\sim$$

BUCK WOKE UP BEFORE RANDI—A rare occurrence. He didn't like the dark hollows under her closed eyes. She lay deeply asleep, apparently exhausted, and he fought the temptation to wake her up. Instead, he snuck out of bed, pulling the covers up over her naked body.

Five minutes later, he walked into his mother's kitchen, which was already alive with coffee and pastry.

"Mornin'," said Chase. "You want something? Ma put me on breakfast duty today."

Buck rinsed out his canteen in the kitchen sink. "Yeah, I want something. What the hell is your problem with my girl? I want you to tell me about that."

Chase exhaled, looking down at the floor. "Yeah, I realized last night when I saw you two together, I got her stupid wrong."

"You did."

"One of those other girls at your house talked a lot of shit about her. Convinced me, I guess."

Buck snorted. "Not like you to be such a dumbass."

Chase scratched his head. "But I did notice she's a little… different. Too fancy. Unfriendly. On her computer all the time, not talking to anybody."

"Because she did a double load at school, working harder than anybody in that house," Buck said, filling a bag with pastry. "It stops now, Chase."

Chase crossed his arms, leaning against the counter.

"Nah, I'm convinced." He turned red. "I was a little jealous, for a minute. Turned my head. I'm over it… Be nice if I found a girl who likes to wear cute dresses."

Buck glared at him sharply. "Nah," he said, "you're destined for a tomboy who can kick your ass. Somebody needs to."

"You going to tell her 'bout everythin'?"

"This morning. Let Ma know we'll catch brunch late."

Back at the trailer, Randi stepped out of the bathroom already dressed. Buck sighed in disappointment, but set the table with his treats.

"I found some cream for your coffee, darlin', but I had to fight a cyclops to win it. I'll claim my kiss later."

She smiled, a hand on her stomach. "I was too hungry to stay in bed," she said.

"Come for a drive with me after you eat. I want to show you something."

He brought up the party as he steered the truck onto the highway. "Darlin', I need to apologize to you about that night."

She stiffened next to him. "I realize now my unlocked room and torn-up projects were all Angie," she said, crossing her arms and hunching up her shoulders. "She attacked me that day, in the library. Went for a full body tackle but missed and ended up being dragged out by campus security. It was a really horrible day."

He shook his head, knocked sideways again by the craziness of it all. Hugh had told him Angie had been arrested for fighting in a Baker City bar last week and had spent the night in jail. He was grateful the lunatic madwoman was out of their lives, for good. He'd have to help Hugh move on, real quick.

"Yeah, it was," he said, reaching out to hold her hand. "Took me a while to get over my self-pity for you blaming me. I'd just yelled at Angie and Sarah before you got there. Found the damn Facebook party invite Angie had posted online and got that down. Went around asking people to leave. Saw your torn-up projects and had a drink to calm down. That's when you showed up."

She squeezed his hand. "Angie went out with a bang. We should paint a picture on a rock to commemorate it."

He huffed. "I'm sorry I dragged you out there, with everything you were doing. I'm learning, darlin', I promise."

She smiled at him, her eyes watery. He had to pull over the truck and kiss her until they both felt better.

Thirty minutes of driving later, they turned onto a rough gravel road winding up through tall pines, ending on a bluff. The Steens Mountain towered in front of them, rugged rock rising above the desert, the valley a long basin below.

"This is incredible," Randi said. "Are we on park land?"

"No, this is private. A rare small lot, small for around here, that came up for sale about two years ago."

"Feels different, woodsier. And this view...I could shout out an off-key 'the hills are alive with the sound of music.' Except, I wouldn't want to spin off that cliff there."

"Darlin'," he said, taking her hand, "the land is mine."

She blinked, staring at him. "Your family bought it to add to the ranch?"

"No, I did. My parents don't own White Horse, they manage it. Ranching is a whole new beast in the modern corporate era, but they're going to be settled for a while. When this parcel came on the market two years ago, I was in a position to act and I knew the seller, who wanted a quick sell. Didn't do too bad on the price."

"Wow, Buck, this is spectacular." Randi blinked, looking around for a minute. "I think you're trying to tell me something and I'm not understanding. What do you mean you were in a position to act?"

"Yeah, that's the thing," he said, relishing the astonished wonder on her face as she looked out over the bluff. "There's a rumor on campus, I've heard, that my family's real wealthy. My grandparents, kind of, my immediate family, no. Not the way they mean. My grandparents, now, they have dozens of grandchildren. Each of us gets a small trust fund, about forty grand, to pay for school or to start a business."

Her brow furrowed. "Is forty-k enough for a down payment on a property like this?"

"No, not even close."

Her eyebrows shot up. "How'd you do it?"

"I gambled on Bitcoins."

"Bitcoins, the crypto currency?"

"That's it. I took my forty and threw everything all-in on Bitcoin. Sold out just in time, during the first rush."

Her eyes opened to wide saucers. "Buck," she said, grabbing the front of his jacket. "What happened?"

"I made a few mill."

"Mill? You mean million?"

"Yep."

"What?" She let go of him and walked away, pacing in a circle through the sagebrush.

He put his hands in his jacket pockets and waited, sucking in a breath. Here goes. Time to get it all out there.

"Buck, you're worth two or three million dollars?"

"Five. This property cost a couple."

"Five! Five is not a few!"

"Hey, don't bust a gut. This is good news. I would have told you sooner, but I didn't want to freak you out."

"I'm freaked out!"

He walked closer to her, putting an arm around her shoulders. "Go into business with me."

"What?"

"You need to finish up your degree for another two terms. After that."

She dropped to the ground, into a crouch with her head between her knees. He squatted down beside her.

"I need your help," he said, "imagining what could be done with this place. Like a resort, with baby-goat-yoga. See over there, what about a swimming pool built like a curving river looking out on this view? The main lodge, up a little higher, and cabins tucked in along the ridge. That little college town we've been living in has given me some ideas about bicycles. Putting in a paved path for the tourists would bring in the yuppies."

She gaped at him. "Buck," she finally said, "everything sounds too amazing to be true… to be doable. I don't really believe it."

"It's perfect for your degree in business, marketing, and design. Especially if you want baby goats. I'm excited about it… Can't stop thinking about the possibilities."

"What about your Masters in Rangeland Management?"

"I'll set up a consulting firm with an office based out of the resort for now. If a rancher wants to work with me, I'll go to them and problem-solve with all my learning."

"Wow."

He kissed her. "We can do it. We'll be a hell of a team."

"This is too much…a dream. I mean, I love it, but I need to think. And my aunt, I'm not sure I could leave her seven hours away…"

"Linda can come live with us later if she wants to, Jack too," he said. "We'll need their help. The first year or two will be rough living, in my trailer, but my parents aren't far, and they'll want us there too."

Buck watched her face. She panted a little, struggling to breathe, didn't understand yet how much he needed her. He wouldn't be able to do any of it without her. She'd been right about him. The drinking and partying were habits too easy for him to fall into. She was a rocket he wanted to hold on to.

"Hugh and my brothers can help us build the cabins. The lodge we'll hire out to an architect, for sure. Point is, in a few years, maybe sooner, we'll be up and running. Could use a charming lady like your aunt to greet guests, teach an outdoor painting class, whatever y'all dream up. We'll get this thing going and see where it takes us. Doesn't have to be forever. It all came together in my head when you told me about your yoga with baby goats idea last fall. But I need to know something before I start this."

"What?" she said, round green eyes blinking at him.

"Will you marry me?" he said, grabbing her hands when she jerked back, to keep her from falling. "But that was just to let you know what's coming. I wasn't asking, yet. I'll wait until spring break and then you'll hear it again, when I have a ring."

She started sobbing, holding him like she might pass out.

# CHAPTER TWENTY-FIVE

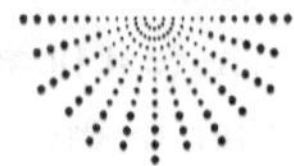

Randi dumped her backpack on the floor and collapsed on her bed. Final exams had ended thirty minutes ago, and she'd lived through them. Barely. Somehow, by the skin on her knuckles, she would pass all the classes, hopefully. One more term to go and she'd own a bachelors.

The picture of Buck on the nightstand smiled down at her. She sighed, exhausted just looking at him. He was a living, demanding, whirlwind. Since the day after Christmas, he had been on fire to break ground on the resort. He worked as many hours as she did, finishing his graduate work and setting a hundred wheels in motion on the property. Surveys, permit applications, assessors, architects, and contractors all danced along to Buck's tune making maps, plans, and contracts.

There was a vigor in him, a purpose, that was new. He hardly drank—didn't have time. At night, he turned that driven energy on her. He wore her out in inventive and enthusiastic ways until she was a melted puddle of bliss. She constantly found herself smiling for no reason. It was unseemly. Uncontrollable.

A little, admittedly insecure, part of herself fretted. They didn't have any plans for spring break. He'd probably forgotten, or thought better of, his promise of a proposal back at Christmas. Working all break would be the best thing. She needed to put in about a hundred hours for her yoga business, and was basically onboard with not taking a break. Of course, she wanted to work. There was too much to do not to.

No matter what happened, her nerves would be stretched thin for the next week, wondering. Rushing was insane. She still didn't know what she would say if he did ask.

"Don't be a chicken," she said out loud, her new mantra for life with Buck.

Her phone chimed in her pocket. The cattle bell, which meant Buck. He'd sent her a video in the text message, and she could feel her eyebrows hit her hairline.

"Hey, darlin'," he said in the video, the camera zoomed in on his nose. He pulled back. "Get gussied up, I've got a little surprise for you. There's a journalist coming, and we're gonna have a chance to talk about the resort. I'm making a video." He leaned in, his eye taking over the screen. "I'm talkin' Instagrammable, babe. Directions are in the Prius. See you at four o'clock, sharp."

She groaned, throwing an arm over her face. Her legs were concrete. The blackness behind her eyes wanted to suck her into the mattress.

Turned out, Buck was a fearless marketer, jumping into the Instagram game like it was a coin-operated bull ride in a honky-tonk bar. The man could ham it up for the camera and enjoyed every silly moment. He was shamelessly using their love story as his narrative. People were noticing. Thousands of them. It was unnerving, and her YouTube page was along for the ride, buoyed by his successes.

Ten minutes later, her phone beeped. She was dozing,

pretending she had time for it. With a sigh, she glanced at the time, and adrenaline shot through her veins. They were going to be on camera in ninety minutes.

Hair done half up half down, makeup set, she agonized about what to wear. The new dress peeped out at her, navy cotton fabric popping with bursts of red, and a set of matching red T-strap heels on the closet floor. All the way from Britain, the midi-dress was snug in the waist with cap sleeves and a V-neck. A dress for a very special night out. She sighed, taking it off the hanger to put on. Maybe she'd get another chance to wear it soon.

Without a minute to spare, she crawled through down-town traffic in the Prius, eyes darting to the dash clock telling her she had nine minutes. Something was happening at the downtown Riverfront Park, making it impossible to park. After circling for a small eon, she zipped into a ques-tionable spot behind a dumpster then jumped out of the car to speed walk four blocks down to the river.

People stood in business doorways, looking toward the park with smiling faces. Her stomach dropped. What on earth was she walking into?

She ducked into an alley, not ready to stumble into the center of all the hoopla. Were those trumpets warming up? A back door was propped open at one of the bakeries. She peeped inside, hoping for a sight line to the park on the other side. Standing on her tiptoes, she could make out a sea of red uniforms. A marching band?

Someone hustled across her line of sight, and she swung around, pressing her back against the cool bricks of the building. A crazy suspicion about Buck's surprise bubbled up. She exhaled. And again. If she breathed for long enough, theoretically her heart would stop racing.

Papa's cheerful face formed behind her closed eyes, round

glasses at the end of his nose, and Mimi's too, with short white curls framing her petite pale face and the thick black sunglasses covering her eyes. Mimi was leaning on Papa's shoulder, both of them smiling at her with joy.

"Buck up, buttercup," she said out loud, pinching the bridge of her nose hard, then exhaling another shaky breath.

Most likely it all had nothing to do with her, and this insane excitement and dread flooding her chest was wasted adrenaline. *Walk out there and get it over with.*

The alley led to a sidewalk on the city-side of the long grassy park in front of the river. She stepped out between packed café tables and startled when Hugh waved, pointing a massive video camera on a rolling tripod frame at her face.

"Randi," a familiar voice yelled. She turned and saw Daisy a block away, standing on top of a chair, waving both of her arms. "Buck! Randi's here!"

"Hi, honey!" yelled her aunt, standing up next to Daisy. "Keep breathing, it's going to be fabulous."

Her aunt pointed up to the sky, where a low-flying plane cruised overhead, a long banner trailing behind it. She gulped, blinking fiercely. The banner said, *I love you, Randi, not just cos you make me randy.*

She stood frozen, and couldn't remember what she was supposed to do. Her eyes frantically searched for somewhere to sit. Not an empty surface in sight, and all the attention was focused on her.

"It's all right, dear," said a raspy soft voice next to her. She glanced down and saw an elderly face, framed by pretty white curls. "Go on, now," she said, pointing toward the water fountain in the center of the park.

Randi dabbed at her eyes. Taking a deep breath, she stepped out into the street.

A scatter of cheers broke out from the crowd gathered on

the sidewalk. Cheeks flaming, she turned back to smile, not able to focus on anyone through the black haze at the edges of her vision. Buck was going to suffer for this. *Good grief.*

The uniformed marching band turned, coming into sharp formation, the drummers tapping out a rhythmic beat. She noticed a choir, the singers crisply clapping their hands and snapping their shoulders.

"When I wake up," they sang out, "well I know I'm gonna be, I'm gonna be the man who wakes up next to you."

She walked forward in a daze, hands covering her mouth, which wouldn't close. The fountain, she realized, was bedecked with hundreds of flowers—pots of blooming tulips, daffodils, roses, and more covered the brick patio surrounding the fountain. All except for a rectangle of space in front of the cascading water.

"When I go out, yeah I know I'm gonna be, I'm gonna be the man who goes along with you."

She stopped in the center of the open space, over-whelmed by music, flowers, and the cameras pointed at her.

"If I get drunk, well I know I'm gonna be, I'm gonna be the man who gets drunk next to you."

Buck walked out, materializing from his hiding spot behind the choir. She startled, a shaky chortle erupting from her throat. He was trying to kill her! She wiped more tears from her lashes.

He smiled—and was unfathomably gorgeous. In fact, she realized, he was wearing an incredible fitted black tuxedo, modern slim legs and all. And the black cowboy hat.

"But I would walk five hundred miles," sang on the choir, "and I would walk five hundred more. Just to be the man who walks a thousand miles to fall down at your door."

He took a moment to look at the crowd and grin. Her stomach fluttered. He sauntered over to her, chin up and a little swagger in his walk. She snorted, smiling. He struck an open-legged dancer's pose and held out his hand. She took it.

"Hey," he said, close to her ear, pulling her in to his chest. "Surprised?"

"To death."

"I'll make it up to you."

They danced the two-step she knew. He'd forced her to practice it with him for the last three months. Line dancing was a part of life now, according to Buck. If it hadn't been so fun, she would have argued more. Air swirling over her as she spun in his arms, it felt like magic. An exhilarating, giddy warp speed formerly only possible in a fourth dimension.

"When I grow old, well I know I'm gonna be, I'm gonna be the man who's growing old with you."

He pulled out all the moves—spins, lifts, arms twists—things she didn't even remember the names of. All she could do was surrender. And laugh. Her skirt spun out into a horizontal plate, and she was grateful the pantyhose had made it on.

The song went into the final verse of *Da da da da*, and echoing *Da da da das*. The next act was about to follow. Her life had taken on the timeline of a reality dating show. They stared into each other's eyes. Turned out she was a romantic after all… She loved him. Every crazy bit of him.

"Da da da dun diddle un diddle un diddle uh da da da," the choir sang out.

He held her close, resting his forehead against hers, as the song came to an end. They both panted. He dropped down to one knee, grasping both of her hands in his. She wanted to shout at him to stand up, she didn't want him to kneel. But, somehow, looking down at his tense face, it didn't seem wrong. Tears streamed down her face. It was refreshing not to be looking up at him for a change.

He cleared his throat. "When we met, I knew I was in trouble. It didn't take more than a few weeks to prove me right. You were what I needed, to become the man I want to be. And in you I found the heart I want to safeguard for as long as I'm living. It scared the piece of shit boy right out of me. I'm yours, always. You can handle me, darlin', and make me a better man with your smile. Come with me through life. Let's create a family, build a business, travel, work hard and play harder. My gut tells me this is right, for both of us. I don't want you to miss out on anything, most of all the love a family can give you. I'm ready. I don't want to wait, but will if I have to. What I'm sayin' is, I want to marry you. Every inch of me loves you. What I'm asking is, darlin', will you marry me?"

She gulped. It was the stupidest, riskiest thing she could do. Marry a guy after knowing him for less than half a year? Insane. She didn't even know his blood type! The prudent thing was to wait, read some books on the subject, and see where they were in a year.

The sun came out from behind a cloud, flooding the park with brilliant spring sun. A trickle of sweat ran down the back of her neck. Her heartbeats drummed by, resounding in her head like a mallet hitting a bong. She was holding her breath.

She exhaled. "Buck Montgomery," she said, her voice choked with tears, "I will marry you. Because you make me crazy."

When they kissed, the crowd erupted into cheers. They spent the next two hours talking to family and friends. A reporter from the local newspaper stopped by. They gave away flowers, and still filled the back of Buck's truck with blooms. Aunt Linda took the Prius, winking at Buck, and zipped away on mysterious "errands."

There was a diamond engagement ring on Randi's finger,

cheerfully sparkling, bouncing back sunbeams whenever she gazed at it. It felt lucky, and that made her heart skip a beat with nervous dread. She looked at Buck and told herself, *Don't be a chicken.*

On the ride home, she actually dozed off for a moment, or possibly twenty minutes, leaning on his shoulder. Had she really taken finals that morning? It must have been a different lifetime.

"Hey," Buck said in her ear, "wake up. Got another surprise for you."

"There better not be trumpets involved," she mumbled. He jumped out of the truck and ran around to pull open her door. She squealed when he lifted her up into his arms.

"Come on, my little ball and chain," he said, hoisting her up to open the trailer door.

Inside, he dropped her down onto the built-in bench seat at the table. On top of the table sat a bottle of champagne chilling in a tub of ice, two glasses, and a wrapped box.

Sniffling, she leaned her head against his neck. "This has all been too much—the show downtown was horrible. How could you do that to me? But," she choked, "I'll never forget one torturous, incredible moment of it. Buck, you're a wonder of the world."

He patted her back. "Stop crying and open it."

With trembling hands, she opened the box. Inside, nestled in sparkling tissue paper, sat two packets. "Plane tickets to Baja!"

"Yeah, what do you think?"

"Wow, just wow. I'm thrilled."

"You can pick the next one. I wanted to surprise you, get that marriage proposal out of the way, so we could relax. And not lose the ring."

"Tomorrow? It says here we leave tomorrow!"

"Yep—wait, sit down—Aunt Linda's been helping with

everything you'll need. All laid out on your bed. You'll have plenty of time in the morning to pack, even do some shopping, before we catch our flight. We're gonna stay in a little resort, with a real big bed and lots of privacy. The wonder is nobody blabbed to you. Lots of beautiful places for you to make videos and for me to fish. Baja's a hell of a deal."

"How—when—Buck, I can't believe you got all of this done."

"I hired an online personal assistant. Sharp kid named Raj. There's more to tell you, darlin'. All that spitballing, daydreaming, brainstorming we've been doing about the resort, I've been acting on. Now, before your brain explodes, I want you to remember that it's all changeable. We'll be adapting and transforming all the time. Point is, we need a name."

"Not the Randi-Buck."

"You got somethin' better? And we need to name the restaurant, too."

"What about Blue Mountain Resort?"

"Boring. Probably taken. But not bad."

"Goat's Gruff? Cowboy Country?"

"I like RandiBuck, no hyphen, capital B. Sticks in your head."

"It sounds like a strip club."

"Here's my confession, I searched online and nobody had it, so I secured domain names. Went ahead and opened social media accounts. And I told the journalist at our proposal we're called The RandiBuck Ranch and Resort, and gave her all those links. Darlin', you can name the corporation, but I want this one."

"Buck!"

"Our website is up. We're taking reservations for next summer. Today was a giant promotion for the RandiBuck

Ranch. Did you see my drones recording us? Nailed the live stream. We've already got emails piling in."

She blinked, adjusting her glasses. "Well, you don't dither over the details. This is really happening, isn't it?"

He kissed her. And didn't stop.

The End

# SIGN UP FOR MY AUTHOR NEWSLETTER

Please help other readers find this book by leaving a review. Also, receive free sign-up bonuses, information about give-aways, coupons, and be the first to learn about new releases through my author newsletter. Sign up today!

www.annaalkire.com

# ACKNOWLEDGMENTS

Biggest thanks, and so much love, to my husband who has weathered my long journey to publishing with grace and generosity. Love you, hon!

Special thanks to my editors and beta readers, who I appreciate to the moon and back, for helping me wrestle my manuscript into something I'm ready to share with the world. Thank you Manda Waller (copyedit), Peter Senftleben (proof), A.M. Vivian, Maureen Saul, Gaby Michaelis, and Max Watson. And heartfelt thanks to my writing group: Irina, Joyce, Gregory, Sharon, Shannon, Chloe, Cathy, and Christine - you're the best!

Humongous thanks to Ashley Santoro, who designed the cover and cheerfully put up with my obsessive edits about the shape of ears.

Thank you to my son for being his wonderful self, calling me 'my queen', and forcing me to call him 'my wizard'. And, of course, thank you to mom, the tireless cheerleader, who actually convinced me I could do this.

# ABOUT THE AUTHOR

Anna Alkire has been a long-term college student, a business owner, and a world traveler. Now "settled"—with a sigh and a cup of decaf—Anna lives in Washington state, where she splits her time between a husband who thinks the North Pole would be a great place to live, chasing her hurricane of a son, learning new handicrafts, and creating worlds full of the kind of romance and fun she most wants to read. Find more about her (and grab a freebie or two) at her website, annaalkire.com.